DANCING WITH DR KILDARE

Jane Yardley

Doubleday

LONDON · TORONTO · SYDNEY · AUCKLAND · JOHANNESBURG

TRANSWORLD PUBLISHERS
61–63 Uxbridge Road, London W5 5SA
A Random House Group Company
www.rbooks.co.uk

First published in Great Britain
in 2008 by Bantam Press
an imprint of Transworld Publishers

A CIP catalogue record for this book
is available from the British Library.

ISBN 9780385609395

'Wish You Were Here'
Words & Music by Roger Waters and David Gilmour
© 1975 Artemis Muziekuitgeverij B.V. & Pink Floyd Music Publishing Ltd. All
rights on behalf of Artemis Muziekuitgeverij administered by Warner/Chappell
Music Ltd, London W6 8BS
Reproduced by permission.

The extract from 'Musée des Beaux Arts' by W. H. Auden is included by kind
permission of Faber & Faber Ltd, 3 Queens Square, London WC1N 3AU, on
behalf of the Estate of W. H. Auden

Typeset in 11.5/14pt Adobe Caslon by
Falcon Oast Graphic Art Ltd.

Printed and bound in Great Britain by
Clays Ltd, Bungay, Suffolk

2 4 6 8 10 9 7 5 3 1

For my mother

PART I

Foxfires

1966 (Childhood)

When Lucia's grandmother booted the girls out of the garden (she was known throughout the village as a cantankerous old trout), they simply transferred their din to Nina's garden down the lane, and hoped for the best.

There wasn't much equipment to lug, just Lucia's drum kit: pots, pans and a cardboard box. Nina played air guitar, while the remaining member of the band was a Paul McCartney lookalike who happened to be imaginary.

Nina counted them into a raucous song of her own composition entitled 'I Love You Baby But I Gotta Catch A Jet Plane To New Orleans'. According to her father the number was promising, if a tad derivative. The girls were ten.

It wasn't until the final verse that Lu realized something was up. Nina had fluffed her lyrics and was making a poor fist of improvising new ones. And she was dragging the tune along like a congregation with an unfamiliar hymn.

'Ni-na!'

Then Lu heard it. Raised voices indoors, male and female. The quarrel's content was indecipherable, misshapen by masonry and the expanse of the garden, but the tone was unmistakable and raw. As Lu listened, the to-and-fro volley of genuine argument disintegrated; the voices overlapped then congealed. This was now a single monster with two heads.

Nina's own voice was scratchy with dread. Staring at the house, she sang haphazardly, the lyric abruptly plotless and soused in baby talk. Her left arm, flexed for her guitar, stuck out unattended with the ugliness of a torn twig. The row had reached its crisis and now shrieked across the garden like whiz-bangs over a trench.

Lu started to say, 'No, Nina, it isn't—' It isn't your parents. Just for once, just for a change. But that was unsayable. Lu rested her spoons on the jam skillet. 'That rotten radio!' she piped up with calculated clarity. 'What a racket!'

Nina abandoned the pretence of her song but didn't move.

'Who'd wanna listen to people yelling in some rubbishy play?'

Then they made out her mother's voice somewhere inside the house, calling to the dog with no more than routine impatience. Above and below her, the cacophony on the BBC played itself out in tears.

Lu watched the distress thaw out of her friend's back and shoulders. The guitar arm slumped. Within the closed house, the Labrador barked with overwrought eagerness.

'Start again?' suggested Lu.

There was a moment of voiceless, saturated relief, then Nina said, 'Take it from the middle eight.'

Lu picked up her spoons.

'A-one, two, a one-two-three four. *I'll call you up on the phone, baby. I got a bag of nickels and dimes . . .*'

1

1989

The storm waited until a couple of hours before the week-end began. After days of buttery autumn sun the sky turned the colour of a tar bucket, there was a flash and a rip, every-one's computer crashed, and the office was suddenly awash with shipwreck imagery, a landlocked maritime disaster: 'It's gone down!' 'I'm sunk!' '. . . all lost . . . lost . . .'

Dr Hannay, who had just lost a day's work on a report about lung cancer, said 'Fuck' and lit another cigarette. The phone rang.

'It's Duane. Lightning's scuppered the mainframe.'

'Ah well, worse things happen at sea. Any idea when—?'

But from the other end of the line came the sonic boom of an airborne secretary. *'Duane Davies?! I've lost the August accounts and my daughter's wedding list!'*

'Got to run and hide!' whispered Duane urgently.

Infected by the general histrionics, a plastic cup keeled over, slopping machine tea across a file headed HANNAY and on to Hannay's tiny skirt and ribbed tights – red and yellow tartan skirt, red and yellow tights, jam-and-custard colours that suited her spiked hair, like a child dressed by a punk mother – pretty much as she had looked on *Top of the Pops* in 1982. Seven years later and Nina was thirty-three, and to the loud relief of her own mother she finally had a proper job. In a perfect world Nina might have written her doctoral thesis on rock music (and finished it in half the time) but instead she went for medical statistics and now worked for a drug company.

As she made for the door and the nearest hand-dryer, her boss appeared.

'Go on, tell me you're another one that didn't save their files!' Glazed with a freaked panic, he fidgeted at his tie as if that might be the very tether he was at the end of. Then he registered the skirt. 'How'd you get drenched through a sealed window?'

'Burst water main in the computer,' Nina told him, cheerfully unfazed, and melted past just as another wave of rain lashed the window so the next blue-white explosion appeared through a rippling film of water, like nuclear war reflected in a millpond.

The corridors were muggy with wet light the colour of smoked kippers, its artificiality somehow palpable in the afternoon's sudden nightfall. Amid the displaced persons swapping disaster stories was a couple lolling in a doorway talking shop.

'Treatment will be coded.'

'So it's a blind trial.'

'And there's four doses.'

'Call it four arms.'

'With a run-in, therapy and follow-up.'

'So three legs. And four arms and blind.'

In the troubled hiatus that followed, Nina heard distant sobbing and hoped it wasn't Duane.

The drenched skirt was too far gone to pat dry, so she had no choice but to ruin it: the rinse-through, the wringing out, the roaring dryer – Nina watched the lambswool morph into a species of cardboard, and fought against sickness of heart. People were wrong who assumed her clothes were a careless snub to convention. Her clothes were art. She recognized the preliminary chill of a disproportionate desolation and set about talking herself out of it. In the deodorized, white-tiled space, Nina in her knickers conjured replacement skirts, silently reciting multicoloured possibilities until the optimism could be trusted to take her weight. Then she dressed, offered the mirror a self-mocking wink and returned to her office.

Strewn across the desk were her printed-out company mails, one of which should never have been left unattended. As near as dammit, it was a love letter.

His name was Richard Quentin and he was one of the medical people at their head office in Boston. The same city was home to another Richard Quentin, a courtroom lawyer of such ferocity he even made it into the British news. Nina had once asked in fun whether she should be addressing her mails to Richard Quentin Jr. Her next was addressed to Richard Quentin IV. 'Not the best numeral in a job where IV means intravenous,' pointed out the father's son. Last spring, he came over for meetings.

Richard was single. Nina was single. He was very tall, with a thick cushion of expensively tamed black hair, and was the immediate subject of intrigued female discussion. Nevertheless, at first Nina had disappointedly written him off, alienated by the ponderous formality of his American business etiquette. Then the initial meeting had been droning on for an hour when a good joke suggested itself from the agenda and Nina cracked it. Richard turned, and in his face she read a kind of recognition, a world-containing smile. Later, Duane took one look at her and said, 'Aye aye!' Richard himself, who would have said he liked his women conventionally pretty, wide-mouthed and power-dressed, spent two lunches and a dinner in the full glare of the waif-like, small-featured Nina with her frankness and eccentric outfits before boarding his flight home wondering what had hit him. A few days later she received a mail clearly still in draft – and as Richard's follow-up was breezily unconcerned, presumably he thought he'd hit *delete* instead of *send*.

> Dear Nina,
> My flight home was comfortable. The flight was. I wasn't, and am still not. There is an unsettled
> You unsettled me. I was moved to
> Nina, I'm moved to write you the kind of stuff that's equivalent to a kid turning cartwheels. Things I haven't written since school. Back then it was sonnets. On a clear day you can still hear the clunk of my rhyming couplets.
> In mid-Atlantic I was dreaming about you. Would you be flattered? Maybe I'm kidding myself that my erotic fantasies would
> If this is midlife crisis (well, I am 40) I don't know if I should weep or cheer.

Other mails had followed, lucid but careful; then slowly the correspondence had evolved through jokey, potentially retractable hints to a state of joyful indiscretion. They hadn't seen each other since that spring, but he was flying over again next Tuesday; in anticipation Nina had been manicured, pedicured and waxed to within an inch of her life. Now her phone rang again. She lunged for the receiver.

'Nina?' But it was an unknown voice, female and elderly, quavering down the line. Beneath the wash of disappointment Nina felt the impact of something more worrying. Drug companies don't employ elderly voices. But her parents were approaching seventy and her mother was away.

'My name's Mrs Peters. I live in Brancaster, round the

corner from your mum and dad. It's about your dad I'm phoning.'

He's had a fall, thought Nina. He's had a stroke.

'I'm so sorry, dear, but he's had a heart attack.'

2

It had happened in the street, a pensioner walking the dog, suddenly clutching his left arm and collapsing. Instant diagnosis by every onlooker who watched TV hospital dramas. He was taken to the Queen Elizabeth in King's Lynn, the ambulance wailing distress along the thread of coastal road from Brancaster.

If you had to drive to Norfolk on any Friday afternoon, the worst of all ways would be from Nina's office via her flat, both on the wrong side of London. She was to remember the journey as a flooded semicircle round a steaming metropolis in a fug of cigarette smoke with whining wipers and the rush hour fully ripe and toxic. Nina eventually fell into the cardiac unit with a headache and tinnitus. By the time a female doctor and two young men came to talk to her, she was convinced her father was dead.

'Mr Hannay is unconscious and very poorly,' said the woman. Nina hadn't taken in anybody's name.

'May I see him?' My voice is clogged, she thought. I'm going to cry.

'We won't keep you long. I understand your mother is on holiday. In South Africa.'

'Cape Town. I've left a message.'

With my sister's houseboy. Nina thought: I wish they didn't know that. She wondered how ridiculous it would sound if she said, 'Please don't hold South Africa against Dad. He loathes the regime, despite my sister.'

The woman, whose accent suggested Nigeria, was asking her something. 'His date of birth?'

'The thirtieth of October 1919. He'll be seventy next month.'

Or not, of course.

'Thank you. I'm sorry to tell you the heart attack was very severe.'

'If Dad pulls through, will you be thinking of a bypass? I've heard—'

'Unfortunately,' began the woman while the other two sighed some sympathy at the floor, 'we don't expect him to pull through.'

Right.

'In the ambulance your father was still able to speak but it wasn't English. Can you—?'

'Finnish probably. Dad was naturalized British as Martin Hannay but he was born in Finland as Martti Hannikainen.' She pronounced his name as her father taught her, purring the *r*. Ma*rrrrr*tti. At this casually cruel trigger, tears pooled in her throat.

'How good is his English normally?'

'Perfect. Slight accent.'

'Thank you. A nurse will show you to his bed.'

'Is Dad too deeply unconscious to hear me?'

'Who knows? Hearing is the last sense to go.'

Nina cleared the sludge from her voice. 'At least he wasn't in Cape Town,' she said loudly, finally unable to stop herself. 'Dad refuses to set foot there under apartheid.'

'No shortage of coronary care,' said the woman, opening the door. 'The world's first heart transplant was carried out in Cape Town.'

And Nina was taken to her father's bedside.

※

If your home was Finland but you were forced to flee, driven from your native soil in disgrace amid a national scandal, then the north Norfolk coast, the upper arc of England's rump, wouldn't be the worst place to end your days: peaceably undulating land, marshes and reedbeds, air thickly textured with the calls of migratory birds. Nina's father had said that this tufty wetland, like Finland's, was temperamentally best suited to the colours of autumn.

On the other hand, he had also told her Norfolk could provide nothing of Finland's glassy air, the rose-coloured granite, the peeling silver bark of birch woods, the hours-long phosphorescent sunsets reflected in mile upon mile of untouched ice and snow. And that if you yearned for the eerie Nordic forests, little comfort could be afforded by turning inland; Thetford Forest has never been backlit by the wintry midnight twilight of July, though its gnarled and knotted pines can present in their gloom the sinister faces of trolls. If the Finnish composer Sibelius had lived in Norfolk, her father had said, no doubt he would still have written music. But not those highly idiomatic works that evoke Finland's landscape. Which meant it wouldn't have been Sibelius.

Nina's parents moved here when her father retired, but he had always chosen the East Anglian flatlands; Nina was brought up in Essex. And now he was going to die in King's Lynn.

The cardiac unit seemed to exist on another planet from the weather, quarantined in its all-day synthetic, plasticky light. He was unrecognizable. A plastic mask glaciated his face; plastic tubes dribbled in and out of the bed. Nina remembered someone at work telling her about his own father's heart attack, the great man suddenly defenceless. 'The shock! I'd always thought he was invincible.' From the time Nina was seven, which marked the onset of what was known in the family as 'Martin's nervous breakdown', she had regularly watched her father cry into his breakfast. Invincible fathers were beyond her ken.

In fact, her feelings were directed at her own helplessness as much as his. He lay there crippled, and there was nothing she could do. She had to stand by and leave it to the grown-ups. I've been here before, she thought, in sudden, savage pain. I should have known to psych myself up for it. If Mum phones, she won't want hysterics from me. She'll have had enough of that already from my sister.

'Hearing is the last sense to go,' the doctor had said. Nina addressed one of the nurses in blue pyjamas who floated round the bed.

'Is it OK if I sing to him for a bit?'

Her father would have found ample black comedy in the situation – tubes in every orifice, the lustily panting ventilators like huffing-puffing monsters in a fairy tale. At all but the very worst of times, his off-the-wall humour was well known. So, 'I was thinking of Tom Lehrer's "The Masochism Tango" or "Poisoning Pigeons in the Park".'

The nurse was resetting one of the machines. She bungled it and the monitor yelped.

'Or a hymn,' amended Nina fast. 'If that's OK.'

Apparently it was, as they let her get on with it, quietly working her way through the hymns of her father's adopted church. In fact, if only the hospital could have re-energized Nina with a sandwich, she might have had a bash at Handel's *Messiah*, 'Hallelujah Chorus' and all. The canteen closed at 7.30. Unluckily, Nina skidded up to its counter at 7.32.

Obsessive by nature, Martin Hannay had thrown himself into the Anglican Church with a zealot's fervour. He'd always been obsessive. But that hadn't always made him a bad father. Until it suddenly went wrong he had been a terrific father. Nina saw herself with her best friend, Lucia. His blond head appeared round the bedroom door yodelling, 'Hymns Ancient and Modern 36, girls!'

'I know that one!' Lu shouted excitedly, her dark head

wriggling up the pillow. 'I've learned them, Mr Hannay. Number 36 is "Christians, Awake! Salute The Happy Morn!"'

'Oh don't, Lu,' Nina, next to her, grumbled into the eiderdown. 'You'll only encourage him.'

'I'll have a little more English Hymnal 149 from you, my girl,' he batted back, meaning, 'Father, We Praise Thee, Now The Night Is Over'.

On Lucia's first visit to the house she had addressed Nina in a stage whisper. 'I need the toilet,' and Nina's father had responded solemnly, 'Hymns 64 and 434.'

Nina had groaned. 'He means it's upstairs. The hymns are "All Ye Who Seek For Sure Relief", and "An Upper Room Did Our Lord Prepare".'

Lucia had stared a moment and then keeled over, screaming with laughter. Pity she'd waited so long to ask. Nina's mother had to mop both Lucia and the cushions.

Nina stayed at the hospital until dawn, give or take the occasional dive outside for a cigarette, shivering beneath a dripping shelter and activating the whooshing automatic doors by the ambulance bay. When at last she fell into bed, her head was full of the hymns' easy iambic heartbeat: 'How *Sweet* The *Name* Of *Je*sus *Sounds*', 'The *King* Of *Love* My *Shep*herd is' . . . the most primal of rhythms – until her mind ran on to 'Holy! Holy! Holy!' and suddenly the metre was slammed out of synch, violent as a seizure. As a heart attack. Nina was knifed awake and lay sleepless, intermittently crying.

'Oh, Nina!' said her mother from the other side of the world. In the background Nina's kid sister, Susan, shouted at somebody about luggage: 'Are you blind? How could that be my suitcase when the master's initials are on it?'

'He's in the best place, Mum,' said Nina. 'Are you able to get home?'

'All the flights are chock-full. André's been on the phone for hours. He's on the other line now.'

The other line? (The *master*?)

A male voice drifted into the air and Susan called, 'Mummy! André's got us on tonight's KLM to Amsterdam!'

'Did you hear that, Nina?'

'He's just sorting out connections, Mummy.'

Nina left them bustling with arrangements. Planes. She had a vision of Richard's plane landing Tuesday morning, his grooming tousled and his dark eyes blinking away the short night and the jetlag. She picked up her keys to head back to the hospital. She was too late. Martin Hannay had quietly died.

'Oh, Nina!' This time it was a cry.

'I know, Mum. I'm sorry.' Nina tugged back her own runaway emotions like a dog-walker catching sight of a rabbit.

Her mother clutched at insignificancies. 'Is today Saturday? Tomorrow will be the first Sunday your father has missed church since 1946.'

'Mum, God will excuse him under the circumstances.' It was what her father would have said.

'Would you be a dear and call Reverend Reece? Tell him we'd like a vigil before the . . . the . . .'

The funeral. Nina heard her mother's voice recoil from those drear vowels and rescued her. 'I expect there are instructions in Dad's will, particularly for the music. I'll look in his desk.'

Nina's father had been an OK pianist and a mesmerizing violinist. He had encouraged his little daughter. Her mind's eye, whose excitation threshold was evidently in chaos, suddenly screened another childhood scene, its soundtrack one of her father's musical arrangements. A violin was tucked under her own small chin, and the world's most famous ballroom champions were dancing. Lucia's parents in practice clothes dipped and swayed across their studio to the bittersweet strains of a waltz played with excruciating sentimentality by an over-excited ten-year-old, milking it. When Lucia's father released his wife from an oversway of such melodrama it would have had them slung off the floor at Blackpool, Lu was moved to tears. 'That is the best waltz you've *ever* danced, *ever!*' she cried at them. 'Nina, what's next? Can you give us a Cuban rumba?'

Now, on the phone, her mother's distress sought practicalities. 'I think Susan's wise to insist we fly first class. She's in a terrible state.'

Clearly. A wail had started up. 'Oh, Daddy! How could you go when I haven't said goodbye?'

'Do you want to talk to her, dear?'

Nina fought the temptation to say she would rather stick needles in her eyes. 'Not now, Mum. I'd better start phoning people.'

'Oh, my love, what an unhappy day!'

Nina was about to say gently that he had died on a beautiful September day, that yesterday's rain had left washed blue skies and the breezy, buffeted, restless golden light of a Turner painting. She stopped. Neither her mother nor her sister was whimsical, only Nina and her father. And now only Nina.

3

As promised, she looked in her father's desk. The will gave extensive directions for his funeral and left everything to his wife. Which did not amount to much. Along an ancient coastline whose towns were built from flint and carrstone, the Hannays managed to live in a tiny box of liverish yellow brick.

It was an orderly will. He'd been an orderly man, small, fair and shiningly clean. When he went bald instead of grey it seemed to increase his air of clinical cleanliness. Her emotions were ambushed by a pair of small, pensionable shoes, their oxblood leather buffed to glow like a sanctuary lamp. He had always taken them off indoors, a northern habit born of snowboots and slush. *Ryijy* rugs testified to his origins, as did the cool elegance of the glassware and ceramics, the oil paintings of muscular swans in quivering courtship between the bloodless watercolours her mother favoured; the sauna. Though extravagant, this had always been planned for their retirement home.

'How does it measure up, Dad?' Nina had asked when it was installed.

'Well, a true *sauvusauna* has smoke. But I'll just send you in first with a crate of cigarettes.' He had railed against her smoking since she was fifteen.

Then he had focused on the sauna his unflagging capacity for worry. Fire hazard. He brought in professionals while his wife blanched over their bills. 'But Martin, you've already filled the house with extinguishers, even upstairs in the *shower*.' That was the same shower where every morning he took a tape measure to assess the progress of a scrawly crack, until Nina's mother stuck up a notice: *When this crack reaches eighteen inches, Martin's house will fall down.*

'Now, Christine, that's just being silly,' he said.

There was Finland on the bookshelves, too, including a whole flock of Moomintrolls, the beguiling hippo-like creatures of Tove Jansson's stories. Her father had read them to Nina at bedtime, in funny voices and translations that were never the same twice running. Moomins had originally lived in human homes, silent behind the tall porcelain stoves: Nina's father embellished one of these into a giant stove of ceramic brick in a sumptuous shade of blue-green. He made the colours sing, literally sing out across Moominland, in the key of F major. And now she had lost him. She didn't feel her bemused grief as something customarily black; it felt more like white noise, mopping up sensation so that she strained to recognize even hunger and thirst through it.

In the sitting room was a boudoir grand piano you were always having to squeeze past, and on top of it his cased violin: seventeenth-century Italian, a gift from a rich uncle when the budding young virtuoso called Martti trotted off to the capital to study music. It was short-lived. His stage fright was ruinous. Other nervous performers threw up backstage. Nina's father threw up downstage. In later life he would say drily, 'It's no mean feat to clean that out of the *f* holes of your violin.'

His family pulled the plug and forced Martti into a stultifying law degree until he was rescued by Joseph Stalin. In 1939, the Soviet military machine rolled into Finland. War. By the time Nina's father returned to college he was an exile in England.

'A violin is a beautiful woman,' he once explained to the seven-year-old Lucia. 'See her waist, her hips, her—?'

'Martin,' warned Nina's mother.

'Whereas *pianos*! A three-legged hulk with a crocodile grin.'

'It's almost got four, Mr Hannay.' Lucia indicated the long drop of the pedal lyre hanging between its legs.

Nina's father gave her a wink that sent Lu into hysterics. 'Martin!'

The inlay of a violin is called the purfling, and 'purfling' became family slang. 'Have you purfled today?' he would demand of Nina. 'I'll have a quick purfle before lunch.' He would mystify people with references to the musical *Purfler on the Roof*. When the teenage Nina gave up purfling as uncool and confined herself to piano, it broke his heart. Now she thought, If I'd understood he would die one day, I would never have done it. Then, Susan will be toting that violin round to Sotheby's before her suitcase is unpacked. Nina found the address book and started phoning.

It was a harrowing task, the words never sounding true. Nina understood her father was dead, but surely it wasn't the same kind of dead as other people's dead fathers? Postal codes in the address book danced before her eyes. Letters and numbers together were always a problem for Nina: they rearranged themselves like unruly toddlers in a giggling fit. At teatime she broke off to phone her own friends: one was still in his office, a computer suite worth several times the value of her London flat.

'Hi, Duane. How's the machinery?'

She pictured him, tall and broad with a blond curly mop like a standard poodle, a look that should have been cordially beautiful but for the hardening effect of a wilful irascibility.

'Totally Jellicoed,' he replied, which was also Hannay slang, Duane having taken a fancy to it.

'More *cod* than *fantabulosa*?' ventured Nina in a slang she thought was his own subculture's.

'I'm not Quentin Crisp, Nina,' tutted Duane down the line. That 'Quentin' came at her broadside with the delicious shock of some opulent up-swelling musical crescendo.

'Actually,' she said, 'I'm after a whopping favour. Samaritans. Tomorrow's my all-night shift.'

'Need somebody to swap? Yeah, I'm up for it. Why, what's occurring?'

She swallowed. 'It's my father. He's – gone and died on me. Heart attack.'

'Oh, God, I'm sorry. So you're in Norfolk. On your own?'

'Except for an enormous Irish wolfhound called Kruger. It's OK, he's not bad company.'

He was sitting perkily, his scruffy knees jutting sideways like jug handles, unaware that dogs are supposed to pine. I'm so like Dad, thought Nina, I even have his pellucid winter-white skin; perhaps we have the same scent and Kruger thinks I'm my father in drag.

'You remembering to eat?' Duane was a devoted cook and knew Nina wasn't. Then he had a different thought. 'Isn't Richard over next week?'

'Yep,' she replied on a fresh wave of pain. 'When the computers are up, can you send a mail to explain?'

'What bloody awful luck.'

'*Que sera, sera.*' Nina was about to add that it was an additional injustice to her father, who would have hated the thought of screwing up her sex life by dying. She stopped, unsure she could voice that even to Duane. The truth was, there was only one person who was never intimidated by taboos about bad taste. And now he was dead.

'If you want me to drive over, just call.'

'Thanks.'

'And don't forget to feed the dog.'

To which Nina explained that the dog was nearly as big as she was, and could probably do his own shopping if she slipped a credit card in his collar and sent him lolloping off towards Sainsbury's.

Drifting back to her father's desk, she was surprised to find its cupboard locked. The hospital had given her his house keys, which he had always kept close ('Martin dear, you're jingling again'). Nina found the missing key on that same ring, as if it had special status. Odd. The cupboard turned out to be packed with manila folders, wedged too tight to dislodge. Brute tugging broke its will and the stack exploded, folders skittering across the rug. Papers shot from an open mouth: music. There were fourteen folders, each plump with music manuscript carefully notated in dark-blue ink. The handwriting was her father's.

He had composed bits and pieces all his life, none of them published. He would joke that an early work sounded like Sibelius's violin concerto chopped up and stuck back together at random. 'If you're going to pillage,' he said, 'choose a respectable source.' His mature works were dabbles. Nina rifled through the files and came to a halt, stunned. This was a massive symphony with a choral movement, like Beethoven's Ninth.

'You aimed a bit high here, didn't you, Dad?' she said aloud.

And when? Her mother would have drawn the line at Martin's shutting himself away to write a cupboard-sized symphony. But the name at the top was Martti, which predated her mother. The choral text was unmistakably in Finnish – inch-long words pebble-dashed with dots:

. . . Väinämöinen kulki äitinsä . . .

'Come on, Kruger.' She scooped up folders by the armful, relayed them to the piano and dug out an ashtray.

Nina could sight-read anything. She had once been a jobbing audition pianist for *The Phantom of the Opera*: all over the world, hopeful singers brought along volumes of opera and blithely handed a full score to the pianist, who generally replied, 'I left my orchestra on the bus.' It was unlikely that anyone other than Nina had been able to work them into something playable on a keyboard. Even for Nina it was no joke to keep track of her father's symphony as the figures were carried by one instrument after another, while the big, loose pages rebelled against the narrow ledge of the music rest and flapped to the carpet.

There didn't seem to be strong melodies you could sing in the bath. The music developed from short motifs that were passed conversationally round the strings, the horns and the woodwinds, while their key and colour shifted in a confident sorcery of modulation.

Why was it locked in a cupboard? Perhaps he had tried to get the work performed but failed, and took that failure badly. All his life, he was the sort of man who might react to any setback as if it were the Curse of the Cat People. Poor Dad.

As she played on, a fine electric excitement began to tickle her stomach wall. I'm no expert on symphonies, allowed Nina, but I can tell dross from . . . Surely this is *good*? Her father had been a wannabe, a failure, a loser, a lost expat two thousand miles from home who nullified every scrap of good luck that ever came his way. She stopped, and the room seemed to tremble. She thought, suppose this is actually remarkable. I could . . . show it to someone? Get it recorded, even. Wring from the world some posthumous acknowledgement. He would have liked that. He would have seen it as . . . vindication.

Nina played on into the September evening, its light stained green-gold by the robinia outside the window. She knew she should finish that address book. But she also knew that tomorrow her sister would arrive, and this closeness she felt with her father, playing his music to a house empty of everyone but his soggily snoring dog, would be blown apart in an entire circus of fuss.

4

'What *on earth* does that man think he's doing? Hey!' demanded Susan in a tone unusual at funerals. 'Yes, you!'

The mourners were lined up on the pavement behind a coffin softened with chrysanthemums. Now Susan was in through the church gate like a whippet.

Nina called out, 'Susan, no! Maybe he's from Finland, and—'

He was doing nothing worse than standing between the leaning headstones and photographing the proceedings.

'Erik?' Nina stopped short in front of the hapless photographer. He was a big, heavy bear of a man her father's age (when must I stop saying 'my father's age'? she wondered with a kick of pain). Amiable eyes wobbled behind the distorting thickness of maximum-prescription lenses. 'Erik Pellinen?'

'And you are Nina? We have not met since many years. You were very little.'

'I'm still rather little,' apologized Nina, and introduced the tall elegant sister glaring at her side. Then she gently explained that nowadays nobody took funeral pictures but the Finns. 'Though I can't imagine why not. I think it's a lovely custom.'

From Susan's scandalized look it was clear she didn't.

'The show's about to roll,' Nina added, to the further disapproval of her sister. She extracted a promise that they would meet later, then rejoined the procession so the Reverend Reece could lead them into the church, described by the delightfully boasting pamphlets as 'in the Saxonshore benefice and a thousand years old'.

While the bishop greeted their mother, Susan hissed, 'I don't know which side to sit.'

'You mean, are we bride or groom?'

Susan ignored this. 'I'm sure Daddy's spirit is hovering around us. Watching from the hedgerows, smiling from the fields.'

To which he would have responded, 'And do-si-do your partner!'

Music was playing, by (of course) Sibelius: the obligatory *Finlandia*. What would I want for myself? Nina wondered, and suddenly ached to discuss it with her father. Pink Floyd's *Dark Side Of The Moon*: 'The Great Gig In The Sky'. 'Go for it,' he would have said.

Then the organist moved on to a piece listed as *Funeral Music by Sibelius*: slow and sure-footed, with frost in its clever open-ended chords. Nina recognized this because her father had used it in his symphony. Lifted it wholesale. So the symphony was just another puffed-up pastiche. Disappointment sluiced over her. There would be nothing she could salvage on his behalf. Even posthumously he was second-rate.

She was tired to the bones, having spent the week running round Norfolk. Susan had been spared the arrangements, the registrar – and the corpse: it was Nina who had accompanied their mother in the hateful task of viewing the body. Their mother had wept, and as Nina had not seen her weep since 1966 it catapulted her back there, to a child's powerless misery. Yet she herself simply couldn't relate her quirky, emotional, exasperating father to that insensible sheeted figure in the chapel of rest. She couldn't relate this social occasion to him either, despite the redolent chromatism of Sibelius.

This was Nina's first acquaintance with family death; all the grandparents had died before she was born. She had caught herself looking for her father in crowds. She kept remembering contact numbers he'd given her over the years, and would conceive the wild idea of trying to reach him on one of them before remembering he had gone beyond the range of British Telecom.

Susan was spared fatigue and upset because she was feeling delicate. Pregnant.

'Daddy never knew!' she had kept wailing.

'Then why didn't you ring and tell him?' Nina had finally been driven to ask, adding before she could stop herself, 'On one of your two phone lines.'

'Because I didn't want to worry him,' Susan had retorted illogically, and demanded that Nina put her cigarette out.

Susan had been a late, thoroughly unplanned baby born when Nina was eleven, and now at twenty-two looked like a better-groomed version of their mother in photographs from the 1950s – tall, dark and glossy with pouty, lipsticky lips. To their father, her unexpected arrival had been nothing less than a gift from his God, sent as a lifeline to rescue him from the mental abyss towards which he was hurtling downhill with the wind behind him.

'Little Susan, my little saviour,' his little Nina had once overheard him say, who had done the best a child could to rescue her daddy from that abyss, and who still had in her nostrils the sulphurous reek of its vapours.

Anxiety neurosis, they called it. He could worry irrationally about anything but his primary focus was cancer. For years, Martin Hannay had suffered a morbid conviction that he was dying, from one malignancy after another, selected from his imagination and a medical text-book. Her mother had once cried out, 'A small child could see you haven't got the thing in that picture!' So it was lucky for them that they had a small child available. Nina must have been one of the few seven-year-olds ever called upon to compare a heat hive with a photograph of malignant melanoma.

That juggernaut of mental illness hadn't rumbled slowly to life on a cold engine and built up speed; it had careened in through the walls of his family's life one morning at breakfast. He had appeared at the door, called his wife outside with the voice of doom, and proclaimed that he had a tumour on his lung. Well, Dad, Nina told him now, you lived till you were nearly seventy and went out un-tumoured to the end.

The church was packed to the doors. Soothed by the age-old doughy smell of cold stone, Nina let the service roll over her with the comfort of those ancient cadences.

'*I believe in God*,' affirmed the congregation in an echoey, lagging monotone. Susan's voice rose piously like a descant. '*. . . the resurrection of the body . . .*'

'*. . . to have our consummation and bliss . . .*'

Bodies, consummation and bliss. Before Richard had got her news he had sent several mails, which Duane kindly posted to Norfolk. They were full of sweet, appealing invitations. Now she imagined a thoroughly un-funereal scene: Richard, with his collegiate air of command and looking her straight in the eyes, was taking her clothes off.

'*. . . we commend thy servant, Martin, the Reverend Hannay . . .*'

And Nina, the vicar's daughter, guiltily returned to her duty.

*

Back at the house there were only three smokers: Nina, a titled parishioner and Erik the Camera, who looked too big for the room. He had been her father's only close friend, and she had never understood why he had suddenly stopped visiting them. She was eleven when they last met.

'Thank you for coming,' she told him.

'I was already in England to stay with my son who has moved to London.' Erik's English was entirely unaccented but wary, as if he couldn't trust it not to bolt and get up to mischief. He fished in a pocket and produced a business card. 'He is a dancer.'

The card said '*Jussi Pellinen*'. Nina read it as 'Juicy' and her eyes flickered away, unexpectedly embarrassed.

'I don't remember you as having a family,' she said.

'In those days I came alone. Now my dear wife is no more.'

'I'm sorry.'

'It was long ago. Sadly, Martti and I had not met in many years. We always think there is plenty of time. Yes, even as we grow old.'

He said that 'Yes' on an intake of breath. As Nina's father had done. Her brain tingled. They sipped their drinks in a silence Erik felt no need to fill. He was a Finn; he only spoke when there was something to say. Otherwise he would be content for the pair of them to sip in silence the rest of the afternoon. But Nina was only half-Finnish; she didn't last thirty seconds.

'What sort of dancer is your son?'

'He teaches tango.'

'Really?' she responded with her first enthusiasm of the day.

'Tango is unofficially the national dance of Finland.'

'Of *Finland*?'

'That is how everyone reacts. It is another of our activities to astonish foreigners, like the wife-carrying contest and the competition for who can sit longest on an anthill.'

Nina laughed. 'Dad never mentioned tango.'

'The fashion boomed after he left.'

'When you used to stay with us in Essex, we lived down the road from the ballroom dancers Giancarlo and Beryl Clark.'

The names apparently meant nothing. Behind the lenses Erik's eyes bulged benignly like friendly fish in a tank.

'They were world champions eight times, and their daughter was my best friend.'

Nina was startled by an intense sense of Lucia, with whom she had lost touch from sheer carelessness after Susan was born and the Hannays moved house. The sensation was of fizzing primary colours, of naughtiness and fearlessness, a spirit supple but not quite malleable. A survivor. Or, as Nina's mother had often put it, a little madam.

It occurred to her that Giancarlo and Beryl would probably have come to the funeral if they had only known. She was sure they were still famous enough to trace. Why didn't I think of it? she asked herself, pained and guilty. Nina had worshipped them: they had charm, charisma, graciousness. But the Hannays moved away, and then Nina reached her teens and came to worship other stars, who weren't very bothered about charm and graciousness. In fact some of them were drugged to the eyeballs, swore and spat at the audience, and bit the heads off live bats.

Erik was saying, 'I fear my son would not be impressed. His dance is the tango of Argentina and he is rather . . .' Erik searched for the expression, 'hoity-toity about ballroom.'

'If he's hoity-toity about the Clarks, he's got it wrong,' said Nina defensively. 'They brought the true Argentinian tango back to our dance floors in the 1960s. To great acclaim.'

'I am corrected,' said Erik formally, but Nina was easily made argumentative from fatigue, and plugged away at her point.

'When they retired from competition they danced it in cabaret. To great acclaim.'

'Yes, I heard you the first time,' said Erik mildly. 'Your sister is telling the bishop she has been pregnant five weeks and two days. I see the precision has embarrassed the gentleman.'

Nina was sipping at a glass of wine. She snorted it up her

nose. The wine hit her sinuses like a belly-flop in a pool.

'That is better,' said Erik pacifically.

'I'm sorry. It's this artificial atmosphere. It's so completely un-Dad.'

The small house was packed. The black-suited congregation, like party-going crows, spilled into the hall, on to the stairs, into the sauna probably. And there was church in their voices. When the bishop had given the eulogy, Nina had realized that if it hadn't been for the Finnish references she could never have identified it as her father's in a line-up of eulogies. Even the Finnish stuff had sounded contrived, the bishop describing her father as a war hero and making a fair old mess of the words Tolvajärvi–Ägläjärvi campaign. But Dad wasn't called a hero for long, she had protested silently. Why insult him by distorting the most crucial facts of his life?

An air of the Apostles' creed still hung over Susan. She wore soft black cashmere and ivory silk, the wide-padded shoulders and tiny waist delineating a chic triangle, arrestingly feminine. Nina, too, was in black: mantilla lace sculpturally folded over jazzy checks, with cute little ankle boots and a leather biker's jacket. Studded.

Susan's voice carried across the chatting and clinking. 'Individual tribes hate one another. Without the whites to keep them apart there would be a bloodbath.'

Erik was asking Nina, 'Do you dance tango?'

'Sadly not. Two left feet. And I didn't know we had any in London. The rest of the world got the stage show *Tango Argentino* but the tour boycotted us. The Falklands War,' she reminded him.

'Our Finnish version is not for the stage. It is a gentle, shuffling motion, whereas true tango has—'

'*Attitude*,' said Nina with relish.

'Indeed. We mostly dance to songs about homesickness. You will know this is another trait – music extolling our homeland: the lakes, forest legends, the seasons, the nesting cranes.'

In September the cranes leave to fly south. Nina had been told this by her father every September of her life. Her eyes overflowed. Erik tactfully let his gaze drift.

'Please carry on about the tango,' she said, making an effort.

'Really? Well, the glory days were the 1940s and '50s, but then came the Beatles. Tango Finlandia was suddenly obsolete and our most famous songwriter took to drink and shot himself.'

'And there was I, thinking this would cheer me up.'

'Ah well, a lot of Finns take to drink,' replied Erik brightly, 'and quite a few shoot themselves. But there is a happy ending. We have a revival. An annual festival, even, though my son hints that this is not for the trendy. For example, "I wouldn't be seen dead at the tango festival." Still, he dances like an angel. He tells me that too.'

'I thought Finns never bragged,' said Nina, smiling.

'Yes? It is also said we are clean people, spick and span, who pay their bills on time. My son lives in a huge dusty flat that appears to have been blasted by a bomb, surrounded by final demands. But our family has some foreign blood. I blame that.'

Nina laughed again.

'Another cigarette?'

'Thank you, Erik, but no.' His tobacco smelled like a fire in a glue factory.

'Forgive me if this remark is misplaced,' he said, puffing, 'but your mother mentioned how your sister was an Oxford scholar. Yet in South Africa she is unemployed. Did your father regret this?'

Erik looked disquieted, struggling to fit this self-assured woman into the jigsaw of qualities that had made up Martti Hannikainen. Nina had gone to university in London and taken first-class honours in maths – which made her the luminary of the family for eleven years until Susan, reading English inevitably at Oxford, inevitably took a starred double First. Immediately after which she married André and moved to Cape Town.

Nina said, 'Dad would have been horrified that she was having babies so young.'

Would he, though? She remembered them all at the airport, the rheumy-eyed tearfulness as he clasped Susan to himself. 'God be with you till we meet again,' he had quoted, the words, not the hymn number. 'My darling.'

His little saviour. If it is unseemly for an adult to feel sibling rivalry, thought Nina, then how uncouth is it to feel this black noxious spew of jealousy *at your father's wake*? Do other people grow up? Is it only me?

She said, 'Speaking of Dad, maybe you can shed light on a mystery. Locked in his desk I found a symphony he'd written.'

'Symphony?'

'Enormous work with a choral finale, no less. It must date from before he came to England. During the war perhaps.'

'Soldiers do not write enormous symphonies,' said Erik.

'Afterwards then.'

'I was with your father then also. He was not composing.'

'Oh.'

She saw her mother edging round the piano with a tray of trembly glasses. Nina should be helping her.

'Your father never mentioned this symphony?'

'No.'

'The score has his name?'

'Well, his former name.'

'And it was under lock and key in his own home? I should very much like to see it, Nina. Where is his desk?' Erik's head turned to the door, the light making sheet metal of his lenses.

'It's all locked up again,' she told him, which wasn't true. There was an unwelcome acuity about the man's interest. The earlier mateyness was slipping away. Her mother was now at her side, gaunt with tiredness, her wavering tray sloshing the drinks out of reach of the bouncing dog. She greeted Erik distractedly and turned to Nina. 'I could do with a hand! Fetch the mushroom vol-au-vents, please. And where have all the peanuts gone?'

Which was nearly a song by Peter, Paul and Mary, thought Martin's daughter. 'Mum, I'll get Kruger out of the way while Susan—'

'Susan says she can't hand out vol-au-vents because she's pregnant.'

A little later, offering coffee in the hope that everyone would take the hint and go home, Nina caught the sound of her name.

'. . . and a gifted pianist. Nina could play at the age of five.' Then her mother's voice climbed a register. '*Now what?* Nina, Susan's just snatched Lady Dorothy's cigarette and dowsed it in her wine glass. Could you calm them down, dear?'

That evening, as she took off her oddball black garments and hung them in the wardrobe, Nina was conscious that something had passed from her. Hymn number 16, she thought. 'The Day Thou Gavest, Lord, Is Ended'. And she presumed that somewhere in the proceedings she must have said goodbye.

5

'It was only a month ago your father was conducting a burial service himself. Howard Mortimer's widow asked for him.'

'Dad must have enjoyed that,' said Nina. 'Well, you know what I mean.'

'Yes, he liked to keep his hand in.'

Christine Hannay wasn't dressed yet. She sat at the kitchen table, her pink scalp twinkling as vulnerable as a fontanelle through a perm from the brutalist school of hair-dressing, its graphite-and-steel greyness further undermining the fatigued beauty of her face, the diluted green of her once-splendid eyes, at sixty-eight. Nina felt a protective twinge and wished she didn't have to return to work. It was Sunday, two days after the funeral.

Had Mum still loved him? she caught herself wondering, and wasn't shocked. Her mother wasn't a woman of passion. A vicar's daughter before she was a vicar's wife, she had a professional Christian's allegiance to Duty. And it was dis-appointingly clear, from certain allusions, that her 'Onward, Christian Soldiers' stoicism had also pertained to her marital bed. Yet Nina's father had loved Christine, and com-prehensively, prompting Nina to ask herself, By what alchemy of genetics could a daughter inherit her sex drive from her *father*? Christine would never have allowed herself to leave her husband, but at his lowest point he was . . . intolerable. Had she ever really forgiven him?

And had Nina?

Now, Christine was gnawing at old worries. 'I am concerned about you being on your own, dear.'

'I'm OK, Mum.' Nina knew what was coming.

'It's a mystery to me why you broke up with dear Gregory. He was such a love. And fond of children.'

'It just didn't work out. I'm sorry too.'

'He was kind enough to send a floral tribute.'

'Yes, Dad and Greg always got on like—' Like a sauna on fire. Two music fanatics together. 'Mum, it doesn't mean I face a future with just the cat and meals-on-wheels. I'm only thirty-three.'

'Your sister's twenty-two, but she is settled with her feet firmly on the ground.'

Or, right now, on the ceiling. From above their heads issued the comic irritation of Susan's noises off, back and forth, up and down, dressing and grooming. She was flying home again on Wednesday and there had been exhausting discussions about her journey to the airport. Susan expected a chauffeur.

'I've already had an entire week off work,' Nina had pointed out reasonably. 'Get a train to London, then hop on the underground.'

'With *my* claustrophobia?'

'Since when?'

'Since I got pregnant. OK?'

'So the train then a taxi.'

'If no one will take me the distance, I'm stranded! In my condition!'

'Susan, of course they'll take you. As a picking ground, Heathrow is to taxi drivers what the Klondike was to Eskimo Nell.'

At which point their mother had reminded them she'd just buried her husband and deserved some peace and quiet.

Now, in the kitchen, Nina waited for the next assault. It didn't take long.

'And there was that wreath from an American.'

Even though she was prepared for it, Nina's heart jumped in her chest.

'Your sister tells me he phoned half a dozen times.'

'Yes, I seem to have missed him.' Running round Norfolk on errands.

'Is this the same American you talked about in London?'

'Possibly,' Nina conceded. She didn't remember having mentioned Richard at all. Her parents had come down the weekend after she met him: perhaps his name had kept slipping from her as involuntarily as the bleeps of Duane's computer.

'The American who fought in Vietnam,' persisted her mother. 'That one.'

My God, thought Nina. The things parents store up.

'Dear, listen to me. Don't get involved with a man who's war-damaged.'

'Mum!' It was a hiccup of horrified laughter. 'Richard just mentioned Vietnam in passing.'

'A man doesn't mention his war unless it's always at the back of his mind. This is one subject I know more about than you do.'

'You've nothing to worry about. Richard's in the departure lounge waiting for his plane home as we speak.' Nina's voice quivered.

Susan called down the stairs. 'I'm going to phone André again, Mummy.'

'All right, but you really must keep an eye on the time. Money is going to be very tight from now on.'

Nina left them to it and went back to loading the car. Kruger (whose colonial name was, of course, Susan's choice) followed her, hoping for a ride. Earlier, Nina had taken him on to the marshes and watched him run, wagging and smiling, across a many-textured montage of silver, brown and sage green. And suddenly she had been convulsed by longing: I want to get away. The idea came from nowhere, fully formed and insistent. And shocking. Away from what? Her yearning had to do with that vast sky, the corrugated sea. Then, looking north across the reedbeds, she had had another thought. It was more than forty years since her father fled his country. The scandal had been started by one man in his home town, who must be long dead by now. Moreover, not many people would be alive still who remembered anything about it. Surely that was strange? That he never set foot in Finland again?

Nina had asked her mother about the symphony but without success.

'No doubt it stems from the foolish days of his youth, bless him.'

'May I take it home?'

'Of course, dear. It's no use to me or your sister, we're tone deaf. And Nina,' she lowered her voice, 'you might like to take the violin. Susan was dropping hints about Christie's. I wish you two would get along better. One day she'll be the only family you have.'

'You'll be around *ages* yet.' Nina kissed her mother on the cheek.

Susan was still on the phone when Nina said goodbye. As they walked down the drive, her mother eyed the car with concern. 'It's terribly old, dear. You said yourself, one day you'll put your foot down and it will fall apart.'

'Mum, that isn't quite what I said, you know.'

Across the road, a sheep with an emerald field behind it strained through a hedge for a blade of grass. Her mother smiled.

'*We have erred and strayed from thy ways like lost sheep,*' she quoted from the General Confession. '*We have left undone those things which we ought to have done, and we have done those things which we ought not to have done, and there is no health in us.* I know you stopped believing a long time ago, Nina, but I'll bet you couldn't recite that without your hair prickling.'

Nina laughed but it struck her that the Christianity of her upbringing should have afforded some comfort now. With a stab of resentment she realized there had not been a nanosecond when she believed her father might actually be up there somewhere.

'Will you be OK, Mum? After Susan's gone too, the house will seem lonely.'

'I've got dear Kruger, and when Susan's gone, at least I'll have my telephone back. Bye-bye, love. Don't do anything foolish.'

Her mother was never entirely comfortable that Nina wasn't about to embark on something totally irresponsible, like ditching the steady job to become a rock star.

6

Childhood

The men at the door were plainclothes police. They were greeted by the family's young Labrador.

'My husband is expecting you,' said Christine Hannay, tugging futilely at the animal's collar. 'I'm so sorry!'

'That's all right, madam,' said the taller of the men, dodging the lunging head. 'I'm fond of dogs.'

'Not this one. He's just been sick in the garden. Down, Tapio!'

Nina's father strode into the hall, right hand outstretched, insensible to the uproar, the perfect English host. 'Do come through to the sitting room. My wife will put the kettle on.'

In the kitchen, five-year-old Nina petted Tapio's ears as he whined at the closed door.

'Nina, don't touch his whiskers, he's been sick all over the roses.' Then she noticed the child's face, smudged with the dried spoors of tears.

'What's the matter?'

'Are they going to take Daddy away?'

Startled, Christine jerked upright. 'No! What a notion!'

'Will they make him go back to Finland?'

'Lovey, they're only here because Daddy wants to become an Englishman. You remember—'

'Is it because of the trick?'

'What trick?'

'The one the nasty man played. Writing about Daddy in the book.'

The kettle was stuttering towards the boil. Christine unplugged it. 'Who has been talking to you?' There was an alien colour to her tone.

'Nobody.'

'Who told you about Daddy and a book?'

'Nobody,' repeated Nina with bewildered guilt. Then, 'You and Daddy did. I heard. Will those policemen take him away?'

Her face was sheet-white and terrified. Christine was nonplussed. What could a five-year-old child in an English village know of plainclothes police dragging fathers away? With one hand she smoothed Nina's spiky hair that would never lie flat, and with the other stroked the dog as if he, too, might be fretting.

'You didn't hear properly, lovey.' Her voice was maternal again.

Nina just looked at her.

'Listen to me. When anyone asks to become a British citizen, there are special police who always come round to talk to them, and see for themselves that they're nice. Daddy's training for the Church, and what could be nicer? You saw the men smiling. They even liked Tapio.'

Nina nodded but her eyes were deep blue and enormous. Christine nibbled her lip. 'Oh Lord, I have to get on with the tea. Let's have a cuddle. Better now? Nobody's going to take Daddy away, I promise.'

The best bone china was arranged on a tray, the translucent bowls glowing the colour of marmalade in sunlight thickened with yellow from the cheap curtains. Christine's movements interrupted the configuration with shadow play. 'I'll be back in a tick.'

While her mother's best hostess voice offered biscuits across the conversational drone, Nina sat on the kitchen floor, confusedly taking stock. Nobody sounded cross, or menacing, or frightened. Had she got it wrong? But if the policemen weren't here to take her father away, why had he been in the shed before they arrived, reciting those words? *Isä meidän, joka olet taivaissa! Pyhitetty olkoon sinun nimesi* . . . The Lord's prayer in Finnish. And what about the rose bushes? Her mother might believe it was Tapio who threw up over them, but Nina, the witness, knew it was her father.

7

She did ditch the job, but merely in exchange for another. It was all part of this strange new mood. *I want to get away.*

Her present company was on the move too, relocating to somewhere cheaper. There were generous redundancy packages so a lot of people made a killing, pocketing the cash and moving straight into a new post. It was therefore unfortunate that Nina resigned the day before the announcement and so wasn't eligible for a penny of it.

'And if you say *que sera, sera,* I'll thump you,' said Duane.

She planned a cracking farewell party – for which Richard was coming over! He had been very kind to her. When they spoke she asked how his meetings went.

'The way meetings go when your mind is fixed on the unhappiness of a friend,' said Richard, which kicked through her senses like cocaine.

Nevertheless, the intrusion of death and funerals had played havoc with their previous courage. Nina's invitation was a mix of excited welcome and no pressure. '. . . but I'll understand if you can't swing a business trip in the present climate of belt-tightening . . .'

She told Duane, 'It's always like this, men and women, one self-assured surge followed by a rapid retreat – it's like some intricate quadrille. You don't know how lucky you are. Remember your joke? An old queen is walking down the street and a bit of rough says to him, "Do you or don't you: yes or no?" And he replies, "Well I don't usually, dear, but you talked me into it." That's the way!'

'Actually, Nina, we're not all tarts,' Duane snapped back.

But even his censure couldn't slap her down: Richard had booked leave and would pay his own fare. Nina, excited as a teenager, plundered her credit card, and soon in her underwear drawer was the sort of lace you wouldn't wear to a funeral.

She had also heard from Erik Pellinen, who had sent her a book: *A Life of Dance* by Giancarlo and Beryl Clark. His son had found it. Nina still had the business card with the phone number of the son's 'huge dusty flat' where Erik was staying.

'That was so kind,' she said when she got him. 'I didn't know they'd written a book.'

It post-dated her days with them. Although Nina herself had brought the Clarks to Erik's attention, the arrival of their book felt uncanny: those sudden flaring memories of her childhood hadn't stopped with the funeral.

'Thank you, Erik,' she said again.

'It seems your friends were indeed famous.'

'Superstars. They worked hard enough for it. If the Clarks weren't travelling the globe they practised ten hours a day. Every year they won half a dozen major championships and another three or four lesser ones.'

'What stamina. Tell me, Nina, have you done anything more with Martti's symphony?'

'Done anything?'

'Shown it to anyone.'

'No.'

'Perhaps I could look myself.'

'Do you know about music? Sorry, I can't remember.'

'A little.'

'Oh.' Away from the funeral atmosphere, his interest felt

helpful rather than intrusive. She had always liked him: Nina could picture Erik playing hide-and-seek with her in the vicarage garden.

'You live in Hampstead, yes?' he was saying. 'A pretty place. We could—'

'Harlesden. Not Hampstead. Not by a long chalk. But I know Hampstead, so let's meet there.'

Nina was right, Harlesden was not Hampstead by a long chalk. No hills, no heath, no blue plaques bragging about Keats and Sigmund Freud. The Harrow Road was an unpretty urban thoroughfare running north-west-ish, which unravelled en route into a ganglion of threads. Harlesden.

Nina had lived in Hampstead until the split with dear Gregory. She had moved out of his Georgian house complete with music studio, and for the first year had shared a rented flat where the costs were low and the parties unforgettable. Then well-meaning colleagues had bullied her into 'getting a foot on the property ladder'. She had bought into the rocketing market last spring. Everyone had promised that Nina could not lose.

The same colleagues, some of whom stabled ponies and could hardly back the Range Rover out of the drive for tourists when there was a regatta, only knew of Harlesden in connection with the notorious high-rise Stonebridge Estate. They were misinformed. Nina's street was tree-lined and lamplit, and you were less likely to meet a mugger in it than outside Harrods. And the whole place had the sort of *zing* you could expect in a district where ninety-three languages are spoken.

The houses of Brickstone Road were built around 1900 in unpretentious rows for the workers. By 1989 workers expected less, and Nina's flat comprised just the ground floor. The small walled garden was her pride and joy – and hers alone, as stipulated by an extraordinary document that also forbade the use of the garden 'for unauthorized erections'.

Colour was central to Nina's inner life. Inspiration for her utilitarian décor had collared her one spangled October day: the no-nonsense beauty of a commercial van in child's-crayon-coloured livery, glitteringly parked under a scarlet maple. And colour flowed from garden to flat in seamless planting schemes that transmuted from soil to container when they crossed the threshold.

The second weekend after the funeral Nina went back up to Norfolk to check how her mother was coping.

'To be honest, dear, friends are a little overzealous with their kindness. I hardly get a minute to myself.'

And Nina tried to interest her father's widow in his symphony.

It followed the old-fashioned format: four movements, the second of them slow. Perhaps being old-fashioned was an occupational hazard of plagiarizing other composers, and this one especially. Sibelius had stopped writing back in the 1920s. Even in his heyday there were critics who belittled him for not following the avant-garde and their icy mathe-matical abstractions: some of Sibelius's most hummable work was rooted in the Romantics. Tchaikovsky. No doubt this boosted his following; he had been staggeringly popu-lar in Britain and the States. When the first talking picture was made, *The Jazz Singer*, his music was included in the soundtrack. An American fan once addressed a letter to 'Jean Sibelius, Europe' and it arrived, no problem: there was only one Jean Sibelius. Nina also knew that although he lived past ninety (he was still alive, just about, when she was born) by then he had been silent for three decades.

Her mother just wasn't musical and Nina couldn't really engage her interest – until the mention of Erik, at which she went off like a firework.

'Don't hand over that manuscript to Erik Pellinen, Nina. The man's very charming but he's an opportunist.'

'Mum? Erik was Dad's oldest friend.'

'Erik kept in touch just as long as he could make use of

our home whenever he flew to England for a dirty weekend. He had a mistress in Romford. From the day we moved to the wrong side of Essex, Erik dropped us.'

'Really? But if he had a mistress, Mum, how come he didn't have a bed?'

'The bed had a husband in it. One afternoon his key turned in the door and Erik left down a drainpipe. Your father thought that was funny.'

'I bet he did.'

'Seriously, dear, Erik takes advantage.'

'He seems to think the score might be worth looking at.'

'Worth money, he means.'

'If so, I'd say he's wrong. There are too many borrowings. But anyhow, Erik couldn't exploit it without our consent. He doesn't own the manuscript. We do.'

'I do,' corrected her mother. 'And we mustn't arouse attention. Your father kept his head down all his time in England. We both know why.'

'Mum, nobody would worry about that old business. Truly. We've been out of the woods for years. The whole thing related to a war nobody outside Finland has heard of.'

'Oh, Nina! Your father was accused of reckless behaviour that caused a death! Think of the gutter press. They would lap up the story.'

Nina could see banner headlines in her mother's eyes: **Dead Vicar in War Shame Scandal**. It was more gently that she said, 'They wouldn't be able to find any story. The British authorities must have decided it was all malicious baloney, otherwise they would never have let him stay. He was vetted, remember.' The shorter of the policemen had worn a hat. She could see him raising his trilby as a choking Tapio wrenched her mother's arm. 'Plenty get rejected, Mum.'

In one of her perplexing changes of direction, Nina's mother asked sadly, 'Is it true that nobody nowadays has heard of the Winter War?'

''Fraid so.'

'It was such an inspiration, Finland's tiny population beating back Stalin's army like David and Goliath while we were expecting Hitler to invade us any minute.'

'According to Dad, we sold them fifty thousand uniforms. Unfortunately they were the same colour as the Russians', so ours weren't a lot of use on the front. He always thought that was hilarious.'

'So I recall.'

'Hey, what does happen if your uniform looks like the enemy's? Do you play in reverse strip like footballers?'

'To return to the point. Please promise me you won't let Martin's music out of your sight. Particularly not in the hands of Erik Pellinen.'

And Nina promised.

8

'Mmmh,' said Erik. The manuscript took up room the waiter made no secret of resenting. The man hovered, clucking, as Erik shuffled the bread and olives on to an empty table.

He reached the choral part. This had rung a bell with Nina. That unpronounceable Väinämöinen – he was a character from Finland's great folk poem the *Kalevala*, full of supermen and magic. Nina's father, a would-be poet himself once, used to read her an English version between Moomins. Sadly, in his little daughter's opinion Väinämöinen was a know-all with a nasty temper, and she would rather have had Winnie the Pooh.

Erik turned another page and said, 'This must be looked at professionally. May I borrow it?'

'Unfortunately, I promised Mum—'

'Say for ten days in the first instance.'

Loosened up by his time in London, his English ran more freely than at the funeral.

'Mum doesn't want any of Dad's music to leave the family. I'm sure you understand.'

Apparently not. 'This work is extraordinary.'

'The size is a bit deceptive,' Nina explained, 'because it

includes separate parts – for each instrument and the choir. The basic score is a hundred and ninety pages.'

'Which is nearly an hour's worth. That is monumental, Nina.'

'Strange that Dad banged it out without telling anyone.'

'And when, my dear? Not at university. We were room-mates; while Martti was studying law I was a chemistry student. And he was not banging out four-movement works for choir and orchestra under fire from Soviet tanks, nor afterwards when Finland was sucked into World War Two.'

'Earlier, then. Dad did study composition.'

'But gave up at eighteen. Such a hefty work would take perhaps six years from the initial sketches. That would make your father how old when he sketched this one – twelve? Martti was not Mozart.'

'So what are you saying, Erik?'

'I have spent days in the library, mugging up. Now I have the score before me – and it can only be a copy of a master-work by a master composer.' His eyes goggled behind their swimmy glass. 'My dear, you're Martti's daughter. Who used the *Kalevala*? And here,' Erik pointed to a page of rushing strings with quick blasts from the brass. 'Whose finger-prints are these? A Finnish genius who wrote a final symphony but never allowed the world to hear it.'

Her mother had said Erik was an opportunist. Right now he looked like a Shakespearean scholar who had just been presented with the Bard's diaries covering the first pro-duction of *Hamlet*. Nina's duck *à l'orange* gave a little jig of excited fear against her stomach wall.

'Oh, fuck,' she said and took a swig of her wine.

They gave up on the food. Erik ordered another bottle of burgundy while the waiter cleared their abandoned plates with a suicidal air. Erik could not keep his hands off Nina's manuscript. Every few seconds he fastidiously wiped his spatulate fingers on the napkin to avoid sullying the neat blue-black of her father's careful penwork. He even put his cigarette out.

'Sibelius is one of our century's greatest mysteries,' he said. 'He was the world's most popular living composer at the height of his powers. He promised a new symphony for years. It never came – and neither did anything else of the slightest significance. At the very pinnacle of his career, the music just stopped. Nobody has ever explained why.'

Nina said, 'Dad told me Sibelius simply retired. How many composers have lived to be so old?'

'There was no question of retirement. He insisted the new work was nearly ready. Season after season he pledged the world première to Boston. You must understand what this meant to them: to be first to perform the new master-piece would be a triumph. When the promise continually came to nothing, their conductor was . . . tearing his hair out,' decided Erik idiomatically. 'He was not alone; critics, journalists and fans were crying with impatience. Other leading orchestras were at their wits' end awaiting a brand-new work that would pack the halls and boost their prestige. It took them a long time to resign themselves. But the symphony never came, nor did anything else except dribs and drabs. Sibelius was effectively silent from 1926 until 1957.'

'Then what?' asked Nina.

'He died.'

'Oh, yes, so he did.'

'Aged nearly ninety-two.'

'So even back in 1926 the man was no spring chicken. Sixty. Surely he stopped because he was past it.'

'Nina, sixty is ten years younger than I am,' said Erik.

'Ah. Sorry.'

'It is not synonymous with brain death. Sibelius was at the top of his game – and he had another thirty years before he started *de*composing.'

'OK, Erik.'

'In the space of just three years before the music stopped,

he gave the world some exquisite works including two more symphonies and his greatest tone poem, *Tapiola*. Not the dying embers of an old man's creative fire.'

'Nicely put. Didn't he turn into a recluse?'

'No. People have said so but it is not true. Certainly in later life he tended to stay at home with his wife and daughters, out of the spotlight. His wife was always very protective. But the house, the famous Villa Ainola, was just an hour from the capital and could be flooded with visitors. Sibelius was a national hero, remember. At one time his head was on our postage stamps. Not a recluse.'

'Right.'

'Eventually the maestro became so touchy on the subject of his symphony that enquiries were forbidden. He famously barked at one intrepid journalist, "You are keeping me from completing it!"'

A touchy genius. Nina thought of the stark photographic portraits: that hairless head scoured with shadows, and dubbed (with tiresome invariability) as 'granite-hewn'. Or walking with a stick, grim and purposeful in a hat you could have played frisbee with.

She said, 'Erik, do you remember? I was about eight. You taped a radio interview – a repeat, obviously, he was dead by then – and brought it to Seaton Bois. Dad borrowed a machine and we listened in the study.'

'His master's voice,' said Erik with a smile.

An interesting voice, roughened by age but not cracked; firm but not hard-boiled. Though the language was alien, even young Nina could tell interviewer from celebrity, the fawning from the fawned upon. And as the virile baritone had ballooned into that austere room, she had watched the men's concentration, the radiance of their reverence.

Erik returned to his thread. 'There were rumours. There are always rumours. Some said the new symphony was still in his head, not a note written down. Others said a pile of unpublished works would appear after the composer's death. But when he died there were no new works. His wife

told of a terrible day when he threw a great pile of manuscripts on the fire. She fled in distress. She loved him and
knew every bar of his seven symphonies by heart, but of the
eighth even she knew nothing. And nobody has ever understood what went wrong with his genius so abruptly and
catastrophically.'

'But you think he did write an eighth symphony. What is
more, you think this is a copy of it.'

'Yes!' With tender idolatry Erik stroked the pretty,
doodle-like characters that were her father's alto clefs.

'Look, I don't mean to be rude, but the idea of Dad
hobnobbing with Sibelius and copying his secret manuscripts is ridiculous. Everything Dad wrote sounded like
that. He was potty about Sibelius; I grew up with his music
wall to wall. Anyway, there's Dad's name at the top.'

'Martti must have brought this manuscript from Finland,
Nina, so of course he doctored the title page. Between
Helsinki and London are six lots of Customs, and in his
backpack a massive work entitled "Symphony No. 8 by Jean
Sibelius"?'

'The whole thing is hopelessly improbable.'

'It gets less so as I talk to you. You grew up with Sibelius
wall to wall? I have just explained the story of the Silence –
and you have never heard it before.'

'Dad's books were in Finnish, and he—'

'Told you Sibelius retired? Never said that another work,
maybe the greatest, was devoured by the stove at Ainola?
Why, unless your father didn't want to bring these facts to
your attention?' Erik's voice had lost its scholarly tone; it
was urgent, and his face shone. 'If this is the lost symphony,
it is one of the most important finds of modern time.
Musicians round the globe will *fight* to get their hands on
it. This will explode upon the world like . . . like—'

Nina stood up. 'I'm sorry, Erik,' she said. 'I absolutely
agree it's peculiar how Dad wrote a gigantic piece of music
and locked it in a cupboard. But if he'd ever met Sibelius, let
alone been allowed to get his mitts on a brand-new

symphony, my father would not have kept quiet. No one would ever have heard the last of it. The idea is one hundred per cent *crackers*, Erik.'

She shunted the papers back into their buff folders, then swept the lot into plastic bags and carried them home to Harlesden.

9

Childhood

It was Erik the chemist who provided Nina's father with irrefutable scientific proof of the existence of God. Her father explained it to Nina when she was nine, on the same day (though the two were not related) that she saw her first erect penis.

It wasn't the sort of thing you'd expect of Frinton-on-Sea, that straitjacket of English respectability between the seaside stripes of Walton-on-the-Naze and the raucous, intolerable Clacton. In Frinton a visitor would find no pub, no amusement arcade, not even an ice-cream van, let alone anything as frivolous as a pier. Frinton was for the peaceful enjoyment of gentlefolk.

Every August the Hannays spent two weeks in a guest house run by a Mr and Mrs Eldridge. They also rented a beach hut in which to change in and out of swimsuits, store the buckets for shrimping, and eat sandwiches gritty with sand. And Nina's mother would sit on its steps in peaceful enjoyment of a book whenever her husband and daughter fled to Clacton to wolf down ice creams on the pier between amusement arcades.

Although Nina's father was raised in a smoky industrial town, like many Finns his family had a summer house beside a lake, so he had interpreted the words 'beach hut' along similar lines. The first time he was confronted with a parade of creosoted boxes like garden sheds, he laughed so much he fell over.

The high point of Frinton was the Children's Special Service Mission. There were services on the beach, and games, and on Saturday nights the Sausage Sizzle, of which the holiday children dreamed all year. The mission workers were Oxford and Cambridge undergraduates, soberly dressed in suits and ties on the beach in a heatwave. Before breakfast they would be down there with shovels and thrusting evangelical energy, to build an altar of heavy, glutinous sand from which to lead their cross-legged assembly in singing 'Trust And Obey' and 'Wide, Wide As The Ocean', accompanied by a cheerful accordionist and a young lady fervently pedalling at a portable organ.

The workers knew about marketing: they assembled the sexes separately, at the 'girling point' and 'boyling point', and counted them, engendering such fever of competition that every child tried to recruit outsiders to augment their team. A couple of hundred children congregated every morning of Nina's holiday. And it never rained on them; the locals talked of 'Mission weather', supplied, of course, by God.

But this year, Nina's father had found another cancerous lump just days before they were due to leave.

'Are you going to be like this for two weeks, Martin? If so, I'll phone Mrs Eldridge right now and cancel.'

Christine hadn't slept. Martin had been up and down all night, doing a contortion act involving a shaving mirror and his rectum.

'Mummy, you can't cancel. Not our holiday!'

'Christine, I have a malignant growth in my back passage.'

'Dr Dolan says it's all hypochondria. That if this goes on, she'll recommend you for St Clement's Hospital. I wish she would.'

'I am not going into a mental home, do you hear? And keep your voice down. I'm expecting a parishioner any minute.'

'And parishioners can't be subjected to this, of course, only us.'

But her father's obsession with his latest death sentence did not abate. On the Colchester Road he was so abstracted he drove up the pavement and his wife shouted that if he didn't pull himself together he'd kill them all.

'Be quiet, Christine. I'm trying to listen to the engine. You hear that? This is catastrophe! We're going to conk out on some country road seven miles from a phone. Listen!'

'Yes, all right,' said Christine, desperate to appease him. 'I think I can hear a funny noise.'

'No, that's a different one.'

Nina shrank into the back seat with the frightened Tapio, biting her nails.

Luckily, the same masculine instincts of self-protection that didn't allow Martin Hannay to display his weaknesses to outsiders also meant he wouldn't start a row inside the guest house. But he dropped weighty hints to the Eldridges about a health problem. 'I imagine the next step is biopsy,' he told them in Nina's hearing but not her mother's.

'Oh Reverend, you had that nasty scare last year, too. We'll be praying for you,' said Mrs Eldridge and made sure he had an extra rasher at breakfast.

There was a lily pond, and rose bowers like sugar-and-wine syllabubs of colour. The romantic Nina loved to sit there, reading and dreaming.

'Mummy and Daddy out?' It was their host. He was an elderly man, his military moustache ginger from the snuff he used, snorting and sneezing. He was good with the kiddies, all cuddles and piggy-backs. Nina loved him.

'They've walked into Walton for a bit, while I learn my scripture for the Tiddlywinks.'

Mr Eldridge sat down beside her. 'Scripture?' he repeated

archly, picking up Nina's TV comic from the folds of her skirt with a crackle.

'No, but I did learn Moses and Miriam earlier on, God's honour.'

'Ho ho ho,' he laughed, like a caricature Father Christmas. 'Don't worry, I'm the soul of discretion. The soul of discretion.' His hand was on Nina's knee. '*Dr Kildare,*' he read from the lurid cover of the comic. '*Sea-Side Disaster – A Call For Help.* Not Frinton, I trust?'

'No, America. Auntie Beryl brought lots back, and my friend Lucia and I share. We've got a real signed photo and his pop record and a pink "Calling Dr Kildare" telephone.'

Mr Eldridge was leaning across her. Something had gone wrong with his smile. He was so close, Nina could see particles of forgotten food in his moustache, like rust. She wriggled, trying to put some space between them, but he was on his knees now, blocking her. The roses were behind and he was in front.

'Be nice, girlie.' His voice was hoarse and pleading. 'Be nice to Mr Eldridge.' Embarrassment and shame roared through Nina's head like a yawn. He was undoing his trousers, the buttoned fly. Nina thought hectically, Buttons are dirty things when they're down there, dirtier than a zipper. Fumbling with fingers and button holes. Down there.

And getting rapidly dirtier. He had his boy's thing in his hand, only it was nothing like those that the boys at school enjoyed waving about. His was big and rubbery with an eye at the top. He had one hand on it, the other on her skirt, pushing it up. Then his thing was against her bare thigh, bobbing ridiculously like a baby seal.

'That's it, girlie,' he said. 'That's right, Rosemary, that's nice.'

It helped, this calling of her by another name. She was a Rosemary, and when it was over she could be Nina again and it wouldn't have happened. In fact it was over rather quickly. His face turned the colour of raw meat and warm sticky sap shot over her thigh. Nina thought he must be dead and this was his spirit escaping. They'd find him dead in the garden with his thing poking out of his trousers.

But Mr Eldridge wasn't dead. He was sitting up. He tugged a handkerchief from his trouser pocket. 'Mop yourself down, girlie,' he said, brisk as a schoolteacher. Nina swabbed at the juice that trickled in repulsive snail-trails over her white skin. She would wash herself properly in the lily pond. 'And I'll have the hanky back,' he said. 'That's right. That's grand.' He was on his feet now. 'I'll leave you to your comic.'

As he went, the silence was scorched by a neighbouring radio. It was the Beatles, which was kind of God, thought Nina. She was also grateful that Mr Eldridge had put her comic down with the handsome doctor's face turned away.

When her parents came back, Nina could see, from the way they didn't look at each other and only talked to the dog, that there had been another row. But she wasn't going to tell them anyway. It was unthinkable to stir more trouble into the broiling seas; to wreck this, the only refuge, Frinton. Her mind was chaotically jerry-building fences to stop it polluting her own refuge. She didn't revisit the event in her head, didn't give it words that would document its reality in her heart. And though she was only nine, Nina understood that Mr Eldridge knew this too, had recognized that hers was an unhappy family and that children in unhappy families don't tell.

Her mother said, 'I've a splitting headache. I'm going to bed. Your father can do whatever suits him.'

'Tell your mother I'm walking Tapio to the esplanade.'

'Can I come too, Daddy?'

'No.'

'That's right, Martin, take it out on a child.'

So Nina did go with him. As Tapio trotted along the greensward, she said, 'Daddy, do you think God likes the Beatles?' and her father said he was sure.

'All music comes from God, Nina – the Beatles or Bartók, Haydn or Herman's Hermits. It's one of the ways He manifests Himself to mankind.'

'So is that how we know God's really there?'

And her father turned to the horizon, then shifted his gaze north towards the shallow, tideless sea of the Baltic, and explained to his daughter the irrefutable scientific proof of God's existence.

10

BY FAX

Boston University Hospital
October 16

Nina, I am so sorry.

Multiple fracture of tib and fib. Not even at work
where I might have sued them into flying me to
London stretched across a row of seats, Concorde out
of New York for preference. No such luck. I fell over my
own feet halfway across the Common, jogging.

Sunny Sunday and the entire damn town is there to
gawp at the foliage. 'Mommy, why is that funny man
rolling on the ground and crying?'

Duane said, 'Shit. Fractures and stuff. Nina, you OK with
it?'

'No,' she said. Then, 'I should phone Interflora.'

'Yeah but – you OK with it?'

'No,' she said.

They both knew they weren't talking about her
disappointment, though it floored her – two rendezvous

scotched within a month. But this was about broken bones and bandages. Whereas her relationship with cancer was a writhing tangle of compassion and impatience, broken bones and bandages tapped into an even darker place and brought out the worst in her.

'Not the worst,' Duane had once argued. 'Some would say it was the best.'

'The worst,' Nina had repeated.

She found herself tortured with the longing to nurse Richard, literally to sit at his bedside and bathe his forehead with cologne. There was nothing about this Florence Nightingale impulse that flattered her own self-image; it was frantic, greedy and self-wounding. The intensity made her feel ashamed, as if the emotional incontinence were physical and she were sitting at her desk in wet knickers. The fact was, Nina reminded herself, that although she and Richard had been colleagues for a year, they had spent only a few working days together and that was six months ago. In her office with the heaped output of a statistical analysis, Nina organized flowers and drilled herself.

At the age of twelve, after crying herself to sleep over some pop star's marriage, she had devised a formula. Sick of misery, she had put his records away and sworn that for a month there would be no more dreaming, hugging the pillow. She had marked off the month in her diary, one day at a time. Alcoholics Anonymous would have been proud of her.

Now she archived Richard's electronic mails, expunged his image from her fantasies and kept her eye on the unsung pleasures of a sense of proportion. Nevertheless it came as an illogical disappointment, how the veto on her sexual fantasizing knocked the stuffing out of her feelings. The affection on its own was like a melody incompetently transposed into some pedestrian key for a dreary soloist. Before her notice was worked out, Richard was dwindling, taking his place among the other ghosts on a company site fading into extinction, entire departments emptied, their very history expunged as partition walls came down.

The relocation benefited many – and nobody more than Duane. 'So I said, "Sorry, folks, but I'm out of here. My phone hasn't stopped ringing since the news broke." And they all turned pale and said, "We're only asking until May, till you've got the system set up in Stoke." So I said, "Stoke? I've got Pfizer offering me midtown Manhattan and you're talking *Stoke*?"'

'Has Pfizer really made you an offer?' asked Nina.

'Well, of course not.' Then Duane reached his punchline. If he would stay long enough to set up their new computer suite, the company would double his redundancy package.

'Bloody hell,' said Nina in stunned admiration.

'You can buy me a drink to celebrate,' said Duane.

So Nina's leaving party was the standard booze-and-canapés with the department, and her lace stayed in the bedroom drawer.

Her next office was a no-smoking zone, and she gave up cigarettes. It wasn't really this that prompted her to quit; Nina would have enjoyed the camaraderie of diehards shivering in doorways in the rain. No, her father's death had undermined a fundamental tenet of her existence (an odd one from which to carry on a career in the medical field), that terminal illness is a figment of the imagination. And because this conviction was irrational, it was susceptible to irrational demolition: though her father never smoked a cigarette in his life, his death demolished Nina's belief that she could chain-smoke without killing herself. So she stopped. She also made her first dental appointment in ten years. Her father not being immortal, maybe teeth really did decay.

The craving for a cigarette was continual, and strong as thirst. She chewed and discarded nicotine gum; her tissues were knobbly with tiny yellow fists that dried out and rolled around in her handbag. And for distraction she had *A Life of Dance*, the autobiography of Giancarlo and Beryl Clark.

Nina was determined to get in touch with them – though

not quite yet. You have to proceed with caution when (a) they're famous, and probably get contacted in the name of friendship by anybody who once stood next to them in a taxi queue, and (b) during the years they knew your family, your family happened to go barking mad.

A Life of Dance was written in both their voices, over-lapping, finishing each other's train of thought, just the way Nina remembered them. *My parents came to England from Italy in the thirties and changed our name to Clark*, wrote Giancarlo, Beryl adding, *Which is a pity. Where I come from in Dagenham, being 'la Signora Castiglione' would have gone down a treat.*

Giancarlo had just turned fifty when Nina last saw him; Beryl was still in her thirties. If the grandmother was still alive she'd be – nearly a hundred? The girls had thought of her as a hundred back then: Liliana Clark, known to the girls as Nonna and to the village as Vinegar Lil.

There was a particular dress of Beryl's that Nina had adored: violet with a diamanté bodice made by a jeweller. One day, Lu and Nina egged each other on to take the dress from the protective bag and climb into it, clutching the scratchy material to their small bodies with small fists. You wouldn't think a fat woman with bandy legs and dressed in widow's weeds down to her ankles could hurtle up a stair-case like a Rottweiler, thought Nina now. Both children got a spanking.

She pictured the Clarks' garden with its chic landscaping. 'Well all right, then,' Giancarlo was saying with hefty reluctance. 'But only for thirty minutes pre*cisely* because I have to be off to the studio.'

'We promise, Uncle Gian!'

'You listening too, Lu? Half an hour, and no tears and tantrums.'

'*Sì, papito!*'

'Please get the whip, Uncle Gian. The whip, the whip!'

So Giancarlo fetched a scaly leather whip, and cracking it viciously like the ringmaster of some psychopathic circus, chased the squealing children up and down the garden.

'Gian!' objected Beryl at the door. 'Nina's mother knitted that jumper and you've got her running hysterical into hedges!'

'FEE-FI-FO-FUM, I SMELL THE BLOOD OF TWO MISBEHAVED CHILDREN!'

'*Gian!*'

Nina had known the Clarks' history the way a child does, with an acceptance that being a world champion and flying all over the planet was just another career option. Reading their autobiography, Nina began to understand how they must have appeared in 1957 when they first hit stardom – like harbingers of the decade just round the corner. There was a hint of rock-'n'-roll in their musicality, a suggestion of awop-bopaloobop. The Clarks had ripped through the dance world like a fresh breeze off a turning tide.

The blurb on the book jacket read, *After they retired undefeated from competition in 1964, their tango cabaret took the critics by storm.* But Nina remembered that, at first, serious commentators had been as hoity-toity as Erik Pellinen's son. Some mordant critic in *The Times* wrote, *Throughout the scintillating performance, one could be forgiven for discerning on Giancarlo's jacket the stigmata of safety pins that usually held the number on his back.*

Her mother said, 'Behave like a little angel today with Gian and Beryl. They'll be feeling raw.' They weren't. They made a suggestion about where the critic should shove his review, and went off to the studio. It wasn't bad press that turned the Clarks upside down. Yet something would do so: before the Hannays moved away, Gian and Beryl had walked out on their cabaret career with no comprehensible explanation to the public, the press, their promoter or their only child. But *A Life of Dance* skirted round it with all the dexterity of champions twirling away from a near collision on the floor of Blackpool's Empress ballroom.

Looking through the photographic plates, Nina got a sight she hadn't bargained for. Those huge netted skirts looked marvellous in the fifties worn as a long frothy pyramid but later, as mini-skirts, the netting stood out like a fairy on a Christmas tree. No wonder Beryl caused a stir, thought Nina. In tango argentino the couples' legs entwine: it must have been quite a spectacle in that frock.

Beryl wrote, *Originally, I favoured twinkle nylon.*

My God, thought Nina, marvelling at human memory. What else is quietly sleeping in my brain on the remote off-chance of being retrieved some day? After all these years that one's still hanging in there, ready and waiting till called for. Twinkle nylon.

_____

11

When Erik's son phoned, Nina had friends round and felt shy of snubbing him in front of them.

'Dad's in a tizzy about this,' he said as his opening remark. 'He's convinced you think he was accusing your father of dishonesty or something.'

That's because he was, she silently replied. He suggested my father stole a symphony and copied it out under his own name. Then, What is it with Sibelius and Finns? Erik was Dad's closest friend since childhood, but one sniff of a Sibelius *hommage* and his deluded conjectures swamp courtesy and common sense.

'It doesn't matter,' she said.

'Look,' Jussi went on, 'Dad said you used to know the Clarks, yeah? Say if this is a bad idea, but you know I teach tango? How about coming along to watch? As a sort of family apology. Just say if you'd rather not.'

She'd always adored tango, and didn't the Pellinen family owe her a nice evening? 'I'd love to,' she said. 'Thank you.'

Her first thought on entering the studio was that Jussi Pellinen wasn't in it. Nobody there bore any resemblance to the bear-like Erik. As Nina tiptoed to a chair she worked out which man on the dance floor was the teacher. Tall, slim, in his mid-thirties; buoyant fair hair, blue eyes set wide over high cheekbones. He looked like a film star. As Nina had been remembering Frinton and comics, she could even name him.

'Bend the knee of the standing leg,' Jussi was telling the women, 'and sweep the moving leg behind you *smoothly*. Then the other leg. The man shouldn't be able to feel you change from one to the other. It's weird for the man, as if the woman's floating backwards across the floor.'

'So basically you want us to float.'

'Got it in one. OK, on with the dance. *Milonguero* style.'

He reached towards a portable tape recorder and the room was suddenly humid. The sorrowful organ-like voice of the bandoneon, the buttoned squeezebox, cried above guitar and violins. The music had the stifled definition of something playing inside a bread bin, but it evoked sticky nights on Avenida Corrientes; men in suits and hats; tango orchestras playing from shellac records on wind-up gramophones. It wasn't the atmosphere of a borrowed studio near Ealing Broadway station on a drizzly November evening. The tune was 'La Cumparsita'. Giancarlo had always joked that it was impossible for anyone to hear it without picturing Jack Lemmon in *Some Like It Hot*, dressed in a frock with a carnation between his teeth, stoically dancing in the arms of Joe E. Brown.

Jussi caught sight of Nina's Nordic features and smiled. Then he called across the music to his students, '*Milonguero* style, remember, so no fancy stuff. You should be cheek to cheek and no room for acrobatics. But just because it isn't fancy doesn't mean it isn't sweet. Remember, you're dressed in silk, dancing in milk.'

Nina was fascinated. The woman was so steeply inclined towards the man that they formed a slow-moving triangle, their backs nearly motionless and their hips apparently double-jointed. Feet brushed, stroked, swept out an arc on the floor. They danced without travelling, as if in a packed dancehall in Buenos Aires or a café between tiny tables on a black-and-white chequered floor. The effect was serpentine, a slow liquefaction.

Jussi appeared to be an effective teacher with his lucid demonstrations and tutting didactics that reminded her of Duane. At the end of the class he turned to Nina and announced bewilderingly, 'Hey, everyone, this is my cousin, over from Finland.'

Later he explained himself. They were in a wine bar, Nina drinking mineral water. One sip of wine, and she'd be inside a pack of cigarettes.

'Yeah, sorry about the fibberoo. What it is, right – my dance partner, Isabella, we had a fling then it went belly-up. Nowadays, she sees me with a woman, I get a bollocking. Easier to pretend you're my cousin. No offence meant.'

'None taken. But isn't that awkward?'

'She emptied a beer glass over my head, Friday. People say to give her the old heave-ho from classes, but Isabella's in debt and needs the work so what can I do?'

'May I ask a question without sounding rude? I had the impression from Erik that you moved here recently, yet your English is colloquially perfect.'

Gratingly colloquial, in fact; Jussi used slang of the 'lovely-jubbly' school, with yes and no rendered as 'pas de problème' and 'no can do'.

'I've been in and out of London for years,' he told her. 'And I learned off of the daddy-o. He's half-English.'

'Of course Erik is!' said Nina, remembering. 'Like me.'

'It's no coincidence, you and him both being half-Anglo. It was because my old man had family here that yours scooted off to London when the shit hit the fan. He crashed out with the Slaters. Slater was my grandmother's name.'

Erik had said Jussi's chaotic flat with its red bills reflected his non-Finnish ancestry. Meaning British. Thanks, Erik. She said, 'I didn't realize the Slaters were anything to do with the Pellinens.'

'No? Your dad and mine were True Buddies.' Jussi made a doleful face. 'So when all hell ... You do know

73

what I'm talking about? This isn't foot-in-mouth disease?'

'No, no,' Nina assured him. 'I know all about Dad's past.' Though not until she had overheard her parents once too often. They had afforded her a sanitized version, around which the details had accreted in proportion to her continuing demands.

It had happened at the weary end of 1945. Nina's father and Erik were demobbed, and home with their families. Their families were lucky: the Winter War alone had wiped out a devastating proportion of Finland's youth. Among the fallen was the only son and heir of a local captain of industry. When the exhausted world was at peace again, the captain of industry published his memoir. It was the rant of a father whose grief had fermented and blown its lid. The book attacked Nina's father, the so-called hero, alleging that in a crucial battle he behaved with criminal recklessness and then lost his nerve and deserted his companion, leaving him to certain death. The son and heir. The author was an influential man hell-bent on damaging the young, surviving Martti. All societies need their scapegoats. Martti was pilloried; bereaved widows, sorrowing mothers, spat when they passed him in the street. He wasn't welcome to return to university; he was unemployable. He fled the following autumn.

Nina said, 'Dad insisted the man was demented with suffering and we should have pity, but all I see is an abuse of power.' She was embarrassed to feel a spasm in her lip.

'Yeah, rotten luck,' said Jussi. 'Anyhow, the pater suggested yours should lie low in London with my . . . great-uncle?'

'Ted and Mabel,' said Nina. 'They died while I was small but I remember their block of mansion flats. I called them Auntie and Uncle and thought living in a mansion was magic!'

I wish I hadn't lost them, she thought. Some steady, elderly couple who loved us might have made a world of difference. Then, I wish I'd had grandparents.

Jussi said, 'So the bit about us being cousins wasn't such a fib. Interesting to hear that the Slaters died. Dad was still popping over to England to see them three times a year until 1979.'

Nina's heart stopped.

'There was a lady concerned,' he went on. 'Some interfering old bag wrote and told my mother. But she wrote in English. Mama's English wasn't up to much, the old man was at work, so she gave me the letter to translate.'

Nina was shocked. 'Did you?'

'No, I invented something. I'm pretty certain she didn't believe me. I'm a useless liar, always have been. Oh *fuck*.' He slapped his forehead theatrically. 'Isabella knows I've only got one cousin and she's met him. *Fuck*, I'm a dead man. Ah well. Cheers.'

'*Kippis*,' responded Nina. 'One of my few words of Finnish. Anyway, that would explain why Dad's English was perfect, if he was exposed to it as a child through Erik.'

'But he never taught you Finnish? Probably not a lot of use in a drug company anyhow. What d'you do there?'

'Work on clinical trials, analysing the data.' That was generally the end of enquiries. Most people thought of statisticians as a species with less razzmatazz than trainspotters. Not this man, apparently.

'Sounds interesting,' he said. 'So it's your job to find a way of crunching the numbers to show their drugs in a good light?'

Nina laughed. 'That's called fraud. Before you ever see the data you put down in black and white exactly what you're going to do. Falsify that and the regulators crucify you.' She imagined the data she'd worked on over the years, still humming inside Duane's computers. When cancer was databased, Nina believed in it. Her illogical, ambivalent attitude had driven her to take up a career in oncology trials while she dismissed as a hypochondriac anyone who said they were unwell.

As a student she had developed a love of analysis for the

sheer joy of turning a hundred thousand data into a picture. From this picture you could not only draw conclusions, you could stop people drawing illegitimate ones, that were not supportable, never mind impassioned wishful thinking and the best motives in the world. To Nina, statistics divorced medicine (divorced cancer) from superstition.

'I couldn't be doing with that,' decided Jussi. 'However bad I dance a tango with a hangover, nobody can crucify me. You ever wanted to be a doctor?'

'I wanted to be a nurse at Blair General Hospital in Los Angeles. Sadly, it was fictional. There was a TV series, *Dr Kildare*.'

'I've heard of it. Richard Chamberlain.'

I bet you have, thought Nina. People must have been saying you looked like him since adolescence. 'It was a phenomenon,' she explained. 'I read somewhere that he was getting twelve thousand fan letters a week.'

Would the series look hopelessly dated now? she wondered. Would the dialogue be too much 'Give it to me straight, doc. Am I gonna make it?'? At the time, the show was cutting edge. She remembered one episode about a teenager and a botched abortion. Nina was watching it at Lu's house. Unfortunately her mother was also watching it, at her own house. She came stout-shoeing and Donegal-tweeding up Church Lane to haul Nina away from the TV.

'Dr Kildare?' prompted Jussi.

'Sorry, that's very girlie and boring. You asked about Finnish. I never learned that but I was handed Italian on a plate. Giancarlo's mother lived with them and I got pretty good.'

'Remember any?'

Nina could see a morning that crunched with frost. Giancarlo and Beryl were Merry-Christmassing the neighbours. She heard their *sotto voce* cross-talk.

She said, 'I could give you the Italian for "Smile at your mother-in-law and don't talk about the show," followed by, "Which show? One that made you rich? Or the one that's driving you nuts?" And I could make a stab at "Don't talk so loud. The vicar can probably understand. He knows Latin." It's a long story,' added Nina.

'All I know of Italian is immigrant slang in tango lyrics. Let's drink up and get some nosh.'

In the nearby trattoria Jussi made an unenergetic pass. Nina turned him down. She wasn't above a one-night stand with a man who was a dead ringer for Richard Chamberlain, but she couldn't stomach the idea of being caught in the throes of passion whispering 'Juicy!'

12

'Samaritans, can I help you?'

There was the tiniest pause, then a woman's breathy rush. 'I'm sorry, I've no right to waste your time.'

In the split second before the caller could ring off, Nina spoke at random. 'Can you tell me what's been on TV tonight?'

'I . . . no. Sorry . . . I . . . wasn't in this evening.'

Then the whole lot poured out.

Her husband had died six months ago and this was the first time she had been out and enjoyed herself – and then she came home bubbling with her evening to find an empty house and no husband to tell, ever again. It was like a climber unstrung, hurtling off a cliff face. Panic-stricken, she had looked up the Sams' number and felt ashamed the moment she got through. Nina knew that if you could just stop this type of caller hanging up in those first seconds, they would talk for an hour. And afterwards they would be able to sleep.

Duane, on his last shift before Stoke, was landed with a manipulative young man who spent an hour threatening to top himself. '*And it will all be your fault,*' Nina could hear him screaming. Which reminded her of someone she nearly married.

She hadn't liked Duane at first. She had detested him. They had met on a Samaritan shift.

'I'm a smoker,' Nina had said, 'so tell me if you're not, and I'll hang out of a window.'

'Rather inimical to the spirit of the Sams, wouldn't you say?' replied Duane. 'Being forced to watch someone commit slow suicide?'

'A simple "no" would suffice,' Nina had snapped back, and spent so much time hanging out of a window she rubbed a hole in a shirt of Victorian silk.

It was a long time before things improved. In an environment where gallows humour was conducive to confidences, Duane responded to the lightest personal question like a bishop's wife quizzed about her proficiency at fellatio. Then late one night about three years ago he came off a long call that he had seemed to be coping with perfectly well, and stayed in the booth. It was quickly apparent to Nina that he was in serious distress. That, she could handle. She made tea and waited. Eventually Duane talked to her. The caller had just come from his lover's sickbed. Deathbed. AIDS-related pneumonia. Then Duane released his own story in an unsightly gulping grief, a cataract of tears and catarrh. It was about cancer and shocked Nina but by the end their views of each other were transmogrified. He was a computer-systems man. When the post fell free at Nina's own firm, it was she who suggested it.

Now, he finished his call and started fixing up the camp bed. 'Triumph of hope over et cetera,' he said. 'What's in the bag?'

Beside Nina on the table was a plastic bag lumpy with her father's books: the epic folk poem the *Kalevala*: one copy in the original, two in English.

'Finnish folklore,' she explained. 'Usually translated as "Land of Heroes". Magic-laden conflicts back when men were men. I could never get on with it – far too much death and shouting at people – but to Dad it was sacred. You know the scene in *Casablanca* with the French on their feet singing the Marseillaise? That's what the *Kalevala* was to Dad's generation of Finns.'

But Duane was tutting at her. 'And to Tolkien! The *Kalevala* inspired *Lord of the Rings*.'

'Blimey. Seriously sacred, then. I know Longfellow borrowed it for *Hiawatha*. That's where he got that wonderful drumbeat: *tum* tee *tum* tee *tum* tee *tum* tee.'

And somehow, in Longfellow's hands it worked better. *Hiawatha* was romantic, the story abounded with happy animals, and nobody ransacked a dead man's stomach to look for spells or committed suicide after sleeping with his sister.

Duane opened a volume embossed with gilt and was confronted with an impenetrable thicket.

> *Vaka vanha Väinämöinen, laulaja iän-ikuinen,*
> *sormiansa suorittavi, peukaloitansa pesevi.*
> *Istuiksen ilokivelle, laulupaaelle paneikse*
> *hope'iselle mäelle, kultaiselle kunnahalle.*

'This is some weird language,' he said admiringly.

And a bugger to check against handwritten words broken up by hyphens above a musical score, which Nina had been trying to do.

She said, 'I'm told it's rich with imagery and alliteration.'

'Hey, I know the Finnish for hero. It's *urho*.'

'How on earth—?'

'*Urho* was the name of Tom of Finland's first love. Oh, *don't* ask "Who's Tom of Finland?"! Homoerotic art. Gay leather scene. Helsinki. Real name's unpronounceable. You must have seen his stuff, Nina – timber men and bikers and cops with enormous wangers.'

'Sadly, Duane, my acquaintance with the gay leather scene is limited.' But she wouldn't have expected to find its roots in Helsinki. 'Dad always said male society was pretty macho.'

'You're telling me. Tom's lumberjacks are to die for.

Anyhow, why are you lugging around three hardback copies of something you don't like, one of them in a language you don't understand? Some kind of penance?'

So Nina told him.

'My Steve has a lot of Sibelius on CD, as I recall,' said Duane. Then, '*Christ*, Nina, if what you've got is some long-lost symphony by a megastar, you'll have half the world's musicians stampeding all the way to bloody Harlesden. *Jesus*, it must be worth a bomb.'

'But since the author was actually a Norfolk vicar, Duane, it's worth twenty quid. Anyway, how's Steve doing?' As a change of subject, it was ham-fisted.

'Still at home. You know what I think of that Queen Mary he left me for but the guy's a good nursemaid.' Then, 'A lost masterpiece. Bloody hell, Nina.'

'Duane, my poor dad did not get hold of Sibelius's final symphony. I mean – how? Anyway, look at this.'

The *Kalevala*. The poem headed 'Rune 41' was marked up: insertions, deletions and a wormery of scribbled marginalia. 'Dad's handwriting. And it exactly matches the choral text. Proves it. These are his workings.'

'Except, Nina, if he *did* stumble on some magnum opus and recognized his national epic in it, mightn't he cross-check with the original? After all, that's what you were doing yourself.'

This had already occurred to her. As is often the way with wild theories, Erik's had hooks, and they were in Nina's flesh.

'What does it sound like? I mean, if it's really him instead of your dad trying to be him, could you tell?'

'Perhaps if I had an orchestra instead of busking my way through on piano. Before this came up, I would have said the thing about Sibelius is you can recognize him from a hundred yards.'

Her father had explained why, and like many a daughter she now wished she'd been listening. The way the brass cried? The harmonic flavour of his shifting chords? Yet it wasn't her father's influence that prompted Nina's pulse to change tempo at those chords, those shifts, or her straining senses to follow the inexorable emergence of some germ of a theme from the thick forests of orchestral background into ebullient supremacy, her mind whiting out in astonished teariness. That wasn't filial loyalty.

Duane went on, 'How about your Greg? Would his synthesizers fake up an orchestra? And he'd keep schtum. Or am I talking bollocks?'

Nina stared at him. 'It's a brilliant idea.' Greg was mellowing. It was a good nine months since he phoned her at 3 a.m. conducting a one-sided row that started in mid-sentence. Even so . . . 'It's a big favour to ask.'

'Might be better to drop it,' concluded Duane. 'If you want my real opinion, this could be trouble with a capital F.'

13

She decided she liked Jussi, and was seeing a lot of him. He was easy company with his un-Finnish chatter and slovenly charm. He allowed her to sit in on his tango classes and luxuriate.

'But won't your dance partner—?'

'It's sorted. This mate of mine's got a thing about fiery women so I manoeuvred them together for a bit. Actually, I think they're getting more than a bit.'

His name wasn't 'Juicy' but 'Yoossi'. He had introduced himself simply as 'Erik's son' and Nina had forgotten that in Finnish the J is pronounced as a Y. Their foreign minister had famously forgotten how to pronounce it in English. In an American hotel his wife wanted orange juice. He was heard seemingly asking the waiter, 'Could you find some use for my wife?'

But that didn't mean Nina was going to go to bed with Jussi. He made passes and she declined them. They bore each other no ill will over it.

Nina had asked, 'But does tango pay? As London never got the show we didn't get the craze. Our dance is salsa.' Jussi had replied that the craze would come and he was establishing his market position ready to rake in the dosh.

Meanwhile he also taught salsa. 'Easy money,' he said. 'Waiting list.'

Not all his classes were *milonguero* style. Others were full of the stagy moves Nina remembered, including the *gancho* or 'hook' – a jack-knife backwards flick of your leg under your partner's standing leg, fast as whiplash.

Jussi would berate the women, 'Stop leaning backwards away from the man. Tango argentino is a conversation between you. Lean inwards – *and look him in the eyes!*'

Nina liked Jussi best this way, informed and impassioned, his 'I kid you not' style of speech vanishing like a dropped persona.

'Tango is not the dance of love,' he told her. 'If you want the dance of love, learn the rumba. Tango is power struggle. The man intends to play the woman like a musical instrument but he can only invite. For example, he invites her to perform a *gancho*. Maybe she will, maybe she won't. In tango the woman holds back. And at its heart there's a kind of lazy elegance. Think of cats; when necessary they can move like the wind but there's a natural inertia. Tango has hesitations and reluctance. The stillness at its heart is far more characteristic than all those flashy legs-in-the-air figures.'

Erik had been right about Jussi's attitude to ballroom. He looked down his nose. Two of his students had a grounding in it. 'Get rid of those horrible head jerks and the ramrod hold,' he reprimanded them. 'Sweet and melancholy!'

'I bet the Clarks' book doesn't mention the spite,' he told Nina. 'It's a vicious little world, ballroom. Couples can step on to the competition floor, get a load of who the judges are, and instantly know they've as much chance as a pig at a baby show. All the backbiting, and rows after a collision on the floor. The Clarks must've been tough cookies to survive.'

'I'll say. Jussi, the first time they won at Blackpool they did it with the crowd baying for their blood.'

'I thought the country loved them.'

'Not at the start.'

In the gridlock of Hanger Lane Gyratory System on the way home from work, Nina would daydream. There was a fancy figure she remembered from the Clarks – the *sentada amor*. The love seat. The woman fleetingly rests on the man's knee sweeping up her legs, then she's back on the floor: a glorious now-you've-got-me-now-you-haven't tease. Nina would amuse herself in the best tradition of daydreams. One day Jussi's Isabella would be unable to make the class. 'Oh, *I* could have a go,' Nina would pipe up, and dance a *sentada amor* to blow everybody's socks off, never forgetting the power struggle and lazy elegance or the stillness at its heart. While decrying every other teacher in London, Jussi had mentioned one he approved of. Nina cowed her misgivings about the two left feet and booked a private lesson.

At home, she wasn't only reading *A Life of Dance*. She bought books on Sibelius. All of them confirmed what Erik had told her. After more than a hundred works and with a fan base of millions, Sibelius stopped short never to go again, like 'My Grandfather's Clock'. And no one had ever explained why.

Certainly the man was plagued with problems. Alcohol, for a start. For many years he was a soak. No doubt drink would have been the ruin of him if his wife, his guardian angel Aino, had not been there to rein him in. He had a tremor, his hands shook like Finnish birches in a gale, but as he lived into his nineties with his faculties intact, this couldn't have been sinister. There were bouts of depression but also long periods of vigorous optimism. Sibelius's crisis could not be attributed to drink, depression or dementia – he just couldn't get that symphony out. Nina thought of those that survived. One Sunday at the vicarage, the suffragan bishop had come to lunch. Her father turned on the radio to a concert and Sibelius's Symphony No. 5 exploded into the air: its swinging hammer theme, the unstoppable outpouring of energy, the sheer physical excitement discharged in that chilly dining room like sheet lightning. Their guest laid down his knife and fork. Nina watched him commit the solecism of putting his elbows on her mother's table. As the final chords subsided he was wiping his face with a napkin.

'Martin,' he said with unsteady anger, 'you have no right to throw Sibelius at a man when he's not expecting it!'

And the composer of those mind-blowing finales – his genius just *vanished*?

Nina turned to Aino's account of her husband destroying his manuscripts, heaping them into her own laundry basket and feeding them to the stove. She called it an *auto-da-fé*, so henceforth that was what everybody would call it. Nina needed the dictionary: *From the Inquisition. Execution, usually by burning at the stake.*

The stove. From nowhere, Nina felt the detestable sensation of skipped heartbeats, like being jabbed with a cattle prod. She had just caught sight of . . . Her heart now in freefall, she turned the pages back.

Colour plates showed the house on the hillside, which Sibelius built for and named after his wife. It was strong and cosy with its shingles, granite and logs, pantiles and pine trees, red and green, holly-bush colours. Ainola nestled in its woody grounds like permanent Christmas. Sibelius had the gift called synaesthesia, a synthesis of the senses. He heard all sounds in colour – birds, children, cities – and saw colour as music waiting to be freed. The photographs showed his stove, a Nordic giant of glazed ceramic brick in a sumptuous shade of blue-green that he chose, said the caption, because it sang to him in the key of F major.

The Moomin stove.

In the vicarage, embellishing his bedtime stories in Nina's unheated little bedroom, her father had conjured the very stove that devoured Sibelius's eighth symphony.

14

Childhood

Today's lesson was about north, south, east and west. Twenty-five children sat in pairs (Clive Mitcham, constituting the carried-over remainder, was tagged on to the Parry twins) working out directions from a grid map. Nina had a problem.

'No, that's wrong,' said the teacher.

'Yes, sir, I know, sir. It's because there's letters and numbers mixed up.'

'So?'

Reluctantly, Nina explained. 'N is the same blue as four, so I can't tell the difference and write the order wrong.'

'The same blue? What does that mean?'

Lucia was in there instantly, backing her up. 'She can't help it. It's like how her Fridays are yellow and Wednesdays are pink.'

'Green,' said Nina, without meaning to. The concept of pink Wednesdays was as unnatural to Nina, as abhorrent, as an orange sea or blue bacon.

The teacher didn't have time for whimsy. Nina was becoming tiresome. Her concentration was all over the place and she was turning into a cry-baby. And this romancing had been going on since the start of the school year. For her composition 'What I Did On My Holidays', which everyone knew the Hannays spent at Frinton, Nina had handed in some nonsense about Buenos Aires. 'That's enough,' he said.

On the page in front of Nina, brash, rusty threes and S's swaggered and sneered like Thursdays.

'She's not making it up,' persisted Lucia. 'There's other people that suffer from it.'

'Not *suffer*, Lu.'

'Like her dad and Sibelius.'

'Who is Sibelius?' asked the teacher.

'Their Labrador,' responded one of the boys and hooted at his own joke.

Then, thank heaven, the door opened and in strode the headmaster.

'Good morning, Mister Caldwell,' chanted the children in tones Nina heard as a pleasant grey, grainy like old photographs.

'What are we pursuing today?'

Against Nina's intense mental opposition, Lu launched her vicarious pride at Mr Caldwell. 'Sir, we were talking about how Nina sees things as colours. Numbers and music and stuff.'

The class tittered and the headmaster turned his searchlight look on Nina. 'Tell me.'

So she mumbled an account of the phenomenon she accepted as workaday: the great gouaches of pop music and plush brocades of a concerto, her arithmetic a *galère* of discordant characters proclaiming their personalities in Technicolor. Every sound had a colour. The commonplace English suffix *-ing* was sunlit gold. Therefore this was the colour of the word sing – and also of ring, king and string, which as a result were redolent of singing, and therefore sang. This symbolism involved a logic that would have been perfectly comprehensible to an Egyptian of, say, the Middle

Kingdom, but it was an unwieldy tool with which to negotiate in Nina's distinctly unsymbolic century.

The headmaster listened grimly. 'You imagine all abstract notions in this manner? So, by his own confession, does Mr Vladimir Nabokov.'

Silence. At least this time the teacher didn't have to ask. His headmaster, on a roll, picked up a stub of chalk and the name *VLADIMIR NABOKOV* squeaked across the blackboard before the baffled eyes of a class of ten-year-olds. Then, *A sorry example.*

'It is a sad thing,' expounded the headmaster with a funereal relish, 'when anybody gifted with talent wastes it. This miscreant,' tapping the blackboard, 'is an author who throws his gift away on dirty subjects that lower both writer and reader.'

At this, their teacher seemed to experience some sort of epiphany. He had been exuding an expression of instant readiness to agree with anything, a rictus smile better suited to the borderline insane or the recently electrocuted. Now he relaxed and muttered the word '*Lolita*'.

The headmaster was piling up the indictment. 'This very week, I unearthed a copy of his infamous book from the desk of one of your coevals. Certain passages have circulated in the playground. I have this to say. As you get older you will increasingly be confronted with that sort of thing. You will do well to remember that in the end it is yourself who is degraded. This unhappy fellow is a prime example of the parable I read in assembly.' At which, both Nina and Lu suspected that reinforcement of this morning's parable was the sole point of the visit and dirty books had been wedged in with some quick thinking and a crowbar. 'We must use wisely whatever talents God has given us. If so, He will reward us by increasing them. If not, they will dribble away.'

'Well said, Headmaster.'

'Nina, to return to your predicament. The author of *Lolita* is not a suitable bedfellow. I advise you to retrain your brain to think in black and white. It will be healthier.'

'Yes, sir, I will, sir,' said Nina fast, before Lu had a chance to pitch in with logical objections.

'Thank you, Headmaster,' said the teacher.

Behind them, a bright boy who happened to be Mr Caldwell's son was scribbling in his exercise book. *V. Nabokov.* There was a pretty good library in Brentwood. They were bound to stock some.

15

The tango teacher's name was Tony Delterfield. His studio appeared to lead a double life. One wall was mirrored floor to ceiling but the other three had spanner sets and gloss paint stacked against them. Nina's first attempt at the notorious right-turning *giro* would be derailed by the sight of a tin labelled *Number 9 Mixed Shag*. No doubt it ensured that nobody developed pretensions as they stalked and swivelled across his varnished floor.

'Tango is a walking and turning dance,' Tony told her. 'No swaying.'

'I know,' said Nina and name-dropped Giancarlo and Beryl.

'Which sounds easy but not when you're walking on the balls of your feet, and especially not when it's backwards.'

'I've practised,' said Nina.

'Also,' Tony persevered, 'beginners have difficulty keeping time because the tempo is so slow.'

'I won't, I'm a musician,' said Nina.

He started the music.

'I know this too,' said Nina. 'It's "A La Gran Muñeca" played by the orchestra of Carlos Di Sarli.'

'It is indeed,' confirmed Tony and proceeded to walk Nina

round the studio backwards on the balls of her feet. But not for long. As well as finding it fiendishly difficult to walk and impossible to follow a lead, Nina couldn't keep time to the music. Another thing she hadn't reckoned on was the problem of trying to relax *in his arms.*

This was bizarre. Her lifelong easiness with men seemed not to extend to an hour-long embrace breathing into Tony's woolly jumper while his body directed hers at his will, all power and purpose. Nina was a divided personality: her brain wanted to learn the tango but her instincts told her to beat the guy off with a stick. Her hands smelled of Tony's after-shave. This said it all: the only times she ever smelled of a man's aftershave were when she'd been to bed with him.

None of which boded well for the *sentada amor.*

When Tony showed her out, something caught his attention. 'Now *that's* a car and a half! That vintage Jaguar E-type. Sorry, I don't suppose you're interested.'

'I am,' Nina told him. 'It's mine.'

'*Yours?* I'm sorry, I shouldn't—'

'You are looking at my share of the only single released by a New-Romantic pop duo called The Look. One day on the motorway I'm going to put my foot flat down to the floor, and the engine will probably leave the chassis behind.'

She had come close to it. These were the nights she played Pink Floyd's 'Shine On You Crazy Diamond' at boom volume, accelerating to its twanging blue sorrow until the rhythm section exploded into the texture of the song and pro-pelled Nina through the black night with a sexual charge singing through her blood and nerve endings, headlights swimming at her, tail-lights shifting in her mirrors as she flew past them at a hundred and twenty-five miles an hour.

'We'll set a goal. The day you master the *ocho*, we'll celebrate by going for a spin.'

'So about three years, then,' said Nina.

✳

Christine Hannay coped with her first Christmas as a widow by putting Kruger into kennels and flying out to Susan and André, where midsummer on the Western Cape would take away the sting – and indeed much of the Christmas spirit. André's generosity would have included Nina but she gave him her anti-apartheid speech, he responded with his evil-pharmaceutical-industry speech and that was that. When Nina drove her mother to the airport, Christine spent the night in Harlesden en route.

'Tango lessons? Can you afford it, dear? They say the economy is on a turndown and your job . . .'

Turndown was rather nice, like a comforter on a double bed. 'I can always get work playing piano. Speaking of which, Mum, I'm slogging through that symphony and I wondered. You remember how Dad used to talk about his uncle Timo?'

'He lived with Uncle Timo while he was at the Conservatoire. That's who bought him the violin. You are keeping it safe, aren't you, dear?'

'Don't worry, it's hidden. When Dad was busy failing his law degree, there was one summer when he didn't go home to Tampere for the long vacation but stayed on in Helsinki.'

'He didn't fail, Nina, war intervened.'

'Anyway, no matter when Dad started the symphony, I know he couldn't have finished it between the end of the war and leaving for England.' Because that's when the shit hit the fan. Nina knew about creativity, knew that you can't get anything done when you're agitated. Grief, yes. Misery? Yes please, by the bucketload, keep it coming, there's probably an album in it. But you can't write in a sick panic. 'But Dad's parents made him spend that summer with Uncle Timo, who was supposed to talk him into knuckling down to his studies.'

'He certainly wasn't working on a symphony, dear. Uncle Timo had been commissioned to keep your father away from music and daydreaming. You have to understand, his family was worried to death. There was to be no career as a violinist, he wasn't interested in law, he was talking about becoming a poet! Uncle Timo kept his nephew gainfully employed doing menial work to show him what life would be like with no profession. He would never have allowed Martin anywhere near a symphony.'

'Look, is there the faintest chance Dad could have met Sibelius but not told us? Admirers were received at Ainola and it was only an hour away from Helsinki.'

'Of course admirers weren't received at Ainola, Nina. The house would have come apart at the seams. Anyway, Uncle Timo had no contacts in that world. He owned a religious publishing house and kept himself to himself.'

'What about that conductor, Tauno Hannikainen? I know Dad said he wasn't any relation but suppose—'

'I'm sorry to disappoint you, my love, but you are not related to famous orchestral conductors. Do think, Nina. Given a connection of that sort, your father would have found a way of tagging along, if only to get out of his studies.'

'Poor Dad.'

'Thank heavens he met me and I brought him into the Church,' said Christine with unconscious arrogance. 'Mind you, given the type of bad lot Martin was exposed to, things could have been far worse.'

'Erik, I suppose.'

'I was thinking of the boy.'

'Which boy?'

'Veikko Virta.'

For an unnerving moment Nina thought this was a character from the *Kalevala*. Then she realized. 'You mean *the* boy? The son of the factory owner who—?' The nasty man who wrote about Daddy in a book.

'Your father never liked to speak ill of the dead, but Veikko Virta was scum.' Coming from her mother the word was like verbal violence. 'He was even running a . . . what do you call it?'

'Brothel?' suggested Nina hopefully.

'For distilling spirits.'

'He managed to run a still in the army? Blimey! I knew the Finns constructed saunas on the front, but I didn't realize they brought their own pub. Did he pull it along behind, bubbling away on a sleigh?'

'Don't be silly, dear. This was while they were all at university.'

'I don't follow.'

'Veikko Virta was a law student with your father. Didn't you know that?'

And just how could I, thought Nina, when his life was never spoken of, only his death? When his very name was never voiced: he was the Boy. She said, 'So he, Dad and Erik were already friends and then they ended up in the same platoon in the war. Was that usual?'

'Why not? They would have been conscripted together. But the boy was actually in a different platoon.'

'Yet he and Dad must have ended up fighting side by side, otherwise—'

'Apparently so.'

'You said he was scum. That implies worse than booze.'

'He was the type to deal in absolutely anything that would make him money, it seems, no matter which side of the law.'

'Including?'

'Regrettably . . . pornography.'

Nina waited.

Creaky with reluctance, her mother went on, 'Cine films. This wasn't some smutty little hobby but a lucrative business. One shouldn't say this, I know, but one can't help feeling that his early death, well . . .' Her voice faded out. 'But this subject is very painful, dear. You were asking if your father could have met Sibelius. I can't think of anything less likely in the whole wide world.'

'That's what I thought.' But louring in a corner of Nina's mind were Duane's words: *Jesus*, it must be worth a bomb. Veikko Virta, son of a powerful family that must have been well connected. And he had dealt in anything that would make him money.

16

Childhood

Worth a bomb.

Nina had always known not to touch Daddy's violin. A violin is not like a piano, which you can treat with a wham bam, thank you ma'am, and call in the tuner. The violin's voice, hauntingly like a human voice, is produced by the bowed strings resonating in the hollow body, and depends for its richness and sweetness on the crafting of the wood and integrity of the varnish. Entire books have been written on so-called magical properties of 'secret' varnishes. All are fragile; they have to be to allow the wood to vibrate freely. To sing. Sunlit gold. The same colour, by happy chance, as the word violin.

Nina had always known to put her violin safely away in its case after practice. As for her father's, it was unthinkable to daub her fingers, with their corrosive salt, on the deep glow and noble crazing of a varnish three centuries old.

His was a beautiful instrument, rich brown and cross-grained, its celebrated purfling a clean ebony line inside the raised edging. The label, which was authentic, read (though in Latin) *Made by Nicolò Amati of Cremona, descendant of Hieronymus and Antonius, in the year 1664.*

Her father only once left it unguarded. A parishioner who had a thug for a husband arrived woebegone in the hall. The vicar had been playing his own arrangement of the Sibelius *Valse Triste* in the drawing room. He recognized emergency and rushed out to the hall to meet it, leaving the violin on top of the dresser, resting on its back, the bow beside it. Some time later, six-year-old Nina entered the room, promising her mother she would practise the piano. There was a variety evening in the village hall on Saturday and Nina, who had not inherited one smidgen of that paternal stage fright, had pleaded until her parents let her perform. She was in there quite a while, in the room with the abandoned Amati violin. But she didn't do any piano practice.

It was lunchtime when her father returned from the cottage hospital. That was when Nina's mother realized she hadn't heard the piano all morning.

'You promised you were going to practise. We said this would happen. We knew you wouldn't be ready for Saturday.'

'I couldn't, Mummy, there's something gone bonkers with the piano.'

'Now, Nina—'

'It wasn't me, I didn't do it.'

'Let's go and see,' put in her father.

'It wasn't me,' repeated Nina on a rising bleat.

There was nothing bonkers about the piano that her father could see. Until the child attempted an arpeggio, and her small fingers slid off the keys. It was as though they'd been greased.

'All right, Martin, mystery over,' said her mother. 'Our new charlady has been over-enthusiastic with the polish.'

Her father laughed. Then he stopped laughing. His face changed and he strode across the room towards the dresser.

Nina's first thought was that it was a different violin. When she heard her mother cry out, 'Oh, Mrs Jellico, what have you done?' Nina was seized by the wild idea that their new cleaner had swapped the antique instrument for a new one. The curved back that had always gleamed with the light and dark flames of maple now shone like the bonnet of a new car in a saleroom. Light from the window hit the polish and bounced off as glare. The gentle rise and fall of its curves, the waist and hips, the belly and neck, all reflected the sunlight by batting it back with synthetic brilliance like a scream. Mrs Jellico had not merely sprayed it and buffed it, she had put on a coating of beeswax. She had treated the Amati to a makeover.

'Daddy!' Nina's voice shattered and she swallowed it.

'Oh, Martin, my dear! *Oh*, Martin!'

'My fault, I left it there,' he said shortly. 'Christine, will you put the violin in its case for me, please? And carry the case upstairs? Thank you. Nina, nothing is ever somebody else's fault when they mean well.'

He took himself off to his study.

It was weeks before he could bear to play again, but he didn't discard his violin, the antique that would have been worth a couple of hundred thousand pounds by the time he retired, had half the value not been wiped out when it was Jellicoed one terrible morning by mistake. He didn't turn it into a catastrophe. The blunderings of strangers, however disastrous, Martin Hannay could rationalize. It was never they who drove him to behave like a lunatic.

17

On New Year's Eve Jussi came over, joining Nina, the cat and the couple from upstairs, Sean and Victoria.

'How's your tango getting on?' he asked.

'Like pulling teeth.'

'Fancy fifteen days in Buenos Aires? I'm off in Feb. Half-term break.'

'Hey, let's all go!' said Sean. 'Where's Buenos Aires?'

In the magical realm of Giancarlo and Beryl's faraway places, but out of Nina's price range. Jussi waved a hand dismissively.

'Nah, you only need the airfare. The accommodation's free, gratis and for nothing. I got a friend with an empty apartment. I got friends with empty apartments most places. If you don't dig sharing a bed with me, there's a spare room,' he added as an afterthought, at which Nina laughed and said, 'Maybe next time.'

Then she had a letter from Boston. Richard was coming over at the end of January. Nina replied that she would be delighted to see him, but by now it was hardly true. When their second attempt had stalled, her self-protective tactics had worked and the width of the Atlantic made its presence felt. By now Nina couldn't imagine what they would talk about. Not her current interests: the symphony was too dangerous, tango lessons too two-left-feet, the Clarks too twinkle nylon to engage him.

Her thirty-fourth birthday came and went, and she and Richard were going to dinner on Friday evening. By Thursday, Burns Day, something odd was happening in the troposphere.

As the British were soon to be told by weather forecasters in tones that oscillated between sepulchral and gloating, all winter there had been pressure and temperature lows over Greenland, promoting storms. Suddenly a big one was sent tracking across the ocean, deepening as it came like some rogue power tool drilling out a trench. By mid-morning the weather map looked like a demented string bag, and by afternoon a vortex. The country was in the grip of one of the most hellish storms of the century. The first Nina noticed was when the sky turned green.

She looked up from her desk, and beyond the lichened bark of the beech trees was a sick glow like the seeping green of a dying LED display.

'Brian, have you got a minute?' she called into the next office.

A man in a grey suit strolled in. 'Christ,' he said. 'Hey, Adrian! Have a shufti out the window.'

'Why, what is it?'

'Fuck knows.'

Then her phone rang. 'Nina,' said a beautifully modulated American voice.

Somewhere in the depths of her mind that voice caused a shuddering ripple, but it was interrupted.

'*Dave!* Get in here. The bloody skies are falling!'

Nina carried her phone to the corner. 'So where are you?'

'London. It sounds like this is a bad time.'

Nina's office was now packed with enormous men hooting expletives.

'Sorry, Richard. How's your broken leg?'

'I'll draw you a diagram complete with rods and bore

holes. They dismantled me before the trip, and the leg will follow by airfreight. Look, I can hear this is a bad time.'

Somebody shouted, 'Here it comes!'

Fat drops of rain hit the windows. Nina's car was parked by the woods.

'Richard, forgive me but there's some murderous storm coming up and—' And our last murderous storm was the day of my father's heart attack. Richard vanished from her thoughts as he was speaking.

'I'll phone back tonight. And I'll buy an umbrella.'

By mid-afternoon the site was evacuated. It took Nina four hours to drive home through distraught woodlands and roads dammed by stricken trees, but her part of London was relatively peaceful. Richard's wasn't. By evening, a stunned Richard had seen central London as a whirligig of fizzing chaos, the air swirling with flotsam and jetsam. When he phoned to discuss restaurants for tomorrow (the worst of all conversations for the non-food-oriented Nina: 'I've heard the Ivy is good but we might have to book') it was clear that Richard had no intention of going out, possibly ever again. They agreed on the dining room of his hotel.

With just enough enthusiasm to bother shaving her legs, Nina got ready and drove through the post-apocalyptic landscape to Piccadilly. From the revolving doors which swung with Friday-night bustle, she saw him through the watery imperfections of their old glass. Dressed as any other American businessman off-duty, and somehow tanned in January, Richard waited with well-bred impatience, his tasselled brogues firm on a floral rug by a florid chimney-piece. In the slow, snowblind seconds before he turned and saw her, Nina thought, Of course he's absolutely gorgeous. It's one of the reasons I fell for him.

Then, racing through the implications like a computer program, her brain made its pronouncement. You are in dire need of a cigarette, it said with vitreous clarity as Nina walked towards the crackling fireplace.

*

'. . . to check him out with some basic neurology obs,' said Richard. 'At which point the guy made it clear he didn't want a physician, he wanted a mechanic, and of the two of us he considered I was the one who needed his head examining.'

Nina, looking at Richard through shimmering thermals of amazed desire, pictured him beside a slain vehicle on the Marylebone flyover ducking the swirling litter and airborne dustbin lids, trying to persuade a frantic van driver with a head injury to count backwards from a hundred in serial sevens.

'Yep, you got it,' said Richard as if she'd described the scene aloud. 'His exact words were, "Look, you tosser, me brain can bleed to death so long as I get this load to Aylesbury. Now shove off and let me phone the road rescue." Poor guy.' He turned to the waiter. 'Another bottle of San Pellegrino.' And to Nina, 'How's your glazed chicken?'

'Fine. Fine, thanks.'

Nina had ordered at random, her stomach fluttering with the low-grade nausea of intense excitement, and she now picked anorexically at a pitted dome of celeriac mash. Richard topped up her wine glass and Nina reminded herself she was driving.

Everything about him seemed manicured: the thick black hair that should have flopped across his forehead was sculpted into a springy wedge. Richard was the sort of man whose hair always looked as if it was cut yesterday. Presumably it had sat tamely in place in a storm-force ten. Nina ran her fingers through her own spiky blonde that always looked as if it had been cut with a knife and fork.

'You said your garden escaped major damage,' he said. 'Do you have a lot of trees?'

She pictured her walled yard, fifty feet long. In her mind she replanted it as an orchard.

'Basically, I have one flower bed,' she explained, wondering how on earth to milk anything interesting from it. 'With stepping stones. Old-fashioned roses, sweet peas, cottage pastels, lit from within by tiny garden lights. Though when they were first installed I half expected the local cats would electrocute themselves peeing on the things and I'd be kept awake by blue lightning forks and terrible searing meows. Hasn't happened yet. When I moved in, Mum and Dad came to stay so I showed them my plans and Mum said, "That's far too much effort, dear," and while I was at work grass-seeded the entire plot. It took *days* to pick it out again. In case you ever need to know this, picking grass seed out of well-turned soil is the fastest of all ways to go blind and mad.'

Richard chuckled, and his endorsement played over her like sunbeams.

'My mom would never do anything like that,' he said. 'She is quiet and shy and kind of grey.'

'Lucky you.'

'But I also have a father, remember, and if the notion took him he would send in bulldozers and turn the site into a boating lake. In fact, that's probably what he's doing right now.'

'Oh, no more for me,' said Nina. Richard was signalling to the wine waiter. 'I'm driving, and we have very unforgiving police.'

Richard gave her a look from which all expression was expunged. Tonelessly, he said, 'You intend going home tonight.'

Nina's viscera contracted with a violence that wiped out all hope of swallowing another atom of that bloody chicken.

'Not necessarily,' she said when she could trust her voice.

'Good,' said Richard. 'Then we'll have another bottle of the chilled Pouilly Fumé.'

And the wine waiter, who had stood through this exchange with his gaze fixed aristocratically on some point in the distance, now gave a fractional bow and melted away with the finished bottle.

18

Richard fell asleep around five o'clock, after which Nina lay awake in the ochrous light that seeped from the street, and watched his flopped body, the long exposed extent of his back, the vertebrae forming a perfect sculptural line like a figure carved from dark and flawless wood. His breathing pulsed beneath the traffic's surges to produce an interesting multicoloured jam of African polyrhythms. If only I had a cassette recorder with me, thought Nina, I'd tape it. She lay between the frazzled sheets, and her shocked body registered an extreme sense of well-being. Always does you the power of good, she thought, to have a really thorough going-over by a physician.

The following evening Richard was flying to Edinburgh. They spent most of Saturday wandering round a London that still bore the marks of a recent disaster, though one that would be difficult to pin down. The plummet to earth of a fleet of light aircraft, perhaps. Crunching through it, Nina threw out the remark about crashing aircraft with perhaps insufficient thought.

She had offered to take him home, desperately trying to remember what state she'd left the flat in.

'Your voice is nervous,' he said with an insight that shook

her. 'Maybe you'd prefer to show me your place when you're better prepared.'

'That is very sensitive of you,' she said.

In fact Richard didn't seem to mind Nina walking him for hours round the seedier parts of Soho on a newly healed multiple fracture to look for a café that was actually in Covent Garden. When they finally found it and Nina was absently ordering a meal she hadn't a chance of eating, the conversation moved to her family, and she told him about the manuscript.

'When you offered to take me home,' said Richard, 'you might have mentioned that one of the century's lost treasures was lying in a bedroom drawer under your pantyhose.'

'On top of the wardrobe.'

A tinge of pink flickered beneath Richard's tan. 'This is a long shot,' he said, his eyes glittering, 'but . . . what else have you got in your flat?'

Nina said loudly, 'A Nicolò Amati violin dated 1664 hidden in the Hoover cupboard.'

Richard gave a shout of laughter and threw his arms round her.

'Look, the violin's buggered,' she yelled into the cashmere and silk of his shaking shoulders, 'and the rest is a fantasy of Erik's.'

'I love you,' he told her, snorts of merriment escaping into her hair. 'You're clever and funny and I love you.'

She hadn't been expecting that. It seemed to Nina that the fabric of the café stepped up to offer its congratulations: the red-painted walls, the ruddy curlicues of lettering on the shining Coca-Cola mirrors, they were the colour of his name. 'I love you, too,' she said and Richard kissed her.

Then he said gently, 'You don't experiment, Nina.'

Not knowing whether this supported his declaration of love or qualified it, Nina was about to object that she would experiment with anything he liked from transvestism to crack when he went on, 'With your sexual power, I mean. You don't show off and . . . tease. Make fun. My ex-wife did when we were first together.'

'Did you hate it?' Nina asked, hoping so.

'I didn't hate it but . . . it felt like I was a prop or back-drop. Yes, you could say I hated it.'

After lunch they wandered aimlessly and he returned to the subject of the symphony. 'Sibelius. A house full of women and a drink problem, right?'

She sketched a punch at him. 'Sibelius had a wonderful family!' Prompted by a harmless craving to show off shamelessly, Nina enumerated them. 'Five surviving daughters, fifteen grandchildren and twenty-one great-grandchildren. Mostly his wife kept him off the booze. Whenever he backslid she didn't speak to him for days and left furious notes round the house.'

Nina thought of photographs of the Sibeliuses *en famille*: pretty little girls in hair ribbons and Aino dressed like a character from Ibsen. A photograph from the time of her engagement showed a striking young woman in leg-of-mutton sleeves. But later there was a telling portrait: Aino in her mid-thirties, looking high forties.

Nina turned sunnily to Richard and his admiring attention. 'You know the most touching thing? Sibelius kept all those notes the same way he kept every love letter. His letters to her were so sexy they must have steamed open their own envelopes. On one of his travels he was worried about mailing that sort of stuff, so Aino suggested he send a big innocent letter and hide a naughty little one inside it. She must have been something rather special, Aino Sibelius.'

A charming notion added its warmth to the colour of Nina's thoughts. In his prime, with that commanding baritone. Murmuring sexual endearments. Oh yes, a woman might revel.

Richard asked her, 'Did you know there's a strong Boston connection?'

'I know he kept promising the world première of this very Eighth to your orchestra.'

Abruptly, a plunging anxiety replaced Nina's enjoyment. She had written to the Sibelius archives in Helsinki and the information they sent her was deeply alarming. First, the evidence supported the idea of a huge symphony. Sibelius had even used the term 'great symphony', which naturally conjured ideas of Beethoven's Ninth, with choral finale to boot. He even estimated the actual size: at one point he sent twenty-three pages to be professionally copied – and said the eventual length would be roughly eight times that. Which was 'roughly' the size of Nina's basic score. But did he ever complete it? Yes, according to one conductor, who claimed to have seen the score on the shelves at Ainola, seven bound volumes *with separate choral parts*.

Even worse, every single article mentioned the funeral piece whose theme popped up in the symphony's slow movement. Apparently, at the time Sibelius was working on the Eighth a close friend died and he had to come up with some music in a hurry, so it was assumed he recycled a theme from his work in progress.

Richard said, 'Can you tell me why the idea upsets you? You really feel this could be something your father—?'

'Stole?'

'Copied out. But never publicized because the composer didn't. It wouldn't reflect badly on him. The restraint would be laudable, surely.'

'Well, that depends on how he got hold of it, Richard. The thing is, my father left Finland under a cloud. And never set foot there again. And since he died it's begun to seem inexplicable that he never went back. And I've recently learned he knew a young man who was on the make, and I keep thinking how this manuscript would have looked to somebody like that. Oh hell, Dad didn't merely know the young man, he was accused of leading him to his death in the war. I'm terrified of what I'll get if I slot those facts together.'

'Hey,' said Richard, his arm round her, squeezing.

'He wasn't a bad man, Richard, he wasn't. I just can't understand. Sorry. Sorry, I'll stop.'

'Listen. You told me once about your father's anxiety disorder. That says this symphony is above board.'

'Really?'

'If it was got illegally, I cannot see him, a man plagued by worry, leaving it in the house to be found after his death.'

'That makes a lot of sense,' Nina replied. 'Thank you.' But it only made sense up to a point. Her father hadn't even reached seventy, his three-score-and-ten, and he always believed he would die a slow death from cancer. It seemed entirely possible that he intended destroying that score when the time came. He just didn't realize the time had come.

Nina and Richard spent the afternoon ambling in and out of cafés, cuddling in taxis. Later, she drove him to Heathrow through traffic clogged with homebound shoppers, to catch the Edinburgh shuttle.

'I'm back Tuesday till Saturday,' he told her, 'and they've put me in a hotel by the river somewhere called Marlow. Not far from your office, I think.' His voice was varnished with the warmth of hunger. 'Nina . . . could you join me?'

So she did. She made some neighbourly arrangements with Sean and Victoria, and spent her nights with Richard in the riotously canopied four-poster of his otherwise hushed hotel. In the mornings, in the shower together, they sang sixties songs at the tops of their voices, Richard demanding to know their colours, laughing against the silvered tones of the water. When they parted at the airport he said, 'Flights between Boston and London only take six hours. We can work it out. I'll be back. I want you. Which I think,' he added, 'constitutes three Beatles songs in a row.'

As an omen, they didn't come better than that.

19

Nina was assessing her garden. Over-wintered berries and red dogwoods obligingly blazed Richard's colour against the architectural statement of her *Fatsia japonica*. It was the morning after he flew home. She had belatedly shuffled out of the bed in which she had been reliving their last night, and was presently daydreaming on a stepping stone in nothing but a vintage kaftan.

Clever and funny, he had said. Well, she could capitalize on that. Nina ransacked the five syllables of his approbation, searching for ideas that were a match. How about Surrealism? The Magritte painting of a pipe with the words *This is not a pipe*? She would plant a floral clock. There must be commercial packs, which could be modified. Nina pictured the traditional colour scheme: sage, misty mauves, very orthodox. Except her clock would run backwards, and round the perimeter in a variety of sedum called 'Dragon's Blood' she would plant the words *This is not a clock*.

On her right was the only one of her garden walls you could see over. Last year something shameful and mortifying had happened. A young mother and child had lived there, and while Nina worked at the flower bed the four-year-old Alicia would keep up a stream-of-consciousness chatter. One summer day Nina picked her up and lifted her over. Eyes comically wide, the child tiptoed across the stepping stones with their overspill of alchemilla and nemophila, spellbound. The rosebuds were opening, the variety called 'Peace', which had totemic significance for Nina because peace itself did, ever since childhood. Because war did. She had wondered, Will Alicia remember this all her life? Will it take up residence in the treasure trove of her mind as a never-quite-placeable memory of an enchanted garden?

Then Alicia had started rubbing her leg. 'Hurts,' she said.

There was no injury Nina could see. She kissed the leg better and moved on, but Alicia wouldn't. She kept whining, 'My poor leg.' And 'Mummy says when I hurt I got to tell.' Over and over and over.

A vast and ungovernable impatience had overcome Nina, swift as a blind coming down, a heavy Venetian blind released with a clatter that set her teeth on edge. Her nails dug into the palms.

'Sweetheart, you don't want to make a big fuss when you're not really poorly, do you? They're horrid things, big fusses when you're not really poorly. Let's pick some sweet peas for your mummy.'

That night, the mummy had stood screaming at Nina's door. 'She *told* you and you shut her up! My daughter's a sickler!' Alicia had been blue-lighted across Harlesden to the Central Middlesex with a sickle-cell-anaemia crisis.

Now, Nina became aware of the new neighbours' garden. There was a concrete path, broken and leprous. One of Nina's overfed stray cats swaggered along it with a John Wayne roll and his eye on a capsized supermarket cart. And in a dereliction of nettles and rusty dock leaves slumped the putrefying corpse of a pink mattress. Rain had unevenly bloated its guts and sodden its exploded stuffing. Even though Nina couldn't smell it from her side of the wall, an odour of sopping rot percolated through her imaginings, the colour of a profound disquiet.

Richard was not merely wealthy but wealthy from the

cradle. Even if American cities actually had such areas of contrasting demographics, it was a racing certainty Richard had never lived in one. For a week, all Nina's thoughts had spoken to her in his beautiful voice. Now it was replaced by the sound of his imagined taxi throbbing some future arrival in Brickstone Road. She stared at the eyesore of her neighbours' back yard, outlandish solutions hurtling through her head: a ten-foot fence (outlawed by her lease). Delivery vans loaded with conifers on hire for the night. Pillars, rods and curtains.

Music was thumping again. The new neighbours played Terence Trent D'Arby at distortion volume, signing his name across their hearts. Sean regularly slammed round there yelling. For another madcap moment Nina pictured herself pleading at their door for quiet, her hands stuffed with twenty-pound notes. Her accelerating anxiety was derailed by a ringing phone. A real phone. Duane.

'Well, thank God,' he said when she updated him. 'I was seriously scared that by the time you two got it together all your bits would have shrivelled up.'

'Thanks for sharing that, Duane. Hey, guess what arrived an hour ago. Orchids. Special delivery on a *Sunday*. Did you even *know* there were places—?'

'Nina. Not putting the dampers on but . . . go easy. You don't really know the guy well.'

'Oh yes I do. This last week, we've—'

'People in the Boston office always said Richard was kind of . . . intense. He gets . . . like, after the divorce he was red raw.'

'Understandably, as she screwed him for every cent she could get. We talked about it.'

'All I meant is, don't go helter-skelter. You know what we're like. Far too ready to lie face down in a puddle if it would spare our beloved getting his feet wet. Hold back a bit.'

The music was thumping on Tuesday evening when Nina's phone rang again.

'It's Richard.'

The highly tuned antennae of her love picked up a subtle but troubling syncope in his intonation. She felt an ice-chip of fear. 'What's the matter?'

'Company's downsizing. Closing half the offices around the Pacific rim. I got the assignment of sorting it out. They're relocating me.'

'You mean ... West Coast?' Nina's brain whizzed through calculations of flight times and time-zone differences. Terence Trent D'Arby stopped as if somebody had shot him.

'Tokyo,' said Richard. 'Fucking Tokyo. They're shipping me out to Japan for two fucking years.' At which he launched himself on a tirade of American obscenities so convoluted that Nina wondered whether they had to be taught in prep school.

20

'I want to turn the job down, but it isn't so easy. Recession's setting in. There's not much else around right now.'

'Is this appointment serious promotion?' And Nina gleaned that it was.

'I'll write,' Richard said.

'But you will be so busy. Please don't give yourself added pressure about me.' She even meant it: it was anathema, to be thought of as psychological pressure by the man she loved.

When they rang off, she made another phone call. To Stoke.

'Fuck, Nina, you two are jinxed.'

'I feel so dreadful I don't know what to do. It's cruel. It's cruel, Duane.'

'Take up Jussi's offer. Fly away to South Tangoland for a couple of weeks. When you were a kid you used to dream about the place, right? Comforts that date from childhood always go deepest.'

So that was what she did.

The empty flat Jussi was borrowing was air-conditioned and on the tenth floor in a residential district several miles from the city centre. Nina had pictured somewhere hermetically sealed and isolated. Not a bit of it. The flat was light and airy with proper windows that opened (some of them never quite closed) to let in the warm, humid, human street-noise from the shops and cafés round a square in the feathery shade of jacarandas. In fact, in Jussi's words, you couldn't walk ten metres in Buenos Aires without barking your shin on a tree.

Duane's instinct was right, it was therapeutic. Nina loved Buenos Aires: the Parisian architecture, miles of green space, flower-and-vegetable stalls and ubiquitous kiosks, and twenty-four-hour bustle that had much in common with the fizzing, spluttering kettle in the apartment's eccentric kitchen.

It was even a city of dogs. Professional dog-walkers strode through the streets with fifteen animals on leads – until another one trotted past, at which they would all go mad and turn him into a maypole.

Regarding the people, the *porteños*, Nina came up with the same word her memory applied to the Clarks: they were gracious. She was also amazed that Anglophilia had survived the sinking of the *Belgrano*. You could even have entirely level-headed discussions about the Falklands War – but one reference to Diego Maradona's illegal goal against England and they shouted the place down.

Buenos Aires was bafflingly inconsistent; every public building and statue was defaced by anti-government slogans, an absolute hysteria of graffiti, yet nobody dropped litter. The *porteños* raged against their country while inflation rocketed out of any comprehensible economic sphere; clinical depression was *de rigueur*, yet everyone – shop assistants, taxi drivers – waved a proud hand and cried, 'So what do you think of my beautiful city?'

Nina could forgive those drawbacks that couldn't be ignored, such as the ridiculous twenty-lane Avenida de 9 de Julio which took a week to cross.

'For God's sake!' Jussi complained. 'And what's *that*

meant to be?' he demanded scathingly of a two-hundred-foot obelisk that pointed arrogantly at Heaven. Nina hadn't the slightest doubt what it was meant to be in the homeland of machismo. She looked at the thing and laughed.

At night she fell asleep to the friendly grey gritty roar of the street. It was curative. Until the second week when she and Jussi came home from a dance at four in the morning and Nina fell into bed with him. She had never meant to. It was the tango, she told herself. You couldn't help it.

Nowadays the young danced salsa but there were still traditional *milongas* where the ageing *tangueros* danced all night. Jussi had even found Nina a teacher, a thin, chain-smoking woman named Monica in a dark-wood studio smelling of jasmine and something earthy that Nina re-captured one afternoon eating an unwashed grape. Under Monica's tutelage and with a string of embarrassingly gorgeous men, Nina began to lose that defensive stiffness and her lope like a vampire's manservant. Monica put her to practising round a swivel chair. 'But remember, a chair is easier. Unfortunately, we must dance with men.'

Unfortunately indeed. The option of replacing all the men in the world with swivel chairs struck Nina as having certain advantages.

So Jussi took her to a *milonga*, Nina carrying her dance shoes in a bag like a child going to a party.

'Jussi, I'm not good enough to tango with people watching.'

'Try doing nothing at all, just follow my lead.'

And when they got back he kissed her, and Nina let him turn her towards his bedroom. Where she did nothing at all, just followed his lead.

It didn't remind her of Richard — nothing about Jussi reminded her of Richard. Sleepless afterwards, she watched his somnolent head on the pillow and thought, The last time I was in bed with a man . . . but it was hollow. The two were further apart than geography.

The next day she rose early and set herself to creating lunch. Cooking was another of the joys of Buenos Aires. Freed from the social constraints of being expected to know what she was doing, Nina would explore the local supermarket where carrots were *zanahorias* (and where, if she was addressed in Spanish, she replied, 'I'm English,' in the abject tones of one confessing, 'No use talking to me, I'm a moron'). Now, stirring the concoction in her pan, she heard the lavatory flush and her senses followed Jussi's footsteps – and she tried to ignore an unpleasant lurch in her stomach.

'Any coffee? It's OK, I'll grab an espresso.'

'Are you going out? I'm cooking.'

'Never eat lunch. See you later, yeah?'

'Well . . . what time?'

'Depends who I run into. And whether I can even dance. Phew, there's no physical exertion quite like sex to take its toll on the body. You OK? How's your ratatouille?'

'My . . . what?'

'In the pan.'

'Oh! It's hash.'

'Yeah?' Planting a quick kiss in the air near the top of her head, Jussi left.

She heard the finality of the door; the whirr of the approaching elevator, the clank of its metal grill, the waning drone. Nina could make out the rattle as it came to a halt in the marble entrance hall. She turned off the gas and picked dejectedly at the tomatoes. Then she took herself off to the park.

Nina was not an ingénue, she'd been round the block, she was no stranger to the sight of a panicked male vanishing through the door crying, 'Is that the time?!' while still adjusting his trousers. What she wasn't used to was having sex *with somebody she didn't want*. Nina plodded sightless and forlorn along the crunchy red paths of the Botanic Garden, glumly conscious that her distaste for Jussi's bed had no right to coexist with feelings of hurt at his small morning-after rejection.

'Why can't you lighten up?' Duane had once challenged her. 'Half-hearted sex is one of the joys of being single.'

Nina saw the justice of this. She wished she could think of last night with pleasure instead of a sense of creeping dismay. But she couldn't. The memory, as she poked at it, dissected it, vivisected the damn thing, elicited a familiar revulsion, an ashamed disgust in her skin, her gut, between her legs. The disgust of Frinton and Mr Eldridge. It was because of this that she had learned long ago not to go to bed with men she didn't love.

The trouble was, the real Jussi was the other side of the city and in his place was a memorized collage of off-putting mannerisms. When he was reading he sniffed. His English was enlivened by that indiscriminate brew of slang so everybody was 'sunshine' or 'old son'. He slept in T-shirts printed with slogans: JUGGLERS DO IT WITH THEIR BALLS IN THE AIR and ACUPUNCTURISTS DO IT WITH A SMALL PRICK. 'Chill, Nina, chill!' was a favourite command, though in that case, she conceded, the man might have a point.

It would have been far better if he had taken her with him today. Nina was no less susceptible than anyone else to the lubricating effects of status, and as a dancer Jussi shed the tarnish of his uninspiring conversation and turned into an artist. Unfortunately, his attraction didn't long outlast the dance floor. She had gone to bed with him last night not because of his sizzling way with a *sentada amor* but because Richard had left her in a sexual state akin to being all dressed up and nowhere to go.

Nina walked all afternoon but it was no good: the limpid blue sky, the palms and eucalyptus trees. Fate had given her Richard and then snatched him away like some peevish toddler. As she thought of his golden body and then of Jussi, a kind of dread seeped into the air and blighted it. Nina sank on to a bench, bowed her head and cried. Nearby, a dog-walker's charges lolled in the shade. At the sight of a sitting target, the entire herd bounded over. In consequence she got sunburned. While Nina cuddled them the dogs licked all the Factor 45 off her arms.

21

'Your . . . boyfriend,' said Señor Ferrari after due consideration, 'tells us every year the Americans will come to Buenos Aires to learn tango. Not ones and twos but in force.'

Not single spies but in battalions, thought Nina. There was a sorrowful note to everything he said, as though he took his cue from the bandoneon. In the afternoon heat, twenty couples danced to its mournful voice as 'A La Gran Muñeca' by Carlos Di Sarli issued from mounted speakers, and the whirr of ceiling fans absorbed its grittier edges. They were upstairs in Confiteria Ideal, a great faded palace of a café with Corinthian columns, mahogany panelling and old, smoky wall mirrors. Señor Ferrari was its principal tango teacher. Not a young man.

It was the hottest hour of the day. A creaky waiter in dentist whites veered between the dancers, holding aloft trays of champagne in chorus-girl glasses. Tired light leaked through pleated net curtains, from the teeming canyon of a road outside. Nina's fraction of the café was reflected in the bevelled mirror at her back and again in the spotty mirror opposite, in a soft-focus infinity, the graininess perfectly suiting the hoary records crackling through the speakers.

'Yesterday came an American dance instructor,' continued

Señor Ferrari, adding with sad pride, 'He took a lesson from me.'

'I hope you charged like sin,' said Jussi.

'Your boyfriend,' said Señor Ferrari again, 'pretends tango is business. Do you believe him?'

'I know it isn't for you.' She smiled and sipped at her third *café con leche*, which was all that stood between Nina and hypoglycaemia. Jussi was always forgetting lunch.

Señor Ferrari returned her smile. 'Tango cannot be about money. It is the sweetness and the sorrow of life. It is the life force. That is why for so many it turns to obsession.' He underscored the word with a frown of unqualified dejection.

Gian and Beryl had mentioned Confiteria Ideal so often that Nina and Lucia even had a game of that name, played in the Clarks' garden with all the delicious rituals of childhood. Wearing Beryl's cast-off evening gowns pinned to fit until the girls looked like voodoo dolls, they set the game between apple trees whose trunks stood for marble columns, while an ancient wicker basket was hung from a branch as the token chandelier. Only the plot was fluid, though at some point either Lu or Nina had to collapse on the dance floor suffering from some ailment in the girls' expanding vocabulary – bursitis, beriberi or bubonic plague – and Jim Kildare would set about saving her life against the odds. Their Confiteria Ideal was a place of pop stars and leggy blondes who could fire a Beretta. It was glitzy.

Now, in the real one, Nina saw it all in terms of confectionery: downstairs, decorative glass cases displayed tiered cakes, puffy meringues and fancy pharmacy bottles of sweets. Upstairs was the creamy marble dance floor, chocolaty panelled wood, light bulbs that glowed vanilla, tablecloths in deep plum. Tempered by the blemished glass, the reflections turned into candied fruit and marshmallows and coffee creams melting ineluctably in the drooping heat of the afternoon.

'Watch the couple in the corner.' Señor Ferrari indicated an elderly husband and wife, the man a collection of bones jigging inside his suit, the woman a rubber ball. Their eyes sparkled. Nina gathered that he was a better dancer than she; he would sometimes essay a complicated finale and his wife would laugh and cuff him.

'Watch. The toe, the edge of the foot, they caress the floor like a cat on the prowl. This is not a technicality, it is a philosophy. Tango did not come from cultured Europeans reaching for the skies, but from African dancers and the cowboys of the pampas. These people understood the earth. Northern civilization tries always to fly upwards with its leaping ballerinas and soaring sopranos. African rhythms and Latin horsemen, they respect the soil. This they gave to tango.'

'That is a wonderful analysis,' said Nina. 'Thank you.'

Her own skills had so improved that her image of herself had changed. This had a downside: nowadays each criticism was a stabbing disappointment and there was an increasing danger that the next time Monica stopped her in mid-step, Nina would tear off her tango shoes, crying, 'I'll never get the hang of this bloody dance, I am GIVING UP!'

After that first night together, Jussi had let her spend the next alone but he was reluctant to let her be. He actually joined Nina when she went out walking, Jussi who would normally take a taxi to travel fifty yards. Yesterday in the Rose Gardens under a perfect summer sky and splendouring sun, he had conjured for her the icescape of a desperate Finnish winter. And for the first time broke through the taboo against a Pellinen mentioning Sibelius.

'We don't get your slushy wet stuff,' he told her, forgetting that she had been brought up on talk of Finnish winters. 'Our snow is the real thing, dry as powder. You should listen to Sibelius's *Night Ride and Sunrise*, about a sleigh ride.'

They had been walking by an extraordinary tree with a hunched root system, sitting with its legs crossed and apparently made of elephant hide as though from some evolutionary confusion over the word trunk. Nina wondered how anyone could feel the need to snow all over the teeming greenery and red earth of Buenos Aires.

As a random diversion she said, 'When I was little I assumed even these parks would have couples dancing. Gian and Beryl made it sound that way.'

'Yeah? Giancarlo was donkey's years older than her, right?'

'Well, fifteen. He'd been someone else's partner but it didn't come together. Gian was already forty when they made it to the top.'

'God! Ancient!'

That nettled her. 'He didn't look ancient, Jussi, and he could move like a teenager!'

'Pushing it, though. Not many miles left on the clock for his sort. Then they retired because Beryl got sick.'

'No.'

'Yeah, they suddenly pulled out of a world tour. New cabaret show that never happened. What was it, exhaustion?'

'Jussi, the Clarks were inexhaustible. They would come off a thirty-hour flight from Melbourne, and the next week they were at Blackpool winning both Latin and ballroom titles.'

'So they lost their nerve, or what?'

'They had nerves of steel. This is the couple that won their first British Open with the crowd trying to boo them off the floor.'

'So they just stopped? Like Sibelius?'

Nina opened her mouth for an acid rejoinder. She closed it. She said, 'Well, yes, actually. Come to think of it. It *was* a bit like Sibelius.'

In Confiteria Ideal the afternoon was coming to an end. 'La Cumparsita' flowered into syncopations and cadenzas, and the dancers closed in a climax of *ganchos*.

As the floor cleared, Señor Ferrari said, 'Time to tidy away. I have been enchanted to meet you,' he added to Nina.

Jussi got to his feet. 'Want me to stack the chairs?'

Señor Ferrari gave a last sorrowful smile. 'Please,' he said, 'take *la niña* downstairs and buy her lunch before she collapses and dies on the floor of my *milonga*. They will give me forms to complete. Believe me, you have not seen bureaucracy until you have seen Argentinian bureaucracy.'

22

Childhood

Lu and Nina sat rigid in the kitchen, eavesdropping. They weren't allowed to be here: Gian and Beryl thought they had been packed off to the Hannays for the morning. But they weren't allowed to be there either, Nina's mother having packed her off to the Clarks. Neither of the girls was particularly acquainted with the laws of physics but they understood that everybody has to be somewhere, and had chosen Lu's because of the central heating. At the best of times the Hannays' vicarage was infested with a micro-climate that bred mildew in the soul, and today it was snowing.

Giancarlo's voice came at them through the wall. '. . . blood out of a stone.'

'No one's asking for blood,' responded the man whose name apparently was Monty. 'We're talking contracts here. Legal obligations.'

'Going round in circles,' whispered Lu. 'They said that already.'

The man called Monty was losing his temper. 'Well, it's a bit bloody late in the day, *four weeks* from opening!

If you'd come to me three months ago, both of you . . .'

Lu said reasonably, 'What's the point of telling me it's top secret and I'm not allowed to talk about it, when they shout so loud the neighbours can hear? We had those reporters again yesterday with Dad doing his "No comment" stuff—'

'Hush up, Lu, your mum's talking.'

But Beryl's voice was obliterated by another blast from the Monty man. '. . . *fifty thousand pounds* and—'

It was the mention of money that did it. One mention of money, and you could guarantee that an adult would materialize at your elbow and evict you from earshot. Sex and babies were a pretty fast trigger, but money was like that passenger ejector-button in James Bond. Lucia's grandmother appeared as if she had come up out of the floor on a spring.

'*Via, via, via!*' she shouted, all jowls and elbows, yanking them to their feet and waving her podgy arms at the door. 'You *out*. Not be here!'

Lu struggled from her grip. 'Go *where*?' she demanded, pointing at the window. 'It. Is. Snow. Ing. *Capisci?*'

'Hannay house. *Subito!*'

'*Nonna*—'

They were out. They were in the garden.

'*NONNA!*'

The back door slammed behind them. Starlings that had been squabbling over bread crusts on the white lawn clacked and chucked in a flapping, airborne stampede.

'Oh, bloody marvellous!' shouted Lu. She turned to Nina. '*Can* we go up yours?'

Nina shook her head. 'We can't, Lu. The bishop's coming for a heart-to-heart.'

'Thought so.' There was no further enquiry. She didn't, for example, ask whether the Reverend Hannay was still away on holiday. She had only been told that once, and had merely blinked a little and then nodded as though it were common practice for fathers to disappear from home on holiday, on their own, without warning, and – for all Lu knew – in the middle of the night. Lu's acquaintance with the Hannays had driven her past wondering whether he had truly buggered off somewhere, or had spontaneously combusted or been either dragged away by men in white coats or throttled by his exasperated wife and buried in the vicarage garden under the peace roses. But what to do now?

Had she been on her own, she would have had no qualms about battering on a neighbour's door and claiming asylum with lurid accounts of her family's ill-treatment. But she had Nina with her, and there would be hell to pay if Mrs Hannay heard they were begging at doors.

'We're stuck out here, then,' she reasoned. 'Serve them right if we die.'

'Why don't we just ring the front bell? Your dad would never—'

'Dad's not thinking straight. He'll tell us to go up yours and close the door again.'

'Oh. Yes.'

Impasse.

There was a pretty sunken area, walled in York stone, across which aubrietia poured purple in spring. The girls scraped the snow from those walls with smarting hands and sat down. Snow settled insidiously on their shoes, clothes, hair. It was a wet cold, acutely hostile to life; your nerves jangled and screamed against its affront. Rubbing at her arms, Nina said, 'You're not supposed to sit still. I read this book. You have to keep your blood moving.'

'I know. What I'm hoping is, somebody'll see us from a window and call the police. If we run up and down they'll just think we're playing snowballs.'

'True,' agreed Nina. 'We're stuck here, then.'

But sit still they couldn't. Their limbs juddered, unwilled. Nina's right foot tapped like a jazzman on benzedrine. Lu leaped up and a shout welled from the depths of her being.

'If this is Scott of the bloody Antarctic, I reckon we've got to the point they shot the ponies! Look, I got an idea. Need buckets and a long stick.'

The stick they dug out from the white grave-hump of a flower bed. Buckets were harder, the Clarks' gardener being a power freak who locked the shed, but from a line-up of white pillows they inferred the snowy burial ground of some cavernous flower pots. 'These'll do the necessary.'

When she explained the necessary, Nina said, 'But suppose it's your *nonna* comes to the door?'

'No. Dad'll answer in case it's reporters. Would *you* want my *nonna* on display to the *Daily Mail*?'

Nina agreed that she certainly wouldn't, and the girls sped round to the front of the house. The Clarks' promotion manager was ranting now. They caught something about the most unprofessional behaviour he'd come across in twenty-five years.

'You first,' said Lu, tamping snow into the pots. Then, in response to Nina's pose, 'No, not like that. More sort of—'

'Like this?' suggested Nina, adopting an attitude of prostrate melodramatic agony she remembered from the victim in a Sherlock Holmes case on the BBC.

'Brilliant. Close your eyes. It's coming.'

It came. Several vile gallons of snow. Repeating the procedure on herself was more difficult and caused Nina to squeal, 'Hurry *up*, Lucia, I'm freezing down here!'

'Just got to reach the bell with this stick.'

Inside the house, the doorbell shrieked. The ranting stopped. The house, suddenly as quiet as an unplugged TV, listened without breathing. Then they heard Giancarlo's approaching footfall before he pulled open the door to find two children apparently sprawled dead on his doorstep under a snowdrift.

23

'*Como estás?*' said Duane from the other end of the phone line. 'I once had a fling with a waiter from a tapas bar. How was Buenos Aires? Go to bed with Jussi, did you?' And when Nina didn't reply, 'Knew you would! Hey, didn't Noël Coward have a song about a Nina from Argentina? As I remember, she despised the tango and declined to begin the beguine.'

Nina had been home five days and this was the first time she'd managed to reach him. 'Duane, you're sounding ominously chirpy. What's wrong?'

'Steve died Wednesday.'

'Oh, no!'

'Has to happen while my best friend's in Argentina. Well, don't cry for me.'

Hesitantly, Nina asked, 'Were you there?'

'I was. Nearly killed me, but I did it, thank God. Funeral's causing the usual nightmare. Steve's family's desperately trying to pretend he died respectably from cancer so we ladies are *not* invited. They're terrified the congregation will be packed with screaming queens weeping operatically into mauve hankies.' Nina pictured him at the phone shaking his blond curls like one of Dickens's little heroines.

'Well, if you're gatecrashing and need a female to stuff a

cushion up her jumper and hang on to your arm calling you "big boy", just let me know.'

'Maybe I'll do it in an Act-Up T-shirt that reads STOP WELLCOME PROFITEERING.'

'Not if you want another job in the pharma industry.'

'There won't be any. Recession is a-comin' in, Nina. It's going to get very cold for R&D.'

This was clearer by the day: budgets slashed, projects abandoned. But to keep her warm there was Jussi. More or less.

'What sort of surprise?' he asked suspiciously when Nina suggested they stay in tonight. 'Sex?'

'Yes, Jussi.'

'No dancing involved, is there? This isn't another of your "strip tango" fantasies?'

'No, Jussi.'

Fantasy was always hard work. The strip tango of Jussi's unhappy memory was Nina dressed in lace basque and stockings, offering to shed them slowly to the strains of 'A La Gran Muñeca' by Carlos Di Sarli. Jussi vetoed this plan on the grounds that it was too much like a busman's holiday.

Yet he was evidently fond of Nina, and she found to her surprise that she was touched. Little by little the habits she had accepted when he was a friend but which embarrassed her in a lover ceased to loom in her mind. Importantly, she liked herself better for it. There was a sense of growing up about this evolution. It is at thirteen, not thirty-four, that it's acceptable for your affection to be obliterated by embarrassment at some behavioural tics that might be ridiculed by the in-crowd.

Victoria from upstairs said, 'You're looking a lot better. Is it Jussi?'

Nina admitted that it was. And when it came to sex, although his repertoire lacked inspiration, the endgame technique couldn't be faulted – and had been known to last up to an hour and a half.

Richard had written from Tokyo, enclosing an exquisite

figure in origami, a tiny geisha, all scarlet and gold. He said, 'The young women in my office are very pretty but they look sideways through their lashes and simper. I miss your frank blue eyes.'

When she first saw the envelope and stamp, Nina's legs were full of air. But my frank blue eyes are on the other side of the world, she sermonized herself.

Though Jussi never would understand that other people ate lunch, he started cooking her dinner. He quickly established that here was someone who would buy junk food scarcely glancing at the packet, so he set about providing Nina with nutrition that might prevent her keeling over from artificial additives before her thirties were out. But unlike Duane, Jussi didn't swing open the door of her mismanaged fridge and stand there clucking, he simply slung out the black and the rancid, and quietly went about providing decent meals.

Duane asked, 'What do you do in return?'

'All the driving.' Jussi had inherited Erik's myopia but not his indifference to fashion. A trenchant optician had said that despite the strongest contact lenses he'd be driving by the Braille method. Luckily, Jussi's friends had cars the same way they had spare apartments.

The 'huge dusty flat' did have a sanitary kitchen, and Nina would find it beset with mystifying vegetable matter. Rutabagas. A sink full of nettles bleaching. He got through unconscionable quantities of dill. He baked in a haze of heat and cardamom that sent her spinning back to childhood when Erik would arrive at their door with a bag of prettily plaited *vehnäpitko* loaves.

Some of the dishes Nina already knew from home, like the delicious mosaic of potato, onion and anchovy called Jansson's Temptation. Those she didn't know tasted a lot better than they sounded (cabbage soup, cabbage pasty, cabbage pie, cabbage rolls and cabbage casserole, for example. Beer soup. Blueberry soup). Others stretched Jussi's English.

'What is it?' she asked of the oven that was flavouring the air.

'*Kalarulla*. Smoked herrings in . . . in . . .'

'In a sauce?' ventured Nina. 'In a pie?'

Jussi reached for the dictionary. 'Smoked herrings in custard.'

And at breakfast. 'What is it?'

'*Mannavelli*.' Dictionary again. 'Gruel,' said Jussi.

Having a boyfriend who taught tango should have meant free lessons. No. Even when she promised to keep her clothes on, Nina ran into the sort of trouble wives have when their husbands teach them to drive.

'I said *right*, you idiot. That's left! We're supposed to be heading over there! I am *not shouting*!'

Nina dared not keep shelling out for Tony Delterfield. Instead she practised at lunchtime in her office: round a swivel chair.

Jussi kept edging the conversation towards her father's symphony with an air of nonchalance so heavy its tremors probably registered in Acton.

'I think you should do something about it.'

'Such as?'

'Such as mail it off to my father.'

'Mum forbids me to hand over the score to anyone.' Nina didn't add that in the case of Erik this would be tantamount to contravening the Geneva Convention.

'Yeah, but suppose Dad's inkling is correct. Then—'

Then the discovery would make headlines, and if her mother was even half right, the Hannays' lives would never be remotely the same again.

Susan's baby was due early in June, and André had sent another airline ticket. Shortly beforehand, Nina took Jussi to Brancaster. It was not a success. Christine winced at his slangy English, and Jussi had a habit of throwing himself into the chintz armchairs that made the springs whimper.

'Nina, dear, he's a freeloader like his father. I do wish you'd find yourself someone with ambition. You have to look to the future. I've nothing to leave you, you know.'

'I can provide for myself, Mum. But you're wrong about Jussi. He seems laid-back but he works to five-year plans.'

It had surprised Nina: Jussi was unthinkingly generous, picking up tabs in restaurants, buying CDs for friends. He never paid a bill until the final demand arrived. All this suggested a man cavalier about money, yet he pored over his business accounts and shuffled money between banks every time the interest rate changed, with the ready confidence of a financier.

'When I think of dear Gregory, who was so hard-working and ambitious.' And fond of children. 'Or there must be professional men where you work. I know this one looks like Richard Chamberlain, but he isn't Dr Kildare.'

'Yes, Mum,' responded Nina, thinking that on the plus side this one wasn't gay, either.

Her mother wore a sleeveless dress. Down her right arm was a puckering like tractor tracks, the scars of a kitchen accident. Nina could never see it without an unpalatable smudge of guilt across her spirits: it was she who had upset the pan. Guiltily now, she offered to drive her mother to Heathrow but apparently a chauffeured car was coming.

'Susan was insistent to the point of hysteria, dear. Let's hope she mellows with motherhood.'

'What, from sleepless nights?'

'There's a live-in nanny and a laundry woman.'

'Of course. Silly of me.'

'Nina, you two must learn to get along. I'm going to suggest Susan interests herself in that symphony of your father's that you like so much. It will bring you closer. I know she isn't musical but there's the *Kalevala*. Susan's a literature graduate, remember.'

And she would hand it over to some musician who'd be suspicious instantly. Panic tightened Nina's throat. 'Susan would only get on her high horse—'

'Not when it's poetry. I'll make sure she gives you a ring.'

'Mum—'

But Jussi arrived in the kitchen. 'Lobster straight from the beach!' He hauled the contents squirming from his box. *'Oh good grief, they're alive!'*

'Well, yeah. I'm going to boil them.'

'Not in my kitchen!'

He still didn't cotton on to his cool reception. ('Should I call her Christine?' 'No, love, I think not.') His innocence touched her and she was irritated with her mother, so Nina dragged him off with Kruger and walked the pair of them all over the Norfolk coast.

'Does this remind you of Finland?' Kruger chased threads of sand that blew across the marshes from the beach like tumbleweed. 'Finland means fen-land, doesn't it?'

But Jussi's powers of description were reserved for the tango. He shrugged. 'Not enough trees. You know, birches and evergreens.'

And pleated sheets of granite under a low skirting sun, glimmering with Uvarovite garnets. Her father used to talk of the muffled echoes of wilderness away from the hubs of synthetic light, the arcing and humming of the electric towns. There were wolves in the forest, lynxes and brown bears, and trolls that were not gentle Moomins but Evil Angels, sprites, ogres, goblins. They would slink through the blue-frosted woods, hunters registering their shadows as a flicker across the marbled gloom or a glimpse of their matted hair exposed by sudden knives of sunlight through the trees.

Nina's father knew the forest in midwinter at dead of night. The Finns had a competitive sport of ski-racing through unfamiliar forest, the night orchestrated by the chuffing of skis and mumbling of trees as they shifted under their burden of snow. Nina knew it was this cheerful competitiveness in the Finnish spirit that drove them to win more than twice as many Olympic gold medals per capita as any other nation on earth, time after time.

The land is furred with forest from Lapland to the Baltic Sea, and the *Kalevala* tells its creation myth: Väinämöinen himself, the shaman, emerging from the waters and demanding that the barren land be sown with trees. He named that land Kalevala.

In the late nineteenth century, the Finns adopted his story as the embodiment of their nascent nation as they struggled to free themselves from the yoke of Tsarist Russia, though they wouldn't win that freedom until the Russians themselves disposed of the Tsar. Finland meant, and means, something to the Finns that England doesn't mean to the English, Nina knew that. And they have rights the English don't have: rights to roam, and be a part of the countryside, and pick its fruits and berries on private land. It is not only the language that is full of imagery: imagery has always held the nation together, leading to a staggering output of poets, artists, a Nobel laureate in literature, and the extolling of a composer whose musical vision of the northlands was enriched by the insights of synaesthesia. The country's great architects draw on its woods and waters and clean glacial lines for their inspiration as far from home as Dulles airport and the St Louis arch. And few of them stay away for long.

The god of the forest is Tapio, and Tapiola his domain. Sibelius's *Tapiola* is a great poem flowing in subtle complexities from a tiny fragment of melody, an eerie soundscape into which howls a winter wind. No one before him had ever made the orchestra sound the way it does in *Tapiola*. But after it, the world never heard from him again.

Though writers on music use colour as a metaphor, it was no metaphor for the composer, who could even hear a shade of yellowed blue in the pitch between D and E flat. In his early days with Aino's family he had suddenly made a move for the piano, announcing, 'This is the impression made on me by this room!' When he built his seventh symphony round a strong-minded motif on the trombone, it meant more to Sibelius than craftsmanship. That theme was the essence of his wife.

Synaesthesia has never been the sole province of genius; Nina's father had suggested it wasn't so rare but said only creative people went banging on about it. He himself had heard D as red and E as mucky brown. For Nina it was the flow of music that she heard in colour – and texture: touchy-feely velvet, dust devils, waves that fizzed like the strange fire-sparks off the crest of a tsunami.

Asked to explain herself – which had happened a hundred times – Nina could only say it was not readily amenable to analysis. Imagine taking the stopper off a bottle of perfume untouched for years, and being commanded to evaluate that thundercrash of associations, sniffing and concentrating and making notes. They would defeat you, flutter away, evanescent. Though not erased: the next time the stopper came off it would all be there again. There was a particular musical idiosyncrasy of Sibelius's, in the climactic surges, that Nina heard as a cloud of boiling iridescent green – like her father's descriptions of the aurora borealis, which the Finns call 'foxfires' after folktales of the arctic fox brushing snow off the mountains with his tail, to fly as sparks in the northern sky. Nothing else ever sounded that way to Nina, only Sibelius. And her father's symphony.

'Is Finland more like Scotland?' she asked, trying again.

Jussi was clutching a curious assortment of string and baler twine he had chased through the stinging sand. 'One of these could choke a seabird,' he explained casually, scraping his knuckles. 'Why don't you nip over there and check it out yourself? See your father's fatherland, sort of thing.'

That was precisely why she wouldn't go. Because he never went back.

'I've always known your dad's story, kind of,' said Jussi. 'From my old man, but I never paid proper attention.'

'I don't mind telling you. Goes back to the war, when Erik and Dad were fighting at Äglajärvi.'

The war itself had never been a secret from her. Nina could not remember when she had first learned what they meant, those chilling syllables. Vicious fighting in the coldest winter for a century, and ending in the worst sort of battle, right inside the village with the enemy holed up in every house, every barn, every shed, and fighting face to face like scenes from the Wild West. In the chaos, Martti and Erik lost track of each other and Martti ended up with the Boy. Veikko Virta.

Nina said, 'They were trying to retake one of the farmhouses, which was bristling with Soviet machine-gunners. The boy was killed. This is where the story gets heartbreaking. Dad didn't leave him there. He knew the building would be destroyed so, at enormous risk, Dad got his body out so he could be taken home to rest. This is the height of battle, remember. Dad was convinced he wouldn't survive the day, but at least the boy could go back to his family.'

An emotion of astonishing violence swept through Nina's veins like fever – a sense of wild and unforgivable injustice. Dad did a great deal wrong in life, but nothing remotely like the charges made against him.

'You might expect the father would be grateful,' she said.

'That was Jorma Virta, yeah? Dead now, but the guy was a big cheese. Owned the city's largest cotton factory.'

'That's him. Said Dad recklessly stormed the farmhouse and left his son with the consequences. Don't ask me how he squared that with the fact that Dad returned to rescue the body. His filthy allegation came in 1945 when the country was at its lowest ebb.'

'Gutted,' said Jussi. 'What a world: you drive out the Soviet army with their tails between their legs, and when it's over the bastards dictate the peace terms and annex half your country anyhow without firing another shot *and* bleed you white with war reparations.'

'But at least Finland kept its sovereignty, love. If you'd lost the Winter War, you'd have been lassoed into the Communist bloc as just another Czechoslovakia or—'

'Yeah? Well, now the Berlin Wall's down and Russia's giving up her ill-gotten gains, we'll have back the twenty-five thousand square miles the thieving bastards stripped from our border in 1945, including a major port and land loaded with precious metals!'

Nina looked at him. This was Jussi speaking – a walking contradiction of most things Finnish: yet he'd latched on to an enmity dating from a decade before he was born.

'Guess I'm preaching to the choir,' he said. 'Remind me. What date exactly was your dad's trouble?'

'The book was late '45. Dad fled the following autumn, '46.'

'You certain? It doesn't make sense.'

'Jussi, I grew up with this.'

'But the dates are cock-eyed. Your dad couldn't've been in trouble in 1946, no way José. I happen to know he . . . Forget it,' decided Jussi, seeing her face. 'Must be barking up the wrong tree. Baying up the mistaken banyan. But can we talk about this music? You *want* the truth, Nina, it's eating you.' His tenor changed. 'Aren't you worried it's actually wrong? Hiding a symphony that's maybe so beautiful grown men would weep?'

24

'Nina? It's Susan.'

Nina's heart stopped. 'Has something happened to Mum?'

'Of course not. André's driving her to the Winelands to see the autumn colour. It's May here.'

'It's May everywhere, Susan. What can I do for you?'

'Mummy tells me you found a lot of music in Daddy's desk. Which nobody knew existed.'

There was a pause. Nina didn't break it.

'A titanic work, she says, which we know he couldn't have composed later than his teens. I asked some people I know. They all say teens are too young.'

Nina said shakily, 'Mum might have got the wrong end of the stick. It's probably just an exercise from the time Dad wrote his violin piece, so—'

'So he wrote that with one hand and a symphony with the other? Mummy says Erik Pellinen is very interested. And she says you've been asking a heap of questions about whether Daddy might have met Sibelius or been invited to Ainola or had some connection through Uncle Timo or a conductor who shares the family name.'

'That's natural enough, Susan. Everything Dad wrote was heavily influenced—'

'Mummy says you've taken home Daddy's Sibelius books even though they're in Finnish. I went to the library, Nina. Sibelius composed a symphony no one's ever heard, didn't he?'

Nina felt sick. 'If you're going where I think you're going, it's nonsense.'

'I'll decide that for myself. I want a copy. Presumably your office has a photocopier. You can—'

'Have you told Mum about these crazy conjectures?' And when Susan didn't reply, 'No, I thought not. Mum would—'

'So it's all right for you to be poring over this music, but not me?'

Nina's nerves got the better of her. 'Susan, I'm a trained musician whereas you couldn't tell a crotchet from a bloody hatchet! The only way you can examine a musical score is by showing it to—'

'You showed Erik Pellinen. Anyway, if you won't make a copy I'll collect the manuscript myself. As soon as it's safe after the baby, there's shopping I need to do in London.'

Now fighting utter panic, Nina said, 'Dad's music runs to fourteen folders of paper. It weighs a ton. No airline will—'

'Mummy says it's a hundred and ninety pages and the rest are individual parts.'

For someone who wasn't paying attention, Mummy made some pretty agile mental notes. How did parents do this?

'Just have it ready for me, Nina, and I'll decide what to take.'

The words 'a flying fuck at a rolling doughnut' clamoured in Nina's brain.

'I think you're under some misapprehension,' she said. 'I'm not your laundry woman, your nanny or your gardening boy.'

'For God's sake.'

'Goodbye, Susan.'

Nina put the phone down, her hands fluttering with a tremor Sibelius himself might have jibbed at.

※

One thing was absolutely clear from Nina's books: when Sibelius failed to get that symphony out he lied his head off.

Yet for a long time things were going swimmingly. He evidently thought the work was nearly ready, and even told Aino how much money it would bring in. This was serious stuff, money. While still in his mid-thirties and already £35,000 in debt, he had the bright idea of building Ainola. Two years later he was £200,000 in debt. But whenever the conductor in Boston requested the score, Sibelius fired off panic-stricken telegrams. And not only to Boston: he had made rash promises all over the place. Now he prevaricated and contradicted himself. As year followed year Aino must have been frantic. Soon he refused to countenance enquiries from anybody. It was now that his legend was born, the touchy genius, the stony-faced god of the photographic portraits. Then *auto-da-fé*.

And once incinerated, could a musical score turn up in Norfolk?

25

Jussi had the London directory in one hand and the phone in the other. 'Dial!'

'I said no!'

She wanted to *see* the Clarks, not have a chat that ended with a cold click. Nina had already found them in the phone book, months ago. They lived just across the river.

'Jussi, couldn't we go up to Blackpool? It's the week after next and I bet—'

'Nina, *please* don't make me watch ballroom tango with their heads flicking about like puppets on a string and some orchestra doing grievous bodily harm to "La Cumparsita". Anyway, in your *dreams* we'd get tickets at this notice.'

There was another hope. Tonight the Queen Elizabeth Hall had a show of tango argentino. Perhaps the Clarks would be there.

Nonnala! she thought suddenly. It had been her father's name for the Clarks' house, using the formula by which Tapio's domain was Tapio-la and Aino Sibelius's was Aino-la. The vicarage garden was, of course, Ninala.

The word Nonna always conjured first a shape (cubic), then hair suspiciously shoe-polish black. Trying now, Nina saw those hard button eyes, rubbery jowls flapping over a neck as creased as the bellows of a bandoneon – and a mouth that twitched higher on one side than the other when she giggled. Which she did.

Nonna legislated an impenetrable penal code, and it sometimes seemed to the girls that everything that was compulsory at the Hannays was banned at Nonna's and vice versa. But unlike the Hannays, Nonna smacked. Yet we weren't scared of her, she thought now with a forgiving nostalgia. Nonna sanctioned merchandise that was vetoed with horror by Christine: Dr Kildare bedlinen, for example. *Whoa*, that was a row! She gorged the girls on good cooking – in olive oil, which in Essex you could only buy from the chemist for clearing ear wax. '*Mangiate!*' she'd command them. 'Eat. Is good!'

She stockpiled gossip magazines, and Lu with Nina at her side would be directed to translate all the idioms in accounts of the despicable conduct of shameless men. The house itself colluded with her management of it, preserving in even the remotest rooms the memory of her sauces and the scent of her lavender water. For the rest of Nina's life, a waft of lavender would transport her back there.

Although the Clarks weren't at the tango show as far as Nina could see, she enjoyed herself. The flying legs, the frying sexuality, the show-stopping *sentada amor*. 'Tango fantasia,' tutted Jussi.

She also enjoyed standing outside when the show ended, leafleting the outpouring crowd with adverts for Jussi's classes. It was a soft cobalt-blue night seasoned with tangy salt from the Thames. When the audience had dispersed into the darkling evening, Jussi returned to the Clarks.

'You said they were once booed at Blackpool?'

'Till the chandeliers shook.'

Giancarlo had retold the story in *A Life of Dance*. They had just qualified for their first major competition, in Berlin. Then disaster. The British ruling body had a row with the West Germans and forced a boycott.

'So the Clarks defied the ban,' explained Nina, 'and danced in Berlin as Italians.'

'Legally?'

'Just about. And took the championship. Then a couple of weeks later came Blackpool.' Nina laughed. 'Even today the idea of a crowd booing my uncle Gian makes me want to kick those chandeliers! You see, the Clarks had turned their backs on Britain to dance in *Germany* as *Italians*. They had tapped into the fathomless capacity of the British for dragging up World War Two. Luckily, it seems our judges wanted a change from the cool English style of the last generation. The Clarks were new and different. The Clarks were *sexy*.'

'So what the hell put the kibosh on their career?'

Behind Jussi, the foyer of the Festival Hall was bedecked with posters for tonight's concert: Simon Rattle conducting the Sibelius seventh symphony. The peacock-coloured background and the conductor's woolly-headed silhouette shimmered in multiple replications, then swam as reflections in the plate glass. The colours sang to Nina, though not in tune with the Seventh but more like the finale of his . . . She slammed her thoughts to a halt. *Of his Eighth?*

Simon Rattle's name in all those reiterations shamed her. Of the two of them, he had the better right to decide the fate of that manuscript. She turned away to the river, the shivering water dyed apricot by light pouring from the Festival Hall.

'Jussi, did Erik ever tell you about his scientific proof of the existence of God?'

'The—? Oh yeah, I think so. Remind me.'

'It's about some inexplicable chemistry that allows life on earth.'

A train rattled across Hungerford Bridge, detonating in her head. Nina's synaesthesia didn't run to conventional irritant colours, flame and orange: she saw pain and rushes of noise as metallic, glintingly cold. Nina waited for the explosions to quieten to patchy pastels, like the after-image from staring at some other planet's azure sun.

'You know we're about ninety per cent water? Well, it shouldn't be a liquid at all but a gas. H_2O is the sister of H_2S – and that's the gas in stink bombs. We ought to be nothing but a puff of air.'

'Yeah? Weird.'

'It gets weirder. To change the temperature of water takes a ridiculous amount of energy – as you find out if you leave the immersion heater on and wait for the bill. If it were any other liquid, cold leaking out of the Antarctic would freeze the Pacific and most of our world would be a frozen waste. And when water does freeze, that's peculiar too. It expands. Hence burst pipes. But everything else *contracts* when it freezes, which makes it more dense so it sinks. Ice expands and therefore floats, insulating the sea below and allowing life to continue under the ice, even in Finland. And as life originated in the sea – though not *necessarily* in Finland – it was able to evolve on our waterlogged little planet. So the inventor of water cheated, and here we are as a result. Proof of an intelligent Creator.'

'You believe that?'

'No, I think it's all accident and something called hydrogen bonding, but Dad believed it utterly. I'm sure he never doubted the existence of God through all his years in the ministry.'

Some molecule moved in the seas of Nina's imagination and she heard the words of the General Confession: *We have done those things which we ought not to have done, and there is no health in us.* Though the ill health was a metaphor, she suddenly found its connection with her father and sin disturbing.

'Nina,' said Jussi, 'you ever think of settling down?'

'Growing up, you mean? Hope not.'

'No, what I meant ... if you fancy having a crack at matrimonials, I wouldn't be averse.'

'Mmmh? Sorry?' The concert had finished. Around Nina poured the exiting crowd, their chatter rippling and lapping. Then the word 'matrimonials' hit her. She swung round.

Jussi's fine-boned features were dark with intensity and a hesitant hand brushed hers. Usually his arm was confidently round her shoulders.

'I've nearly got the money for my own studio,' he said, 'and when the tango revival hits London I'll be at the forefront. You love it too, tango. Wouldn't be the worst of partnerships, would it?'

The crowd drifted, dissipating across the South Bank, swimming in the periphery of Nina's startled senses. A partnership. A Life of Dance. Do I love Jussi? He can be very lovable. I'm a lighter, nicer person in this relationship. And love grows in a good marriage, everyone says so.

Beside Nina a man's voice said '. . . the Piccadilly line and we can walk from Green Park station . . .' His tones were beautifully modulated. American. And everything else fell away.

Jussi could see her face. 'OK, it's too soon,' he said quickly. 'Let's wait a bit, yeah?'

✳

When they got home, Nina had a phone call. For some inscrutable reason tonight was suicide night in Ealing: there was a man on the Town Hall roof shouting, 'Stand back or I'll land on you!' and another one lying across the tracks waiting for the midnight express out of Paddington. The Sams rang to ask Nina to man the phones while they did their stuff. She and Jussi hadn't been in bed long. Not long enough.

As Nina left, he called brightly into the hall, 'Can't promise to keep it hot. Might have to go into dry dock,' at the exact moment Sean and Victoria were coming through the front door.

As it happened, both situations were quickly defused and by 3 a.m. Nina was home. She knew something was wrong the moment she turned her key in the lock.

Light spilled from the kitchen. She heard a sweet,

unmistakable electrical whine. Adrenaline kicked through Nina, clenched her gut, lightened her head. She was along the hall and into the kitchen. On the pine table was her father's manuscript. Jussi was lining up the pages and photographing them under the searing blue-white light of his flashgun. Followed by the whir of the motordrive.

'*What are you doing?*'

She lunged at Jussi, who was wrong-footed and astonished.

'Hey, calm down and listen.'

A cartridge of used Kodak film bounced from his pocket. There was a brief comedy routine in which the pair of them leaped around while it shot from their grasp like wet soap. Nina lunged again and walloped her shoulder.

'For God's sake, Nina, I'll give you the bloody film!'

She tore the cassette from the camera. The film split, a billowing tangle of lethal-edged ribbons that sliced the pads of her fingers. On and on went the row, with Nina stymied and now boiling with agony. '*How could you?*'

'Because somebody bloody has to! You got the only copy on earth stuffed in a suitcase growing mould, and anybody could steal it or . . . I know you, you'd be bloody *devastated. And* it might be worth an absolute—'

'It's not worth a cent to me, you idiot,' she yelled. 'The copyright belongs to Sibelius's heirs!'

Jussi stared at her. 'My God. You *know* this is the eighth symphony.'

The flat was suddenly full of spinning light – whoop-whoop lights strobing blue through the bay windows, bouncing out of the open door and blatting along the hall. Someone hammered at the front door. The police. Nina's neighbours had phoned the police station at the end of the road and demanded they get round there and sort out the noise. The Terence Trent D'Arby neighbours.

PART II
Rainlight

26

Childhood

In a winsome curtsey, her father's verger tweaked the satin skirts of his frock and the petticoats rustled, suggestive as the whisper of sheets. The headmaster reached for the man's hand.

'To meet you today for the first time,' he said, 'well, it is like a lonely traveller coming across some bright little . . . floweret,' he decided, taking inspiration from his buttonhole carnation.

'Do you mean me?' squeaked the verger.

'I do! Oh, Donna Lucia, do you know what a man longs for when he's lonely, desolate and wretched?'

'A drink?'

'What a woman!' responded Mr Caldwell, admiringly.

The audience loved it. Even Nonna, whose habitual facial expression would cause the blood of any comic actor to run cold, was laughing and clapping her liver-spotted hands. Her own manner of dress was sufficiently close to the play's setting of 1892 to cause consternation backstage. 'Bloody hell, we've got Vinegar Lil in front!' one of the actors had whispered. 'She'll think we're taking the piss!'

Lu and Nina had been allowed to sit in on the dress rehearsal. Now they squirmed with laughter in advance of every joke and addressed Nina's parents in knowledgeable asides.

'They haven't got the name wrong,' babbled Lu to Christine Hannay. 'It really is "Loosia", not "Lu-chia" like me. I asked.'

'It's because Charley's aunt is from Brazil,' put in Nina. 'Where the nuts come from.'

'So we gathered,' responded her mother wearily. 'Now be quiet, the pair of you.'

'*Basta*,' hissed Nonna, reverting to type. '*Silenzio*, Lucia!'

The girls were ten years old, or nearly ten-and-three-quarters if you asked them. It was October 1966, and this was their own headmaster trying to woo Charley's friend, who had been coerced, for complex reasons, into masquerading as Charley's aunt.

Before the lights had gone down in the village hall, Mrs Hannay had attracted sympathetic attention that she was ill-equipped to cope with. The skin was stretched taut across her handsome features and there were muddy rings beneath her slanted green eyes. Her husband, too, looked drawn but misery was more readily camouflaged by a vicar's gravitas than by his wife's habitual brand of bright, impersonal efficiency. This evening's entertainment was a fund-raising event. Throughout the short scene from *Charley's Aunt*, the Reverend Hannay twitched a dutiful smile whenever the villagers' laughter penetrated the deafness and blindness of his own preoccupations.

It was now widely believed across his two parishes that there was a question mark over their vicar's health. Letters and cards of good wishes had been dropping on to the door-mat all week, which Nina's mother acknowledged as best she could. For more than three years they had battled with this in secret. Now the secrets were dribbling out. Christine knew the bishop was no fool, and the day could not be far off when he would ask her directly whether the recurring theme of cancer signified a different sort of problem. And what was she supposed to say then?

Worse, people within their immediate circle were becoming aware of the marital disharmony, the rows stirred up by Martin Hannay's inner chaos like toxic waste leaking from a damaged hulk. It seemed miraculous to Christine that the trouble had escaped detection for so long, considering how the church's extended family flowed through the vicarage at any hour of the day.

The problem was that her own resistance was breaking down. At first she had offered reassurance and support. When this was rejected outright, when her husband wouldn't listen to a word she said, when the family life she provided failed to make any dent in his deepening depression, she began to respond to his unreasonableness with exasperated snapping. This rapidly progressed to shouting matches. Although even these could be shut up like a trap whenever anyone came into the house, recently the shouting had started to give way to distraught weeping, which couldn't. Earlier today the choir mistress, a buxom woman in a twinset, had let herself into the house, her arms full of organ music. At the sounds of distress coming from the bathroom, she had bounded up the stairs to find Christine slumped against the bath wearing nothing but her girdle, still not dressed at midday, uncontrollably crying while the Hannays' yellow Labrador barked hysterically and a desperate Nina pawed at her mother and shrieked through terrified tears.

The instant Nina's father heard this new voice fluting from the bathroom, he flew out of the bedroom where he had been alternately storming and sulking, and tried to take control.

'Flora, please give us five minutes.'

'It might be better if I helped Christine.'

'No, no, we mustn't trouble you.'

'Martin, *I'll* get Christine dressed,' insisted Flora with gentle authority. 'Nina, you take the doggie. Martin, find

Nina something nice to eat. Chocolates if you have any. And a glass of milk.'

Her good-natured determination succeeded in bustling the vicar out of the room, and he retreated with heavy reluctance down the Victorian staircase and into the cold enormity of the kitchen. There was never any question of finding treats for his daughter. He paced, biting his nails and straining to hear what was being said upstairs, while Nina sobbed by the boiler, tense, white and agonized, compulsively stroking the dog. Tapio was shivering, his buttocks shrunken and abased, his muscular tail in a servile curl between his legs.

Nina blurted out, 'Mummy won't tell her you're not really ill, Daddy.'

'Quiet!' commanded her father.

Earlier, he had fussed round his collapsed wife, desperate to calm her crying, well aware that the female voice carried a great deal further down Church Lane than did his own ranting tenor. But his every word provoked his wife to further outbursts, so he left her huddled on the floor, the suspenders of her roll-on girdle dangling obscenely in the dark cloud of her pubic hair. Perhaps their daughter's crying would drown his wife's and the whole terrible mess be interpreted as the tantrum of a child.

Would he have felt less paranoid about their crises being overheard and his failings broadcasted to the world, had he not been the vicar? No. Martin Hannay wasn't the only father in Seaton Bois to put up a public front while directing all his inner turmoil at his family. And did he recognize that his cancer scares were absurd? Inevitably. It was inescapable. At least, he always recognized that his *previous* scares had been irrational. But equally he always knew the latest wasn't, that this time it was real and would kill him. To that agony was added the excruciating pain of having nobody take it seriously, and the humiliation of realizing this was his own fault for crying wolf so often.

Neither of them could have said what had started today's

row; it was simply that Martin's mental illness was driving his wife into a lunatic asylum. Every now and then he would see a psychiatrist, referred by their family doctor and dragged there by Christine. The latest had listened while his patient held forth on aggressive skin cancers, and had then written a prescription for tranquillizers that Martin Hannay would refuse to take. Martin's knowledgeable discourse was so alarming that by the time he left the consulting room the psychiatrist had his own trouser leg rolled up and was examining a mole on his knee.

Their family doctor was a shrewd Irishwoman named Mary Dolan. She had spent years in India among children who were dying of dysentery. She had trouble sympathizing with nonsense.

'Mr Hannay, let me admit you to psychiatric care. I do understand that in your position a local hospital would be embarrassing, but St Clement's is in East London.'

She was wasting her breath. The night before the village hall event, she wasted some more.

'Anaplastic astrocytoma,' repeated Dr Dolan, her bifocals slipping down her bony nose. 'A brain tumour. What is the basis for your diagnosis, Mr Hannay?'

The basis was a headache. His wife was in no doubt as to its aetiology. 'What do you expect?' she had demanded at breaking point. 'You knock back sleeping pills as if they were sweets. Of course you wake up with headaches. It's a wonder you wake up at all!'

In Dr Dolan's surgery, Nina's father quoted extensively from the chapters in his medical textbooks that dealt with brain tumours. Christine had thrown one lot into the dustbin but he had gone straight up to London and replaced them from money they could ill afford, so she never did it again. When he finished the recital, Dr Dolan swivelled her chair to face him square on.

'Mr Hannay,' she said patiently, 'you're an intelligent man. You readily admit you're a hypochondriac.'

'I do indeed.'

'Therefore you know this is fantasy.'

'And you, Dr Dolan, know that the incidence of brain tumours is the same among hypochondriacs as in the population at large.'

Dr Dolan shut her eyes.

'I am a hypochondriac who has anaplastic astrocytoma.'

'For heaven's sake, man, all you've got is a headache! Patients with brain tumours suffer far more severe—'

'What percentage of them survives, Dr Dolan? You must concede that if only they went to their doctor earlier, the prognosis might not be so grave.'

'There is nothing whatever the matter with you. Take an aspirin!'

'I've taken so many aspirins my ears are ringing like a muffled peal at a state funeral. I need a specialist. Tell yourself it is for reassurance. And when he confirms—'

'But you would *not* be reassured. You'd be back within the month with self-diagnosed leukaemia.'

At this, his eyes turned wild with fear. 'Why leukaemia?' he snapped. 'What did you pick up from my last blood tests?'

In this morning's row his wife had shouted at him, 'How that woman resists the impulse to stuff a medical textbook up your bottom is a mystery only the saints could explain!'

Flora Latimer helped Christine into her clothes with the minimum of fuss and not a trace of curiosity.

'I'm so sorry,' Christine kept saying in hiccups.

'Not at all, dear. Happens to us all.' Though as Flora wasn't married, thought Christine, she could have only limited experience of the intolerable behaviour of supposedly decent men.

'Now, which dress shall we put on?' Flora brightly addressed the poverty of the Hannays' wardrobe. 'Let's refuse to be bullied by the rain. How about this lovely orange?'

At which Christine broke down again. Erik Pellinen

always commented on that dress. He should have been here this weekend, but blizzards closed the airport. And though Christine resented being made an accessory to his adulterous liaison, there was no doubt that in the presence of his placid friendship Martin always picked up, and the influence buoyed him along for a time afterwards. When Erik's telegram arrived, she had felt as if a vital support had been withdrawn and she was now bereft.

The Seaton Bois Amateur Dramatic Society took their bows, the verger acknowledging the wolf-whistles with a flounce of his skirts. When the applause decayed, Mr Caldwell swapped to his other role, that of tonight's Master of Ceremonies.

'Ladies and gentlemen,' he began with delectation. 'We come now to the highlight of the evening. This is a couple needing no introduction – but I'm not going to let that deprive me of the chance to give one.'

Light applause and laughter. Nina and Lu sat bolt upright and nodded with proprietorial approval.

'I'm sure I speak for us all when I say my heart swells at their recent inclusion in Her Majesty's Birthday Honours list.'

'My son!' said Nonna audibly.

'Following their retirement from competition two years ago – undefeated, as we all know – their cabaret shows have sold out quicker than a Beatles concert. But tonight we are privileged to watch them dance for the price of a ten-shilling ticket for a good cause. It is my immense pleasure, nay, my delight, to introduce the incomparable, the bedazzling, eight times World Ballroom Champions – Giancarlo and Beryl Clark, MBE!'

At the dress rehearsal there had been problems with the technical cue for the music. Meaning the tape recorder jammed. Tonight a slow, drifty version of 'The Anniversary Waltz' started up obediently and the dancers appeared, Gian lean and dark at forty-nine, Beryl young, pretty and ruthlessly groomed. She wore the violet dress beloved of Nina; under the rigged lights her diamanté glimmered like Christmas. Giancarlo in white tie and tails took her hand, encircled her waist, lifted her above his shoulders – as though (the audience would tell one another later) she weighed no more than a songbird. In this balletic attitude they spun slowly to whooping applause.

'Up on the roof,' whispered Nina and Lu to each other.

Nina turned to her mother. 'In cabaret there's roof, floor and basement – floor is normal dancing and basement is when you're crouched down.'

'Shush, Nina.'

'Yes, but on the roof you have to be perfect because people notice every mistake.'

Giancarlo gently replaced his wife on her feet and they took up the standard hold for the waltz. Now it was Lucia's turn. 'They couldn't do a Viennese one, Mrs Hannay, cos dust makes the floor too fast for fleckerls.'

'*Fleckerls?*' queried the postman on Lu's left.

'Lu, you really must be quiet.'

On silent feet, Giancarlo and Beryl circled and dipped across the tiny stage. Later, everyone would say the Clarks were the only couple in the world who could dance a perfect waltz on a postage stamp.

'Nice rise and fall, Nina.'

'It comes from starting the rotation from the feet, Lu.'

'That's right, Nina. Too many couples think you rise by lifting the ankles and lower with the hips.'

'If the pair of you don't shut up, I'm taking you out.'

'Christine!' This was Nina's father. 'It's *your* voice everyone can hear. Be quiet!'

The girls were silenced. Nina felt an ache start in her throat. Onstage, the dancers broke the rhythm with syncopated pivots.

Lucia said, 'Left whisk coming up, Nina, and untwist into a standing spin. This audience will go mental.'

But Nina was aware only of her parents behind her, their

antagonism. Pains clawed at her gut. Round and round went the dancers. The audience roared.

'Big top coming up, Nina.'

'I know,' said Nina, rallying. 'Then the contracheck.'

Lucia's knowledgeable babble froze. She pursed her lips. 'Contracheck is tango.' Her voice was tightened by a fine disgust. 'It's a throwaway oversway!'

'That's what I said. I *did*, Lucia, I said throwaway oversway!'

'You got it wrong,' said Lu, flatly.

With the controlled slowness of world-class dancers, Giancarlo and Beryl swung quietly into the picture line that is more frequently photographed than all others: each dancer with a leg extended behind, their bodies swayed back, their arms outlining a perfect oval. The audience sighed extravagantly and then held its collective breath as the Clarks maintained the line. Nina adored an oversway but she saw nothing of this one. Humiliated misery at her stupid mistake raged through her veins out of all proportion. Everything was out of proportion nowadays. It was as if she had been skinned. Beryl's violet blue dissolved in coloured water and tears dribbled, tickling, along Nina's nose. She sat silent and unseeing as the couple gently righted themselves and began their Argentinian tango.

'Oh, I say!' muttered an elderly gentleman as Beryl wrapped a long leg round Giancarlo's waist and leaned against him in a swoon. Nina saw nothing and heard nothing. Her parents stared rigidly ahead, above her shaking shoulders.

The dancers segued into the ballroom version. As they drew out of their final figure – which this time was a contracheck – their daughter said loudly, 'Good one, wasn't it, Nina? Too many couples have the man looming over the lady as if he's Count Dracula going for her throat.'

27

All Saints, Seaton Bois, was an approachable country church whose rose-coloured brick and shingles set amid hawthorns and yews produced an abstract artwork in red and green. Seen from the approach in Church Lane, the colours always reminded Nina of that villa in her father's books. Less trouble had been taken with the vicarage, which stood solid on the other side of a prettily poisonous yew hedge, and was set back behind deep, tree-shaded gardens that wrapped round the house and dappled the mean light of the drawing room. The house had hatchet-faced bay windows, ceilings that were echo-high, and sparse furnishings. In the kitchen, under a spidery calligraphy of cracked plaster, a row of servants' bells hung like crotchets on a musical stave, silent for three decades, like the vicar's hero.

Seaton Bois had old views about new money. Giancarlo and Beryl just about got away with it – their manners were regal, and the Queen herself had awarded them the MBE. But Nonna didn't, Nonna with her seamed face and broken English, shapelessly dressed in rusty black, rocking down the road on legs that couldn't stop a pig in an alley.

On this Sunday afternoon, the Clarks were on their way to Weald Park. The weather had begrudgingly provided a weekend respite. Rain had washed summer into premature autumn and then battered the tinted leaves off the trees. Twenty miles away in London's theatreland, on most nights Leicester Square was a sea of black umbrellas waiting for the Clarks at the stage door. The poor summer and wet autumn of 1966 gave a further melancholic cast to the besieged misery beneath the busy, smiling surface of the Hannays' vicarage.

Giancarlo and Beryl had taken today off from the studio. 'It's *The Black and White Minstrel Show!*' cried Gian, swinging a squealing Nina into the air. The allusion was to the cars, one black and one Old English white, and both required for this expedition because they were E-type Jaguars, two-seaters, and no matter how the girls pleaded, Beryl refused to let them travel in the boot. The arrangements also meant Nonna stayed home as she certainly wouldn't fit in the boot. She had packed them a picnic tea: cheese, home-baked bread and the pimento olives from a jar that she'd learned to put up with in England. 'And when you home again, ravioli and *Sunday Night at the London Palladium.*' She loved the spangled chorus girls high-kicking in leggy unison.

'So what have you been up to, Freddy?' asked Gian as the car turned into Ongar Road. A playground nickname: the singing duo, Nina and Frederick.

'I've got my Grade 6 violin and piano soon.'

'Pretty impressive for ten.'

'And I've been teaching Lu to purfle.'

'We know.'

'But Lu can't get on unless she has a violin of her own.'

'Nonna says no.'

'But now you're home—'

'We're not, sweetheart. We're in the studio or on the cabaret floor or heading for another airport.'

'Yes, but once Lu gets some proper practice it will stop sounding like Nonna says.'

'Like . . . ?'

159

'Like a yard of pigs being castrated with house bricks.'

Giancarlo snorted and the car swerved. 'Nonna also says no violins, Freddy. By the way, we've mended the lovely straw donkey you bought us, and put it out of reach of pussy-cat claws.'

This was a souvenir of Weston-super-Mare, famous for its donkey rides. The Hannays hadn't gone to Frinton this August: Martin couldn't face the Eldridges, still alive after two consecutive years predicting his demise. Christine was surprised how readily Nina acceded.

'How's your friend Tapio, the god of the forest?'

'Tapio's ever so well, thank you. The vet took the lump away and he might be all right for years. Years and years,' repeated Nina absently. 'I don't think he'll ever like the vet, though. When he saw where he was, Tapio sat right down on the path, boff!'

Gian remembered one of Martin's stories from when the dog was a puppy. The bishop had graciously dropped in en route to the cathedral to welcome the new lay preacher. While he sat and talked, Tapio sat and chewed. When the bishop got to his feet there was a window hole at the back of his robe, right through his trouser leg, displaying his sock suspenders. But since the Clarks' latest return from abroad, Gian had noticed there were no more anecdotes from Martin; the reflex by which the man could fashion a decent joke out of the air had vanished. And his daughter's speech had developed a worrying childishness. As he remembered, Nina at seven had sounded like a college student.

'Daddy still got his headache?'

'Yes, but it's getting better,' invented Nina. 'I expect it will have gone by Wednesday.' She wound the car window down. Then she wound it back up again. She opened and closed the glove compartment.

'Good,' said Giancarlo. 'Is Tapio the reason you've been bandaging our cat?'

'No. Anyway I've stopped. Tyger doesn't want me to.'

Which he knew to be true; Tyger had not taken to life as

a three-legged cat with one paw in a sling. Gian had never heard a noise like it.

'You're not worrying about Tapio?'

'No,' repeated Nina, surprised. Truly, she wasn't worrying about Tapio. Nina had started by assuming the lump was harmless, and then when it turned out to be malignant she accepted the vet's assurance that her dog might still live for years. Just as she accepted her mother's assurances that Daddy had nothing wrong with him, nothing whatsoever, despite his opinion to the contrary. Besides, Tapio must be all right or her mother would be upset. That time he went missing for two days she was in such a state she cancelled a Charity Morning. No, the bandaging was to do with *Dr Kildare*.

There had never been any doubt in Nina's mind that Jim Kildare could cure human cancer, or if he couldn't, his middle-aged mentor could: Dr Gillespie with the deep facial grooves and the waistcoat. And so, somewhere in the swollen sea of Nina's terrified powerlessness was one small island of solid practicality: she could play at hospitals in preparation for the day she would be allowed to assist some handsome doctor who happened to be the spitting image of Richard Chamberlain. He would find a cure so marvellous that nobody need ever fear cancer's thuggery again. Nina began with bandages. Everyone has to start somewhere.

Every year since she was five, a new *Kildare* series had begun in the spring and finished in the autumn. To the dismay of both Nina and Lu, the latest had just ended: last Friday evening the sacred slot was given over to a Sherlock Holmes mystery. The long, cold winter had begun. Never a self-analytical child, Nina did not wonder why the break was so much worse this year than before; she was not aware that her love for Richard Chamberlain was directly proportional to the collapse of her father's mental health. She only knew that the thought of waiting until March for the next series was simply not tolerable. Perhaps if I pray really hard

God will bring it back next week, she thought. If I'm a good girl at school and don't keep getting into trouble with Mr Caldwell . . .

Nina's fidgeting had dislodged her seatbelt. Giancarlo reached across and clicked it back in place. He said, 'Lulu tells me the kids at school have been nicknaming her "macaroni".'

'No, only half macaroni. Like they say I'm half Eskimo.'

'Half *Eskimo*? Do you mind?'

Nina shrugged. She was a vicar's daughter; you grow up suffering worse epithets than that. In Gian's day, these things had been settled by brawls in the yard. Of course, in his own case, apparently being named Jan hadn't helped. He had tried to establish from Lucia just how badly Nina was affected by Martin's illness, but his daughter had shut down like a portcullis. Does Nina actually talk about it even to Lu? he wondered, and decided probably not, that the shame of having a mad dad would keep a child silent more effectively than any legislation on the subject from home. He suspected it was only on TV that trembly-lipped children confided, 'I'm sad because Mommy and Daddy are always fighting.'

Ahead on their right, a mass of greenery now resolved into Weald Park. Giancarlo slowed the car. Behind, Beryl did the same. Together, heel to toe, the long, low E-types swung into the entrance, swept across the asphalt in a broad arc and then, with a carefully controlled reverse turn, circled into adjacent spaces and came to a halt precisely together. Choreography.

'OK, girls, let's head for the hills!'

Beryl's blonde hair was loose today and she wore a mini-dress with a geometric design and smart leather boots. Lucia was in a hipster mini-skirt and ribbed jumper while Nina wore a corduroy skirt and jerkin made by her mother. The point of today's jaunt was to fly a kite. This was an exquisite souvenir of the Clarks' latest trip to Japan: a huge man-shaped creation, hand-painted on Washi paper and held by bamboo spars. The figure represented a sword-toting warrior in disconcerting pink. As they trotted towards high ground, Lucia and Nina carrying the kite between them, the warrior's legs flapped as loose and bone-less as a clown in a comic tightrope routine.

Beryl said to Nina, 'Lu was telling me you're going to do some practice for tomorrow's school test.'

'It's a pretend eleven-plus exam, Auntie Beryl. Mr Caldwell's going to give us lots between now and the real one.'

'He's only giving us two,' corrected Lucia.

'Three.'

'No, the third one's the real one.'

'No—'

'The precise number doesn't matter,' broke in Giancarlo.

'I think practice is a great idea,' added Beryl. 'You haven't always been doing what you should for Mr Caldwell, have you, lovey? I heard.'

'He tells me off for not doing news.'

'What's news?' asked Giancarlo.

Lucia answered him. 'Just writing about something we've done at home. Not this weekend because of the test tomorrow, but on normal days we're meant to hand it in, Monday.'

'Nina, lovey,' said Beryl, 'surely knuckling down would be less hassle than getting into his bad books?'

But as with her feelings about *Dr Kildare*, Nina could not have explained. At home the trouble would start Sunday afternoon. One parent or other would throw at her, 'Have you done your news?' Nina always said yes. She had to. If she said no, a lot of noisy telling-off would ensue – which inevitably, albeit mysteriously, developed into her parents' having a row of their own, even though this was the one topic on which they were in perfect agreement. The rows clawed at Nina like some sea creature clamping her gut. She even had a name for this: worry pains. But by saying she'd done it, she dug herself into a hole. She couldn't start now without the risk of being caught out as a liar and told off. Which would inevitably, albeit mysteriously, develop into . . .

'Could it be,' pursued Beryl, 'that you don't want to write about home because you're not supposed to tell anyone about Daddy's little problems?'

Lu jumped in. 'Hey, Mum, Nina gets enough of this from Mr Caldwell without you having a pop at her. Loads of people don't hand in news. Clive Mitcham never—'

'Yes, but Clive Mitcham can't even write his name,' said Nina.

'He can.'

'No, he can't.'

'Enough!' said Giancarlo. 'Anyway, it's time to get this show on the road.'

The sky was busy in the wind. Boys and their fathers raced down the slope with vividly coloured canvases. The successful ones sailed overhead like giant butterflies. Fifty feet above them, a purple box-kite was twitching round a crimson diamond, trying to bring it down. Giancarlo took hold of their own.

'Can you both hold the strings without an argument?'

'What argument?' The girls stared at him.

'Good,' he said after a fractional pause. 'Lulu, give me your right hand. Now yours, Nina. When I tell you, run down the hill. If the kite catches the wind, unravel the strings little by little. If it doesn't catch, then come back and try again. Have you got that?'

'Yes, Dad. And we can see what everyone else is doing.'

'Hold tight in case it gusts.'

'Yeah, yeah, Dad, we heard you. Now you've got to let go or we can't run anywhere, can we?'

So Giancarlo reluctantly let go and the girls took off down the hill. As they veered into the wind their Samurai whipped upwards, flapping his legs. The girls stopped running. The wind tugged the string. They screamed and clutched. The warrior braced his back, flipped, and flew. He was up. Way above their heads his dolorous figure gazed dejectedly down at them. Giancarlo grabbed the strings and reeled him back in, like a fisherman.

'Gian,' protested Beryl, 'they did everything right. The kite was up. If the children lose it, they lose it.'

'Yes, dear, and I'll trot back to the Shizuoka prefecture and pick up another one.'

'If the girls don't wreck it, the cat will. We went through exactly the same thing with that Hawaiian grass skirt which you wouldn't let them wear and then you left it lying around for Tyger to knit into a raffia mat. Let the children have some fun.'

Nina and Lucia were looking accusingly up at him, blonde head and dark head and four enormous eyes fixed on his. It was an attitude they might have been taught by the Hannays' Labrador.

'All right but *hold on*,' he directed them, and unenthusiastically loosened the grasp of his long dark fingers on the strings.

'I've climbed hundreds of trees, Beryl, don't be silly.'

'Not for thirty years and not when a broken leg would end your career.'

'I'll go, Auntie Beryl.'

'No, Nina, it's taller than it looks.'

'Beryl, what the hell does that mean?'

'In trouble?' A small, tubby man in glasses and a jolly-looking woman tilted their faces towards the upper branches of the oak. With them was a gangly lad of perhaps twelve. The Japanese warrior, bobbing above the greenery, offered them all a ceremonious bow. The man ran an eye over Giancarlo. 'Would have thought you could nip up there without much trouble,' he said.

'Unfortunately,' responded Beryl, 'my husband is a dancer and the slightest injury would put him out of action for weeks.'

'Dancer?' repeated the man in the same tone in which he might have said gigolo. He looked at his son. 'Well, I don't think this rapscallion is much of a dancer, eh, Michael? So how about shinning up the tree, son?'

'Oh, please—' objected Beryl.

'Look to it, Mike. Like lightning, lad.'

The boy started up the tree. He made short work of the first ten feet, his lace-up shoes finding easy footholds on the trunk. When he was secure in the lower storeys his father turned back to Giancarlo.

'So what do you do – ballet? Tap? Fred and Ginger?'

'Ballroom and Latin American. Tango, slow foxtrot, cha-cha-cha. That sort of thing.'

The man's distaste deepened. 'Not full-time, surely? Is there a living in that?'

The children exploded.

'They're Giancarlo and Beryl Clark!'

'Famous stars— '

'On TV and— '

'OK, girls, that's enough.'

'Ah well,' said the man. 'We don't watch a lot of the old goggle box, do we, Mike?'

Mike was by now a respectable way up the oak tree. The wife smiled at Nina. 'Are you going to be a dancer when you grow up, like Mummy and Daddy?'

There was a pause in which the girls blinked at her.

'Oh, Nina isn't—' began Beryl but Nina broke in. With strained over-enunciation and declamatory volume she told Weald Park, 'No, but I'm going to play violin waltzes for Mummy and Daddy, and when Mummy and Daddy are in Argentina I'm joining a tango band, and while Mummy and Daddy—'

'OK, sweetheart,' said Giancarlo, running a hand through the child's hair. 'You've made your point. Is Michael all right up there, do you think?'

'Oh, Mike will be all right,' replied the man breezily. 'You're all right, aren't you, Mike? Yes, Mike will be all right.'

In response to some more cheerfully barked instructions, the boy untwined the kite strings from the branches of the oak and then lowered it down to his father without a tangle or a tear.

28

'It's me, Christine. I've brought Freddy back.'

'Thank you, Gian. Do you want to come in? I've just made a pot of tea.'

'Thanks. I will.'

'Tapio, down, lovey. Nina – before you rush off, have you done your news?'

'I understand there's a reprieve this weekend, Christine.'

'May I put a record on, Mummy?'

'It's nearly bedtime.'

'But only nearly. May I put a record on, Mummy?'

'In your father's study, then. Martin's out,' she explained to Giancarlo. 'One of the Young Mothers' group has had a bereavement.'

'I'm sorry to hear that.'

'It's common currency so I'm not betraying a confidence. I was there this afternoon.'

They drifted down the hall. Nina, with the still-bounding Tapio, made for the study. A light rain had started up again, pizzicato like violins in a symphony.

Early in Martin's decline, Christine had tried to lift his spirits with a stereo system bought with the money her father left her. The hi-fi was sequestered in the study, where shelving was clumsily erected to house yard after yard of gramophone records. As well as Sibelius, there were some surprises. The American humorist Tom Lehrer, for example, whose jolly songs of subversion, drug-peddling and murder Nina and Lu knew word perfect. The collection also included every Beatles LP. Christine accepted from Martin that the Fab Four had great musical merit. Unluckily for Nina his best efforts had failed to secure her anything by the Rolling Stones: the vicar's wife had taken one look at Mick Jagger and banned the lot of them from the house.

Nina knelt by the shelves. *Richard Chamberlain Sings*. Even her mother approved of his old-fashioned crooner style. Nina slid the record from the sleeve with its lovely photograph and placed it on the turntable. Track five, 'Three Stars Will Shine Tonight: Theme From *Dr Kildare*'.

The theme as it was used for the series was a big dramatic number. In taming it into a ballad for the actor to take to the top of the charts, the colours were transmogrified: whereas the original rolled out of the TV set in waves of wet blue, Richard Chamberlain's song was sweet and un-insistent, like photographic tints on old postcards.

The music was in waltz time. The girls had never yet persuaded Gian and Beryl to dance to it. They said the tempo was wrong, Lu's tears and other emotional blackmail notwithstanding. But her parents did use a couple of other tracks for practising. 'And I bet Mum pretends she's dancing with Richard Chamberlain,' said Lu, though Nina suspected privately that Giancarlo might be the only man on the planet you'd think twice about before you swapped him.

One two three, *one* two three . . . In the cold space of the despondent study, Nina waltzed in the arms of the handsome young doctor. When the song finished, he told her he had to return to the hospital.

'Dr Gillespie's waiting,' he said. Then, shyly, 'What I'd really like, my darling, is to have you by my side. Would you come with me?'

She smiled serenely and turned to Tapio. 'Stay there,' she ordered him, and shot upstairs. A minute later Nina was back, lugging behind her a canvas holdall misshapen with Kildare merchandise and accepted as the girls' shared property. Nina retrieved Dr Kildare's Thumpy Heartbeat Stethoscope and set about listening to Tapio's chest.

Thump-thump. Thump-thump.

'Oh dear,' Nina said portentously in her Dr Gillespie voice. 'This is the seventy-fifth case of smallpox since Tuesday, Jim.' Then she pulled from the bag a heap of hankies and toy-town bandages and set about swaddling the dog.

First she tied up his front feet. Then she wrapped her largest handkerchief round Tapio's head, tying a bow at the top like a pudding cloth. Nina considered her handiwork. He looked like a cartoon patient with toothache. Then she had another go with the stethoscope. 'The X-ray shows a lumbar puncture in his EKG, Jim.' Nina's voice trailed off in deep medical gloom and she started tying her patient's ears together.

At this, even the long-suffering Tapio rebelled. He was on his knees like a half-risen camel, hobbled by the hankies, and frenziedly shaking his head. Somehow this sort of thing never happened to Dr Gillespie. His patients stayed where he put them.

'All right, Tapio.' A moment later the liberated animal was out of there and down the hall.

The record was coming to an end. She thought of her bed. Love ached in Nina's bones, and in bed she could resume the storyline with a pillow to fondle and long suckling kisses. In bed she was also free of a nibbling and unwelcome feeling about Lu. Though Nina never acknowledged a sketchy jealousy, one of the boys at school had pointed out that pale little Nina was less likely than the dark, mischievous Lucia to win the love of an international heart-throb. But in bed, Nina was miraculously less pallid, in both face and outlook. She could never have called it happiness, this longing, with its raw vulnerability to tactless comments and the whim of BBC schedulers. Her feelings for Jim Kildare lay hot and irresistible across her sore senses.

She knew nothing really about sex. Her parents' teachings on the dutiful pursuance of baby-making had not sat comfortably with the hateful recollection of Frinton, so she had dismissed the whole lot, pushed it away, thrust the entire conundrum forward from her confused present into a grown-up future, to wait for her in that unimaginable world where you knew everything and controlled things. Nevertheless, Nina understood that her love was physical, that it nagged, like a full bladder, from within a strange synergistic alliance of her body parts: her pillow-enfolding arms, her wet-kissing mouth, and that supremely private place down there. She wouldn't imagine this handsome man naked, yet she knew that if she did, it would not prompt the familiar tormenting dreadfulness in her belly that gripped her whenever she couldn't stop herself remembering Mr Eldridge.

On the other hand, if she went to bed now she would miss Uncle Gian, for whom her love was unqualified happiness. She made her way to the drawing room. As she approached, she heard her own name.

'I expect Nina's kept you up to date with our dirty linen.'

'No, no, she's discretion itself, Nina. But I realize your life isn't plain sailing. And it's getting worse, isn't it, Christine?'

Tapio had been slurping water in the kitchen. Now he jammed his dripping muzzle into the backs of Nina's knees.

'. . . a terrible war,' Gian was saying. 'Is that where this all stems from, do you think?'

'We do, yes. So many of his fellow soldiers were killed in front of his eyes. That takes its toll on any man. You were in North Africa, weren't you?'

'Yes, but my brother was captured at the fall of Singapore. Paolo never talks about the camps. He says if you were there you know without being told, and if you weren't you could never understand.'

'Don't you mind going to Japan?'

'Many in our audience weren't even born during the war.'

'Nevertheless. Forgiveness is the most strenuous of the Christian virtues, I know. I'm not convinced Martin has ever forgiven the Russians. It was such a terrible business.'

'Yet Martin can joke about it. I remember him having us in stitches with a story about a Finnish raiding party on skis. Dead of night, sneaking up on the enemy fast asleep, totally secret, totally silent. Or would have been, except the commanders were both partially deaf and had to holler orders into each other's ears. I can't carry off the mimicry but Martin was wonderful.'

'Yes, he wasn't in that raid himself. Martin got the story from a poor lad who was dead a couple of weeks later. It was Martin who risked his life to rescue the body.'

'Heroic.'

'That wasn't his only act of heroism, Gian. He played a crucial part in the first major victory. Of course, he doesn't talk about that. The Finns are even more reserved than the English, you know.'

Nina, on the other side of the door, felt a wretched tingle of embarrassment. Her mother, with her slender legs curled under her on the sofa, made it sound as if modesty was what prevented Nina's father disclosing his war history. That wasn't the version Nina understood. He didn't dwell on his war because of the terrible thing done to him afterwards, which related to that same boy her mother was talking about in quite the wrong tone of voice.

Though that was a secret, the war itself wasn't; the names Tolvajärvi and Äglajärvi had been part of her lexis since infancy; in fact it was clear even to Nina that her father couldn't stop himself mentioning them – references to the war slipped from him like the secrets of an over-stimulated child. But he never talked the way her mother was doing now. It was as though she was showing off.

Christine's voice went on. 'The men were dropping from fatigue but they still had to slog on, fighting entire Soviet divisions that were armed to the teeth. Then Äglájärvi. It was too much for a sensitive boy like Martin. One day some backlash was inevitable.'

'How terrible.'

'I've no doubt your brother saw even worse, Gian.'

'Afterwards Paolo had to forgive himself for surviving. I suppose that's how Martin felt too – guilty for staying alive?'

'Perhaps.'

'So when the war was over he came here, married you . . .' Christine smiled.

'. . . took holy orders. So when he reaches his forties Martin is happily married with a quiet country parish and a healthy daughter – and suddenly he comes to wonder how he has been so lucky when his comrades perished in ice and snow. He decides his luck must be due to run out. He broods. He starts to wonder if it is already running out. From there it's a short hop, skip and a jump to the conclusion that it *has* run out. That he has cancer.'

Nina's mother ran a hand over her eyes. On the coffee table was a bowl of garden roses, blowsy and overblown in October, yet somehow undiminished. The peace rose.

'Does Martin believe this is some sort of divine retribution for surviving?'

'That would be blasphemy, Gian, so let us hope not.'

'I don't know how you both stay sane.'

'I'm not sure we do. You're a good friend but I really mustn't talk about Martin's cancer fears. I'm the vicar's wife.'

'Christine!'

'Clergy wives can't have confidential friends. You asked about the war. Martin readily admits his anxieties are rooted in it. How does your brother cope, if you don't mind my asking?'

'With unrelenting cheerfulness.'

'Oh.'

'Plus at least once a week he wakes up from nightmares, crying. He says he doesn't. His wife says he does.'

'Oh Gian, what a world we've brought our children into. But Martin is still a conscientious priest. I've no doubt that right now he's dispensing comfort to that poor mother. Martin always says he succeeds because his aims are modest – merely to calm a despairing soul to the point where they will get a little sleep. It's only with his own family that he allows himself the luxury of letting go.'

'How intolerable for you. Well, if we can give you any help looking after Nina, just say so.'

'I'm grateful. Thank Beryl, won't you? And now I'd better get the child to bed.'

At which Nina crept back to her father's study to repack the medical equipment. She heard the goodbyes at the front door, and then listened to Gian's tread through the clammy dark that cloyed at the windows.

29

In an assembly hall panelled and floored entirely in wood like some seagoing vessel, twenty-five children sat at small wooden desks and tackled the mock-exam paper in front of them.

In the scribbling silence, Nina winced against the noises in her head. Voices, male and female, shouted at her, jagged and steely and remorseless. The phenomenon was familiar – shouting filled Nina's head whenever the ambient condition was silence. It was like a song stuck on the brain.

There was a choice of titles for the composition. When they got back from Weald Park, Nina and Lu had devised a collection of adaptable plots with the aim that at least one of them should fit one of the options. Nina decided on 'A Stranger Arrives'. Picking through her plotlines, she rejected the smallpox story and the one about Moomintrolls and settled instead for a tale set in a dance studio. A city gent in a bowler hat turns up out of the blue and asks for lessons. Lu had worked on the technical bits and taught them to Nina.

The third step of the fishtail, Nina wrote now, *is the only step which is danced outside partner but not in CBMP.*

It looked impressive, written down.

The teacher thought Albert would never be able to dance it but Albert had a wonderful understanding of musicality, floor-craft and body flight. Then he did a waltz to the Dr Kildare *music and the teacher said—*

The teacher said, 'I'm going to stop you in two minutes.'

Nina had never yet got a composition finished; she was invariably developing the middle ground when time was called. At the next desk, Lucia chewed the end of her pen. Nina wrapped up her story by having Albert find a lady to share his new life with, though there wasn't time to have the happy pair win at Blackpool.

During geography that afternoon, the headmaster appeared in Mr Ellis's classroom and asked to borrow Nina Hannay. Well, for once she couldn't be in trouble over her news. Probably he wanted her father to give a talk or something. Nina followed Mr Caldwell up the twist of stairs to the top classroom. This was home to the Special Class. For their final two years, an élite group took certain lessons up here with the headmaster. If today had been a normal Monday, Nina and Lu would have spent the morning doing poetry, which was not taught to the common herd.

'Well, Nina.' Mr Caldwell took a seat behind his desk. Her composition lay open on it. '*The third step of the fishtail,*' he read, '*is the only step which is danced outside partner but not in CBMP.* What does it mean, Nina?'

Clearly she was in trouble, but why? Her mind raced.

'Which particular dance involves the fishtail?'

'I . . . I don't know. Uncle Gian and Auntie Beryl could tell you.'

'Indeed they could, but as a matter of fact, I already know the answer. The gentleman dances it in a quickstep. And what is CBMP?'

From a pile of papers, he retrieved a page of neatly feminine handwriting. Lucia's.

And the skies came crashing down. Nina knew what had happened. This outcome, that she and Lu would choose the same story and use the same rehearsed lines, had not occurred to either of them. In the slow-motion thinking that comes with catastrophe, Nina found a resentful moment to realize it hadn't occurred to Gian or Beryl either, while they were encouraging this very project.

If she explained herself, would it make things better or worse? Which would the headmaster consider the more culpable – copying Lu's exam paper, which was clearly what he believed, or planning it together in advance?

Mr Caldwell was saying, 'It stands for Contrary Body Movement Position. Now let me read from Lucia's essay: *The third step of the fishtail—*'

'I didn't copy it from Lu!'

'You were seated at adjacent desks.'

'I've heard them say it loads of times so I put it in my story.'

'So did Lucia. Hers was also about a man who went to a dancing class. Wearing a bowler hat.'

Nina burst into tears.

'I had hoped the new term would bring a turning over of new leaves.'

'We wrote our stories before, for practice!'

'Nonsense. You didn't know what today's titles would be.'

'It didn't make any difference.'

'When I allowed you back into Special Class for the second year, it was on the understanding that you bucked your ideas up. And here you are, cheating in an exam and lying. I'm removing you from Special Class.'

'*Please*, Mr Caldwell!'

'I'm replacing you with Teresa Pears. She deserves the chance. Now go back down to Mr Ellis and carry on with your geography.'

Lucia was scandalized.

'You tell your mum and dad to ask mine what happened,' she said.

They were walking home, Nina with dawdling reluctance.

'Nina, they *encouraged* us. He won't chuck you out when you were only—'

'But then Mummy and Daddy will go and see Mr Caldwell and he'll tell them I haven't been doing my news.'

Lu stared at her. 'You are going to tell them?' And when she didn't get a reply, 'Well, that's stupid for a start. They'll find out for themselves and go bandy. You tell your mum the minute you get in the door. That's what I do when it's Nonna.'

If it had been Nonna she would have had the hide off them, Lu or Nina, whoever was in striking distance when the crime was discovered. On the other hand, at least you could guarantee that Nonna would be available to listen to the charges. When Nina got back to the vicarage, her mother was with the Women's Institute. Nina recognized the familiar soundtrack of chatter and china even as she was opening the back door. She walked down the hall to her father's study.

'Yes? What is it?'

'It's only Nina.'

'I'm busy. Can it wait?'

'Yes, Daddy.'

A female voice reached her through the door, ragged from distress. He was good with people like that. He would be tied up for some time.

Tapio had obviously been shut out of the drawing room. He trailed behind her, wagging. Nina led him out to the garden and threw sticks, her senses focused on the house behind her, waiting for the conversational upsurge that signified the spilling of the women's meeting into the hall.

In the garden, the pyracanthus hedge blazed with berries reddened by all the rain. The busy-lizzies were turning to jelly in flower beds soggy with leaves. A low milky sun cast half-hearted shadows; Nina's and Tapio's flitted over the lawn, crossing and re-crossing. This end of the garden was glebe land and used by the local bowls club. It looked as if they had been here this afternoon tending the grass.

Keeping track of who was expected round the house had become second nature to the Hannays; her father in particular had self-preservation instincts honed as sharp as if by a whittling knife.

There was a whole hour before the Women's Institute left. Nina dropped the stick and started towards the house, Tapio pushing at her hand with his nose. She tried to say, 'No more, Tapio,' but her voice stopped working. Worry pains dragged at her tummy. As she opened the back door her mother came into the kitchen, her face tightly shuttered.

'I've a splitting head,' she said. 'If I'd known you were home, I would have asked you to start on the sprouts. Didn't you see them on the draining board?'

'I was playing with Tapio.'

'In the muddy garden? Oh Nina, look at him!'

'I'll clean his feet up, Mummy.'

'No, you'll only make matters worse.'

'Daddy's got somebody in his study.'

'Good for Daddy,' responded her mother curtly, and wrestled with the dog, who was never good at co-ordinating the lifting of one paw at a time.

Nina peeled the sprouts, notching little crosses into the stalks and dropping them into a pan, her courage draining away like water down the plughole. The potatoes were already boiling when her father joined them. He didn't look at his wife or she at him. Nina saw two chalky tablets in his hand. She blurted out, 'Mummy's got a headache, too!'

'I'm not surprised. Your mummy's been busy.'

'That's a stupid thing to say, Martin!'

'Why has Mummy been busy?' asked Nina against her will. Nobody answered.

'She was only doing tea for the WI,' Nina explained, in the faint hope of clearing up a misunderstanding.

'He's being sarcastic. Take no notice. Dinner will be ready in five minutes.'

'I'll have mine on a tray in my study.'

'You can have it in the garden shed for all I care.'

'What's Mummy done?'

'I cleared out the loft,' snapped her mother, slamming a lid on a pan. 'Last June, for pity's sake. Your father didn't realize until October. But when has he ever given a fig about the house or how hard I work to stop it falling down around our ears?'

'The loft wasn't falling down around our ears, Christine.'

'Your father wouldn't have known for another decade if he hadn't taken it into his head to go up there this morning to look for a couple of old books he probably left in Tampere in 1946!'

'Daddy, you *did* know. Because of jumble for the summer fête. You said—'

'It never entered my head that your mother would clear out every possession of my own.'

'Martin, you hadn't touched anything in that loft in fifteen years!'

'We've only lived here five, Christine.'

'Yes, and which of us dragged those carrier bags here when we moved from Southend, while you swanned off on parish business with the rural dean? Not again. This time we travel light.'

'Funny how it's only my belongings that have to be jettisoned.'

Nina's head swivelled from one to the other like the conning tower of a submarine. 'Travelling light where? We're not moving, are we?'

The idea was devastating: not even her home was safe.

'Your mother seems to think so.'

'Her mother understands her father is going to pot! That he'll have no job this time next year and we'll have no roof over our heads.'

'Has the bishop said something, Mummy? Are we—'

'I'll be dead this time next year, woman.'

'You insisted you'd be dead last year, Martin, and the year before that.'

'Rest assured I won't disappoint you this time. I think I had double vision this morning.'

'You will turn this child into a hypochondriac with your tumours and double vision! That's exactly how she'll grow up.' Christine distractedly stroked the dog. In pain, she always turned to Tapio. With Nina's attentions and Christine's petting, he was the only one in the house turning a profit.

'But what did Mummy throw out?'

'He doesn't even know. He's been shouting all day but hasn't been able to name a single thing worth sixpence. Now shut up, Martin, before I go mad.'

Plates rang, pans clanged. Steam whitened the window like a pressing ghost.

'Here's your dinner. Eat it where you like or hurl it on the compost heap, it's all the same to me. Nina, have you washed your hands?' Nina was rummaging through the BBC's TV guide. '*Nina!*'

'Sorry, Mummy. I'm looking for *Dr Kildare*.'

'You know it isn't on! Sit down at the table. My head is breaking.'

So was Nina's. She hadn't recognized until now that the nausea and the cold creep of her skin were offshoots of the pain thrumming behind her eyes. As she tried to swallow the meal in front of her, nausea rushed into her throat and she fled the table to throw up her dinner into the sink.

Her mother pushed her own plate away with a clatter. 'Not anything more today! I can't stand it!'

30

Sunday night after Evensong.

School had been terrible all week. Stuck at a desk with Clive Mitcham when she should have been upstairs with Lu reading *Oliver Twist*. Lu had tried to exonerate her friend by appealing to Mr Ellis but he only said, 'I'll have no excuses, Lucia. Nina has to learn that cheats never prosper.'

She knew she must tell her parents before Mr Caldwell got in first, but each night her courage failed. Her home life was deteriorating as inexorably as the shortening days. Martin slammed doors and shouted that he was going out, and stayed out. Christine snapped at both of them and kept Tapio with her. Nina's faint hope was for Sunday after Evensong, with her parents softened up by candlelight and *The day thou gavest, Lord, is ended*.

They had started off for church in the dead sunset of another poor day. By the time they returned to the un-smiling house, any beneficent effects of the service were unravelling like wool cuffed round the carpet by Tyger.

'. . . Because I have mending to do, Martin, that's why.' Tapio bounded into the hall. 'I can't send the girl to school looking like a diddicoy, and I'm worried sick about money, in case you hadn't noticed.'

'Nina, go upstairs! Christine, I provide a regular income. Plenty of families in this village—'

'For how much longer?'

'Not much, I imagine. But then you will have the life insurance.'

'Mummy, may I put a record on?'

'You won't have a job much longer because you're losing your grip.'

'So you said. Last Sunday after Communion you told me I was like some doddery old minister who should be put out to pasture. How very supportive. You know what it costs me in stage fright before every sermon—'

'I did *not* say that. I said you'd got through the service on a wing and a prayer.'

'All right, Christine, if we're in penury as you say, I'll get you the money. I'll go up to London first thing tomorrow.'

'What idiocy are you talking now?'

'I'll sell the violin. Despite the ruined varnish it should still bring you in the price of some clothes.'

'No, Daddy!'

'That is a spiteful thing to say! I've *never* suggested—'

'Nina, I'll drive you to school on my way.'

'If you want to save me money, Martin, you could sell those wretched medical textbooks. You could contain yourself when you buy gramophone records. You could—'

Nina's father froze. In a ghastly metallic monotone he said, 'I shall do better than that. As you obviously wish to deprive me of the one pleasure left me at the end of my life, I will not merely stop buying records.' His voice rose. 'I'll bloody destroy them!'

He wheeled away down the hall.

'Don't you dare!'

'Mummy—'

'Martin, have you gone mad?'

'You begrudge me my music, do you?' he shouted from the study. 'Well then, *you* have it. Here it is, Christine. And here. And . . .' The sound of an avalanche drowned him out, a crash of wood collapsing on wood.

'*Martin!* Nina, go upstairs. Now!'

Her mother was running, Nina and Tapio at her heels, running to the study.

It was the lower shelves that had caved in. He was crouched there, tugging at his albums. They were tight-packed. He wrenched. He hurled them at the walls, his beloved music. There were 78s in the collection, irreplaceable. The antique shellac smashed like eggs. He tore plastic sleeves off vinyl and with air-ripping savagery cracked the discs against his hi-fi cabinet, their grooved splinters spinning off the wood and shattering against the wall.

'You bitch!' he screamed. 'Begrudging me the only comfort I have in this filthy rotten life . . .'

'*MARTIN!*' His wife threw herself at him. Tapio yelped and barked, half wagging, half panic-stricken. 'Nina! Get upstairs.'

Nina couldn't. 'DADDY!'

Missiles flew from his fists, skimming across the floor, shelling the desk, slamming against the high ceiling. The carpet crunched with shards. The bookcase was vibrating, its volumes creeping forward together like an army in stealth. His desk light shattered. Another shelf keeled over, upturning a regimented line of LPs. They rained from the up-tipped wood, their sharp corners and raw plastic edging striking his face and hands and eyes.

'Bloody cow!' he shouted in fresh agony. 'You think I'm mad? You've driven me bloody mad!'

'NINA, GET OUT, GET OUT!'

'*DADDY!*'

He shook his wife off and lashed out at the highest of the shelves, words barking from his mouth in another language, alien and terrifying. Then the entire fabric collapsed, shelf after shelf smashing and echoing like a forest under a bulldozer. Her mother grabbed Nina and pushed her into the hall. She slammed the study door. From behind it issued a wordless roar and the utter mayhem of a man smashing up a room with a plank of wood.

Christine finally got her daughter to the bedroom, left her struggling into her pyjamas inside out, and flew back downstairs. Nina strained to dissect the sounds from below. They reached her through the inscrutable channels of the Victorian house, throttled and tortured by wood and pipe and plaster: a singsong voice and strange dark vocal booms. Then her father started crying. He howled like an animal in a trap. The air was drenched with him. Nina shook and whimpered. The noise went on and on, on and on, wailing into the night.

Some time in the small hours her mother carried her to bed. Christine had found Nina inexplicably curled up on the thin, comfortless carpet with the eiderdown right up over her head like an animal hibernating. Like a Moomintroll in winter.

It was Tuesday evening before Nina set foot in the study again. Her father was out and her mother in a Flower Roster meeting. Nina had overheard Christine talking to their cleaner. 'Terrible accident, Mrs Jellico . . . Fell right over on top of Martin, he might have been killed . . .' Nina stepped gingerly inside. The room was tidy and tight-lipped. The shelves had gone. The desk looked forlorn in its bareness. Deep scratches cicatrized the cabinet of the hi-fi. In the corner was a small neat pile of surviving LPs. Nina crept over to them. There were just two of Sibelius, their covers creased; the rest were the random debris of four centuries of Western music. But at the bottom were all six of her Beatles albums and Richard Chamberlain.

From inside Nina's relief a subversive thought percolated upwards like a bubble of caustic gas: wouldn't it be easier to pardon the fury of a father whose control mechanism had completely flipped, than of one who could still pick and choose what to throw?

31

Like Nina, Lu's favourite waltz after the *Kildare* theme was *Valse Triste*. Mr Hannay's latest arcane eccentricity was to ban it from the house.

'Nina,' he had said warningly as she started up on the violin.

'But Daddy—'

'No Sibelius.'

Her father had outlawed the playing of any Sibelius, even (and at this, Lu concluded that he was definitely round the bend) *even when he wasn't there*. Nina had assumed hers wouldn't count. She was wrong. Nina or David Oistrakh, it was all the same to her father: there would be no violin arrangements of *Valse Triste* in his vicarage. Luckily, Lucia saw an opportunity for a spot of emotional blackmail at home.

'Seeing how us three are the only proper friends Nina's got,' she told her parents, then it was only fair that the girls be allowed to accompany Gian and Beryl to the studio next weekend, where Nina would play the *Valse Triste* and they would dance. They wearily surrendered.

'Bring books to read,' ordered Giancarlo the following Saturday. 'And after that one dance, anybody who makes a noise will be immediately packed off home in a taxi. Understood?'

'*Capito*, Papa!'

'I don't want any arguments.'

'Gian, they've said they understand.'

In the studio, the dancers took up their ballroom hold and Giancarlo politely asked Nina where the waltz came from.

'Sibelius wrote it for a play called *Kuolema*, which means death.'

Gian dropped his arm from Beryl's waist. 'Death?'

'Yes, that's right.'

Gian looked at his wife. 'Well, darling, we won't often be asked to perform the dance of death on a wet Saturday morning in Ilford. Let's give it our best shot.'

Afterwards, when Lucia stopped crying and the arguments died down about following it with a rumba and the *Kildare* theme, Gian directed them to the office – where he forbade the girls to touch anything or swing backwards in the chairs or make any mess on the carpet.

'We'll levitate, shall we?' suggested Lu, flouncing off the sprung dance floor. '*Hover* all day in mid-air.'

It must have been an hour before Nina became aware of raised voices in the studio.

'Oh, not again.' Lu snapped her book shut. 'They were at it yesterday, too, before they left to do the evening show.'

'*Why?*' asked Nina, utterly dismayed.

'Choreography. Dad keeps changing his mind. It's for next year's show, not the one they're already doing.'

'Yes, I know what they're working on.'

'Well, that's more than they do themselves,' said Lu resignedly. 'Mum says Dad keeps changing horses in midstream and Dad says it's all very well for her, he's the one has to do the creating and make the show logical right through. When he puts everything together, it does tell a story.'

'But it's a love story about a girl and her tango teacher,' objected Nina.

The Clarks' cabaret always told a story: the first a history of tango's development in Argentina, the second the story of tangomania coming to Europe. Gian had had them in giggling fits over that one. Europe, 1913: women's hats being remodelled to stop the feathers sticking up the gentlemen's noses; special underwear to allow titled ladies all that lunging and swooning without their whalebone corsets impaling a lung; the Pope demanding a demonstration of the dance from a nun and a priest before he had it banned. But about the new one Gian had been strangely reticent.

'Well, Dad says the thing's all bits and pieces and doesn't go anywhere. He even fixed up a camera and filmed it. When they watched themselves, Mum said it looked brilliant and Dad said it was all hopeless and they'd got to begin again. That's when the ding-dong started.'

The voices in the studio lost the intricacies that characterize conversational speech, and slammed at the air in the high-pitched monotones of fulminant quarrel. Beryl was yelling, 'It's cabaret, for Chrissake, man, not the Ballets Russes!'

'They'll calm down in a bit,' predicted Lu. 'Mum'll cry and Dad'll stop yelling and it'll end with them saying there's ages yet and it was exactly like this last time but the show turned out great in the end.'

'But it wasn't like this last time,' contradicted Nina.

'I know.'

Horrified, Nina watched Lu's sangfroid crumple. Her friend's lips trembled. Lu could throw a tantrum fit for a theatrical stage but she had never trembled, even in the face of Nonna and Mr Caldwell. These were the twin pillars of Nina's only remaining shelter: the rock-solid equilibrium of Giancarlo and Beryl, and Lu's emotional stamina.

'I'll go and make a cup of tea.' Nina ran out of the office.

The shouting continued, churning through her insides. 'So are we just chucking it? Another week's work?'

'If it doesn't gel we can't patch it, Beryl. Nobody's going

to pay West End prices to watch a show that goes off at half-cock.'

'It *doesn't*. We take it from the *voleo*, then we have the fans, followed by a slow *syncopated paseo* – that's absolutely gorgeous, the audience will—'

'Can't you see the whole sequence is nothing but a collection of fancy figures with no artistic cohesion? It doesn't lead anywhere! If I trot out just another tango show, our adoring little world will turn right round and bite me in the balls.'

'I think your Latin temperament is getting the better of your judgement!' Beryl charged out of the studio, full-pelt into Nina, who trailed behind her into the galley kitchen. 'Never get married, Nina.' Beryl banged the kettle under the cold tap. 'I've no doubt your mummy will tell you the same. There's more difference between a man and a woman than between a human being and a monkey!'

Gian was suddenly at the door. 'Beryl – *basta! Non parlare così davanti alla bambina.* Where's Lu, Nina?'

'In the office, Uncle Gian.'

'She all right?'

'Yes, Uncle Gian.'

'You all right?'

'Yes, Uncle Gian.'

'Well, don't worry, everything's fine. But your auntie Beryl and I think you should both be getting home now. I'll take you across to the station for a taxi.'

Nina knew what Giancarlo had just said: 'Don't talk like that before the child.' Protecting the children. Now there was an idea.

32

Then her father announced that he was having Tapio put down.

'Mummy will explain,' he told her.

But Mummy refused to explain, saying she wasn't doing his dirty work for him. Her voice was desiccated from crying.

Nina was pole-axed. She fought against hysteria that would drive him deeper into madness and obliterate any chance of a reprieve. She said desperately, 'Tapio isn't ill yet, Daddy. Look! He's happy and eating and everything.'

'Tell her, Christine.'

'No, Martin. You explain why you're having the family pet destroyed. If you can look the vet in the eye and tell him, you can tell your daughter.'

But nobody seemed able to look anybody in the eye. It took most of Friday evening for Nina to piece together the facts: her father couldn't bear to watch Tapio day after day knowing a malignancy was growing inside him; he looked at the dog and saw cancer spreading through his system like some devastating metaphor; he couldn't cope with the knowledge that the day would come when Tapio would have to be put down. So he was putting him down.

'But Daddy,' Nina said with unassailable logic, 'we're all going to die some day, and you're not having *us* put down.'

'Answer that one, Martin,' said her mother.

When he didn't, Nina petitioned God. In case he didn't have ideas of his own, she designed elaborate scenarios in which her father's drive to the vet tomorrow would be blocked by mighty oak trees strewn across Ongar Road. She petitioned herself to sleep, her bed a zoo of bandaged toy animals. By Saturday morning Nina had felled much of Epping Forest, but when her father crawled out of bed and got through the daily kitchen conversation ('What do you want for breakfast, Martin?' 'Christine, I'm a man in torment. I don't care what I have for my wretched breakfast!') Nina's faith had grown shaky and she was left with the simple ache of grief.

The dog didn't much care what he had for breakfast either, he just wolfed it down and waltzed the drooling bowl round the kitchen floor with his nose, colliding with table legs until Christine took it from him and put it in the sink.

'Can't he have some more today?' said Nina. 'A second breakfast?'

Nobody answered.

'Come on, Tapio,' she called with a pathetic manufactured brightness. 'Let's go and play in the garden.'

Her mother seemed to notice her for the first time. 'Nina, that's your Brownies uniform. Why are you wearing it on a Saturday?'

'For good luck.'

'Take it off. I have enough washing and ironing to do. Anyway, it's too cold for that thin cotton.'

In hastily assembled trews and a home-knitted sweater, Nina romped in the damp garden with the arf-arfing Labrador, singing an appeal for clemency. A simple refrain turned out to be more soothing than clever lyrics. Nina sang hers to the tune of Crimond.

'O Lord my shepherd, save our dog
O please, Lord, save our dog.
I'll work at school, obey each rule,
If Jeeeee-sus saves our dog.'

Then again. *'O Lord my shepherd, save our dog . . .'*

Round and round, steeped in the matchless misery of a child, powerless and absolute.

The rain had drizzled away, leaving watery sunlight shining through the clouds in streaks of mother-of-pearl. The upper leaves of the sycamore ran with yellow as if the summer colour were bleeding through the tree from the top. Nina ran up and down the garden throwing a soggy tennis ball. She had found it green from algae beside the roses, peace roses, weary and dropping. And useless.

Would the vet refuse? But her father was the vicar and Tapio did have a cancerous growth. She knew the vet wouldn't refuse. She played with Tapio for an hour. It seemed longer to Nina, her senses taut from trying to intuit the dog's preferences for his last gambol in the garden while sensing the progress of events in the closed house behind her, all the while singing her begging prayer and avoiding any serious insult to the pampered lawn of the bowls club. When eventually her father appeared, Nina's arms hurt from throwing, and her hands were blue.

'Nina.' He had his coat on. The lead was in his hand. 'I have to take Tapio now.'

'I don't think you can get into town,' she managed to say. 'The roads have got a problem because of falling trees.'

'You've made that up. Come on, now. Tapio! Here, boy!'

Nina watched the dog bound across to her father. 'Daddy, Mr Hoxton might say he's been cured.'

'There's no cure for this sort of tumour, Nina. You know that.'

'No, but there might be a miracle. Ask him. Promise you'll ask him, Daddy, *please*! *Please*, Daddy!'

'Tapio, stop jumping up or I can't put your lead on.

A nice drive in the car, boy. You like the car.'

But he hates the vet, she thought. Mr Hoxton was to Tapio what Mr Caldwell was to Nina. Father and dog retreated. Then she heard the voice of Flora Latimer. The back door opened on to the sound of running water and her soft vowels, and shut again. If it was a secret that Tapio was to be put down, and no doubt it was, Nina decided she had better stay out here or she'd give the game away.

The sun had given up and it was drizzling again. There was busyness next door outside the church. Of course, a wedding this afternoon. Car doors slammed and the confident voices of happy people with a job to do carried across the hedge. It seemed incomprehensible to Nina that a couple could get married today. The triteness of the noise was an abomination, getting on with life as if her suffering were irrelevant. Everything was hateful. The puddled flower beds smelled sour from windfall apples puckered by the rains. Familiar images loomed with intolerable ugliness in the rainlight: her mother's washing line with its old metal poles askew, scabrous and the colour of pain; the last tattered rags of leaf hung from the cherry tree and two bare branches stuck out in an ungainly V as if its legs were open.

Her father's car started up in the drive. From the house came a crescendo of distress. Her mother's. Beneath it, Flora Latimer was speaking. She sounded as though she might have her arms round Christine. Nina imagined the cushioning comfort of Miss Latimer's marshmallow bosom. 'Must go and supervise the flowers . . .' sobbed her mother, and sank back into smothered incoherence.

Nina, also brokenly weeping but alone, heard the car wheels crunch away down the gravel drive. She thought, If God does let this happen, would He at least let Tapio come back to me sometimes as a ghost? I won't be scared, she implored Him. If that isn't allowed, could I at least have his doggy scent and a haze of golden hairs? A sense of that galumphing comradeship and trust, to fill the hole?

33

'Ah, Christine! Are you here to collect Freddy?'

'In point of fact, Gian, Martin and I wondered whether you'd like us to take care of Lucia. Until this blows over and . . . Beryl comes back home.'

'Oh. Well, I don't think . . . I mean, Nonna's here. But come in, come in. The children are in the bathroom.'

Lucia wasn't, she'd returned to the kitchen for a glass of milk. Overhearing this exchange, she told herself that if ever there was a choice that deserved that line about the devil and the deep blue sea, it was the choice of being looked after by either Nonna or the Hannays.

Nonna was on her way up the stairs.

'Ah. Good evening, Mrs Clark,' said Christine with condescending articulation.

The old lady shuffled her bulk and looked round. 'Mrs 'Annay,' she said with a nod of deference to the hymnary odour that trailed behind Nina's mother like must. Nonna held up a bottle of something chemically orange. 'For the girls. To wash the hair.'

'How very kind, Mrs Clark. *Grazie.*'

'*Prego.*' Nonna sketched another nod and dismissed herself.

'Come in, come in,' repeated Giancarlo over the hot

thunder of Nonna's retreat, and led Christine through to the sitting room. Whenever the Clarks were home, Beryl's invariable first act was the one Lucia called 'chucking the cushions about'. This was a generic term that covered the business of nudging all the furnishings out of the military alignments perpetrated on them by Nonna. The walls were painted a fashionable magnolia, tinted after dark by cones of pearly light moulded by turquoise lampshades. A silvery haze of Chinese rugs muted the effects of the angular furniture, and the sleeping cat formed a cushion of its own in the middle, precisely where the central-heating pipes ran under the floor. Christine sank into the latest sofa from Terence Conran.

'Good of you to think of us, Christine, given how things are in your own household.'

'But my duty is to offer comfort to others. And to count my blessings, not rage against fate.'

'Yes. How unbearable.'

Here we go, thought Lucia. Even when they're claiming to be concerned about us, this is what it always boils down to in the end: them, them, them and to hell with the kids. It should be against the law for any grown-up to shout at another grown-up when there's a child in the same building. Not to mention decisions like walking out with a suitcase and moving in with Gran or sodding off to *Japan* or Melbourne, Au*stralia*. Or destroying healthy animals.

'WHERE'S TAPIO, WHERE IS HE, WHERE IS HE?' she had demanded, ransacking the vicarage while Nina sobbed.

Mrs Hannay had appeared at the door. 'Now, now, Lu, that's quite enough.'

'WHAT'S HAPPENED TO HIM?'

'Poor Tapio had a tumour.'

'*Had?*' Lu pounced on the past tense like an angered grammarian.

'The vet put him to sleep. It was a kindness. Nina, don't

you think Lu might be better off at Nonna's? I have the Sewing Circle here in half an hour.'

Lu had seen Mr Hannay in the drawing room. By the light from the window he examined his bare arm: turning it, rolling it, kneading the skin with his index finger then exploring his armpit, his eyes focused and fixed on a mole on the forearm held just inches from his face.

Now she heard her own father offering to go to the kitchen for a pot of tea, and Lucia jumped to her feet.

'Not for me, thank you, I'm swimming in tea. I've just come from the Christmas Committee.'

'I'd offer you a proper drink but I suppose—'

'Thank you, but we don't. Martin saw too much of the effects of alcohol in Finland.'

'So be it. How is he, honestly?'

'Terrible. This afternoon he put his violin away, vowing never to play again in the short time left to him.'

'But *why*?'

'Oh Gian, don't ask for reasons.'

'Can't the doctor help?'

'Martin won't be helped. Make no mistake, he's in great pain. This headache isn't put on. And imagine what it must be like to believe you've a disease that needs urgent attention but nobody will acknowledge it. And he doesn't sleep. That's been a lifelong problem. But the time was, he could be persuaded into sleep by a comfortable bed in complete silence aided by earplugs and a blackout. Now he has to be bludgeoned into it with pills. So it's followed by a hangover. Anybody's judgement would be impaired. But he does work hard, even now. He never lets down his parish, one can say that of him.'

Yes, that's another thing that should carry a custodial, thought Lu. The show must go on. Anyone talking about how the show must go on should get sent down for two years without parole.

'Christine,' said Giancarlo, 'forgive the question, but . . . is he a suicide risk?'

The pause was so long before he got a reply that Lu wondered if Mrs Hannay would stalk out, affronted. But the reply did come.

'Yes. He is. Every time I come in through the door and the house is silent my heart is in my mouth, terrified he's cut his throat.'

'Oh God. Do you mean that specifically?'

'It's the term he uses.'

'Christine, could I talk to him?'

'You could try. Lord knows, he won't listen to a word I say. But Gian, this wasn't my purpose in coming round. I'm here to ask if there's anything I can do for you. Do you know where Beryl has gone?'

'Yes, to her mother's in Dagenham. We've got a show tomorrow night. Beryl won't cancel, we never cancel, we've danced through flu, never mind a marital bust-up. It's just that she refuses to live at home until I change my attitude to working on the next show.'

'That's booked for February?'

'Première in Düsseldorf, then London, Tokyo and so on. Except there's still no bloody show to première, if you'll pardon my Italian.'

'Perhaps Beryl's simply exhausted. The schedule you both work to. Your third new cabaret in as many years!'

'It's not the workload. We've always done this. No, it's me. I'm cracking up. The choreography we've rehearsed, it's enough for half a dozen perishing shows but I can't get the damn thing to drive forward. It's just a lot of fancy steps. I must have ditched the entire design and started from scratch ten times. Throwing out the baby with the bath-water, I don't doubt. I can no longer tell them apart.'

'Gian, have you considered that *you*'re exhausted? We're none of us getting any younger. You'll be fifty soon.'

'Age is irrelevant.' Lu heard the rap in her father's voice, and then an apologetic laugh. 'Sorry. That's a sore point from our competition days when I was sharing a floor with dancers half my age. And wiping the floor with them, I might add. No, I've just . . . stalled. I even hired a cine camera and filmed us, to put some distance between me and the performance. Hoping it would look better from the outside. It didn't.'

'Yet you know you can count on your audience loving it. Of course, I realize there are always critics sharpening their pencils.'

'Yes, but Beryl and I have always had judges with sharp pencils. At Blackpool you get just one hundred seconds for each dance. A single error and you're sunk. And we thrive on pressure. Remember, it was Blackpool in semi-riot that made us.'

'But isn't this different, Gian? With dance as an art form . . . your judges aren't marking you against pre-agreed rules, so it's more difficult to gauge and, well, more frightening?'

'Oh, make no mistake, cabaret is gladiatorial combat,' said Giancarlo. 'And yes, however harsh the pressure of competition, you know what the rules are. Even if you intend defying them,' he added with a bleak laugh.

In the kitchen Lucia dropped the biscuit tin. Her father's laugh broke off.

'Ah,' said Christine. 'Little pigs have big ears.'

And *that*, thought Lu, slamming the cupboard door, should carry a suspended sentence, 'suspended' as in hanging by a rope. Hanging and flogging, she concluded, and thudded back to the bathroom where Nina was having her rat's tails smoothed out by a grandmother with a grip of iron.

*

'I know what we'll do today,' said Lu as they trundled home from school. 'Something you got to do some time, Nina.'

It was a letter.

'*Dear Mummy*,' dictated Lu. '*I keep trying to tell you some important news from school but it's difficult with you and Daddy always so busy . . .*'

It was therapeutic to write it out, externalizing a fear that cankered Nina's waking life and terrorized her dreams. Her fantasies, too, were darkening. In bed she went to Hollywood, a beautiful young nurse at the scene of some catastrophic studio accident. The strewn and moaning cast included guest stars from the last episode of the series: Jack Nicholson got off with two broken arms while William Shatner, as the wicked ambitious Dr Noyes, was left to bleed out, uncared-for, under some tortured bedlam of girders. In the rustling authority of her uniform Nina knelt lovingly beside Richard Chamberlain and bandaged his wounds. Not just in bed. Even in the classroom her mind would slip away to an ever more severely wounded and increasingly needy Richard Chamberlain, because the only comfort he would accept was hers.

When she took her letter home she was greeted by Miss Latimer.

'Sweetheart, your mummy's having a lie-down. I thought you and I might play some gentle piano duets.'

'I've got to give her a letter.'

'Not now, lovey. Leave her be for a wee while.'

It was half six before her mother appeared. 'Flora, I'm so sorry. I didn't realize the time.'

'Not at all, we've had oodles of fun, haven't we, Nina?'

Her mother's face was parched, her beautiful eyes dead.

'Would you like me to cook?'

'Thank you, but no. I've got fish fingers and chips, which won't take twenty minutes.'

'Then I'll be on my merry way rejoicing. If you do want anything, just pick up the telephone. Night or day, I won't mind.'

In the kitchen, her mother moved like a woman in water. The chips bubbled in the pan. The empty spaces that had belonged to Tapio's bowls and basket were slowly being encroached upon by the dance of everyday objects round a busy kitchen.

'Mummy, I've got something I wrote you.'

'What do you mean? Oh Nina, why are you fiddling with the paper? Your fingers are soiling the pages.'

'I'm looking up *Dr Kildare*.'

'*Dr Kildare* has finished! Will you please wash your hands for dinner?'

'Perhaps it'll come back, though, Mummy. Perhaps Sherlock Holmes isn't on tonight.'

'Stop being so babyish. You know perfectly well—'

'Perhaps God will bring it back.'

'God?' It was a sob. 'If God turns His eyes to this household, He'll find rather more momentous problems to sort out than some footling television programme.'

'But He might, Mummy.'

'For pity's sake, Nina, *Dr Kildare* has finished for good. There won't be any more. The American TV company isn't making any more. They filmed that final series months ago and packed up and left. Now do as I say and wash your hands.'

'*NO!*' The scream came from her gut, her hair, her knees, her finger ends. '*NO! NO! NO! NO! NO! NO!*'

'Stop that!'

'*NO! NO! NO! NO! NO! NO!*' Nina was flailing. She caught the pan handle. The chip pan spun off the ring and bounced against the corner of the oven. The air writhed with flying fat. Nina was shielded from it, shielded by her mother.

'*Oh* God. Oh no, no, no.'

'*NO! NO! NO! NO! NO! NO! NO! NO! NO! NO!*'

Christine yanked at the material of her dress, tugging it free of her chest. She lunged at the kitchen tap. Water whooshed out in a thick pillar and bounced like a fountain. She thrashed her arms under the water, splashing it over her frock and face. Boiling fat was a puddle on the floor, spreading outwards in an ideograph of its own whim. The other pan, too, had toppled, greasing up the floor tiles with fishy fingerprints. Nina was still shrieking. When her father drove up he could hear it before he got out of the car, the same monosyllable at the same pitch over and over, like a looped tape.

34

The run-up to Christmas was usually an enchanted time for Nina. The Hannays had always celebrated the season with allusions to Martin's homeland. The first Sunday of December was Little Christmas with a party round the Christmas tree and the piano. Nina would spend her evenings eagerly twisting straw and sticks into geometric shapes based loosely on the *himelli*, the traditional multi-layered mobile that hangs from the ceiling, delicate squares within triangles within octagons. Nina's own limping octagons were displayed beside a proper one that Uncle Erik had brought over from Tampere. There were lanterns, sing-songs and sheaves of straw for the birds. Nina's father had also tried to interest Seaton Bois in a Christmas Eve ceremony with candles in the churchyard to honour the departed. But that one didn't fly.

'You mean the *graveyard*, Reverend? In the *dark*?'

Besides, most of Seaton Bois's departed had been ashed in a crematorium.

But this year the vicar absented himself and left his wife to manage, her right arm still in bandages. The bishop would usually drop in but this year he was on church business in Africa. 'Five weeks,' Nina had overheard her mother tell Giancarlo. 'I imagine it's our last respite before the roof caves in.'

Her father took to going off in the car, sometimes all night. Nina would see her mother sag in relief when the car grated home on the gravel, and then watch her stiffen as though the key that turned in the door were ratcheting her muscles tight. Nina's own attention was trained on a home-grown tradition: the school nativity play. Her parents would be in the audience and she still hadn't told them she had been expelled from Special Class.

If this were anybody else's parents, diversionary tactics might be possible, a sprained ankle, so they would just rush in and out without a chance to chat with the headmaster. But when your father is the vicar, custom compels that they hang around interminably afterwards, sequestered in the staffroom for tea and chat. She knew she had to tell them before Mr Caldwell reeled off an inventory of her delinquencies and branded her a cheat and a liar.

But she couldn't.

Lucia played a saintly Mary opposite Christopher Caldwell's Joseph. Nina was cast as Herod. Wearing a curtain and a paper crown edged with cotton wool, she ranted across the stage ordering the massacre of the innocents. Her fiery performance was much enjoyed by the audience. As she sang an aria of her own devising, 'I'm King of Judea and exceeding wroth', it was clear to Nina that the King of Judea wasn't on his own. Her father in the front row had clamped his features into an expression of such caricatured fury that she was reminded of the Japanese warrior on the kite. Her mother was leeward of his anger and also unsmiling.

Somebody's already told them, realized Nina and felt ill. But who? Mr Caldwell hadn't been anywhere near the parents, far too busy fussing backstage and winding up the nerves of already overexcited children until one of the magi was sick in the wings. Nina continued her scene in misery. The headmaster's story should have fallen upon parental temperaments softened by pride in their daughter's performance. Instead, his every word would aggravate an anger already torrid from sitting in silence, stewing.

'*The wise men have mocked me!*' Nina shouted at little Billy Weeks. '*But the boy shall die. I don't care what's right or wrong.*' Tears squeezed from her eyes.

'Nice little actress, that girl,' commented the verger to his wife.

When the play ended with a botched epilogue and a couple of choruses of 'Ding-dong Merrily', her fellow actors rushed off the stage, twittering like exotic birds. Lu was in a hurry to get to Nonna, black-hatted as though attending a king's funeral and making exaggerated claims about her granddaughter's star potential. Nina's parents appeared backstage and didn't look at her.

'Mummy—'

'We'll be talking to you later. Mr Caldwell, congratulations. Always such a tricky thing to pull off and the children obviously enjoyed every minute.'

Her father still looked quite seriously deranged. Nina registered Mr Caldwell's startled reaction. But the angry face is meant just for me, she thought. He used to be able to hide it when he wanted to.

A harassed Mr Ellis joined them and they withdrew to the staffroom and closed the door. Nina sank on to the lino tread at the bottom of the staircase that led up to Special Class. The corridor crackled with discarded crêpe paper and smelled of all her Christmases: pine needles and spirit gum. Behind her the school was a great multicoloured noise like some vast sea of baubles or balloons; she heard the retreat of parents and their charges, heard their chatter wrap round the building, taut yet fuzzily soft like the skin of a peach. Footsteps and babble dispersed into the lanes of Seaton Bois. Cars revved. After a while, the only human sounds were enigmatic janitor noises and the drone behind the staffroom door with discreet percussion of china. Now and then Nina made out Mr Caldwell's voice with an undertow from Mr Ellis. She could guess what was being said.

Who had told them? Had her parents been accosted by someone else's? With what motive? She was prepared to bet it was to gloat.

The staffroom door eventually opened in a series of heart-stopping stages, the rattle of the handle merely a preliminary. '. . . Funding for carol sheets,' Mr Caldwell was saying before the door was finally thrown ajar. Nina's father had lost his mask of insanity but his gaze drifted over his daughter's head in a deliberate refusal of contact. It was then just a matter of minutes before the Hannays were out of the school.

'How could you let us in for this?' Her mother was close to tears. 'The horrible creature was wallowing in it!'

Meaning the mother of Teresa Pears, whom Mr Caldwell had promoted in Nina's place. 'Lying in wait for us!' Ostensibly to say how sorry she was about Nina's failure: it was a shame, a clever kiddie like that, but at least it gave the others a chance.

'Wallowing in it!'

'Christine, wait until we get home. You're talking about a parishioner.'

When they did get home everything was terrible. 'They say they can't do anything with you,' reported her mother tearfully as her father paced the drawing room. 'You won't concentrate in lessons, you haven't been handing in your news—'

'Which you lied to us about!'

'Every Sunday you gave us your word—'

'Then cheated in an exam! When Mr Caldwell told us, do you know how I felt? As God is my witness, I felt as if I'd fathered Myra Hindley.'

That Nina was rapidly beyond reach of the recital, that she was crying with such abandon that for all she knew her father could have been hollering elk-hunting songs in Finnish, failed to modify his tirade. Then he shouted that he was going to bed, and her mother shouted back, 'Well, thank you, Martin, for leaving me to cope – she's your daughter too!' and this auxiliary row was just ripening when the carol singers arrived, shuffling into position beneath the Norwegian spruce on the lawn to flute *Tidings of comfort and joy* from beyond the drawing-room window.

35

As good Christians, the Hannays were bound to forgive their daughter on Christmas Day. Nina woke to find splintered fingers of frost across her bedroom window. The garden beyond glittered under impeccable icing and a brittle sun.

'Daddy, Pakkanen and Kova Ilma have been in the garden!' meaning Jack Frost and Sharp-Air from the *Kalevala*.

At the end of her bed was the usual stocking of tangerines and chocolate pennies. But every year of her memory, Tapio had bounded into her bedroom with the chocolates in a little bag tied to his collar. Her presents proper were even better: *colour*-illustrated Moomintrolls from Uncle Erik, and from her parents the Beatles' *Revolver*, the Beach Boys' 'Good Vibrations' and a copy of *The Wind in the Willows*. Tomorrow she'd get more from Gian and Beryl. Boxing Day was traditionally the day the Clarks distributed the non-family presents. It was a wide distribution. They were generous people.

The Hannays opened the front door to find the frosted step loaded: a coconut, two gift-wrapped boxes of mixed nuts, a brace of pheasant and a big rubber bone with a ribbon from somebody who hadn't heard about the Hannays' sad loss.

In the bustling vestry the choir was already robing, in an atmosphere that bordered on febrile, with a lot of talk about LPs. As they processed up the aisle, Nina counted the congregation out of professional habit. A good turnout. Today Giancarlo and Beryl joined them, even bringing Nonna and Lu to church instead of to the Catholic cathedral in Brentwood. Nina had known that Beryl was coming home for Christmas. ('Sleeping in the spare room,' Lu had reported gloomily. 'The pair of them need their heads banging together.') Later Lu would confide that the whole church-going activity was a con trick to make the village think everything was happy families.

After the service Nina stood with her parents in the porch, happily stamping her cold feet while everybody wished everybody else a Merry Christmas. She listened with ungrudging pleasure to Lu's recital of her presents, which would soon be the girls' common currency anyway: a record player of Lu's own, a transistor radio and a flamboyant doll in a kimono, which Lu wasn't allowed to take to school, or into the garden, or leave unattended near the cat, or play with at all unless she'd washed her hands. 'So what's the use of that?' she demanded. 'Anyway, they *know* I wanted a violin, I *told* them.'

But this morning, Lu's parents did not look like people who would be told. They shook hands, hand over hand, with the mobbing congregation, some of whom were hurriedly discussing the propriety of asking for autographs in a church porch, and never once looked each other in the face.

'Mum had a right old shindy with Nonna,' confided Lu to Nina under cover of the jollity.

'With *Nonna*? But your mum *never*—'

'Sssh! She's got ears in the back of her head. Mum shouted that she was taking me with her to Gran Colby's in Dagenham. Said she wanted to sever Nonna's unhealthy influence and medieval methods of child-rearing.'

Yes, well, Beryl had a point, but '*Dagenham?*'

'Don't worry, Gran Colby would never stand for it. As it is, with Mum there she can never get into her own bathroom.'

Giancarlo was nodding cheerfully as deaf Mrs Withams hollered advice about his quickstep. Now he rattled out some fast Italian sideways at his wife. '*Sorridi alla tua suocera e non parlare dello show!*'

'*Quale?*' she shot back, smiling. '*Quelli che ti hanno reso ricco? O quello che ti ha fatto impazzire?*'

'*Non parlare così forte, Beryl. Probabilmente il prete ti capisce; sa parlare latino.*'

'Yes, but,' whispered Nina to Lu, 'they'll be off to the continent, February. Your mum might take you to your gran's and dump you there.'

'They're not off to the continent, February, it's all cancelled and kaput. Jellicoed. The whole tour. Don't tell anybody, it's top secret. Dad has agents and people on the phone all day long.'

'What's top secret?' Giancarlo's dark hand was in Lucia's hair.

'Nothing, Dad.'

'Good. Not a day for secrets, is it? And how's our Freddy?'

'I had a Beatles LP, Uncle Gian, and the Beach Boys' "Good Vibrations" and *The Wind in the Willows* by Kenneth Grahame.'

'What a marvellous collection of presents!'

Nina's eyes happened to fall on Nonna. She was in her best Sunday black, hugging a buffed handbag, two foppish feathers cobbled to the outmoded hat. Above an all-purpose smile her eyes were flummoxed and scared. In the pressing crowd she stood in a kind of lacuna, as if her force field repelled the matter around her – an isolated old woman, never accepted by the village, who had just been threatened with the confiscation of her grandchild.

Nina, in a paroxysm of scarcely comprehended guilt, called across to her. '*Nonna, buon natale! Ho avuto in regalo dischi dei Beatles e dei Beach Boys ed il libro* Il Vento nei Salici *di Kenneth Grahame!*' At which Giancarlo and Beryl exchanged the only direct look to pass between them for the entirety of Christmas Day.

Miss Latimer always joined the Hannays for Christmas dinner. Nina's father, soothed by the healthy size of the congregation, seemed to have regained his sense of humour. Urged on by Miss Latimer and Nina, he retold stories that had made them laugh in the past.

'And she said, "Vicar, I'm only thankful Jesus doesn't know or he would turn in his grave!", thereby undermining every tenet of Christianity in one short sentence.'

'Oh, dearie me,' laughed Miss Latimer, dabbing at her eyes as she had last year.

It was in the evening that everything went wrong again. The vicar had excused himself and wasn't missed, the assumption being that he was either working on the next sermon or in the lavatory battling with his wife's sprouts. He wasn't. He was on the stairs, crying.

He chose the stairs! thought Nina disloyally as her happiness was plunged into blackout like fused bulbs on a Christmas tree. The stairs, where he was bound to be stumbled upon, and possibly by Miss Latimer.

'Daddy?'

'Go away, Nina.'

Tears trickled over his cheeks to the thin lips. He was licking them! She stood, useless and dithering, revolted by the wetness that dribbled into his ungainly open mouth.

Then Flora was in the hall. Nina clumsily tried to direct her away but she walked briskly across to the Reverend Hannay, now snivelling into his hands.

'Martin,' she said gently, 'wouldn't you be more comfortable upstairs?'

'I'm sorry, Flora. I can't seem to rise above the fact that this will be my last Christmas!'

'Up you get now. Ups-a-daisy.'

The noise had brought Nina's mother from the dining room. 'Oh, Martin. Today of all days,' was all she said.

'I'll never see another Christmas!'

'Really? If one of us won't see another Christmas, it will be me. I feel like death, though far be it from me to have feelings.'

She did indeed look like death. Her face was the same pasty yellow as the anaglypta on the walls, and her brow oozed an unhealthy sheen.

'You're ill, Christine?' He dropped his hands. 'Have you got a lump anywhere? Have you seen Dr Dolan?'

'When have I had time to see Dr Dolan, with you in this state and parish duties and a home to run, and a child who's a continual worry?'

'Christine.' This was Flora. 'Let's not—'

'Answer me!' demanded Nina's father. 'Have you got a lump anywhere?'

Flora held up her hand like a policewoman directing the traffic. She had been watching Christine Hannay. As well as her church duties, Flora was a probation officer – and not only with boys. 'Christine, a quick word in private. Nina, dear, would you be an angel and make a nice pot of tea?'

Nina shuffled off to the kitchen, her father behind her, wild and sobbing.

'Did you know Mummy was ill?'

'No, Daddy!'

'Two of us! And nothing to leave you except my paltry life insurance!'

By the time Flora reappeared, he had orphaned Nina and assigned her to the care of the bishop, and a distraught Nina was pleading with him to bequeath her to Giancarlo and Beryl.

'Martin, go and talk to Christine. Nina, sweetheart, your mummy isn't dying, I give you my word. Now let's cut the Christmas cake while they have a little chat.'

36

Susan was born in August of the flower-power summer of 1967.

By then the vicarage was full of purfling again and Sibelius on the radio. Almost immediately, her father had started making an effort, trying to pull himself together. Her mother hadn't; her mother spent the rest of the Christmas holiday snapping at them both and shaking her head with a look of disbelief.

'I'm going to get better now,' her father promised.

He did get better. Because he allowed Dr Dolan to send him to St Clement's Hospital.

'*Oranges and Lemons, say the bells of St Clement's,*' he quoted to Nina. 'You see, it's no more scary than a nursery rhyme.'

He spent two months in hospital and re-emerged extremely shaken but on the mend. The truth was, he found it very scary indeed. His wife was to say that his contact with frankly psychotic patients did as much good as all the anxiolytic drugs and ECT, that the experience sent him scampering back towards normality appalled. He had been an obsessive worrier all his life, and that wouldn't change. He would be prone to episodes of clinical depression. But the florid madness was over.

The Hannays were moving to an undemanding church on the other side of Essex. The bishop felt that far too much information was batting round the community, and it wasn't appropriate for a vicar to have his psychiatric history common knowledge throughout two parishes. So the Hannays would move and Martin, who had embraced the Church in the belief of steady promotion through archdeacon, suffragan bishop and perhaps even full diocesan bishop, would never even rise to the position of rural dean.

Nina passed her eleven-plus exam despite Mr Caldwell and was due to start at grammar school in September, so it made sense for the family to move during the summer.

The rumours of illness that departed the Hannay household drifted down the road to take up residence instead with the Clarks. In their case it was the fault of the newspapers.

'HEALTH WORRIES DOG GIANCARLO AND BERYL' screamed the *Daily Mail*. The *Express* didn't mince its words. 'CLARKS CANCEL TOUR AMID CANCER FEARS'. The Clarks' misfortunes were even reported in *The Times*, the paper whose early reviews had borne the unmistakable whiff of ballet buffs going slumming:

> Yesterday, the dancer Giancarlo Clark refused to answer questions about the health of his wife, Beryl. There has been speculation ever since the Clarks cancelled the world tour of their latest cabaret show, which should have come to London in April. Tickets had already sold out and were changing hands on the black market for up to thirty guineas.
>
> The veteran ballroom champion, who celebrates his fiftieth birthday this month, declined to answer questions. The Clarks' tour promoter, Mr Monty Epstein, issued a brief statement to the effect that the Clarks are looking forward to returning to the stage as soon as possible and exciting audiences with another landmark show.

But there never was another landmark show. The Clarks repaired their marriage, started teaching full-time and repeatedly promised that by the following year they would stage the new cabaret, until Giancarlo refused to discuss the subject. Eventually even the most tenacious journalists gave up pestering him about it and the public was left to shrug and write it off as a mystery. Nina was soon at a new school with a set of foxy friends to whom ballroom dancing was decidedly not hip. The letters to and from Lucia dwindled and the girls lost touch.

At home, life settled down. While Christine was convinced her husband's recovery was due to St Clement's, her father credited Susan.

'This wonderful gift has healed me,' Nina overheard him say, gazing at the baby with tears in his eyes. 'Isn't she lovely? Isn't she a miracle? At last, I have something to live for.'

PART III

Saxophone Blue

37

To a police officer on the beat in the spring of 1990, a post-
ing in Harlesden brought its standard city share of burglary,
street and car crime, enriched by drug-related violence from
the Stonebridge Estate and the insidious beginnings of a
gun culture. Plus a smattering of 'domestics', sometimes at
three in the morning.

'Now why don't we all calm down?'

'Nina, I'm sorry, I was only—'

'If you say sorry one more time, Jussi, I won't be bloody
responsible!'

'*Madam!* Either we calm down or the pair of you are
under arrest for breach of the peace!'

As a Samaritan, Nina was used to unfathomable
ructions, and she found it in herself to be impressed
at how this couple was handling hers. They were fit and
good-looking and their self-assurance spoke with quelling
authority to that part of the mind trained to obey the
grown-ups. PC Bowers and WPC Rycroft, though a
decade younger than Nina, were unmistakably *in loco
parentis*.

'Let's all take a seat. Can we move these papers out of the
way, sir?'

Jussi shot Nina a terrified glance registered with interest by the police.

'Music, is it, sir?'

'No, no, I'll do it!' Pouncing on the heaped sheets he flipped them over, face down.

And then, incredibly, the phone rang.

'Go ahead and answer it, madam. We'll sit here and have a chinwag with the gentleman.'

Jussi gave Nina another panicky look. Desperately worried, she made for the sitting room. The voice at the end of the line was distraite.

'Your sister's had a girl! Seven pounds three ounces and absolutely adorable. They're naming her Martina. That's in memory of Susan's father,' added Susan's mother.

'Lovely,' said Nina. 'Susan all right?'

'Splendid. Well, she's sleeping now, bless her heart. Dear, you *must* come out here to see your baby niece.'

'Can we discuss this tomorrow, Mum? It's quarter past three.'

'Good heavens, is it?'

'But it's sweet of you to let me know.'

'Nina, they'll be your only family one day. And Mr De Klerk has released Nelson Mandela.'

'And the day he calls free elections, I'll be on the next—'

'Oh Lord, you're as stubborn as your poor father.'

Back in the kitchen, the police were comfortably seated at the table, turning the pages of Nina's manuscript while Jussi watched with a weighty air of nonchalance. When their walkie-talkies squawked he jumped.

'Everything OK?' ventured Nina nervously.

'I'm hoping you'll tell us, madam. You see, in our job we develop a nose.' He canvassed his colleague. 'What's your nose telling you, Siân?'

'That something is dodgy, Matt.'

'So we're hoping you'll give us an explanation. Let's start with why Mr Pellinen doesn't want us anywhere near this music.'

As Nina would tell Duane the following evening, Duane being newly returned from Stoke, an unfortunate offshoot of Jussi's ingenuous nature was that he was a spectacularly incompetent liar. 'The police didn't take their eyes off him. If I'd fabricated some tale he would have gone, "Yeah, nice one, Nina!"'

'So in the early hours of this morning you were telling the uniform branch about Sibelius's eighth symphony?'

She had tried not to, and began convincingly enough. 'This is something my late father wrote. The row was because Jussi's father wants a share.'

'I was only making a duplicate,' objected Jussi with a voice full of hurt. 'In case somebody steals it.'

'You mean somebody might break into this flat in order to steal it, sir?'

'Exactly.'

'And why would anyone do that, sir?'

'Oh, Jussi!' Nina tried a smile infused with suffering honesty. 'Look, he's persuaded himself that my dad copied the music from a masterpiece that has since been lost. Believe me, this is of no interest to you.'

'Does it have a name, this lost masterpiece?' asked PC Bowers easily. His pencil quivered over his notebook. There was a longish pause.

'The composer does. His name was Sibelius.' Feeling entirely surreal she went on, 'Sierra India bravo echo Lima India uniform sierra.'

Duane was now wiping his eyes.

'It wasn't funny, Duane, they stayed bloody ages. A second pot of tea and a couple of lectures.'

'And a notebook account of your dad's iffy symphony. You believe Jussi?'

'Absolutely. He'd never hurt me deliberately, you know him. But the duplicate was meant for Erik. After the police left I cornered him into admitting it.'

By then a threadbare dawn had been picking out the white and blue from Nina's garden. 'Please give me the whole story,' she had requested patiently. 'Have you been photographing it piecemeal for weeks?'

'I snaffled a few pages and ran them off on a photocopier. I could look through the score and tell you.'

'Now, please.'

He identified four pages at the close of the symphony's first movement and a random half dozen from the third. Nina remembered there was a rollicking good theme in the third movement, which Jussi's sample had apparently captured.

'So what did Erik think of them?'

'Said he still needs the whole thing to . . . Oh shit. Look, Dad thought I had your blessing.'

Now, in Duane's flat, Duane was shaking his head. 'Nina, you got to find out who really wrote it. Preferably before I'm charged with receiving stolen goods.' He pointed at Nina's suitcase. She had given in to Jussi's insistence that the place for it was behind the alarms and surveillance cameras of Duane's gated apartment block. 'And the same goes,' Jussi had added, 'for that seventeenth-century violin in the Hoover cupboard!'

Duane thought of something else. 'Before I forget, I'm organizing a pub crawl this weekend. You two up for it?'

Normally they would be. Jussi liked Duane, who didn't patronize him like some of her friends. 'Jussi's a tango dancer,' Victoria had introduced him at a dinner party. 'It's very artistically respectable.' But this weekend was out.

'Oh, I'm sorry. Jussi called in every favour he's ever been owed. We've got tickets for Blackpool.'

38

Inevitably, one of his international legion of friends happened to have an empty flat near the Winter Gardens at the time of the British Open. By Friday afternoon, Nina was watching the contestants rehearse under the chandeliers and opulent Victorian ceiling of the most famous dance floor in the world.

In the Clarks' day, dance was dominated by the British. Nina knew there used to be a spectators' section known as the foreigners' gallery; nowadays a joke was going round that the British fans would fit into it. Dancers wore tracksuit tops proclaiming their affiliation: Japan, Austria, Germany, Poland, Italy. Finland. Young women with tanning-parlour faces and their hair throttled into submission practised their leggy 'high développé' with protective robes over their dresses. Round the perimeter of the ballroom, couples had set up home in the alcoves: a tailsuit hung from the handle of a firepoint cupboard over an open suitcase with something draped across it, orange and feathered. Nina wondered, Why are glimpses of backstage so touching? Latin tassels peeking from under a tracksuit top, girls crouched in corners checking their false eyelashes, all swank to the wind.

The backstage atmosphere was even more pronounced in the exhibition hall. There were stands selling dancer's tan, hair jewellery, floral leggings. And frocks.

'Look at this,' demanded Jussi. 'God help us! What's the British word? Not kitsch.'

The British word was 'naff' but Nina had no intention of telling Jussi or she'd hear nothing else until they left Blackpool. The object of his derision was a tailor's dummy wearing a fuchsia-coloured creation in voluminous georgette. Feather boas fluffed the sleeves and bounced from the scalloped hem.

Jussi read loudly. '*Also available in electric lime, Benidorm blue and fluorescent tango!*'

'Yes, I know,' said Nina patiently, 'but stop thinking of these as evening wear and try to see them as theatrical costumes.'

'For what – a drag act?'

'Jussi, keep your voice down.' They were drawing a crowd.

In the ballroom for the afternoon heats, he started again before his bottom hit the chair. 'Are you telling me the garb looks better in here?'

On the dance floor three couples collided. The air was suddenly full of feathers like a pillow fight.

'No,' said Nina, 'it looks like it was concocted by a five-year-old and a dressing-up box. That's because the ballroom is still half empty.'

'How can that possibly make a difference to the *clothes*?'

'I've absolutely no idea, but it will.'

And however unlikely, Nina was right. Once the taped music was replaced by a band and the house was packed and febrile, the formerly seedy, end-of-the-pier-matinee atmosphere was all tautness and exhilaration. Under the glittering cones of the spotlights, iridescent skirts flounced and rippled like exotic sea urchins in a tropical ocean. Even Jussi shut up except for the occasional technical remark such as 'Those two are tricky little dancers.' For Nina, it was bliss to be in this buzzing electrified place where the rumbling floor transmitted the energy of the competitors into her bones. And the compère was her uncle Gian.

When he first took the stage, Nina's excitement was so intense it blotted out coherent thought, but when that ebbed she saw that Giancarlo was the same handsome man, elderly but not remotely frail, and very obviously enjoying himself. He wasn't the only one. All round the ballroom strangers exchanged comments, knowledgeable and opinionated. '. . . love the technique of the Italians . . .' '. . . fallaway reverse into the slip pivot . . .' '. . . this cross-fertilization of steps will ruin the tango, you mark my—'

When Giancarlo introduced the judges, the band struck up fanfares. 'And from Richmond in Surrey, Mrs Beryl Clark, MBE!'

And there she was, still perfectly blonde and, as far as Nina could see, still thirty.

'Keeps herself looking good for mid-fifties,' said Jussi. 'Facelift, you reckon?'

'Oh, Jussi!'

Once the contestants were winnowed down to the finalists, tiny Nina couldn't see the stage above the agitated spectators and realized she had no hope of getting anywhere near the Clarks at the end of the night. Nor would they possibly remember her if she did, not in this context, on their home ground. Her besotted daydreams looked infantile now. When the finals finished, long after midnight in a cataract of flowers, Nina's eyes ached from the livid light of flash photography.

'Hey, stay with it!' demanded Jussi. 'You can't stand around with your eyes closed or what chance have we got of elbowing our way to the front?'

'We've no chance anyway. Might as well give in gracefully.'

'After schlepping two hundred miles? I should cocoa. Watch it, they're starting to shift. Nina, *go, go, go!*'

It was a long time before the crowd thinned. The stage was a workshop of huge men dismantling equipment. Beryl was nowhere to be seen, only Giancarlo, still discussing and congratulating. Nina hung back, creakingly shy. She could see his eyes, those dark Italian pools, and a further recognition hit her. Tapio. Giancarlo Clark was the only man she'd ever met who had the irresistible eyes of a Labrador. She turned to Jussi in panic.

'He'll never remember me. I'll prattle like a fool and the poor man won't know what to say.'

She was wrong.

'*Our* Nina? It *is*!' He was down from the stage and she was squashed in his arms, breathing aftershave and an intense maleness, its pungency sharpened by the heat. Then, 'Wait, wait, I have to find Beryl . . . June, have you seen my wife, she was—? *Beryl!* Come and see what I've got! It's Freddy!'

Through a spasm of giggling tears Nina said, 'Nobody's called me Freddy in nearly a quarter of a century!'

Jussi melted tactfully away with a delighted smile that reminded Nina why she hadn't thrown the teapot at him the night of the police.

'Nina Hannay! After a week like this, too – brand-new Blackpool champions and little Freddy!'

Suddenly Beryl was there. 'But we saw you on TV! *Top of the Pops*. Ages ago.'

'You really saw me?'

'Lucia did and phoned us. "Turn the telly on right this instant!" she said.'

'And there you were with your hair all pink and green,' finished Giancarlo simply.

Nina blotted her messed mascara. Beryl's make-up was discreet and flawless. 'How is Lucia?'

'Ah, there hangs a tale. Lu is in the middle of a divorce.'

'Oh, I am sorry.'

'Us too,' said Beryl. 'Perfectly lovely husband. Heaven knows what's the matter with her.'

'He's a dentist, Freddy. Toronto.'

'Orthodontist. They've a daughter, Melanie. Eleven now.'

'The same age you were when we last saw you!'

'Toronto,' repeated Nina, winded with disappointment. 'But will Lu be coming home now that she's . . . er . . . ?'

'Don't ask us,' said Beryl. 'We'll be the last to know, we're merely the parents.'

'And grandparents. Heigh-ho.'

'Speaking of which, Nonna's ninety-five! Gian's brother Paolo lives in Rome now, and she's there with him. Home at last! But how about your own parents?'

Nina explained. Gian said sadly, 'So Martin has passed on.'

Then Jussi was brought over, who looked gorgeous and talked intelligently about tango finlandia.

'Yes, we've heard there are festivals,' said Beryl. '*So* glad. I remember soon after we came up through the ranks, Finnish tango went down through the plughole. Terrible for a dance to become extinct,' she added, sounding like Nina's friends talking about the rainforests.

Gian said gently, 'Beryl, darling, we mustn't forget the time.'

'Oh, Lord!' She glanced at her watch. 'We would dearly love to take you off for a drink but we're booked to go out to dinner.'

Nina became aware that waiting on the outskirts of her own effervescent group was a cluster of about twenty people in evening dress. The Clarks were booked to go out to dinner with a large party in formal attire – at one o'clock in the morning. Their stamina had obviously not waned much. Then Nina realized that among the people she was merrily delaying were the newly fêted champions.

They all walked out together and an elderly gentleman asked Nina about herself. '*Statistician!*' he responded with rare vivacity. 'Has Gian got you sorting out our skating system?'

'What's a skating system?'

'Oh *don't*, my dear,' advised a woman in Thai silk. 'We've got statisticians trying to come up with a better method for settling championships when there's a tied score. People come to blows.'

It was a warm night and enchanted. A mineral tang came off the shining metal sheet that was the sea. With the lights strung along the promenade and decorative ironwork rimed with silver from the moon, the scene looked as if men in top hats and ladies in bustles might materialize from the wedding-cake façades of their hotels for a late-night stroll by gaslight. Nina would have emptied her bank account for the chance to join the dinner party.

'I've got a solution to your scoring problem,' said Jussi. 'Make them dance a Viennese waltz as a tie-break.'

'By George, the lad's cracked it!'

There was a hushed discussion going on, which determined that if the Clarks turned up at their restaurant with two unplanned guests, the chef would throw them all in the Irish Sea, so they parted in a flurry of contact details, walking backwards and waving, their laughter buffeting from one to the other, to be picked up by the sea breeze and twirled away as light as a feather blowing off the hem of a dancer's frock.

39

The next morning was Saturday. Jussi phoned Tony Delterfield and asked if he could stand in at the classes for another couple of days.

'Cheers, mate. It's Nina. I owe her a heap of favours and . . . No, we gotta get back for Tuesday, anyhow. She's needed at work.'

For some kind of announcement apparently, so Nina's boss had informed her when she had asked for time off. 'The entire site is being corralled first thing Tuesday,' he had said, and added, 'Keep that strictly under your hat.' At which Nina had turned cold.

Meanwhile, with an energy that was the afterglow of Giancarlo and Beryl, she had a mission to accomplish. Instead of heading home from Blackpool, Nina drove Jussi across the Pennines towards Brancaster and her mother's empty house.

'Hello, dear!' said the neighbour. 'Yes, of course I can let you have the key. Is this your boyfriend?'

The house felt stale and smelled of hot carpets. After a quick coffee, Nina and Jussi were back in the car. It was a short drive but they weren't greeted with the same enthusiasm at the end of it.

'The booking is for another three weeks,' objected the receptionist.

'I'm not concerned about the money—' Nina began until Jussi kicked her.

'While you're revising the bill downwards,' he interrupted, 'someone can fetch the dog.'

The receptionist bristled. 'I'm sorry, sir, but I can't just hand over an animal to anybody that asks.'

'You know it's illegal to hold a dog against his will?' countered Jussi. '*Habeas corpus.*'

'I don't believe you said that.' Nina couldn't hug him because Kruger was hurling himself at them. 'What do you know about *habeas corpus*?'

'Busted once for possession. I'm practising to get the hang of this lying lark. Well, sunshine,' he enquired of Kruger. 'How d'you want to celebrate your release from choky? Beach?'

So the three of them crammed into the tiny cabin of Nina's E-type, Kruger's enormous body pressed against the glass like a bottled dog. First, Holkham Bay: tangy pine woods, samphire and a mile's walk to the sea.

'Hey, Nina, what's a naturist?' hollered Jussi, standing beside a sign, to which a naked man in the dunes shouted back, 'There's clues around if you look for them, pal.' And when Kruger had run off his hysteria Nina took them to the bird sanctuary at Titchwell Marshes.

Titchwell had become the focal point of Nina's fascination with this coastline. She was fast forgetting that until her father died she had never given it a second thought. It was a landscape of lagoons and water plants like floating meadows, of copper-coloured butterflies and watery light. Wind waved the bulrushes and blew the lagoons indigo and black like the colour shifts of shot silk. The marsh marigolds of spring were giving way to a sprinkling of magenta, volatile in the shifting shadows of the never-quiet reeds. There was a map: *wet grazing meadow, freshwater and brackish marsh, tidal saltmarsh* . . . Nina incanted the words like a spell. Unbidden, the thought whistled through her mind: If Tuesday brings redundancy, then good! It's my chance to get away.

Where had that come from? She didn't want to get away, not from Jussi. Besides, the statement was nonsense. Nobody could get away. House prices were falling, and the forecast was particularly grim for areas like Harlesden that hadn't attracted the yuppies. Sean and Victoria regularly updated her in death-knell tones. Yet it persisted, her wild optimism: at last I can get away.

Mobs of birdwatchers were marshalling on the boardwalk, kitted out like paparazzi. Great flocks of birds twisted in the air like fishing nets thrown into the wind. Nina remembered that Sibelius had felt such an affinity with wading birds, he had convinced himself he was descended from them.

'Last time, I asked you about Finland,' she said to Jussi.

'I remember. You should go over and check it out.'

I want to get away. Was it Finland she had been yearning for on the Norfolk coast ever since the September day after her father's funeral? The symphony had been singing in her head all morning. Her translation of the orchestral score to piano was improving, and she could make better sense of it. The first movement opened with the woodwinds spinning amiable spirals of gold, until the brass pounced in with a motif that developed first as foxfires and later, in the last of its many iterations, as rustling browns like the Finnish *Ruska Aika*, russet time, autumn.

Could it really be Sibelius? And even greater than the other seven? *If*, then surely – this was a new thought – surely there was a more generous interpretation to be put on her father's legacy? Maybe it was an extraordinary gift from him, deliberately left behind knowing Nina would play the music through and recognize the provenance of its streaming colours. But how could it be? She reminded herself that Aino insisted the Eighth hadn't survived, and Aino was a scrupulously truthful woman.

Every biographer hammered the bloody fact to death.

Nina was developing a daunted fascination for Aino Sibelius. Ferociously right-wing, who ran her home to principles of discipline so exacting, her dazed visitors recalled the court of the Russian Tsar, she bore six daughters and devoted her life to the protection of a moody genius. She berated him when he came home sozzled or was wallowing in one of his sloughs of self-pity, and she ensured he wasn't subjected to the disturbances that pester lesser mortals. Disturbances such as the kids, whose chatter might sully the colours of his musical palette. Can't have that. So they were hushed.

The house had no electricity, no running water; water was drawn from a well in the garden. A lot of it: the genius would not be short-changed on his bathwater. Nor on much else, Sibelius being the flamboyant spendthrift he was, the man who would throw a crayfish-and-champagne party to celebrate a win on the horses. During the war, as Europe was torn to pieces and Finland bled from the heart, he actually demanded special dispensation to have his cigars imported from Havana. He spent his life borrowing and Aino spent hers making do and mending. Nina thought of the photographs of Ainola in its cabin snugness, Moomin snugness – and wondered what in God's name it had been like for a child growing up in that dysfunctional household.

'Fancy coming home with me for a trip?' Jussi was asking.

'That's kind. But somehow . . . It's because Dad never went back.' Nina didn't add, And I've always believed your country treated him shabbily.

'Yeah, I know he never got over the shame and disgrace.'

'Well, that isn't quite—'

'It's weird though, Nina. You know how your dad got some poetry published? It throws all the dates haywire. I tried asking my old man but he cocked a deaf 'un. I reckon those two old boys never told the truth.'

They had reached the creek. It was low tide and heaps of razor-fish shells lay stranded on the shingle, pointing seawards as neat as bamboo. Afternoon light crackled like static along dunes of sugary sand.

'Those poems were in the national papers,' persisted Jussi. 'Big big deal and your dad thought, Hey, maybe I can be a poet and live in café society and never go back to law school.'

'Something like that.'

'But when? Once old father Virta's book came out, the shit was flying. Our papers would never have carried your dad's stuff.'

'The poetry pre-dated the scandal.'

'Couldn't've done. My father kept the cuttings of those poems. I've seen them.'

'Strangely, so did mine. So have I.'

'Not being rude, Nina, but you can't read them and I can. I had another look last time I popped home. They're about the news. After the war, our new president buried the hatchet with the Russians. That's what your dad's poems were about – reconciliation.'

'I know. I'm his daughter. Why are you telling me this?'

'Because the new president wasn't even sworn in till March 1946. Fact. It's not like your dad was writing under a pseudonym, it's Martti Hannikainen. So *either* the national press was promoting Public Enemy Number One, the outcast who was being gobbed on in the street, *or* my dad and yours have spun everyone some cover story to—'

'Jussi, just shut up!'

He stopped dead, startled as a smacked toddler. 'You don't have to scream, yeah?'

But she did. She had to drown him out. She wanted to flee, to outrun the implications of Jussi's words. Her features contorted. 'Does it never occur to you it's in bad taste to accuse your girlfriend's dead father of lies and cover-ups? You and Erik and your hellish conspiracy theories, you—'

'For Chrissake, Nina!'

Kruger had never liked discord; he was barking in pitiful agitation, sending shells flying. But nothing else was flying.

The shore, the creek, the lagoon behind them, were devoid of visible birdlife for fifty yards. The violence had driven the nesting birds from their eggs. Nina registered the damage through the sickly colour of a fury she hated to give up. A distracted insight fought for attention. How easy to let go and cause mayhem. How easy not to give a fuck what harm you caused.

40

Her company was cutting down to a skeleton staff and out-sourcing, a word being chanted around the industry like some sinister mantra. Nina was offered a month's salary.

'Frankly, I expected a week's pay and a good luck card,' she said. 'Anyway, I've already got some work giving music lessons. I'm not worrying.'

Duane said, 'I've read this recession's even more dire in Finland. The disintegration of the Soviet bloc obliterated your markets.'

Jussi shrugged. 'Dire always brings out the best in us.'

They were on that pub crawl. Apparently it wasn't a celebration. 'Friend of mine in New York just heard his T-cell count has fallen below 500.'

'You been tested?' asked Jussi, who could somehow ask questions like that without causing offence.

'Yeah, negative so far. Meanwhile, you two. This bloody symphony in my flat.'

'I'm making progress, mate. I've got Nina to admit she has to hear it through properly. She's going to talk to her ex with his music studio.'

'I didn't say definitely . . .' The terror at Titchwell Marshes had not endured. Nina had grown a skin around it, perhaps stimulated by the counter-irritant of redundancy. But in its choppy wake her worries about the symphony veered and yawed. She wanted to know, she didn't, she did, she didn't. It scourged her sleep. Sometimes her father was there, doodling at the piano with frowning inspiration. But more often she got Aino Sibelius demanding her property back – sprightly for one who had died in 1969 – supported by a plainclothes policeman raising his trilby.

'Nina,' said Duane in a less heckling tone. 'Talk to Greg and see how it sounds on synthesizer and *then* decide if you've got to worry yourself comatose.'

'Sure, no probs,' said Greg. Nina had invited him to the Mean Fiddler with warnings of an ulterior motive.

She had played keyboards on their one hit single. Greg wasn't pretty but he photographed well, and had looked good in eyeliner and the spangled theatrical glamour required by the New Romantics. A good musician generally and a clever songwriter, he went on to write hits for other people, and these days was a successful independent producer. Nina had started by being in awe of him, of his talent and incandescent ambition, of that inexorable drive like a masonry drill, which had so captivated her mother. But what had beguiled Nina were Greg's sudden, painful vulnerabilities, the infrequent cameo glimpses of a little boy unsure of his place in an industry of tinsel. During the four years they lived together, the balance of power was inflexibly in his favour for three and a half, until it keeled over with giddying abruptness. Since the break-up they had successfully passed through Greg's acrid recital of grudges (months) to a queasy ceasefire and recently a determinedly amnesiac friendship.

'How long will you need the studio?' he asked. 'I'm free Thursday evening.'

'Actually,' said Nina, 'it might take longer than Thursday evening.'

Indeed. She would have to play each instrument's part on

the synthesizer keyboard, right through the orchestra and choir. For a hundred and ninety pages.

'I'm only asking one evening a week,' she added hurriedly, seeing Greg's gobsmacked expression.

'Good,' he said faintly. 'What the hell's it for?'

'Can you keep a secret?'

So she told him.

'Fucking hell!' said Greg. Here we went again. 'Jesus Christ. You are *serious*? *Sibelius*?'

'How long will it take to record, do you reckon?'

'Eh? How long? Well, if you and an experienced engineer did it one evening a week, I'd estimate a couple of years.'

'You are joking.'

'No. My God. So Duane's got Sibelius in his trousseau drawer? I bet he's giving you grief.'

'A couple of *years*?'

'Look, this is too good to miss. London's full of musicians who could do with the work. Hell, for this I'll bring in the buggers by relay.'

'Oh, but Greg—'

'Trust me, I'll spin them a yarn. So that nobody hears the texture building up, which might shout "Sibelius", we'll record each part separately against nothing but a click track. It means the finished article won't exactly swing – but no news will leak out. I don't want the world's journalists camping on the pavement either, or they'll get an eyeful of the A-list babes sneaking out my back door at breakfast.'

'You are a prince among men,' said Nina.

Greg was as good as his word. Unfortunately, his response to Jussi, as Nina's lover, was sulky sniping, but as Jussi was never jealous of anyone he let them get on with it. On Saturdays Nina would arrive in Hampstead after lunch just as Greg was getting up. Never on his own: at some point she would run into a female in a towelling robe.

Nina was perversely glad of her own small pains of jealousy, the spasms of undead emotions directed at the bed that had been hers, in the house that had been her home for

235

four years – and where, thanks to Greg, she had written up her PhD in a very un-student-like luxury. They weren't an emotional washout, then, those years. They left behind traces sufficiently alive to feel pain.

By high summer Nina had a recording. She had come close to abandoning the job. The synthesized voices were nauseating: an electronic syrup of wordless ululation. Nina assumed the whole symphony would be a similar mush, like some concoction glugging out of a tin marked 'Orchestra Melt'.

When Greg was mixing the finished work down, she made them both some coffee under the suspicious eye of a stunning young woman in a bathrobe at five in the afternoon, and went back to the studio. Nina knew what was in store: the corrosive disappointment that comes of wrestling with a serious artistic project and getting a turkey.

No. Never mind the fakery or the strict-time plodding of a mechanized score without conductor, life and verve; never mind that she'd put in some inexplicable clunk and howl which Greg said sounded like somebody slamming his penis in the fridge door. Nina had said you could recognize Sibelius from a hundred yards. She would have known this one from the other side of London. The rustling strings, the effulgent horns, the fragments of forest woodwind, she was listening to the 'idiosyncratic orchestral colouring' of which the critics talked – and which she had known all her life.

'My opinion?' said Greg. He was perched on a stool, bare-chested and a cigarette in his hand that Nina could have wept for. Presumably the robed girl was upstairs, chafing. 'My opinion is that if it looks like a duck and quacks like a duck, it's a duck.'

41

One person, at least, was relieved. Duane. He didn't have to take the manuscript back.

'Greg's security has beams like something out of *Topkapi*,' Nina told him. 'But actually I'm after a new favour. Could you get hold of a pc on the cheap?'

'Sure. You intend doing some outsource work?'

'Nope. There's this thing called the skating system. Sounds interesting.'

'A-one and a-two and a-three and a cha-cha,' counted Beryl to a floor of writhing Latin dancers. 'Maxine, lovey, you have to improve your inner-thigh awareness. I could drive a coach and horses between your legs; you've got one knee pointing east and the other west.'

The dance studio was an extension to the Clarks' beautiful little house 'halfway between Richmond Park and Mick Jagger', as Nina put it, to which Giancarlo responded, 'And if he wants lessons in slow foxtrot, he only has to ask.'

When the classes were over they walked in the garden.

'I've written to Lucia,' Nina told them. 'Sent a résumé of my life and a photo of the cat.'

They talked about their respective teaching. Nina paid

the mortgage with music lessons – but also taught adult numeracy for peanuts. In an overheated room in Harlesden High Street, she oversaw men and women with little schooling patiently learning arithmetic to improve their employment prospects.

'And you love it, I can tell,' said Beryl. Then the phone rang and while Beryl was gone Giancarlo asked about Martin's later years – so Nina gave him the lot.

'I don't know what to think. Any expert could provide a conclusive yes or no, but I daren't let them near it because of Mum. You see, Gian, there's a story we never told you.' And with a feeling that this would provide a sympathetic context in which to view her father's worst excesses in the 1960s, she explained to Giancarlo about his flight from his homeland.

'I often wondered if there was something,' said Gian. 'I meet a lot of Finns in the dance world and they don't like to stay away from Finland long. How dreadful. Martin's very homesickness must have been tainted with resentment.'

'Exactly.'

'But regarding the music, I don't know any more than you. I knew your father had seen the Sibelius symphony but I didn't realize he'd copied it out.'

Nina stopped walking. 'Sorry?'

Gian carried on serenely, 'There's no need for your mother to worry. Martin told me in confidence. I never repeated it.'

'Dad told you he'd seen the Sibelius no. 8?'

'Well, yes.'

'But *nobody* has seen the Sibelius no. 8.'

'I know. He explained all that. Martin said that a few years later it went up in flames.'

Nina gave a shout of laughter. She snorted and blew her nose. The hysteria infected Giancarlo. They stood there in the garden, snorting and giggling.

'Shall I begin at the beginning?' he suggested eventually.

'If you would.'

'You might not even remember but when you and Lu

were children, Beryl and I abandoned our cabaret at devastating cost to our reputation. I literally couldn't get the show on the road. When I was at my lowest ebb and your father was . . . well, one evening I went round to talk to him. I hoped he would feel less isolated to realize we can all behave irrationally and muck everything up. We talked for hours and he told me Sibelius's story – a perfectionist who threw his magnum opus on the fire. And your father said the music wasn't just legend; he had seen it.'

'When? How?'

'He didn't say. I'm sorry, Freddy, how frustrating for you. All I know is that Martin was privileged to see the score of a symphony Sibelius never released.'

Nina's brain seemed to be feeling its way through a gluey fog. 'Then it really *is* the lost Eighth?'

'Seems the likeliest explanation if you think it would be too much for an amateur. Of course, our cabaret still went to the fire, so to speak. Martin wasn't attempting to talk me out of chucking the show, that was already lost. No, your father's point, like mine to him, was that I wasn't alone. He'd seen the same calamity befall Sibelius.' Giancarlo produced a sour smile. 'I realize the parallel between a lauded classical composer and a ballroom dancer wouldn't go down well with everyone.'

But Nina wasn't listening. In her head she heard the cross-hatched strings, the keening clarinets, the foxfires.

'I see how Christine would be concerned to keep it in the family,' he went on. 'How many people know?'

'Mmmh? You mean, how many know Dad's manuscript is fishy? Well, there's you, me, Jussi and his father, Susan – and by extension André – my friend Duane, my ex-boyfriend Greg, an American named Richard Quentin and the Metropolitan Police.'

Giancarlo looked at her.

'That's a tale for another day.' Then Nina's composure blew like a nobbled nuclear reactor in an action movie. *Wheeeeeeeeeeeeeee!* She spun across the garden with aeroplane arms, a whirligig on the lawn. 'I'VE FOUND THE GREATEST LOST MASTERPIECE OF THE TWENTIETH CENTURY,' she shouted across the privet hedges and quiet wealth. 'Do you hear that, Richmond? I, little Nina Hannay—'

'Freddy. Nina.'

Her arms flopped to her sides. 'What's wrong?'

'Can you trust all those people? If Martin's history gets bandied about, Christine will be devastated.'

But now that the obfuscating doubt had been effaced, the truth was suddenly and glacially clear to her. 'Mum's worries are baseless. No one will care less about Dad, only the music.'

'Oh, sweetheart, you're wrong. The worst elements of the press could take a very nasty line.'

'They won't give column inches to some classical composer with a four-syllable name.'

'They might to a vicar who fled his country in a scandal involving a dead hero, and apparently smuggled out the world's only copy of a masterpiece that's worth a jackpot. It's a story with legs. And now Martin has gone they could write whatever they liked. There's no libel law for the dead.'

'I know.'

'Christine deserves better. She had a bad enough time when Martin was ill.'

In a more grown-up tone Nina said, 'I would trust most of those people to the ends of the earth, and the dodgy ones can't get hold of the score and who would believe them?' She added lightly, 'When Dad was ill I had a bad time too, Uncle Gian.'

'I know, love. I'm concerned about you as well, and what this symphony will stir up.'

'Mightn't it work as catharsis? If I try to see it as a gift to me from Dad? This wonderful work of genius?'

The symphony as a concept had its own colours independent of the actual music, and for months now they had been confused, shifting with the angle of her parallax view: an edging of migrainous worry-colours; a splash of Sibelius crimson, based on his name. But through it all, Nina had retained as her primary impression a sense of the symphony as *manuscript*, and its colourist was her father. The sensation was of grand blue arabesques as if from a scribe so inspired he was writing in the dark. She went on, 'Mightn't it heal old wounds?'

'That is exactly the line of thought that worries me, Freddy. Don't look to that music to be therapeutic. Your mother's instincts are right. It's trouble. They were two very troubled men, your father and Sibelius. It's not a happy combination. Their symphony isn't going to heal anything.'

42

She lay across Duane's leather chesterfield with her head on Jussi's lap and Kruger's head on her knees. Among Duane's furnishings in metal and matt black was his Bang and Olufsen. From its speakers flowed Sibelius's eighth symphony.

'We're the only people ever to hear this,' she kept squealing.

'So it would be nice to actually hear it, Nina,' responded Duane.

'*Modal flavouring; background of restless diminished chords,*' she quoted from the books. A drum roll thundered and Kruger woke up with a snort. The music slipped briefly into *Kalevala* rhythm, that trochaic drumbeat of the Finnish language, foreshadowing the choral finale. Nina could also hear some of the molten light of the sixth symphony, which Benjamin Britten had loathed with such fervour he accused the composer of writing it drunk.

'Listen up, it's that big climaxy bit. I always say there's two types of "*Ah!*" in music: there's the satisfying one when a chord is exactly right, but the other sort makes your hair stand on end and you go "*Aaaaaaaaghh!*" like you've been plugged into the national grid. It's a bit like orgasm – the sighing type is very nice, thank you, but not a patch on hollering like a stuck pig.'

'No doubt they'll put that in the sleeve notes,' said Duane.

'His is the most sublime sound ever produced by the human spirit.'

'That accolade might be convincing if you hadn't previously applied it to "I Am The Walrus", "Macarthur Park" and "Shine On You Crazy Diamond".'

Duane's immovable scepticism was eating into Nina's exhilaration. To buzz around in a euphoric fever felt like an actual duty, but first there was Giancarlo's foreboding and now Duane. Jussi, too, was getting pissed off. He had not been a passive accomplice: over the last few days they had worked together, cross-checking her books.

'What's your problem, mate?'

'Well, I'm not the statistician here but I reckon if something's highly improbable then it didn't happen. Maybe Giancarlo misunderstood.'

'No way.' That was in unison.

'All right, but tell me this. We're saying Nina's dad not merely copped a look at this music but had it long enough to copy out an entire cupboardful. How?'

Nina said, 'Let's start with a plausible who. The boy – I mean Veikko Virta – was from a powerful family that could have had access to a celebrity. And we know he was a crook.'

'But if crookery was all that was needed to get hold of this, Nina, somebody would have prised the draft out of that house while your Boston conductor was firing off telegrams and bashing his head against a wall.'

'His name was Serge Koussevitzky.'

'And all you *know* is Veikko peddled porn. So what was he doing at Ainola in the first place – taking dirty pictures of Sibelius in the sauna?'

Nina felt the weight of her upbringing and winced.

'And as your father *wasn't* a crook, why did this Veikko give it to him?'

'We've got it worked out,' put in Jussi. 'Veikko wangles his way in via his old man, gets his hands on the score and thinks he's on to a nice little earner. He's no musician so he's bound to show it to Nina's dad, who puts him straight that it isn't worth diddly squat on the black market.'

Bolstered by Jussi's confidence, Nina clarified the point. 'You see, this is worth a mint *now* but not back in the 1930s. Think about it. Nobody could have performed the thing because it was hooky and would have to be hidden away. But unlike some hooky painting, you don't get much pleasure from staring at a musical score. Unless you're a top-flight musician, and any conductor who got wind of it would have assumed Sibelius himself would release a printed version pronto. *We* know the Eighth would never see the light of day, but *they* didn't.'

'So Veikko goes back to his blue movies,' continued Jussi, 'and Nina's dad returns the symphony to the maestro, anonymous. But not before he's made a copy to feast his eyes on. It makes sense. You can't have a problem with that.'

Duane sighed like a musical glissando. 'Jussi, Nina, loves, I've got a major problem. You two just made it up.'

Nina flung herself into the couch cushions, irritation inflaming her like prickly heat. She burned to head straight for the nearest music college, slap the manuscript on a desk and watch academics slaver over it. But she could see Giancarlo's eyes dark with disapproval and her mother's headlines blazing in the redtops: **Dead Vicar in War Shame Scandal**.

'OK, so what are you saying?'

'Veikko Virta is your family's bogeyman so you've written a script that casts him as a bumbling idiot and your father as the hero. But there isn't a scrap of evidence to back it up. *And* it gets us no nearer explaining how a small-time crook smuggled fourteen folders of paper out of a fortress run by a paranoid superstar with a wife who was an armed sentry all on her own.'

'Ainola wasn't a fortress. It wasn't, Duane. Apparently

they didn't even lock the place at night. Until 1952, when they woke up one morning to discover they'd been burgled.' She laughed. 'My first thought was the burglar was Serge Koussevitzky on the ransack because he couldn't stand it any longer, but he was dead by then. It turned out the intruder was some escaped murderer. How about that? Only the best when you're a living legend.'

'Ha!' said Jussi.

'Anyway, if Sibelius didn't compose the bloody thing, who did?' Nina waved a hand at the Finnish forests that poured from Duane's speakers in further modulating shades of green. Her frustration was corroding her tolerance of the pseudo-orchestra. This particular passage had a sturdy simplicity that deserved testosterone, a manly augmentation of the sonorous trombones and tuba, not this smeared melody beneath a sheen of strings. The entire section gave off a cutesy gloss like satin in a Gainsborough portrait. She debouched her cassette from the tape deck and dropped it in her handbag with a clatter.

Duane had his answer ready. 'The smart money is on your father. No, Nina, he *didn't* have to write it in a foxhole on the Russian front. You found this in 1989, not 1939. He had fifty years to put it together. If he once copped a look at the real thing, all the better. Your father was an expat longing for home and this was the closest he got, writing the lost symphony.'

'Rubbish.'

With a new edge to his voice Duane said, 'Look, I'm throwing you two a lifeline. The alternative is bloody awful, you just haven't twigged it yet. Your dad copied the score before mailing it back? Why'd he need the players' and choir parts? He went to one hell of a load of trouble to have a score ready for *performance*. Which is fine if it's his own work and he intended starting a Sibelius tribute band in his old age. But it's a whole different shooting match if that music was stolen, and smuggled out of the country, and dates from a time when half the world's orchestras would've given their kidneys to get hold of it. Don't go there, Nina. Your dad wrote an *hommage*. End of story.'

This time it was Greg who was in a bathrobe, pink and pine-scented from his sauna and his plunge-pool. Nina had forgotten how Finnishly clean Greg was, how fastidious and sweet-smelling. She had a vision of him in their early days, in a health spa – flailing out of the bubbling water of the Jacuzzi, actually gagging because a couple had wandered in from the gym area for a soak, still sweating in their lycra. 'There are fucking *rules*!' he'd yelled behind him, stumbling away across the tiles.

Today Greg was muzzy from a very bad night: a pop princess he'd been dating had finished with him. There had followed an eviscerating row in which he had stopped her leaving by locking the front door and throwing the keys out of the window.

'But Greg, love—' began Nina.

'Heartless bitch,' he raved. 'She *knows* I'm not well, I've been having dizzy spells and there's a pain behind my eye. Just here.' Greg stabbed at his eyeball with a vicious forefinger. The white was already bloodshot. A fuzzy zigzag ran from his iris like a scrawl.

'Lovey, have you been trying to demonstrate that a relationship with a chart diva is better than a poke in the eye with a sharp stick?'

'Not funny, Nina.'

'When did you first tell her you were ill? When you fell for the girl and started feeling insecure?'

'It's not made up! I'm a sick man.'

It was evening before she recounted the conversation with Duane. Greg scoffed at her.

'You say Veikko wouldn't have found a market? I bet he had some pretty shady contacts abroad.'

'Yes, porn kings. The last I heard, they don't do thieved symphonies on the side.'

'Crooks know other crooks, and this would've been an

absolute goldmine. Nina, you're wrong about a buyer needing to hide it away. Any *American* could've bought it without breaking a single law. Which meant the seller could name his price. The US hadn't signed up to the copyright convention. Any American who got hold of that score could've performed the thing coast to coast, fetching up in Carnegie Hall if the fancy took him.'

'That can't be right.'

'Hell, I'm a producer, I could copyright you blue in the face. I'd guess that back in Veikko's day, that unpublished symphony wasn't covered *anywhere* beyond local law. The minute it left Finland it was naked as a newborn babe. Therefore – goldmine!'

'Greg, you knew Dad. He would never have schemed to defraud anyone and least of all Sibelius.' She suffered one of her moments of drenching empathy. The essence of her father was in her eyes and ears. It was disordered, and there was a lemon-sour tang like slow bending notes from a blues guitar, but nothing cynically self-serving that would fit a fraudster and a thief.

'Nina, *I'm* OK with Duane's theory that your dad bodged it together himself during all those decades stranded in bloody Essex. *You're* the one who insists on dragging this Veikko into the story with some aborted racket. I'm only pointing out—'

'That as rackets go, it would have been a corker.'

'Of a lifetime. The score is protected now, of course; the US has ratified the convention. I could give you half an hour on performing rights, too, but not tonight. It's nearly 2 a.m. and I got to be up at lunchtime.'

43

When Lucia and Richard both landed at Heathrow on the same day, Nina should not have been so astonished; as a statistician she knew that rare events tend to cluster. She caught herself thinking of it as a good omen.

Nina couldn't pretend Richard was just a friend from the past but she insisted he wasn't a dangerous one; the Tokyo job had now been extended to three years. Richard was simply not available to her. I have become ... what? She searched for the expression. Comfortably numb, decided Nina. Her judgement failed to remind her that she had made that assumption once before, driving to his Piccadilly hotel.

'Jussi, you remember the American who wrote to me from Japan? He's in London on a trip and he's asked me to dinner. Is that OK? The point being—'

'You two have a scene once? No probs. I'm cool.'

'Thanks, love.'

'I'd kind of prefer you didn't screw him but ...'

'No, Jussi, I was not asking—'

'... just so long as there's no porkies.'

'No *what*?'

'Porky-pies, lies. If it transpires, you'll tell me, yeah? Hey,

I'm worried about Fearless. Think I might shin up that tree with some tuna.'

Fearless was Nina's ironically named housecat, who hadn't clocked the fact that the flat was now dog-free. Nina had collected her mother from Heathrow and driven her and Kruger home to Brancaster. ('Oh, thank you for liberating the poor little lad from kennels, dear!')

Nina had spent much of her life subservient to the whims of animals: it was very easy to love a man who would climb a twenty-foot tree with a plate of tuna fish to coax down a pampered cat. Whenever she looked into the future she unthinkingly pictured Jussi there.

'Why hasn't anyone married him?' her mother demanded. 'Are you sure there isn't something he's not telling you?'

'Oh Mum! Jussi's an open book.'

About everything: the girl he lived with for years until she left him for a fashion photographer who promised to launch her career; even the prostitute on his sixteenth birthday, who demanded cash upfront and said she'd meet him round the corner. Which was the last he saw of her.

Nina knew her feelings for Jussi were of a different species from the convulsion she had always called love in the past. Therefore she should have known better.

'Hell, you look wonderful,' said Richard.

'But how are you?'

'After day-long meetings with an eight-time-zone jetlag? Not fresh as a daisy.'

There were marks of chronic tiredness about him: a loss of weight that angled the cheekbones, a jittery exhaustion in his eyes whenever the smile left them. As they sat down, the restaurant was half empty. After the main course, when she went off to the loo, Nina was astonished to discover the place was chock-full and chirruping like an aviary. She hadn't noticed.

He asked whether she was involved with anyone and Nina replied, 'Yes. Happily. And you?' to which he answered,

'Approximately,' and she didn't invite him to expand and didn't like the way her stomach jolted.

Richard was clearly a man who hadn't talked about himself in a long time so Nina let him, gently drawing out pent-up grievances against the company that had packed him off to do two men's jobs, reeling from airport to airport.

'Is your Boston house empty?' she asked in a pause.

'Rented. My illustrious father takes care of that and no doubt wrings the last cent out of the intimidated tenants.' Richard smiled. 'Let's change the subject. There's few things less attractive than a grown man in full-blown complaint about his father. Makes him sound like a thwarted kid.'

Perhaps not with this particular father. Recently, Nina had come across an article about him in one of the Sunday supplements.

> This prosecuting attorney is no Kennedy-style Bostonian, but neither does he share his far-right platform with the usual suspects. Richard Quentin III has no time for the traditional "free speech and liberty" right-wingers of America. Regarding their extreme manifestation, the gun-toting "I'll say what I goddamn like" survivalists, he would not spit on them if they were on fire. This is a short-sharp-shock prosecutor, a hunter down of obscure laws, curtailer of freedoms, shutter-up of dissent. This is a Banned-In-Boston Bostonian.

The son signalled to the wine waiter, and Nina wondered, Is that air of easy command born of the numerals after the family name? When his fingers reached for his glass, the memory of them making love to her scorched through Nina. She was suddenly aware of Richard looking at her, a smile playing in his eyes, and with a mix of misgivings and thrill she imagined he had read the desire in her face.

He said, 'I have something for you.' From somewhere he produced a rose, one long stem. But not the usual clichéd florist-shop bloom. This was a garden rose, ivory and pale gold suffused with carmine. The peace rose.

'You once mentioned the name,' said Richard.

There was even a scent, and though she grew peace roses in Harlesden, Nina was catapulted back to Seaton Bois. 'Thank you. For you to remember—'

'Mostly I'm an ignoramus about flowers but there's a story behind this rose, did you know? I read it in an airline magazine and thought of you.'

Nina was about to leap in with 'I've known the legend all my life, isn't it wonderful?' She stopped. She made herself shut up. She said instead, 'What story?'

He stroked a petal. 'Seems it was bred in France shortly before the war. Then the Nazis came. The grower couldn't bear the idea of his beautiful rose falling into their blood-stained hands, but how could he keep it safe? In the end, the American ambassador smuggled the seedlings out of the country – on the very last plane to leave before France fell. The rose was then quietly propagated around the world. It was launched after VJ Day in a celebratory release of flying doves, and when the United Nations assembled for the very first time, each delegate was given a single peace rose as a symbol, a blazon. Just one stem in a vase. Peace.'

Nina thought, If I open my mouth, I'll say something irrevocable that I'll hate myself for when I get home to Jussi. She sat quietly, turning the stem in her fingers.

They left the restaurant after midnight and Richard walked Nina to her car. He was flying back tomorrow lunchtime 'after a breakfast meeting'.

'Richard, at this rate they'll kill you.'

'*They* don't know about this one. It's with a head-hunter. So wish me luck.' Then he kissed her cheek. 'That green lace against your white skin,' he said. 'It's so beautiful I could cry.'

When she reached Brickstone Road, Nina realized the journey home had failed to register the faintest trace on her memory. That she might have been driving in her sleep.

44

Beryl had always been quick and sharp. 'Don't marry Jussi if you're in love with another man.' Giancarlo dragged the wrought-iron table on to the lawn. She threw across her shoulder, 'Not there, Gian. Left a bit.'

'That's three inches south-south-west, is it, dear?' asked her husband mildly.

'Mum, Nina did not say—'

'Oh yes she did, Lu. Don't, Nina. There's enough divorce in the world already.' And Lu laughed.

The adult Lucia who was Mrs Daniel McIntyre had greeted Nina at the door with 'God, all those chestnuts about feeling like you've never been away – you could para- phrase for an hour but they'd still be the truth. And look at you! That's a decent pair of pins you've got there, girl.'

'Lu!' Beryl had objected. 'What a thing to say.'

'God, it's good to see you, kid. I feel ten years old again, on stage with a tea towel over my head and you behind the curtain singing "*They can't hide, they can't flee, I'll track them down, you just watch me.*"'

'Yes, lyrics were never my strong suit. Hello, Lu!'

Beryl said, 'You'll have to be quicker off the mark than that, Nina, to get a word in edgeways.'

Lu was small and dark. She didn't have her parents' beauty but there was her old enticing air of mischief. Nina, overwhelmingly grateful that she hadn't changed, experienced an extreme sense of freedom, of letting go, like a gargantuan sigh. She had returned to the one person who knew her. This had no counterpart in her feeling for Gian and Beryl, with whom she was, as ever, in love to the point of hero-worship. Faced with Beryl's unfussy femininity and the liquid grace of her walk, Nina always felt a spasm of resolve to dress more smartly, and not slouch so much, and stop saying fuck so often.

She guessed Lu was very attractive to men: probably more so than Nina's indisputably beautiful sister. Susan was presently at 39,000 feet, pointing towards Heathrow. Yet another good omen buggered, decided Nina, who had been commanded to turn up at Terminal 3 for half six tomorrow morning to chauffeur her sister to Norfolk.

Beryl's barbed comment about divorce had missed its mark on Lu. Nobody was in love with anybody else. 'We'd find it easier to accept if they were,' agreed Gian and Beryl. Lu had simply decided she didn't want to live with her husband any more and their daughter would cope perfectly well.

'How?' demanded Beryl. 'The poor thing will be tossed back and forth across the Atlantic like some parcel lost in the mail!'

'Melanie's a coping sort of girl,' said Lucia. 'And she's at boarding school anyway, loving it.'

'Nonsense.'

'*Mamma, ascoltami*. Melanie will be fine. *Papito*, can you hand me the scones? Nina – cream? Or do you value your arteries?'

When Lu asked, 'So what's Jussi like?' Beryl replied instantly.

'Extremely handsome. Reminded me of what's-his-name.'

'No kidding, Mum.'

'You know who I mean. The TV heart-throb. Richard Chamberlain.'

'*Really?* Hell, I call that a result! Actually, I thought of you a couple of months back. Some oldie-goldie channel was rerunning *Kildare* and it was the one where he's in love with that girl who's epileptic and she's a surfing fanatic and one day the surf's up and she has a fit on the crest of a wave and drowns. Remember?'

'Find me something that will serve as a surfboard and I'll act out the entire episode here on the lawn, grand mal convulsions and all. She and Jim recited poetry to each other: *Tyger, tyger, burning bright.*'

'Tyger,' repeated Gian. 'Didn't we have a cat?'

'Who was previously called Fluffy,' said Nina. 'Which reminds me, one of my strays is a ginormous tom I call Charlie Wade. Do you—?'

'Oh my God, he was a patient who was grossly over-weight and . . . oh my *God*, he had this rhyme about himself: "Charlie Wade makes lots of shade." '

' "Fifty whales on fifty scales . . ." '

' "Wouldn't weigh what Charlie weighed!" '

'You two should get therapy,' said Beryl.

'Did you see him in *Shogun*?'

'Yes, Lu.'

'*Thorn Birds?*'

'Yes, Lu.'

'Hey, but I bet you didn't know he was—'

'Yes, Lu! I did. My friend Duane told me.'

'Yeah, I was heartbroken, too. Thirty-four years old but I'd never given up hope that some day he'd marry me.'

Duane had mentioned it to Nina one midnight on a Samaritan shift, with the careless authority of assumed prerogative. She had stared, then yelled with laughter. Duane had responded grumpily, 'Don't you dare say "What a waste"!' The revelation about her childhood fantasies had reminded her of another eye-opener when, emerging into teens, the thought had hit Nina the vicar's daughter that religion was a human construct: and that on the balance of probabilities, underscored by the memory of all those unanswered prayers, she couldn't see any sound reason for believing a word of it.

When tea was over they watched a video: Lu and an energetic Melanie in Rome last April – with Nonna.

'*Buon. Gior. No,*' articulated Nonna on the assumption that the camera was partially deaf. Then her puffy hands flew to her face and there was a coquettish laugh. She was not much fatter and only marginally more jowly, and after the first shock of recognition Nina saw something unexpected: she saw Lu in her, in the shared hairline and upward twitch of the mouth at the left corner. It had skipped Giancarlo and shown up in Lu. You don't notice these things when you're a child.

Afterwards, out of earshot of Gian and Beryl, Lucia said, 'Tell me about Jussi properly.'

'Well, he's funny and kind and very lovable, and I wish my mother could see it.'

'Yes, but your mother's disapproval isn't a basis for marriage, is it?' reasoned Lu. 'If you'd married all the men your mother slagged off, you'd have a male harem including every Labour prime minister and the Rolling Stones.'

'Now there's a thought.'

'And this Richard?'

'Eight thousand miles away.'

'But still in love with you? Tell me to mind my own business, kiddo, people do it all the time.'

But it was inarguable that Richard was still in love with Nina. The day he flew home, she had received a delivery from a florist. A dozen peace roses. Nina expected Lu to laugh. She didn't. She said, 'Run it past me again. He knew you weren't single but sent roses *to your home?*'

'I can only think he didn't hear me properly. He can't have done.'

'Tell me Jussi wasn't there when they arrived.'

But it was Jussi who had answered the door. Nina, astounded, stammered, 'This doesn't mean . . . It was only dinner.'

He interrupted her. 'Better hammer the stalks, yeah, or they'll wilt.'

'Richard couldn't have heard properly,' said Nina again.

Lu just raised her eyebrows. 'Jussi sounds a good guy. I'd stick with him. Oh, and you can help me find a flat.'

'And a job? I warn you, they're thin on the—'

'Lord, no, I walked into a job the day my plane touched down. Simultaneous translator working for some Americans in the West End. Top dollar.'

'If I'd known the West End was paying people to translate American,' said Nina crossly, 'I would never have gone back to music.'

45

'*Crescendo* is Italian for growing. Therefore getting louder. Same root as the word crescent, because the moon grows.'

'But we still say crescent when the moon shrinks, so that's just stupid,' responded her student, whose name was Rebecca, and with whom this banter was part of the deal. 'Anyway, I *know* crescendo, Nina. It's that other thing I can't remember.'

'Plagal cadence,' said Nina patiently and sang an *Amen*.

'I want one of your spelling-out thingies. Six letters beginning with P,' continued Rebecca as if it were the *Times* crossword. 'What words begin with P?'

Thinking of some of them, Nina sighed. 'How about . . . Pandas like abusing gherkins at lunchtime. Pants look absolutely gorgeous around Loretta.'

Rebecca shrieked. 'No, do *piss*.'

'Pissing lager at George accelerates lunacy. Meanwhile back at this music lesson.'

'Bor-*ing*.'

Nina was inclined to agree. It seemed to Nina that of all subjects on the face of the planet, music is the least rewarding to drum into the head of an unwilling pupil. Rebecca was sixteen and according to her father, 'The girl is perfectly capable of passing the grade exams if only she will apply herself.' Nina would rummage through the syllabus for just enough hilarity to keep Rebecca awake. And then add a sprinkling of obscene mnemonics.

She felt sorry for her. At Becks's age, she thought, what was I doing? Lashing out against my childhood. Trailing home at 10 p.m. with my school uniform determinedly askew and my features smudged from marijuana – preferably just as the parochial church council was leaving by the vicarage door.

Nina remembered her father's voice as she came up the path. 'Christine, you've tried tearing into the girl. You've cried and threatened. Nothing has worked. At least *try* my way. Greet her with, "Good evening, dear. Your dinner's in ruins but I've made sandwiches."'

And if Mum had taken his advice, thought Nina now, maybe I would have jacked in my rebellion before a really nasty evening at the police station.

Susan had once shot at her, 'No wonder I was such a well-behaved teenager – Nina at sixteen constituted aversion therapy. God, my poor childhood!'

'You had it bloody easy,' Nina had flung back. 'You weren't even born when Dad—'

'Stop it, you two!' Their mother. 'And Nina, don't let your father hear you. He didn't choose to have a breakdown!'

Her earlier teens. Nina had been asked out by a folk singer at their local club. He was twenty-one. She was fourteen and her parents had never set eyes on him. Her mother was out at a charity day. Her father said, 'He's picking you up in his car?'

'Brentwood High Street.'

'Well, you can't trust the buses. I'll give you a lift.'

He had never worried about people. It was her mother who imagined murderous rapists lurking behind the smiles of strangers, never her father. She was a teenager, she would date them with or without parental permission. He'd been a teenager himself.

It had not dawned on Nina before now, how unusual it was for a man of that generation to be quite so free of all the common paranoia and prejudices. 'Christine, wearing his hair down to his waist is a fashion, not an indication of moral turpitude,' he had insisted about some other hapless boyfriend. And, 'Of course rock bands are singing about sex, so did Frank Sinatra, it's what makes the world go round.' And after an evening with Duane, 'It's no business of ours who the man chooses for his bed. All we need know is he's a good friend to our daughter.'

He did give her that ride to Brentwood, dropping her off with a wave. But only after a tearful quarrel in the kitchen when he harangued her until Nina promised that the moment she got in that stranger's car she would buckle up her seat belt. Car crash catastrophes were another thing altogether.

Now she tried to drag Rebecca's attention back to the piano.

'You'll like this one,' she said, 'because it's horrible. Horror movies sometimes use it.' Nina played a middle C followed by F-sharp.

'*Gross!*'

'Exactly. Called the Devil's interval, or *diabolus in musica*. Medieval churchmen believed the Devil had corrupted it.'

'But as we don't believe in devils and it's yuck, why do people like me have to learn it?'

'Well, jazz uses it and Jimi Hendrix did, and—'

And recognition hit Nina like a thud in the midriff. Of course. All the clues had been telling her the same thing, and she had not been listening.

Sibelius had also used it – to great effect in his Fourth, hammering it out against a dark, brooding background. In Nina's symphony it was there again, this time played against something jolly, tempering the sweetness. Self-referential but with a twist.

'Nina? You've gone off on a mong.'

'Just a moment, please, Becks.'

Devils. The god of the forest was not the only genie of those gloomy northern woods, there was also the Demon. His was a mumbling forest with strangled, desperate under-growth struggling for the light, and gargoyles louring from its knuckled trunks. In winter the trees were coated with ice, hung with ice; icicles rubbed together in the wind and sang like the cries of ghost-children. Sometimes creatures crept out of that alien darkness – shrunken humanoids, to insinuate themselves into the lives of innocent human families. Changelings. Trolls.

The *Kalevala* chorus, forest music, the *diabolus in musica* . . . The sense of disquiet that for the past weeks had woken with Nina and walked with her, a softly snarling menace, now bared its claws and roared. Fear. But I don't know why! she thought in chaos.

'*Nina?*'

'Sorry, Becks. Where were we? Plagal cadences.'

'P . . . p . . . pelicans leer at gussets and laugh,' decided Rebecca. 'Penises leave a glow after looting. Prick lubrication adds great arousal, Lenny.'

'Amen to that,' murmured Nina.

46

Did the entire symphony tell a story? Well, perhaps not anything quite as intellectually crass as a *story*, but an evocation of tales from the *Kalevala*?

This was where Jussi came into his own. In his school-days Finland still taught in the bardic tradition, with poetry and folk songs. He knew his *Kalevala*. To Nina, his lively collaboration was a welcome sunspot in her abruptly darkening agitation.

The choral text was taken from Rune 41: Väinämöinen's Harp Songs. 'Why've they translated it as harp?' demanded Jussi. 'It's the kantele!'

'I know. Like a zither.'

'Väinämöinen invents the first musical instrument out of fishbone. It's a creation myth. But not a bloody *harp*.'

For context, Nina had to start with earlier runes. Unfortunately, the only verse translation was high Victorian and could make toes curl. Wading through verbal mud thick enough to suck her boots off, Nina read of a boat, a tempest, a monster pike. A man of courage was needed. Väinämöinen was that man. First came a lot of ranting at his companions: 'Feeble . . . insane . . . witless!' though in Nina's opinion they were doing their best. He polished off the pike with magic, and like any self-respecting hero handed the fish over to 'the Maidens' and demanded dinner. Apparently, they rendered it 'toothsome'. Then the hero announced that what this expedition lacked was a harp fashioned from the bones. He called upon his colleagues but of course it was the pike-slaying story all over again: they were useless and Väinämöinen had to do it himself. The first musical instrument was born.

Nina read this tale rolling her eyes and tutting like somebody's mad granny. It didn't help that earlier she'd found a character called Soppy Hat. 'This stuff is Moomins gone homicidal!'

With a certain *Schadenfreude*, it struck her that Väinämöinen got his comeuppance from posterity. One of the Sibelius tone poems depicts his fruitless attempts at impressing some less complaisant maiden; the music shrieks out her scathing laughter – and those shrieks went on to inspire the soundtrack for the shower scene in *Psycho*. Väinämöinen would be mocked on countless screens, to innumerable viewers, in perpetuity.

Jussi said, 'Look, the choral stuff uses the next rune along and you'll like that.'

So Nina moved on, and realized with a lighter heart that this was nowhere near as silly. It told of Väinämöinen picking up his invention and playing it.

> *Now resounded marvellous music,*
> *All of Northland stopped and listened.*
> *Every creature in the forest,*
> *All the beasts that haunt the woodlands . . .*

'Oh, Jussi, it's Hiawatha! *From the hollow reed he fashioned / Flutes so musical and mellow / That the brook, the Sebowisha / Ceased to murmur in the woodland.*'

'Well, yeah, the guy borrowed it from us. Want me to run the tape back to the movement before the choir comes in? If that's a storm, we've nailed him.'

It was a storm. The music rolled and reared. That wasn't all: a recurrent voice on oboe leaped away from the strings, and the last time it was repeated the theme was modified into a minor, mournful, dying chant. 'Oh dear God, it's the pike. Väinämöinen's killed it. Jussi, tell me I'm imagining this.'

'It's the pike, all right.'

'Oh God. Sibelius was fascinated by creation myths. He did fire, air and water in tone poems. Our first movement opens in the same colours as *Tapiola*. Could that—? Remind me how Väinämöinen created the landscape.'

'He comes out of the ocean on to barren land called Death's Domain and commands the Spirit of Arable to plant it. Life out of death, sort of thing.'

Jussi reran the tape to the beginning and leafed through the *Kalevala*.

> *Birches rose from all the marshes,*
> *In the loose soil grew the alders,*
> *In the mellow soil the lindens;*
> *Junipers were also growing,*
> *Junipers with clustered berries,*
> *Berries on the hawthorn branches . . .*

She could see it all: the springy marshes, the berry-bejew-elled fields, the mossy, spice-scented forest under the thin white nightlight of a northern summer. These were not quiet lands. Väinämöinen's later songs would tell of hares and bears, wolves and weasels, slinking lynxes. There were squirrels stop-start-darting across the pungent forest floor.

Then, as the music developed, it veered away from that benign domain. Across its pastoral geniality came the clang of those two notes, shockingly ugly, and again, and again, swinging like a wrecking ball. The *diabolus in musica*. This forest was suffering. Nina was aware of a giddy delusion that the kitchen table was pitching away from her: the light-headed mélange of intoxication and buzzing terror that comes with the approach of confirmation that a discovery is real – and that it's momentous.

'If we're right,' she said unsteadily, 'then the symphony starts with the creation myth for Finland, and later gets to the storm that culminates in the greatest creation of all, the musical instrument. I think this bit with the Devil evokes winter closing in, but how does that fit with the myths theme?'

'Dunnó. And there's the whole second movement to account for.'

'That's got the theme Sibelius reused for his friend's funeral. The movement starts off ice-blue and angry, and ends up sky-blue and lyrical. What other creation—?'

'Väinämöinen tells a yarn about how metal was born. What d'you call it? Bog iron.'

Nina thought, Please tell me I'm not listening to a slow movement about bog iron.

'Plus the first cure for pain.'

'Yes?'

'He's done his knee in and it's killing him,' recounted Jussi, who was no bard himself. 'The Old Man of the Hill takes away his suffering with a balm from God. So that's another one. The power of healing.'

The newborn forest suffering its winter, the hero in pain, and God's merciful creation of both spring and the power to heal. 'Jussi, I think we've got it,' said Nina.

She understood her fear now. Nina knew what Greg would say: 'This will go platinum! Record buyers are always mad for musical pictures. Think of *The Sorcerer's Apprentice* and *Danse Macabre* and Beethoven's *Pastoral*. And Nina, if this hits the CD charts, the tabloids will snout out your dad's history like pigs after truffles.'

There had been a small but life-threatening realignment of the tectonic plates of her world. And her mother's world. A symphony that told a story: the concept summoned the metaphor, was inextricable from the metaphor, about having a life of its own. There was no chance of holding this back. It would make a break for freedom all by itself.

'No, Nina!' Jussi put his arm round her. 'You're safe. After all, no one's going to shop you.'

'I can think of one who might,' she said.

'Mummy says you've got Daddy's copies of the *Kalevala*.'

'Only because Mum asked if you wanted any books, Susan, and you said—'

'Nina, I'm not accusing you of anything. Please can we get through one phone call without you flying off the handle? But you've had them for months and I would suggest it's my turn.'

And it probably was.

'So when you come up to Brancaster next weekend, will you bring both translations plus the Finnish original? I'm thinking of learning Finnish.'

At which Nina's weak hope was doused, that her sister's request was innocent. Their mother had told her about the *Kalevala* and Susan was clever enough to wonder whether Dad's copy might be marked up. Which it was. Pencil marks all over the harp songs. The literary Susan was perfectly capable of recognizing a creation myth when she saw one, and if she passed *that* on to some musician . . .

'Susan, must you? I'll have to shell out for replacements.'

And if Susan makes some obnoxious remark about my inferior finances she can stuff the bloody *Kalevala*, decided Nina. But even Susan didn't do that.

'Perhaps I'll just take the Finnish and order translations from Hatchard's. I can read them to Martina,' she added sweetly. 'How Daddy would have been proud.'

47

Nina dreamed, guilt-dreams. But not about her mother; the pangs that gnawed her by day ceded their place at night to that other mother, married to that other difficult Finn.

That other drama queen. Their second daughter, an acclaimed actress, always said he could have made a living on the stage. During a trip abroad he was ill, and terrified everyone with messages ending 'Farewell!' Ah yes, thought Nina, I've been here before. It wasn't only Aino who protected him, his entire nation was in on the act, in a mind-boggling conspiracy of mollycoddling. Even his age was unmentionable. But despite Nina's awed respect for the woman who in some parallel universe might have run an army, she suspected the Sibeliuses were one of those families where you admire the long-suffering wife but it's the selfish husband who enchants you.

His charisma was shaped by lifelong intimacy with womanhood: raised by a mother, two grandmothers and a couple of aunts – then his beloved wife and daughters. The tragedy of his life wasn't the eighth symphony, it was the loss of their little Kirsti from typhus. And he had the virtues of his failings: he was tolerant of failings in others, and as money meant so little to him he was a soft touch, so plenty tapped him. He kept his friends, and those he worked with the closest adored him. Sibelius was extraordinarily funny, frequently kind, endlessly patient.

That granite-hewn individual never existed; he was ever a crayfish-and-champagne man at heart (and at ninety he pointed out that he was still going strong while all the doctors who forbade him to drink or smoke were dead). Behind the shaved cranium of the solemn neo-aristocrat was always the spirit of his youthfully lush hair and lively moustache. Even the depressive gloom that he hawked and carked into the diary he himself called a 'spittoon' was interspersed with sparkling letters and endearing recipes, including punch based on brandy, wine – and jam.

So could it be, Nina wondered, that his legend is faulty in other respects, too? Was he really a more contradictory character than most, or might we all look like that under the biographer's lens?

Duane said of *course* tango is a gay dance: with all that intensity and attitude, tango is irredeemably high camp, a musical incarnation of a slit dress on a gay icon. He decided to take lessons.

'I need something physical to remind me there's life before death, but if I spend any more time in the gym I'll look like Arnold fucking Schwarzenegger.'

His new muscularity gave him a heavy-duty look at odds with both the sleepy disorder of his curling hair and the critical intelligence of his eyes. Nina thought of the genres of gay appearance he liked to catalogue for her in mocking enjoyment, and wondered what possible phylum would include Duane.

He turned to Jussi. 'How does it work? Do I need a couple, him to demonstrate and her to partner me?'

'Nah, I'll do it,' said Jussi instantly. 'The way true tangueros learned in Buenos Aires, man to man.'

Nina's heart turned over. Not every straight man would

happily volunteer to spend a couple of hours a week in Duane's arms.

She, too, was dancing again, an occupation to deflate that ballooning dread. Nina blew her Rebecca money on Tony Delterfield. It was the same studio, his busy shelves now enhanced by a fez and a Henry vacuum cleaner, under whose affable gaze Nina, proficient at last, consummated her lifelong affair with tango argentino.

It seemed to her that the erotic charge of dancing tango, as opposed to watching it, owed little to the man's embrace and not much more to the sexuality of the music. What did it was the *discipline*. The honed precision of the steps, the execution of exquisite bodily movement within the profound restrictions of free will exacted by the dance, recalled for Nina experiences of sex when she was lovingly, consensually, forbidden to writhe. The person she became, the tango dancer with her haughtily heightened femininity, was something of poetry. It was about the strength in her back, the torque in her hips, the taut of her calves, the whip of her foot. She became the cadences of Maya Angelou's *Phenomenal Woman*.

So it was all the nicer that she had an audience. Duane.

Tony didn't mind his sitting in. 'Argentinian men can still tango together,' he explained. 'It's the upside of a machismo culture.'

'I don't understand,' said Nina.

Duane did. 'If queers don't exist, you've no need to worry about your friends mistaking you for one.'

At home there was a more unsettling tweak at her sexual feelings. Richard had written to say the meeting with the head-hunter had been fruitful.

> To cut a long story short (not my paramount skill.
> I am credited as the only man ever to get the word
> antepenultimate into a telex) the new position
> means working out of Boston and controlling the
> European office. Two men's jobs again, but the
> European office is in London.

Nina replied with a flustered letter so concerned with saying she was happy with her partner that she forgot to congratulate him.

'So has Richard always been single?' Lucia asked over a trattoria lunch.

'No. Divorced.'

'Recently?'

'Immediately before we met. I gather it was a match pushed on him by the family when he returned from Vietnam. Very WASP, very suitable and very much a money-grabbing bitch. He was sore.'

'Is that a one-off, or is sore something he's prone to? Sorry, none of my business. Children?'

'No.'

'What if the guy's resolved to sweep you out of Jussi's arms?'

'Maybe I can't be swept.'

'Good. Jussi's adorable.' Lu had come to Harlesden and Jussi cooked. ('Hope I've rendered it toothsome. Mind the bones.' He had found her a pike.)

Talking now with her mouth full, Lu went on, 'There'd be one advantage to Richard – you'd mostly be on opposite sides of the Atlantic. If Dan and I had done that, we'd probably still be having swinging-from-the-chandeliers sex instead of a divorce.'

To Gian and Beryl's dismay, their granddaughter wasn't coming to England for the summer but was off to some camp in the Rockies. 'Mel's always been happiest in paramilitary organizations,' explained Lu cheerfully. 'All my fault, I expect, for not breast-feeding.'

'DIDN'T YOU, LU?' responded Nina in an affectionate parody of Lucia's own pitch. Other diners were turning to look.

'God, no. Breasts are sex organs. I said to Dan, imagine if your willie produced milk. How would you like the thought of—'

A passing waiter stopped dead. Lu told him to mind his own business in fast Italian.

'Oh yeah – Mum and Dad tell me you're plugging every possible scenario of dance scores into a computer. What is it? You don't have to kill yourself impressing Giancarlo and Beryl Clark. You'll always be their little Freddy.'

'No, it's interesting. Though maybe only to statisticians.' Nina explained about first-past-the-post systems and the problems when they fail to give an outright winner. 'I'm analysing made-up scores until I hit on the method least likely to land them with a champion that's against all common sense.'

Lu said, 'Or the ballroom fraternity will have collective hysterics like the world's started spinning backwards and we'll all be dead by Tuesday. *Capito*. Hey, I tell you, girl, I'm grateful to Nonna for the language. This translation lark is making me money hand over fist.'

Jussi's weekend classes were over for the summer so he joined her in Brancaster again.

The house was too small for four adults and a crying baby, particularly when one of them just wasn't baby-orientated. The arrival of a screaming, colicky infant when Nina was eleven, to a mother worn grey and frazzled, rather spoiled the whole theme for her. Luckily Jussi had enough baby orientation for the two of them. He padded up and down the garden with Martina in his arms, singing her tango ballads.

'Hey, Carlos Gardel, d'you want a coffee?' called Nina.

'Shhhh! I've just got her off!'

'Well, Nina, you won't have to employ a nanny when your time comes,' said Susan, laughing.

But it wasn't all laughter. While the other two put Martina to bed, Susan beckoned Nina into the sitting room and shut the door. 'I want to know what you're up to with that symphony.'

'Oh, Susan!'

'Do you know the name Nils-Eric Fougstedt? He reported seeing the Sibelius no. 8 in the composer's bookcase. Seven volumes including separate parts. Just like Daddy's. And one of the grandchildren rummaged through Sibelius's desk one afternoon and reported that the music was a sort of cantata. That's a choir, isn't it? Just like Daddy's.'

'This is fantasy.'

'What key is it in?'

'Why?'

'What key is it in?'

Nina thought, If Mum insists I hand over the manuscript, Susan will check it out. And if I've lied . . . 'It's *anchored* in G minor,' she said cuttingly. 'Like "Shine On You Crazy Diamond". Why?'

'The archives include a short sketch from no. 8 – in G minor.'

Where the hell did she find that out? demanded Nina of her head. Even I didn't bloody know that. She said, 'If you start brandishing your wild theories—'

'If they were wild, you wouldn't be in such a panic. I want a copy.'

'I'll burn the fucking thing first.'

'Really, Nina? Funny how people keep destroying that symphony yet somehow it bobs back up again like a message in a bottle. Anyone would think it *wanted* to be heard.'

Jussi still hadn't registered their mother's antipathy. 'Dad's over next week, Mrs Hannay, and he'd love to catch up. I'm thinking about a dinner party.'

'Thank you, but parties tire me,' was her mother's ungracious response, making Nina blush for him.

By Sunday evening she was grateful to be out of there. She broke the speed limit most of the way home down the M11, splattering insects until the Old-English-white paintwork of her E-type looked as if it had been in a bullfight. When they ground to a halt in the enchained traffic of the

North Circular, Jussi said, 'Have you thought any more about us two moving to Seriousville?' Then he caught the look on her face before she could hide it. 'Nina? You got something on your mind? If so, I'd rather share it.' And when she didn't reply, 'Hey, you up the duff?'

Nina managed a laugh. 'No, Jussi. Sorry.'

Then a different intuition prodded him. 'Is it that American?'

'I haven't been seeing Richard,' she said quickly. 'Only that one dinner.'

'Was he why you suddenly wanted to clear off to Buenos Aires last Feb?'

'But that was . . . before us.'

'He still out in Tokyo?'

'He's home now. Boston. And he'll be coming to London.'

Every word I'm saying is calamitous, thought Nina. 'Jussi, I'm happy with you.'

'But not in love with me. OK, you never said you were. Not something a person can force. You in love with him, Nina?'

In agony, she thought: I must not keep silent. Silence, that recurring bloody theme. She thought of Greg, his manipulative bids for sympathy, his exhausting self-pity. By the time any woman left Greg she felt as if she had been fed through an industrial shredder. Jussi's very dignity made you ache not to hurt him.

'Perhaps my feelings for you are better than that,' she said. 'The heady stuff has drawbacks. Maybe this is more . . . nourishing.'

'Yeah. Speaking of which, if we ever get out of this traffic I could do with some nosh. How does reindeer with bacon grab you?'

'Where on earth—?'

'I cheated. It's venison.'

When they got home, Nina watched miserably as Jussi pushed his exquisitely prepared food round his plate. The radio was playing the Vivaldi *Four Seasons*. Nina hated *The Four Seasons*. If she had done a Sibelius and portrayed 'the impression made on me by this room', it would have been a chilly cube unthawed by the brilliant August evening, while Vivaldi's spiky white violins needled her sensitive skin.

'Heady stuff,' quoted Jussi. 'I once fell for a woman and couldn't think of anything else. My girlfriend didn't know. I felt I was patronizing her.'

'It isn't like that,' said Nina dismally. 'Jussi, *please* don't force my hand!'

'This is not about you, get it? *I* can't take it. Being with someone who's in love with another guy. I'd rather we went belly up. Nuff said,' he concluded. 'You gotta do what you gotta do. Just so long as he treats you right. If he doesn't, you'll tell me, agreed? Just tell me, Nina, and I'll deck the bastard.'

48

The couple of weeks that followed were hideous, she and Jussi back and forth from each other's flats clearing the debris of their short shared life. Nina verged on pleading to change his mind. What stopped her was foreknowledge of the question he would repeat and the only answer she could offer. She wanted them both. Well, hard bloody cheese, she told herself. All her reference points had shifted. It was like being stuck in the mental equivalent of a revolving door – every few seconds the same fact would come round again and wallop her in the head.

Richard had meetings in that Piccadilly hotel again and when Nina walked in he was waiting on a floral rug beneath a chandelier, and she couldn't stop her nervousness from babbling rubbish about déjà vu.

The maître d' steered them to the middle of the restaurant. 'We would prefer a corner table,' said Richard in his investigator-meeting voice.

'Certainly, sir.'

The heady stuff, thought Nina as waiters came and went. Those schmaltzy magazines of Nonna's: *How to tell if it's real love*. When he walks into a room, does it feel as if all the lights have come on? Yes, she thought, this is indeed a phenomenon of light. A room without Richard's luxuriant tenancy has a wan cast, muted and substandard. Ain't no sunshine.

His tiredness had deepened and he had lost more weight. The thinness and shadowed eyes seemed to correspond in some deep aesthetic fashion to his black gloss of hair and clever fingers, so that Nina had an abrupt impression, despite the welcome benignity of his smile, of an intense pianist at a lustrous concert grand.

'How are the shrimps?' Richard asked of her starter.

'Mmmh?'

'The food.'

'Oh, the food. Yes, fine, thanks.' She glanced at her plate. 'Though if it were me, I'd have gone for dill in the sauce for subtlety, and perhaps a squeeze less of lemon. Slightly too strident a high note against the groundswell of Dijon and—'

'Nina, I want you to know I didn't break up your relationship lightly.'

'You didn't break up anything, Richard. My partner did.'

'I think I'm trying to say,' he smiled, 'that my intentions are honourable.'

This was another flying visit, literally – Richard was off again tomorrow afternoon. He handed her a printed page of dates: his travel schedule and free time in Boston.

Nina read it with flares of concern. 'Richard, there's a limit to the number of times I can fly the Atlantic.'

'You mean financial? I could help.' He smiled apologetically at her hesitation. 'OK, suppose I spend my frequent-flyer miles on you? Believe me, the only thing I want for myself is a couple of weeks' break from airports.'

And Nina said, 'That is very sensitive of you,' as she had once said before.

After the main course, when he asked if she wanted anything else or was it time to retire? her voice failed so she merely shook her head.

'Just the check, please,' Richard told the waiter. Then he

reached out his hand across the swept tablecloth. The senior-management expression that had attended the discussion of his itinerary fell away, and in his eyes was a simple urgency that shivered through her skin.

The following morning they were in Covent Garden again, talking about her father and Veikko.

'Everything goes back to that damn war,' said Richard, 'which I'm ashamed to say I'd never heard of. What was it about, do you know?'

'Leningrad. Stalin guessed Hitler would set his sights on it and Finland might be a stepping stone, so he demanded a whacking great tract of land as a buffer.' Nina gave a grim laugh. 'Even I could have told Stalin where that would get him. The Finns are a very stubborn bunch, they don't *do* mind-blowing gall. Basically, they told Stalin to stick his demands up the nearest tank.'

'Brave.'

'Or potty. We're talking about Finland with a tiny population and no preparations for war, and the Soviet Union with 170 million people and the biggest military juggernaut in the history of the planet. So they bombed Helsinki.'

'This is 1939?'

'Autumn. The Soviets seethed across the entire country, and the world waited for Finland to be annexed to the Soviet Union in a matter of days. The world was wrong. The Finns sent them squealing home, whipped and humiliated.'

'How?'

'I told you, they are a very stubborn bunch.'

The vim and gusto of Covent Garden were an unalloyed pleasure to Nina but not to Richard. For Richard, the borrowed va-va-voom of being in a crowd, the reflected warmth of its vivacious persona, invariably wore off round about the second serious buffeting. She drew him away to a side street where a busker on steel drums was transforming a cerulean Bach prelude into concentric yellow rings.

Good old Bach. At the same age at which Sibelius ground to a standstill, Johann Sebastian was cheerfully knocking out the B Minor Mass despite being virtually blind.

What went wrong? Nina wanted to shout. *Auto-da-fé*. Was he insane with temper? The swung-open door of the glossy, singing stove, the laundry basket slammed down, the skittering paper sheaves hurled on to the fire: his work, his spirit, his life's blood. Aino fleeing the room. Nina thought of flying shellac and the tortured jackets of LPs thrown at the wall of a wintry, disapproving study.

Yet long afterwards Sibelius confided to friends that he was still optimistic of finishing that symphony. So was he subject, year in year out, to electrified, near-manic surges of resolution to resurrect it from his head? And did they fall softly away in the oblivion of an all-forgiving exhaustion, or plummet in yet more agony of failure and self-loathing?

Richard was saying again, 'It all goes back to that war. We need to find out exactly what your father was doing during the time he knew this crook, Veikko.'

'There's only Erik Pellinen,' said Nina with a sudden massive sense of Jussi.

'Nina, someone else claimed to know things about your dad. The guy who wrote the book defaming him. Veikko's father.'

Nina stopped walking.

'Or there's Plan B. Lock the damn thing away and forget it.'

'I don't see how the book could help. I already know what it says.'

'Well no, from what you tell me you only know the strapline. Nina, Veikko was central to the biggest thing that ever happened to your father. The scandal. The book must have talked about how the author's son related to the man he was defaming.'

'Richard, it must be out of print.'

'If it caused such a stir, there will still be copies in a library somewhere. You don't have to get the entire book translated, you merely scour the text for his name and pick out those excerpts.'

Merely. Merely translate embittered accusations against my father. Which Richard doesn't see as a problem because of his own father.

Last night, lying in their warm breathing darkness and dizzy with love, Nina had asked about that relationship. What Richard told her was shocking. He had not been drafted to Vietnam; his father forced him to go by pulling him out of Harvard. 'Medicine can wait, son. Your country needs you.' So Richard enlisted for a tour of duty. In a sleepy drone, he had talked to Nina about Vietnam, a story of Chinooks, flak jackets and the Ho Chi Minh trail. His style and register changed, a slippage into dark inflections that had no place in a fancy hotel in Piccadilly but belonged elsewhere. Like to 1968 and The Doors.

'I survived,' Richard finished sleepily, 'but we don't talk about it much.' Then he added something Nina had heard once before, on a drear October night. 'If you were there you don't have to be told, and if you weren't you'll never understand.'

Now, he turned her towards him. 'You're letting this drive you crazy. So either overcome your qualms and investigate what your father was doing, or draw a line under it and move on. Surely I'm right.'

But his logic took no account of the heckling inner voice of family obligation. Nina couldn't decide whether seeking out Virta's book would constitute a blood disloyalty to her father. Or whether, given the blinding mess he'd landed her in, she continued to owe him any such abstract loyalty at all.

49

The librarian at Tampere University gave her other numbers, and eventually she was put through to a man who spoke English and had in front of him a book called *Muistelmat*, meaning 'memoir'. By Jorma Virta.

'But I am not able to send,' he explained. 'One moment, please.'

The hammering of Nina's heart was sickening. She was half afraid he was about to say, 'Didn't *Muistelmat* valiantly expose the yellow-bellied cowardice of that cur and disgrace to his motherland, Martti Hannikainen?'

He didn't. 'A colleague knows of another copy. Would you be willing to return—?'

'Yes. Thank you.'

'Your address is?'

Lucia's translation service was one of the few in London that worked with Finnish. 'If you really want to go ahead with this,' she said. 'Not just because Mr Wonderful suggested it.'

Mr Wonderful's stock had never been higher. This morning's post had brought her tickets for the end of the month. The outward flight was purchased with air miles but Nina's homebound journey would be via New York –

from where she would fly back to London on Concorde.

'I know you get a kick out of speed,' said Richard's letter. 'Also, it's a great weekend to be in Manhattan. There's a music festival including Sibelius in the Park,' and he itemized a few more events before wandering off into a sexual reverie.

'Do you miss Jussi?' Lu asked her.

'Chronically. Richard likes my letters to include everyday trivia. I start off and realize I can't go down that road because it would be full of allusions to Jussi. I feel as if a happy slice of my life has been amputated.'

'I know,' said Lucia. 'The ex has to be expunged unless you want to seriously piss off the replacement. It's called not being able to have your cake and eat it, kid.'

Richard had done a computerized trawl for information about the Eighth, and the printouts he sent her showed he had been derailed en route:

```
Students' Exam Answers
Q: Whose 8th symphony is known as
   the 'Unfinished'?
A: Sherbet.
Q: Which symphony was dedicated to
   Napoleon in 1803?
A: Beethoven's Erotica.
Q: What is the name of the simple
   tuning device used to establish
   the pitch of A?
A: A pitchfork.
```

Apparently Beethoven wasn't the only one writing erotica.

'I've done a deal with a publisher,' announced Duane.

'You've written a *novel*?'

'Didn't want to tell anyone till I'd clocked up my first rejection slip. Seems I got lucky.'

'Duane, that's fantastic! Which publisher?'

'You won't know them. It's gay porn.'

At which Nina laughed.

The idea had grabbed him one morning on a bus, so he made a detour into Soho and returned home loaded with books. 'I had to figure out the formula.'

'What is it?'

'Launch into your first bit of sex by page 6. That's just a warm-up, the hero indulging in some fantasy, three pages max or you're wasting your powder. Then another five of plot and it's time for your first proper sex. This is still early days, so a bit of slow undressing followed by some oral, sort of thing. The good stuff won't come to a climax, if you'll forgive the pun, till maybe page 30.'

'What counts as good stuff?'

'Threesomes, foursomes, touch of S & M. But before you get there, Gay Hunk arrives. He's the guy your hero is aching to get into bed. The whole book is working up to the big one with him.'

'It's a love story!'

'That's right. And on the way, the hero beds various lesser hunks, some in series and some in parallel, and approximately every six pages.'

'Can I read it?'

'I'll print you off a copy. It's called *The Code of Highwaymen*. Historical settings are very popular. I've done a four-book deal.'

'This is fantastic!'

'Only sort of. Hunk is based on somebody. Don't get excited. It won't work out.'

Because the man was married.

'Oh, Duane,' said Nina.

'Shouldn't you be railing at me for enticing a man to cheat on his wife? Shouldn't you stand up for the sisterhood?'

So Nina reminded Duane of her experience of sisterhood. 'Well, you know the problems,' she said. 'You've heard them from mistresses who phone the Sams.

Though you're no fool, so your situation is probably better.'
'I doubt it,' said Duane.

*

Muistelmat was a hardcover volume running to a hundred pages and a dozen photographic plates. Nina stood in the small communal hall in her nightie, flicking through. When her father smiled up from a photograph she felt ridiculously ashamed, as if he'd caught her in an act of deviousness. His name was in the index:

> *Hannikainen, Martti, ix, 4, 9, 11, 15-16, 19, 22-6, 32, 35, 37, 45-6, 48-9, 58, 69, 71, 73-4, 84-6, 90, 92, 96-8*

Nina stared. Her father was mentioned on each of . . . *thirty-one pages?* The photograph showed him in a tweed suit of impossibly wide trousers with turn-ups, a pipe fashionably clamped between his bared teeth. Pictures of Veikko presented the boy's development from babyhood to the front line, swaddled in white camouflage against a white background in a white-spotted world. His mouth was broad and his hair richly curled. An attractive young man.

'You all right, Nina? You look like you've seen a ghost.'
'Sorry, Victoria.' And Nina let herself back into her flat without thinking to ask after Victoria or Sean.
Being unable even to grapple with the language was infuriating.

> *Äglä järvellä, muutamia kymmeniä kilometrejä Tolvajärveltä pohjoiseen . . .*

Even familiar words were in disguise. Presumably *Äglä järvellä* was something to do with Äglä järvi. The baffling inflections applied equally to the word Hannikainen, so it was an arduous business for Nina even to identify the name of her own father. She found it most prominently in two photographic plates. Letters. The crease lines and quiet ink had the gravitas of history. One of them stopped her heart; it was her father's. In the same well-behaved penmanship as his music manuscript, he had apparently written to Jorma Virta on '*25. joulukuuta 1939*'. Christmas Day? The battle of Ägläjärvi came just beforehand. Had her father written to Jorma Virta three days after the son died in that benighted farmhouse?

The other was from someone Nina had never heard of, and was peppered with the names Martti Hannikainen and Veikko Virta.

The Winter War. Nina saw herself at eight. Her father had persuaded Dr Dolan to refer him for hospital tests but it was Christine who took the phone call with his results. Martin had appeared behind her, his face the colour of ice.

'*Mita kuulu?*' he had demanded, forgetting which country he was in, his voice cracked with fear. *What is heard?* Meaning, what news? A terrible question weighted with the anxiety of an entire nation, the bitter music of the Winter War: *Mita kuulu?*

Today was Saturday. Nina would have to wait two days before she could even take it to Lucia's office, where it would join a backlog. Her reaction to the delay involved a warped logic. Next week she was flying to Boston and Richard, therefore time would stand still. Anything scheduled for after Boston was never going to happen. She spent most of the day scouring the text and attaching Post-it notes until the book bristled. But Nina suspected all she really needed were those two letters.

50

Susan flew home the following Friday night. As she didn't mention the manuscript again, Nina in return did her duty and they met up at Heathrow for Nina to wave her sister and sleeping niece through Departures.

Susan's entire demeanour was different. Chatty. She even complimented Nina on her clothes.

'I can't get away with anything like that because I'm so tall,' she said of Nina's crochet-and-appliqué sweater and tiny skirt of green tulle, 'whereas on you it looks terrific. Taking good-quality fabrics and reworking and mixing, they're the principles espoused by Gianni Versace.'

Nina assumed Susan was mending fences, ashamed of her earlier behaviour.

It was here in Departures that Nina and Richard had said goodbye two weeks earlier. Perhaps helped by this beatification of Heathrow, and touched by Susan's pretty tearfulness at going away, Nina was conscious of unexpected pulses of family feeling. She had lived away from home for much of her sister's life but there had been a time when it was considered cool to have a cute toddler in the house. Prolonged antagonism had never sat easily with Nina; as she drove home she relaxed into the fragile affection with a sense of discarding a cumbersome hostility that had out-lasted the demands of its *casus belli*.

At home, she had great fun reading *The Code of Highwaymen*. Not because of the sex. That was mystifyingly unerotic. There was nothing in Duane's characters' physicality and slow undressing that spoke to Nina's own feelings about men. Yet her previous dips into pornography had generally managed to raise a flicker, and sometimes a firestorm, including lesbian erotica and some nasty stuff that Nina would rather not dwell on. It was as if male gay imagery was aimed at circuitry that her brain simply didn't possess. But Nina was delighted by the love story.

'Read it, Lu, it's lovely.'

'Gay porn.'

'Oh, you just skip those bits.' They were sitting in Nina's kitchen with the door open to the soft day and a motif of jasmine, pursued in varicoloured containers from table to garden path. 'There's a highwayman who turns out to be a goodie and a country house full of beautiful young men. There's even a marrying-off chapter when the highwayman's feisty moll teams up with Hunk's fiancée while the men walk off together into the sunset. And it's beautifully written.'

Even Duane's stock phrases ('Lu, when did you last see the word debonair?') couldn't subdue the fluency of his prose. There was a powerfully lyrical scene in a bathroom, all lavender-scented steam and watery reflections from the bathtub, whose poetry so affected Nina that she mis-understood the term 'rimming'. But all she could gather of Duane's lover was that he had a predilection for men in silk knickers, which Nina hoped was fictional.

'I like Duane,' said Lu. 'He's got a mouth on him like a landlady with a lemon up her arse, but I like him.' Then she added, 'Is he seriously screwed up?'

'He's lost his ex and three friends.'

'I meant deeper than that. Don't tell me if you're not supposed to.'

'Let's just say he'll be more relaxed when he gets himself back to work. If this recession ever eases.'

Seriously screwed up. That Samaritan shift in which Duane cried – it was nearly four years ago now. With the chronology of hindsight, Nina could class it as an unavoidable crisis between Steve's positive test result (followed immediately by his leaving Duane for another man) and his death last February in the Royal Free.

'I caught the gist of the call,' Nina had said gently as she rested a cup of tea on the plywood desk of the booth. 'A young man whose lover just died.'

'He held his hand.' Duane's voice was throaty and lost. Then he told her.

Duane's mother had come home from hospital to die. He wasn't allowed in the room. Everything was whispers and soft footfall, and terrifying appliances wheeled through the door. The sounds from within were intolerable. There was an afternoon when his father was at work and the nurse was in the kitchen. He opened the bedroom door. He was five.

'The smell!' he told Nina. 'One AIDS support meeting, this bloody nurse wouldn't shut up over coffee, told me he could smell cancer. There's nothing he could tell me, I know, I've fucking smelled it.'

So had begun a phobia on which thirty years and several thousand pounds' worth of therapy had failed to make the smallest impression.

'I can't step into a sickroom. Steve knows. It's why he left. He read it on my face the day we got the results. I wasn't worrying if I'd caught it. I wasn't seeing *him* at all but . . . bed sheets with hospital corners and equipment like a fucking octopus. Tubes. They were *skewered* into her arms, there were fucking *pins*. And this black metal can the size of a turbine engine, this malevolent monster with its paw clamped on her face, it was suffocating her. Her chest was . . . and the sound . . . dragging, panting, dragging!'

So he did the only thing a five-year-old son could do. Rescue his mother from the instruments of torture. Tear the mask from her face and the tubes out of her arms.

'THAT FILTHY NURSE!' he shouted at Nina. '"What have you done, you evil boy? Your own poor mother's life blood, you horrid little tyke!" An hour later she was dead!' Duane was now beside himself.

Nina said, 'You understand that your mother was unconscious? Morphine. That's why her respiration was depressed: she was comfortably slipping away in a sweet dream. And a little blood goes a long way. You didn't kill your mother, Duane. The nurse was obviously a child-hater.'

'I *understand* because I've heard it hundreds of times at fifty quid an hour. I've had desensitization therapy with oxygen cylinders and . . . It's irrelevant what I *understand*. I *know* she was lying there being tormented and then I . . . Three people close to me pegged out and I didn't get further than the doors of the fucking ward. The guy on that phone held his lover's hand. I picture how it'll be with Steve and I *ache* to hold his hand. I'd give half my own fucking life.'

Nina sat quietly stroking his shoulder while Duane wept and shuddered.

'Therapists all tell me to get involved in some capacity that doesn't mean being with patients. I do volunteer work for the Terrence Higgins Trust, stuffing envelopes. I'd do that anyway, I'm a faggot, for Christ's sake, a shirt-lifter, a pillow-biter, I read the tabloids, I know we have to fight the propaganda. It doesn't help me one fucking iota.'

'Well, no,' said Nina. 'How could it? Your mother wasn't dying of AIDS, she was dying of cancer.'

'I can't go near cancer.'

'I can think of one way you might. You're an IT man. Know anything about the VAX-8600? Twenty miles from here is a security-controlled suite with two of them, caged and in need of a zoo keeper.'

So: 'Let's just say Duane will be more relaxed when he gets himself back to work.' And Lu didn't probe.

When she left in the evening she did take *The Code of*

Highwaymen – and something else, her own phenomenon of luminosity, so that Nina sat on in the inertia of a tender gloaming and a minor sense of loss. It would have been nice if someone else were due in her kitchen, to fill its space with his undemanding chatter and a carrier bag of dill.

∗

> My dearest Richard,
> . . . The bathroom was misted with lavender-
> scented steam and a rippled webbing of
> deliquescent light. Slow heat massaged my breasts,
> my white thighs, my . . .

His Boston house was still occupied and his address would be changeable for a while, so Nina had to mail her letters to Richard's office. In case they were opened by a secretary, she always wrote a big innocent one and hid a naughty little one inside it.

This was an unusual juxtaposition, Nina decided – soft porn and military history:

The Finns' labour force was outnumbered forty to one. Some of their guns dated from 1887. However, they learned on the hoof. They took a cheap weapon invented in the Spanish civil war and renamed it the Molotov cocktail. Also, the Finns were world-class skiers; their deadly night patrols caused mayhem.

Anyone might assume the Russians knew something about snow, ice and long dark winters, yet they found this landscape utterly alien, and countless numbers simply froze to death in it. While their soldiers faded out of existence in foxholes in temperatures of minus thirty, the Finns built saunas on the front line and rolled in the snow. This was their home ground.

And that was the decisive factor. The Finns would pull through because they knew exactly what they were fighting for whereas the conscripted Soviet soldiers hadn't the faintest idea what they were doing in a frozen hell pitted against an enemy that had guerrillas on skis. Finland humiliated Stalin while the world learned a third word to supplement its vocabulary of sauna and Sibelius. *Sisu*, meaning indomitable grit. It translates best as 'balls'.

Every account she could lay her hands on coruscated with Finnish heroism, and the pacifist Nina had to stop herself punching the air with a fist and shouting 'YES!' whenever a Finn cut down a tank with a petrol bomb.

The conflict was shot through with her father's own brand of black comedy. The Finns had *bicycle* battalions. There was the 'Sausage War', where a Soviet patrol found themselves in the Finns' kitchens and fell on the sausage soup, only to be mowed down and merrily toppled into the cauldrons. And way up in the Arctic, under skies black with bombers, the Finns somehow destroyed two entire Soviet divisions and left the battleground heaped with *twenty-seven thousand* enemy dead, who froze solid as they fell, their death throes grotesquely preserved like some macabre sculpture field. No war journalist had ever seen anything like it.

Nina closed her books. She had just made a connection. '. . . *whereas the conscripted Soviet soldiers hadn't the faintest idea what they were doing in a frozen hell . . .*'

She remembered Richard in the small hours talking of bombing raids and billions of US dollars. 'That jungle breathing, shifting, you never knew what was going down, never knew what the hell would come out at you, and never, never, never knew what the fuck you were doing there.'

And suddenly, after all these years, Nina understood why America had never stood the slightest chance of winning the Vietnam War.

51

'Tomorrow,' said Richard dreamily down the phone. 'The sweetest word in the world.'

Tomorrow she was flying to Boston. Unluckily, his house wouldn't be ready for them until Friday night. It was apparently full of men and machinery, re-sanding floors and carpet cleaning. Nina misunderstood.

'Did your tenants leave the place in a terrible state? How awful.'

'It's just the annual workover.'

'Right,' she said, refocusing.

'I guessed you would rather keep these dates because of the festival.'

'Absolutely.'

Saturday morning they were flying on to New York for the big finale weekend of Manhattan's Festival of Twentieth-century Music. This included something in Carnegie Hall for whose tickets Richard must have pawned an heirloom. In New York he had taken a suite for them *at the Plaza* and then she would fly home on Concorde.

'You don't have to win my heart,' she told him tenderly. 'It's already won, stuffed and mounted on a trophy board in the hall.'

'Shit, I *wondered* what that shrivelled red thing was that the workmen just slung in the dumpster.'

Waiting for the house, they stayed five days under yet another hotel chandelier; five days and nights of hunger and laziness, learning each other.

It was a source of joy to Richard that Nina liked to watch him just ordinarily naked, crossing from bedroom to bathroom. 'To all of you out there,' she announced from their bed, 'Richard Quentin is this immaculate creature in a hand-tailored suit. But I know him tousled and naked – with his air of command annulled by the defiant flush of an unshameable ecstasy.'

'The pungency of contrast,' responded Richard. 'Maybe we miss out these days, surrounded by our blizzard of sexual imagery. Picture a Victorian gentleman seeing his bride in a nightdress for the first time – *with her hair tumbling loose.*'

She had packed her basque and stockings but it became clear that he preferred ordinary cotton briefs – and liked to uncover them for himself. 'It's more erotic to think I've taken you by surprise.' Therefore hundreds of pounds' worth of lace stayed in Nina's suitcase along with her cassette recording of 'A La Gran Muñeca' by the orchestra of Carlos Di Sarli.

'It's a world apart from my married life,' he told her one drowsy afternoon.

'Was it bad from the start?'

'No. I'd returned from Vietnam, I was worn down, I wanted to be in love and Anita was a socialite with a wide circle of friends. It was nice to have a ready-made life. I silenced the inner voice warning me that what she wanted was the family status.'

Nina was exultantly gratified at the implied comparison, and subsumed a tiny concern for the quiet rancour of a long hurt that she heard in his subtext.

For Nina there was an unexpected luxury in being out of her depth in this unknown town, reliant on him. The only shadow was cast by the temporariness. When she first arrived and they had sat and talked in a Laocoön tangle of silk and tailored wool, Richard, suddenly impatient, had unwrapped her and led her to the bed. And in the moment that he entered her, the thought hit Nina: I go home on Monday; I live alone; how will I cope after a week of this?

Despite Carlos Di Sarli, the cassette player did get an airing. 'I feel privileged,' said Richard with New-World solemnity as the finale closed on a hair-raising high note. If this were ever sung by a flesh-and-blood soprano, she would have to go for that note bald-headed against an astonishing discord from the orchestra. It was a *drive-by* discord. Richard asked intelligent questions about the Kalevala, the newly invented harp that was so beautiful Väinämöinen wept as he played.

> *From his eyes the tear-drops started,*
> *Flowed adown his furrowed visage,*
> *Falling from his beard in streamlets*
> *Trickled on his heaving bosom,*
> *Streaming o'er his golden girdle . . .*

Nina said, 'Now look at the Finnish.'
'OK, but I can't get the Finnish to look back.'

> *kaunihille kasvoillensa,*
> *kaunihilta kasvoiltansa*
> *leve'ille leuoillensa,*
> *leve'iltä leuoiltansa*
> *rehe'ille rinnoillensa,*
> *rehe'iltä rinnoiltansa*

She smiled. 'See those paired lines with alliteration? They aren't really identical, there's a subtle change *inside* the words. Repetition with knobs on. I think it's saying, "From his visage to his beard, from his beard to his bosom" in a "knee bone connected to the thigh bone" sort of way.'
'Clever.'

'God, don't you wish we could hear it belted out by a real choir? Male voices take one line then females the near-repeat. Call and response. Whether classical or delta blues, call and response works every time.'

And you would weep, wouldn't you? she thought. Today harp-songs, tomorrow Bach and Beethoven and the Beatles. And a genius whose hallmark was an ability to construct entire movements from the tiniest seed of a motif; who in his second symphony wrought magic from nine B flats in a row.

With one of his flares of perspicacity Richard said, 'You look flat. Saddened.'

What Nina felt was a protective disappointment on behalf of the symphony, not its composer but the burgeoning life force of the piece itself. She tried to put her thoughts in order. 'We're all so cerebral in our reactions. Analysing and dissecting. My fault for making it mystery instead of music. I've stopped everyone from doing the decent thing.'

'Which is?'

'To listen and weep.' She thought of her father's suffragan bishop unexpectedly hit with the Fifth.

Richard thought about this. 'Isn't that inevitable, given that we only have an approximation? It's a remarkable job, but it's an engineering job. Surely it takes the inspired hand of a conductor to make grown men weep.'

'Oh God, Richard. If it really is Sibelius, then how can I be right, depriving it of that inspired hand?'

On Friday they checked out and Richard led her briskly across the Common to Beacon Hill. It was a poor afternoon, prematurely autumnal, the light livid beneath a roll of lugubrious cloud. Nina was chilly in a skirt of layered scarlet voile, red sweater, black tights. Beacon Hill reminded her of Hampstead: Georgian houses, mellow red brick, the same smell of refinement and money. Richard's house was in a square with a railed arboreal garden; the roots of ancient trees heaved through the prettily undulating sidewalks. His front door was open beneath its decorative entablature and the whine of vacuum cleaners issued from inside, insistent as a domestic fight. Richard stopped on the threshold in mid-stride. 'Fuck,' he said quietly.

'. . . in the master bedroom, if you will,' said a voice which then turned towards them. 'Richard!'

'Sir.'

'About time. The supervisor tells me you haven't looked in since he got here.'

'I'm looking in now. Nina, my father. Sir, Nina Hannay from London.'

A manicured hand reached for her own. 'How do you do?'

Nina registered the discreet shout of expensive tailoring. Her own froufrou skirt squeaked like twinkle nylon.

'I don't think I know any Hannays,' said Richard's father. 'Are your people from London?'

'No, my late father was a clergyman in a country parish.' She said it on the off chance that this evoked a kind of rural idyll populated with Miss Marples, sufficiently quaint to surmount the lack of social status.

'Ah,' responded Richard's father in a tone indicating that it hadn't. 'I hope you enjoy your stay. Son, will you call me when you get home from New York? Before seven. Your mother and I are dining with the Frobishers. Goodbye, Nina.'

'Fuck,' said Richard again as the handmade shoes withdrew across the square. Nina followed him into the busy echoing alien hall, his father's 'Ah' in her ears like tinnitus.

Richard said, 'Do you want anything from your case?'

'Now?'

'I thought we might grab some coffee on Charles Street.'

'Don't you have to stay?' She indicated the buzzing machinery.

'Nina, do you want anything from this case or not?'

'No.'

'Then let's get some coffee!'

They sat in a coffee shop that was all potpourri and dried

roses. Nina's heart ached in her chest. The ice-cold indignity of having let Richard down thrummed through her. She was mortified. She was misreading it.

'He fucking snubbed you.' Richard turned the reeking cup in his hands. '"I don't think I know any Hannays," for Chrissake.'

Nina unclamped his hand from the blistering china. 'Darling, I didn't help. Perhaps I could have dressed more conservatively. I hadn't expected—'

'Me neither. I intended easing him into our lives gently.'

'Richard, I'd love you if your family included Vlad the Impaler. Anyway, you haven't met my mother. Snub? She can freeze engine oil at fifty paces.'

'Why the fuck was he even there, getting his hands dirty? That's his agent's job.'

'Agent?'

'Takes care of both houses. There's a smaller one on Willow.'

Nina sipped her coffee to cover her surprise. That Richard didn't own the property he lived in had simply never entered her head. Yet it should have done the moment she set eyes on that square. The house required him to be independently wealthy. Or dependently wealthy. Dependent on his father.

She said carefully, 'You're his only child. It's natural your father would take a dim view of—'

'A girl from the wrong side of the tracks? Baby, I know I have a numeral after my name but this isn't *Love Story* and I am damn sure not Ryan O'Neal.'

'OK. I'm sorry.'

'Is that a feed?'

Nina laughed.

'Let's move on, shall we? Want to see Symphony Hall? We can stand and stare and think of poor Serge Koussevitzky.'

As they rode a cab across town he determinedly moved the subject on. 'I read that Sibelius abandoned his Eighth because he was scared he could never live up to all the hype. You think that's it?'

'Maybe,' said Nina, 'but in the latest books, scholars have started suggesting he just lost his way, musically. Too far from the action, stuck out there in Finland.'

'Artists do get petrified by their own success, afraid any follow-up would be greeted as an anticlimax. The author of *To Kill a Mockingbird* was too scared ever to write another book.'

'It very nearly happened to Pink Floyd,' pointed out Nina.

'I don't remember that.'

'No? *Dark Side Of The Moon* sold twenty-nine million copies and spent two hundred and ninety-four weeks in the UK charts alone. Anything after that was bound to be a disappointment. It was two and a half years before they released anything else. People said the band just couldn't follow their staggering success, they'd lost their bottle, they were falling apart. In the end, we got *Wish You Were Here*. Well, it was pretty comprehensively slated. *Creem* said they were in a virtual slump and *Melody Maker* a creative void. That's "Shine On You Crazy Diamond" they were rubbishing. Philistines!'

Richard said, 'I suppose Sibelius's equivalent of *Dark Side Of The Moon* was his entire back catalogue. How could he follow that?'

'Except I've been reading that he was well used to bad crits. Plenty of respected names thought his stuff was all mannerisms and no substance. And his fourth symphony was trashed by half the musical world but that didn't even slow him down, so *why*?'

Yet somehow there was always the niff of failure about him. In early years he was another failed violinist, never quite the virtuoso for a soloist's career, and it haunted him even when he'd won the acclaim of influential figures among the creative élite and popular veneration. And finally he became the statesman; the head on the postage stamps. The creative has-been.

But Sibelius had just lost her attention. 'Is that Symphony Hall? It's beautiful!'

As they walked past a poster advertising the 1812 Overture, Richard said, 'Tchaikovsky married a Nina, didn't he? Though I seem to remember she was . . . well . . .'

'A raving nymphomaniac is the term you're groping for. At least, according to the movie with Richard Chamberlain. I'm sorry, darling, but you're the second Richard in my life. The first was Dr Kildare.'

'Yeah? I still want to murder the guy. When the last episode aired, my girlfriend sobbed right through and wouldn't let me slip my hand in her blouse.'

Nina thumped him and laughed. 'That one alone had Jack Nicholson *and* William Shatner.'

'Wrong episode, Nina. The final show had Richard Beymer of *West Side Story*.'

'In Britain we got that earlier. The BBC must have shown them in a different order.'

'Impossible,' contradicted Richard shortly. She was displeased to hear a clipped impatience. 'Kildare was found guilty of misconduct and lost his licence. It would have looked ridiculous.'

'Nevertheless—'

'Nina, you're just wrong. You've misremembered. Let's move on.'

She bit her lip. 'Richard, that last episode is carved so deep in my memory it would show up on a CT scan. I'm telling you.'

'You can't tell me. You're wrong. Accept it!'

Nina came to a halt, nettled by a deeply unpleasant irritation. She wasn't used to being so peremptorily contradicted. Even Duane, her touchstone of rude behaviour, didn't say, 'You're wrong. Accept it,' about something he couldn't possibly know. There was no hint of joshing in Richard's face or the language of his body, drawn away, not sharing her space. She couldn't work out who contradicted first: had her own persistence rankled him into a grievance about a TV show that finished in 1966? Or was there another source of his choler, which he had turned on Nina merely because she was there? Forcing a mollifying tenderness into her voice she asked cautiously, 'Do we need to finish a previous discussion? About your father?'

When he said, 'I *hate* being made to feel in the wrong,' she heard it as some dangerous escalation, so the relief was like brandy in her veins when he continued, 'I will not run my life dissecting my father's every word or I'll end up like my mother. Hasn't voiced an opinion of her own since around 1952. Let's get some food and forget him.'

They ate deli food in a dining room that was a period piece of Chippendale and watered silk. The September evening had turned wintry so Richard lit a fire; it bubbled behind a protective screen, its murmurings the only sound in the millionaires' enclave. Nina thought of her own utilitarian flat. God knew what Fearless might do to that brocade couch.

'Roll on New York,' said Richard sleepily. 'If we're feeling clever there's Schoenberg at the Juilliard. We might even find some music that's coloured orgasm purple.'

'I should *never* have told you that!'

'Or we could stay in bed.'

In the end, that was what they did, even missing the Carnegie concert he had been talking about for weeks. And at six on Monday morning as Nina dressed for Concorde, a thought flickered across her mind, brief as a drifting cloud. Could this festival have been a pretext and the dates chosen *because* Richard's house would be uninhabitable for most of the week? Which meant I was less likely to run into his father?

And his father was less likely to run into me?

52

Richard had secured her a window seat on the right-hand side of the plane, from where Nina would have a view of Manhattan at takeoff. She gave a little bounce in her seat like a child.

'One *does* object,' said a voice in her left ear, 'to the pricing structure.'

Nina spun round. 'Sorry?'

'Two cabins but one price. Ostensibly we're all the same, but try telling that to a Concorde aficionado who finds himself at the back with no view but wing.'

Her neighbour was British and in his middle fifties. Although he wore a Ralph Lauren polo neck there was an air of bow tie about the man.

'Your maiden trip?'

'Yes,' Nina admitted. Then, in response to the extreme psychological pressure crashing over her in waves, 'Yours?'

'Mine? Good Lord, no! I've lost count. Are you expecting to fly high enough to view the curvature of the earth?'

'It would be nice,' said Nina warily.

Her companion clucked. 'Doubtful. These days you can't guarantee sufficient altitude for the eerie glow, either. In the seventies we'd often spend the entire flight up there. At 67,000 feet you *really* get a glow.'

And the pilot gets ten years, thought Nina. Sixty thousand is the legal limit. Was she in for four hours of fishermen's tales? Then, thank God, the captain came over the PA. He talked them through the procedure and then, 'Cabin crew – take your seats for takeoff.'

'Set The Controls For The Heart Of The Sun', thought Nina.

In the vertiginous moment when the wheels lifted off the runway and her senses whited out, her window was full of New York City, epitome of all cities, its glimmering geometric skyline thrusting out of the silvered water into the cabin. The plane climbed and the city swerved and was dwarfed, and was gone. On an elegant display banner, numbers spun like fruit in a one-armed bandit. Nina thought, I am careering up through the earth's atmosphere towards twice the speed of sound. Her neighbour watched with a condescending smile.

She said coldly, 'There is an advantage to being a novice. The thrill of the first time.'

'Oh, I think we're all enjoying ourselves. It's just that we're not trying to stick our heads out of the window.' He nodded at the book in Nina's lap. 'Sibelius. The dear old granite-hewn master. Serious stuff for a young lady. Are you a musician?'

'No, but back in London I've got the world's only copy of his eighth symphony,' she said. She was tempted to say.

'Musician?' persisted the man. 'Mmmh?'

'I'm a lady pianist,' said Nina, letting him have it. 'I also have a PhD on non-parametric methods in clinically applied statistics.' She smiled. 'It was a terrible thing to explain at student parties over the noise of the disco.'

Then, with steel-cold conviction, Nina thought, He's going to trump me. The patronizing bastard will turn out to be the world's premier transplant surgeon who hurtles round the globe from crisis to crisis like Red Adair. He's got a human heart on dry ice in his hand luggage and a celebrity patient waiting on a table in the bloody arrivals lounge.

Worse.

'Stefan Oxenford, orchestral conductor,' he told her, holding out his baton hand for Nina to shake. 'En route from the Juilliard to our dear old Albert Hall. Of course, I'm a Schoenberg man myself but I expect you saw we've got Simon on board. Actually, the plane's positively stuffed with us all. I hope you caught the festival.'

'Simon?'

'Rattle! He's at the front. Delightful chap. Pop along after they've served us lunch, and mention my name. So what do you think of these rumours – any truth in them, do you think?'

'What rumours?'

'Apparently somebody made a handwritten copy of the lost eighth symphony and a Manhattan academic is tracking it down. Enormous work, a hundred and ninety pages including a choral finale.' He turned to the purser. 'Do you have the Krug Clos du Mesnil '79?'

When they reached 55,000 feet the captain announced that they had officially achieved astronaut status.

With infuriating complacency Stefan Oxenford said, 'Purely arbitrary. You need minimum fifty-*eight* for the curvature and glow.'

But Nina's glow had dissipated. 'These rumours,' she said. 'Do you know the details?'

'I only know the net is buzzing with the stuff.'

'The . . . net?'

'Usenet. Information technology, my dear! Some academic at the Manhattan School of Music was overheard on the phone with person or persons unknown, so the story goes. He himself appeared to be in possession of excerpts but his protagonist knew the location of the full score. *I* suspect the whole thing dates from April Fool's Day.'

'Who's the academic?'

'Oh, rumours like this are never dignified with names. An unidentified prof was heard saying this was the most important thingamabob of the et cetera. *Do* go and ask Simon, he'd be charmed.'

Nina distractedly accepted a glass of the Krug from the purser and downed it with a speed that made both men wince. She reminded herself that she wouldn't have been allowed to smoke even if she had been allowed to smoke.

Erik! thought Nina. It's bloody Erik. Mum was bloody right. He's probably still in London. When we land at Heathrow, I'll go screaming round to the flat and bloody kill him.

What could this prof actually know? Presumably he had those four pages Jussi photocopied from the first movement and an uncertain slice from the storm later on. Oh *Christ*, Jussi will have innocently told Erik about the myths. That's enough information to send any musicologist frenzied. He will dig and dig, and what will he find? Erik's son's ex-girlfriend, daughter of Martti Hannikainen. I'll *kill* him.

'Poor old Sibelius.' Oxenford's condescension was oily. 'Lumbered with longevity. If only he had popped his clogs at a decent age like poor deaf batty Beethoven, the world would have had seven symphonies, a couple of them really rather splendid, plus some quite astonishing tone poems, and thought itself lucky.' He tucked into his ballontine of salmon. 'As it was, that brooding elderly presence set back Finnish music for ever. Young talent couldn't get a look-in, so it fled abroad.'

As the journey was utterly wrecked, Nina knew she must make the effort to salvage something, if only Oxenford's musical insights. She said unevenly, 'You blame his old age?'

'Not for provoking the crisis, only for dragging it out through three excruciating decades. Nothing mysterious about the Silence: a simple case of blue funk in the face of too many folk crying, "What will the genius give us next?" I'd say he was always up against a deadline. When he hadn't come across with the goods by the mid-1930s, the world's expectations had surpassed anything he could possibly meet.'

'Even worse than trying to follow up *Dark Side Of The Moon*,' said Nina. 'Sorry, I was being flippant. It's an album by a rock band.'

'*Now* who's patronizing whom?' demanded Stefan Oxenford.

When the complex implications of that remark had subsided, Nina said, 'I read that Sibelius was just too isolated. Too far from the action and out of touch.'

'Well, no one was saying that at the time of the Seventh and *Tapiola*. Surely your books don't suggest the tide of fashion turned so fast he was left stranded in mid-symphony?'

'Wasn't he always lagging behind the trends? He had some derisive critics. Benjamin Britten said—'

'Benjamin Britten could have written another opera in the time he wasted thinking up pithy sound bites. Sibelius has always had his detractors but he was a key player, never you doubt it. But hopelessly thin-skinned, which you just can't afford to be in our business. Do you know *Kullervo*? He withdrew it after the première and nobody heard *Kullervo* again in full until after his death. Mind you, that said, the thing's pretty awful so one sympathizes with the chap. But the sublime *Tapiola* very nearly didn't see the light of day at all. He did his damnedest to claw it back from the publisher and bury it.'

Oxenford had started on the grilled sea bass with caviar sauce. 'It's quite simple. The old lad was trying to knock out the last one while the musical world was on its feet clamouring, "Maestro, why are we waiting?" I don't suppose being a national hero at home helped, either – though one can hardly blame the Finns for making a fuss of him. Until Sibelius, the only Finn the world had heard of was Father Christmas.'

Nina realized it was now half an hour since she had even looked out of the window. The cabin display told her 1,390 mph. Oxenford sipped his wine.

Nina sipped hers and said, her voice squeaky, 'I've been pulling your leg. I do know the rumours.'

'Ah.'

'There's this friend of mine,' she went on, sounding like a letter to an agony aunt, 'and it crossed his mind that the manuscript might exist but it's copycat.'

Oxenford humphed. 'Well, in 1935 a journalist did say that if Sibelius didn't hurry up, somebody else would write the Eighth for him.'

'Exactly. So I was wondering. How difficult would it be, given that he had so many mannerisms to exploit? Musical fingerprints.'

'Not a hundred and ninety pages with a choral movement,' Oxenford replied instantly. 'Ask any art forger – in fact we probably have a couple on board. They don't go to the trouble of knocking up a canvas ten foot by five if the artist can be faked in eight inches square. Which this artist could be. His Seventh runs to what, twenty minutes? Anyone shamming it would have fabricated another of those.'

'I wasn't thinking sham, just *hommage* by a gifted amateur.'

'Well, that's utterly implausible. Such a work would be pushing it, even for a genius.'

'Yes but my friend says the choral part apparently has a *Kalevala* setting, so suppose a fellow Finn—'

Oxenford chuckled. 'I bet it does. Remember his *Väinö's Song*? Tells the story of an old man coming home. Sibelius held it back for years, and I don't blame him. He could just hear the critics: "A-hah! The hunter home from the hill – this is the swansong of an old master ready to hang up his crotchets and learn to grow a decent vegetable marrow." If I'd been him, I'd have made damn sure I had another *Kalevala* piece up my sleeve to put the kibosh on that particular insult. Especially given how pathologically touchy the old boy was about his age. Your friend say anything else?'

'Well—'

'Listen, if there is a symphony out there, which I don't believe, and complete with choral movement, heaven preserve us, you can forget copycat. The reason Sibelius's fingerprints are all over it is because Sibelius left them there. But I assure you the Eighth doesn't exist. Aino insisted it didn't survive and she was a scrupulously truthful woman. Let her husband rest in peace.'

'This is your captain again, ladies and gentlemen. We'll shortly be starting the descent into Heathrow. Unfortunately, weather conditions didn't require us to fly high enough to see the curvature or the famous glow but I hope you enjoyed the experience.'

'Bad luck,' Stefan Oxenford commiserated kindly.

They were at Terminal 4, where he was watching tiny Nina lug her overloaded case off the carousel. She set it rockily on the floor and sorted out her hand baggage.

'You are sure you used to fly at 67,000 feet?' she asked, giving him a last chance to retract.

'Lord, yes. The cabin scintillating like . . . the internal palate of a synaesthetic composer.' His smile invited her to admire the imagery.

Nina dropped her voice. 'The reason I ask is at those altitudes you were being *fried* with radiation, so for a man of your age you have to think of prostate cancer. Get it checked urgently because once the disease is advanced many surgeons still play safe by removing the testicles. Anyway, I mustn't hang around. I want to catch up with Simon Rattle and gush at him like a schoolgirl.'

Her baggage was nicely tagged with an elegant blue C. She intended to keep that on the case until it rotted. Dragging the lot behind her, Nina slogged through Customs and went home to Harlesden on the bus.

53

'It wasn't my dad! Nina, *listen*. It wasn't Erik, it was Susan!'

'What do you mean, Susan?'

'I didn't call you because there was nothing to be done, she'd flown off.'

'Jussi, what are you saying?'

'You remember Dad was coming over, yeah? I told him to bring those pages I photocopied, so you could watch me shred them, but then we went pear-shaped so—'

'You gave Erik's excerpts of the symphony to *Susan*?'

'Don't be stupid! It was the night she flew back to Cape Town. I was out giving Duane his lesson. When I got home again Dad was nearly hairless. Susan had come round.'

'How?'

'Nina, I'm trying to tell you. She was on her way to Heathrow and got the limo driver to do a detour. Dad did his best to tell her to sod off. Said he couldn't hand over Martin's music without your mother's permission. So Susan told him to phone your mother. What else could he do? He phoned your mother.'

'Hell.'

'And *she* said my dad had no right to Martin's music in the first place, and to hand it over to Susan pronto.'

And how did Susan know Erik had those excerpts in the first place – cosy conversations over bloody babies? She pulled herself up. This was *Jussi*.

He seemed to have read her mind. 'Nina, I didn't tell Susan Dad had the music.'

'Forgive me, I'm nearly out of my head.' Then, 'Oh, *fuck*, I was with Susan at check-in! She even made me help with her bloody suitcases and *that* was inside. The bitch.'

'No, she put the pages in her holdall,' corrected Jussi miserably. 'Then she got back in the limo and Dad watched them drive off.'

'*Fuck, fuck, fuck!*' said Nina.

'What's she done, you reckon?'

'Toted it straight round to some musician who posted it lock, stock and barrel to New York.'

'But Susan wouldn't want your father branded as—'

'She's just arrogant, Jussi. All that matters is her curiosity has been piqued. She probably had some vague notion of a professor going, "Ah yes, I can confirm this looks very like the symphony Sibelius talked about for thirty years but never published," and then just mailing it back to her and getting on with his day.'

'She hasn't got much to tote.'

'The fuck she hasn't.' Nina's vocabulary seemed to be stuck in a groove. 'Those extracts include a full recapitulation of the opening theme and an important bit of development from the third movement. And . . . oh *no*.' Susan had their father's copy of the *Kalevala*, marked up. The harp songs that weren't a bloody harp. No doubt she'd forwarded a copy of that, too. Any academic seeing the third movement in that context would recognize Väinämöinen's storm and wretched pike, and from *there* . . .

'Oh Jussi, we've got a rabid professor on our trail with the smell of blood in his nostrils.'

The following evening, Duane said, 'You have to hand it to Susan, she's clever. Your mother told her Erik was nosing round the symphony. She knew he was coming to London because Jussi was trying to get up a dinner party. Susan wonders if your boyfriend made a copy for his father. A hunch. What she probably hoped was that Erik had the lot. The only thing Susan needed to wangle out of Jussi in Brancaster was his London address and the fact that he was out Friday evenings. She caught Erik on the hop and bluffed.'

'The bitch put down the phone on me.'

'When?'

'Seven o'clock this morning. And eight o'clock. And nine o'clock.'

'Nina, Susan didn't start this. Be reasonable. You've been sounding off about that symphony since practically the day you found it. You do have to take some responsibility here.'

But before Nina could retaliate, the phone rang.

'Samaritans,' she said. 'Can I help you?'

Despite his refusal to wade in on her side, it was Duane who accessed Usenet for her. His married lover, Jeremy, was another IT man.

'Somebody's started a newsgroup,' explained Duane. 'I've printed off the messages.'

They were much as Stefan Oxenford had described, though not as elegant.

```
HEY ALL YOU SIBELIUS FREAKS OUT THERE,
HAVE I GOT NEWS FOR YOU — A PROFESSOR
AT MSM HAS A BIG LINE ON SYMPHONY 8.
I MEAN HE KNOWS SOMEBODY THAT HAS . . .
THE . . . SCORE!!!
```

The writer was one kuutar@msm.bar.com. Nina knew that Kuutar was the Finnish moon spirit:

```
Right now all I'll say is male, Senior
Faculty, Composition, and the name is
from south of the border.
```

A tease, this Kuutar.

```
Here's something to give all you guys
a boner — we're talking 190 pages
rounded off with a CHORAL SECTION FROM
THE KALEVALA, VAINAMOINENS HARP SONGS!
```

This was followed by a reference that made Nina want to string her sister up from Harlesden's Jubilee Clock.

```
All the info fits with what we know
already about number 8, even the key
of G min.
   Ready to hear the story now? Once
upon a time, my children, Kuutar was
innocently walking into the office of a
certain professor when he raised his
voice in anger, yes kiddies, in
anger...
```

The arch tone was nearly intolerable but Nina fished out the facts. Kuutar heard this professor shouting down the phone about 'the greatest find of the century' and insisting that the caller come across with the goods in their entirety. Kuutar had the sense not to wait around to be seen, and therefore overheard the rest through the door. When the man calmed down there began a long discussion. Yes, well, it would be, thought Nina furiously. Susan talks for bloody hours on international calls. Then she realized: he must have addressed her by name. But which name? God knew, there were enough Susans. But anyone searching for a Mrs Susan Van der Merwe would ultimately home in on Cape Town.

Well, Kuutar must have been gratified: that gloating announcement was like a grenade lobbed over a wall.

```
   ... South of the border limits it to
```

3 people on the faculty, Gomez, Santana
or Llames . . .

. . . So we have a choice of 3
candidates for caller 1, right? Then I
better point out its CALLER 2 thats
got the damn symphony and that gives
us a field of around 3 billion, which
is the population of the world that
has access to a phone . . .

YIKES. 3 billion possibilities yet? How
about, soon as we track down this Prof
then the number of the party he phoned
is logged in the switchboard records of
his outside calls? I'm on the case
right now.

. . . Hey stop crabbing and rejoice,
somebodys found the Sibelius 8, this is
AWESOME

Richard said, 'Oh my God.'

'Mum will blame me, you can bet your life. Susan's as wriggly as a barrel of eels.' But Nina didn't voice her foremost thought: What will your father say when the Hannay name hits the international news?

'Want me to make some enquiries about the faculty? Maybe one of those three names has a Cape Town connection.'

'Clever thinking, Richard. Thank you. According to Usenet, MSM is putting out the line that it's a hoax. The three suspects deny all knowledge. But nobody can track down this Kuutar.'

'That means he's logging on from a computer with multiple access.'

'She,' corrected Nina. 'Kuutar is feminine.'

'That reduces the field. I'll ask our computing people to keep tabs on the bulletin board.'

Which was getting fuller by the hour.

```
. . . to figure out what we would pre-
dict for number 8. The direction
Sibelius was taking could only lead to
increasingly crystallized overarching
cadences and . . .


. . . Hey, remember I told you to get
hold of the phone list of outside
calls? Ive done it. I got the list. I
also got the Prof. How? Look, Kuutar
is NOT a degree student because degree
students do NOT sail into professors
offices without knocking. Think about
it. And out of our 3 Hispanic mavens,
who has females in his postgrad team?
Only Alejandro Santana, folks. I'll
start checking those phone numbers. And
keep you posted? You betcha.


Q: What do you call a girl that dates
   MSM professors?
A: A symphomaniac
Q: What's a suspended chord?
A: Rope for lynching MSM professors
Q: What's the meaning of the term
   atonal music?
A: Some day, somehow, someone is going
   to atone for it.
```

The following evening, Richard phoned to say the MSM switchboard had been jammed for three days and there was already a paragraph inside the *New York Times*. 'It's OK. The tone is sceptical.'

As yet.

'I'll mail it to you,' he promised.

But the computer printout in his next letter didn't look like Usenet. There was a thick wad of sheets, all with similar headers:

Series 1 (60 min, black/white) . . . Series 5 (30 min, color)

Then some details caught her eye under 'Series 5'.

Out of a Concrete Tower
Special Guests: William Shatner, Jack Nicholson

She flicked to the concluding page.

Reckoning (final episode of "Dr. Kildare")
Special Guest: Richard Beymer

Her own Richard had gone to a great deal of effort to find a complete listing of *Dr Kildare*, which, in his eyes, demonstrated that he had been right in Boston, and she had been wrong. And posted it to her.

54

The next day, the story progressed to page 2 of the *New York Times*. When her mother phoned for one of her chats, Nina felt her own guilt as a chemical fog, stinging like smoke from a factory stack.

'It was a year ago today, dear, that I flew to Cape Town. Little did I know I was saying goodbye to your poor father for the last time.' Then she said something unexpected. 'I've been thinking a lot about the past. Although I was horrified when I discovered I was expecting Susan, Martin was right that the baby was a godsend, because of the change it wrought in all our lives – his, mine and yours too, dear. Our little saviour, he used to say, because the upheaval kept us all too seasick to look backwards, and drew a line under those dark years. He was so good, you know, making sure you were never left out. He worked so hard to compensate for the past.'

His little saviour. Had she misheard, all those years ago, her resentment of this sudden sibling warping his words in her ears? *Our* little saviour?

'Mum,' began Nina and hesitated. 'Did you completely forgive him?'

'Oh darling, completely is a big word. Forgiveness is the most strenuous of Christian virtues.'

Which Nina knew.

She started working unpaid days at the adult numeracy centre, did extra shifts at the Samaritans. She told Jussi, 'It's not to my credit. Psychologists call it projection. I'm in such a mess, I want the world to help me so I'm helping the world.'

'Don't beat yourself up about it. There's plenty of people, when they're fucked up they turn vicious. You turn into Mother Teresa. Problem is, this isn't working. You don't sleep, you don't eat. If the worst happens and the excrement impacts the electric extractor system, how you going to cope? You need to reboot. How about gardening? That always calms you down.'

Nina took Jussi's idea and bounced it off the wall. She didn't want to work in her beautiful garden, she wanted to give it to people. So she threw a party in it.

'An afternoon-to-midnight extravaganza,' repeated Duane, 'with Greg's sound system and theatrical floods after dark. So, point one, the garden will be trashed.'

'There's patio space and stepping stones.'

'And guests who'll fall on the booze and collapse on your cosmea. Let's move on to point two. You're talking cables and hi-fi equipment. Might I ask what you'll do if it rains?'

But it didn't rain.

Sean and Victoria joined her in a spirit of Blitzkrieg defiance. They'd had a bill from the taxman: 'I would never insist on tax *person*,' said Victoria, 'as I would for more respectable professions. Hang person, for instance. Or mafia hit person.'

All the neighbours came so there was no one to call the police. (And the Terence Trent D'Arby couple had moved on.) Greg brought half the clientele of the Mean Fiddler. And grumbled about her Pink Floyd.

'Here, I've brought something. You like medical men. Give Dr Dre a spin.'

The Director of Ealing Samaritans arrived with his teenage children who had obviously been shanghaied into it, expecting pineapple chunks on sticks. As they copped the extraordinary walled flower garden dripping with lights and blasted with Marshall amps the son said, 'Wicked!' and the daughter said, 'Oh Dad, this is *so* embarrassing!'

Nina loved having the place full of happy people, her garden a moving coloured collage, an art installation. But nobody could have called it a day off. It wasn't long before Duane took her aside. 'New York just came online,' he said, talking out of the side of his mouth. 'Jeremy's calling me back when he's downloaded.'

I feel like a world leader being updated on the Cuban Missile Crisis, thought Nina.

An hour later he was at her elbow again. 'Mostly it's about crystallized overarching cadences.'

'What fun.'

'But they're on to Cape Town. That joker with his list. Alejandro Santana made only one long call that day. So far, the Usenet guy's only got the country and city codes.'

A voice called, 'Freddy! We made it! Lu's on her way with some man, apparently. We don't ask. Oh Nina, you *are* clever!' Gian and Beryl had emerged into the garden.

'NINA! MORE GUESTS FOR YOU.'

Lucia's man was extremely good-looking. 'This is Tod. Tod, Nina's my best and oldest friend. And that handsome couple by the hollyhocks, staring at us like morality campaigners monitoring four-letter words on TV, are my celebrated parents.'

And there was Jussi. 'Anything more happened?'

'It's spinning out of control. I have to phone Susan.'

She got André. 'We know,' he said. 'I've handled Susan's crises before and I'll handle this one.'

'But what if they get the phone number and—?'

'Then we'll double-lock our double gates, retreat behind our barbed wire and set the guards and dogs on them. If I were you, Nina, I'd worry about what I was going to do in an unprotected ground-floor flat in Harlesden.'

At which he put the phone down, leaving Nina to shout,

'Bloody *chutzpah*!' just as her ex-boss appeared in the doorway.

By mid-afternoon Duane had moved on to point three. Nina's cassette tape. 'I bet one half of this party knows you got a dodgy symphony and the other half has read all the bumph on Usenet. At some point, the two factions will meet up and take your flat apart. Get the tape upstairs and lock the door.'

At dusk, care of a friend of Greg's, the night lighting came on, haloing the guests in St Elmo's fire under the sodium glow of the London sky. And downwind of some rather good ganja, Duane agreed to dance a tango with Jussi.

The gangsta rap was taken off the sound system to be replaced by a tango called 'Feline'. The men were floodlit on the patio. They faced each other, not yet in hold but eye to eye, two fit, muscular men with locked gaze. As Jussi moved, Duane mirrored him. It *is* feline, thought Nina, they are cats squaring up for a fight. The men circled each other, and Nina pictured slouch hats in alleyways, *compadritos* with knives up their sleeves. They stamped and clicked their heels. Jussi reached out and took Duane into hold.

It was entirely unlike watching a man and a woman. So much more upper-body tone, so much more resistance in the arms. The sheer speed and momentum this produced was savage. You could feel the whip in the whiplash *ganchos*, the lasso in the decorative twists, the power in the rotating hips, shoulders, buttocks. The music marched on, *one* two, *one* two, the time signature of an army on the move, of controlled aggression. The time signature of sex. These men were no longer fighting.

Really, the sexual imagery was overpowering. The entwining limbs came together with a snap but the release was serpentine. Every move was a thrust, fast in but slow out. Every hesitation was inflamed. When Duane wrapped a muscular leg round Jussi's waist the party guests let out a shout. The tempo was speeding up. On the final bar, Jussi spun Duane round and bent him over backwards like a flick-knife. The party whooped and hollered.

After that, everyone was dancing tango: girls with girls, fathers with daughters, women with total strangers who bent them over in a Valentino swoon, their eyes on fire.

'Hey, Nina, your turn,' called Duane, and grabbed her.

Unnoticed by anyone in the garden, Nina's phone rang. One of her teaching colleagues was wedged in the kitchen, and heard it. The call was Richard.

'Who? Nina? No way, my friend. There's upwards of five dozen people between me and her. Anyhow, right now Nina's dancing a tango. From what I could make out through the window, she had one leg clamped on the guy's thigh and the other wrapped round his neck in a headlock. When the girl's back on her feet, you want me to say who phoned?'

'If you would. Tell her that while she had her legs fastened round her boyfriend, Richard called.'

'Sure thing.'

She put the phone down and had forgotten all about it before she got back to the kitchen.

55

Nina's garden wasn't exactly trashed, but it had taken a battering.

She wasn't distressed. The eloquent debris – green bottles, dropped chicken legs, orphaned clumps of grapes and tomatoes – were to Nina another collage, a welcome prolongation of party atmosphere. When the doorbell rang, she had an armful of broken cosmea. A man in a smart suit said, 'Miss Nina Hannay?'

'Yes.'

'Detective Chief Inspector Nigel Lowry.' He held up his ID. 'New Scotland Yard.'

He wouldn't sit. 'I prefer to nose around. Goes with the training. Nice garden,' he added at the window.

Nina's trembling hands were betraying her. She put them behind her back. 'Everything's upside down. I had a party yesterday.' She tried a smile. 'But no one called the police.'

'Unlike an earlier occasion,' he smiled back. 'Last May. Two uniforms were called out.'

Nina made no reply.

'Thing about our job is everything has to be reported. The motto says if it isn't written down it never happened.

We record a summary of the incident and the cause of the fracas. In your case the cause was a pile of handwritten music, and your male companion believed it was a lost masterpiece by the composer Sibelius. Might I trouble you for a cup of tea, Miss Hannay? I'm parched. Milk and two sugars.'

As Nina moved round the kitchen she said, 'My male companion was wrong. The music was written by my late father in his youth.'

'Your father was a composer?'

'A wannabe. Studied composition.'

'Where?'

Nina hesitated.

'Where?' repeated Lowry.

'Helsinki,' said Nina reluctantly.

'*Finland*. Now that *is* interesting!' His nosing had now brought him over to the fridge. Sprawled across the enamel were Duane's printouts. Lowry picked them up. 'I was going to ask if you'd come across this tittle-tattle.'

'What is this about, please?'

'These very rumours, Miss Hannay. Somebody is feeding snippets of music to an American professor, and one way or another his friends are letting slip it's the eighth symphony of Sibelius. Of course, we leave copyright matters to the civil courts. But for crimes of theft, dealing in stolen goods and conspiracy to defraud the composer, the heirs and the publishers, we have various departments, some of them with international contacts in countries with extradition treaties. Ah, lovely,' he added because Nina had poured his tea. 'You see, Miss Hannay, there's a strategy sometimes used for art theft. Leak a few details, let the market heat up, then sell at fever pitch. Take the money and run. If such a crime had a British connection, it would come to us.'

'So you've come to me.'

'Just for a chat. This Kuutar,' he waved the printouts, 'she's talking about a Sibelius score that runs to a hundred and ninety pages with a final movement for choir. Last May you were in possession of a score that your boyfriend said was Sibelius, it ran to a couple of hundred pages and included a lot of singing. Have you got it here, by the way? I'd love to take a look.'

Nina said carefully, 'I haven't. And for my own reasons I'd rather not tell you where it is.'

'Pity.'

'Mr Lowry, I assure you I'm not preparing to sell any score, by Sibelius or anybody else.'

'Delighted to hear it. But how about your sister?' He sipped his tea. The mug clunked as he reset it on Nina's table.

'My – sister?'

'That's who sent the snippets, isn't it? From Constantia, near Cape Town. She posted them to Santana with a précis of pivotal information including some verses from Finnish poetry. Then it was leaked by a Miss Janis Klein aka Kuutar. That would suggest it was smuggled out of Finland. Which is where your father was, in the days when he was still Martti Hannikainen.'

Even the pronunciation was correct. Nina thought, This is one of the few times in my life I've truly wondered if I'm having a nightmare. And she realized this was precisely his intention: the caricatured TV persona, snide and smart-arse, was calculated to the point of being rehearsed. To frighten her.

'Any relation to the conductor?' he asked lightly. 'Reminds me of those lager commercials. Perhaps Hannikainen reaches the parts other conductors cannot reach. And his largo is probably the best largo in the world.'

'Mr Lowry, this is a series of stupid blunders. My sister isn't a criminal, she's merely criminally arrogant. I'm sure even Scotland Yard knows that life is more cock-up than conspiracy.'

'Yes? I don't have a sister myself but I've got a brother. He's a bit like that. One in every family, perhaps.'

Then a thought prickled Nina's mind. 'If you linked this with my name on the police computer, then—'

'Now, now, Miss Hannay, if we had innocent members of the community on a police computer, that would be illegal, wouldn't it? No, it's just that the incident was out of the ordinary for Harlesden, so one of the officers remembered it.'

'And reads musical gossip on Usenet?'

Lowry sketched a vague wave. 'Oh, it was mentioned to somebody who passed it up the line till it reached a colleague who has musical connections and also happens to be computer literate. Call it a string of coincidences. We all deserve a bit of luck sometimes. Anyway, I've said what I came to say. Prevention is always better than cure. No doubt your friends in the medical world would agree, both here and in Boston, Massachusetts. Thanks for the tea. I'll see myself out.'

When he left, Nina stood by the sink a moment absently running water for the wilting cosmea. Then she fled to the bathroom and was violently sick.

56

'Let me check,' said Richard's staff assistant. Then the chirrupy voice resumed, '*I'm* sorry, but Dr Quentin is busy right now.'

'Could you let him know it's terribly urgent?'

Nina never phoned Richard in tones of high drama. He would call back the first chance he got. When he hadn't done so by evening, she phoned again.

'I gave Dr Quentin your message. Like me to remind him?'

'No, he must be really tied up. I imagine he'll call later from home.'

But he didn't.

The following lunchtime Lucia said, 'Kiddo, you look grim. Still hung over from Sunday?' Then without waiting for a reply she handed Nina a Jiffy bag, stiffly disfigured by a hardback book. *Muistelmat.* 'Good news, by the way. I got fifteen per cent discount. Invoice is inside.'

'Thanks.'

'If you want to tear the bag open and devour the contents, go ahead. As Jussi says, I'm Coolio Iglesias.'

'Does he?'

'Did to me. Nina, what's up?'

She had spent a white night sweating under a strangled duvet.

'You're too shattered to even tell me. Okey-dokey, it'll wait.'

When she got home, Nina wrenched the staples from the padded envelope and started on the typed pages that rendered into English her marked-up sections of *Muistelmat*.

Nina knew to expect a rant. The author had been synonymous all her life with a violent tirade thrown down in grief. It was clear immediately that the voice of *Muistelmat* was quietly measured. Most of the pages told her nothing useful; she had wasted her money. According to the random glimpses afforded by her mistaken Post-it notes, the Virtas' home was a happy one and Veikko grew up a happy boy. His father went on to introduce the cast of the drama to come. Martti Hannikainen was described as 'The son of a lawyer, he failed to live up to his early promise as a violinist.' There was detailed coverage of the Tolvajärvi–Äglajärvi campaign. And those letters.

25 December 1939

Good Mr Virta,

I would not intrude upon a father's grief had I not something to say that might be one drop of consolation in the sea of anguish. I was with your dear departed son when he was taken from us. I write to tell you the end was quick and merciful. Our enemy has done many terrible things, but this at least was fast. A bullet to the heart. The assassin met the same fate and fell within moments of your son, at my own hands. I was glad to be the instrument of it. I pray with you and I partake of your sorrow.

Martti Hannikainen

The other letter was prefaced by an explanation:

```
Rifleman Kaarlo Sippola had no family at
home. A lonely boy, he wrote letters to
a Little Lotta.
```

Nina found 'Little Lotta' in one of her books: *A kind of Girl Guide outfit. Among their duties, they wrote letters to servicemen who had no family of their own.*

```
This teenage girl I will call only by
her Christian name of Elina. Kaarlo
Sippola was wounded at Ägläjärvi and
treated in the field hospital. The wound
became infected and he died. That letter
was his last. More than five years
later, Elina brought it to me.
```

So a lonely dying boy wrote his last letter to a girl he had never met. Nina fetched her history books. Somehow, the idea was unbearable that she might read through this letter, trip over obstacles of incomprehension and *then* have to turn back to the books. She must possess a solid framework within which to read the story that blew her father's life apart.

Järvi means lake; on a map the region looks as full of holes as a lace curtain. The enemy had the only high ground, and by a filthy stroke of luck the one hill boasted a brand-new hotel – a stonking great structure of granite and logs from whose windows the Soviet Army aimed its formidable firepower in warmth and luxury. All they lacked was bloody room service.

The Finns didn't even have heavy guns. That hotel had to be taken by infantry soldiers moving uphill from foxhole to foxhole while the enemy fired on anything that moved. Erik and Martti.

Nina knew what happened inside: among the torn and bloody dead, survivors huddled in the debris – boys, kids, shivering with terror, openly sobbing. Russian front-line rumours said the Finns tortured their prisoners to death. It would haunt Nina's father all his life, the memory of those shell-shocked boys in despair. But his platoon had just taken the hotel. The Finns had won the battle of Tolvajärvi.

Desperate with exhaustion, having barely slept for days, they slogged on, the heroes of Tolvajärvi, a gruelling push across snow and ice fields with the Soviets in the air, bombing and strafing the road.

The Finns stormed Ägläjärvi village at noon on 22 December, the only daylight a long dawn around midday. Nina's picture of it went beyond the recital of battle plan and chaos; she could taste the desperate cold, the jagged rage of machine-gun fire, the evilly glinting bayonets. Her father watched one of his friends kippered with bullets fired by what they had taken to be a corpse on a kitchen floor. He lost track of Erik. In the yard of a timbered farmhouse he found Veikko Virta clambering through a sandbagged door together with another soldier, a boy, just eighteen. Nina had never known his name. Until now.

```
25 December 1939
Hello Elina,
I write from the field hospital. How I
hope you have joy at Christmas, though
we know how it is at home.
   The surgeons amputated my left hand. We
make tired jokes that it is good I never
learned to play piano. I am afraid. I
have seen soldiers with my wounds, who
develop weakness and then fever. They
rage. There is much to rage against but
it is never lonely here. Lonelier at
home, perhaps, where no soldier can tell
```

the truth. Fellows return from furlough
exhausted with pretending.

Poor little Elina! I write as if you too
were a weary soldier in foot-rags! My
heart is so troubled. I must not meet the
Lord God without recording what I know.

A farmhouse, once with its daily life
of a working family and horses in the
fields. Such dreadful things have
happened in this war even to horses. The
enemy does not have our compassion for
animals. I was with my friend Veikko
Virta, you know him well from my letters. Another of our soldiers appeared,
an acquaintance of Veikko from Sixth
Company, Rifleman Martti Hannikainen. He
was asking about a man named Erik but
Veikko could give him no news.

The outbuildings were in ruins, the
farmhouse door strewn with enemy dead.
Veikko believed all was safe. He had the
courage of a lion and he was also
shrewd, but he was wrong this time. We
heard movement above and withdrew. Veikko
threw another grenade at a window. When
the dust died down, we entered the farmhouse a second time. More smoke, more
ruin, though the stairs were intact.

Machine-gun fire exploded from above. A
cat was crying, a terrible sound, not
bearable to hear. Then I knew there was
no cat, the mewing was me. I rocked on
the filthy floor among the corpses,
cradling the remains of my fingers. I
suppose Veikko and Martti Hannikainen
went together up the staircase. I heard
no more from machine-guns but perhaps it

was only that the Reds' automatic
ammunition had run out and they still
had handguns.

I heard shots and the foreign shout of
a dying man. I heard bodies hit the
floor over my head. I expected to die
then. A heavy tread came down the stairs
and a voice called 'Kaarlo!' It was
Martti Hannikainen, and he carried the
body of good, brave Veikko. He told me
the farmhouse might be torched and we
must not leave our friend to burn. To
carry the body endangered him greatly,
and I did, too, with my slowness,
stumbling along and crying. These were
good things for him to do, Elina, to
carry Veikko from the house and wait for
me.

Those are the events to which I was
auditor: a pistol shot, a body hitting
the floor, another shot, another body
going down, shouting in Russian. But I
did not hear them in that order. Just
two men fell. The first to die was
Russian. So the second was Veikko, and
he fell after the enemy was dead.

57

There was no further reference to this from Jorma Virta. He had not compounded the libel with speculation of his own; the numerous other references to her father were innocuous: his attendance at Veikko's funeral, his demob, his work on clearing bomb damage. As though, thought Nina, Virta had no intention of allowing the reader to forget the name.

'*Hei! Kansa Taisteli!*'

'Do you speak English?'

'Yes. Tovio Kuusiniemi speaking.'

'My name is Nina Hannay. I'm doing some research.'

'We are a magazine of military history.'

'I know. In 1945, the industrialist Jorma Virta published a book entitled *Muistelmat*. Does that . . . do you know the name?'

'No.'

'It contained an allegation that a soldier named . . . named Hannikainen . . . that he deliberately . . . shot the author's son. Dead. It caused a rumpus.'

In the nauseating seconds that followed, Nina registered the man's negative reply before the first syllable was out.

'I am sorry. I do not know this.'

Bitter hopelessness sluiced over her. Two quiet lines in a book. She could not stop herself picturing the scene Kaarlo Sippola presented of her father murdering Veikko with a handgun, but 'scene' it was. Cinematic. She saw her father on set in an artfully directed movie, just twenty years old, his uniform distressed by Wardrobe. It hadn't the power to appal her. What frightened Nina was that none of it, not the accusation itself nor Jorma Virta's understated authorial voice, fitted the tenor of the story she'd been given all her life. She could not rest, could not cope, *could not go on breathing* without an explanation. Her father was slipping away from her like mist through a sieve. She would have to fly to Finland and do the research herself. Nina saw an unspeakably tedious drudge in newspaper morgues searching for his name or some linguistic inflection thereof. Of photocopying and shelling out for translations, of money bleeding into hotel bills and plane fares. The weariness weighed down on Nina as if she'd already had weeks of it.

She said, 'Martti Hannikainen helped take the hotel at Tolvajärvi. Virta's son was in Pajari's midnight raid on skis.'

'Heroes, then. I am surprised to hear of a murder allegation.'

And did they get you to trade your heroes for ghosts? 'Wish You Were Here'. God, I wish you were here, Dad, to talk to me.

'Possibly this is of interest for our magazine,' said Tovio Kuusiniemi. 'I know a historian in Tampere whose specialty is the post-war years. I will ask.'

'Would you? That is so—'

'But what precisely is your question?'

*

'Oh God, Richard, I've been worried sick!'

'I did try to call.'

'*Really?* I—' Nina had twice phoned the engineer to check the line.

'You were dancing a tango.'

'But that . . . that was Sunday. It's now Friday.'

'I left a message with one of your guests. Apparently you were too busy with your dance partner.'

Nina's head clicked through readadjustments. 'I told you I was having a party.' And when Richard didn't reply, 'I danced a tango with Duane.' Still no response. 'It was Duane. Duane Davies.'

'You don't mean from IT? *That* Duane Davies?'

'Yes,' agreed Nina, vastly relieved. 'That Duane Davies.'

'The guy that stung the company for double severance pay just to relocate two VAX-8600s. *That* Duane Davies.'

'What do you mean, stung? He negotiated it. Don't be ridiculous.'

'He is some negotiator.'

'Richard, stop this.' She was near panic. 'Duane is one of my closest friends. He is also gay. He is so gay, he publishes gay porn. In Duane's own words he's as queer as a coot, a football bat, a pint of Thursdays. Duane dances a mean tango but preferably in the arms of a debonair male with rippling muscles.'

'Gay porn,' repeated Richard. 'Nina, I'm in the healthcare industry. You will not endear this guy to a doctor by saying he works on HIV-promoting activities. I also assumed you had a more finely tuned sense of erstwhile corporate loyalty.'

Since Sunday, Nina had had a plainclothes policeman in her kitchen and had read an account of her father as a killer. She had also imagined Richard in trouble too desperate to confide in her, in car crashes, in traction. She had imagined him dead. She felt as if her nerve endings were sticking out of her skin. Now she was aware of a searing distaste, a refusal to be subjected to this. Nina was convinced there was no such expression as 'erstwhile corporate loyalty', and that Richard did not believe HIV could be contracted from reading fiction.

She said, 'Tell me you didn't turn your back on my panic-stricken messages because somebody told you I danced a tango with my own friend at my own party.'

'The fact is, Nina, I've had the week from hell.'

'Oh? I think we should talk again when you've got that edge out of your voice.'

Richard cut in. It might even have been an apology. If so, he was too late. Nina tugged the plug out of the wall and threw the phone across the room.

58

He didn't call her the following evening. He immediately flew to London and called her Saturday morning from Heathrow.

'It felt like the right thing to do.' Richard's voice was bleary from a night flight and a jetlag that told him it was two in the morning. 'Though admittedly the idea doesn't look quite so clever from here.'

Nina could hear it, the sleep and stubble and ruffled hair. As she had always loved him best.

'Look, I behaved like a fucking idiot,' he said. 'I know this is a crummy excuse but the house was broken into Monday. Burglars were scared off by the alarms, but I've had police and . . . It's still no excuse. I'm a moron. But can I see you?'

Now? Her hair would have to be washed and her leg waxing had expired. She tried to remember where she was in her pill cycle. 'Where will you be staying?'

'How about Harlesden?'

Nina estimated it would take Richard nearly an hour to get there, most of that time reaching the front of the taxi queue. After she put the phone down, she stood a moment, dithering. Then she began.

She changed the bedlinen, ransacked her wardrobe,

leaped in the bath, razored anything that bristled, washed her hair, dressed, made up her face. Then she got the Hoover out.

The problem was Fearless, whose unstable coat continually spilled over the soft furnishings and wove itself into a mohair fuzz. Nina swept through the flat with the Hoover extension on full power, sucking up the occasional clunking pencil and pinging pin. Then the cat jumped back on the sofa and Nina realized the problem was better tackled at source. She put on her gardening gloves and held Fearless down with one hand while she ran the Hoover extension over her with the other. Turning the yowling, scrabbling cat on to her back to do her tummy was no joke, and there was a nasty moment when Nina saw the tail sucked up the pipe, but she finished the job and slung the Hoover into the cupboard. Which was when she gave some thought to what she was going to do with Richard.

Nina imagined Brickstone Road as though in double exposure, the neat street she first moved into with its new conversions and peppy optimism – and now, discouraged, a place of blown litter and dog mess, of weed-eaten concrete in a forest of FOR SALE signs. Her flat was now worth half her mortgage. *He is not a snob*, she shouted at herself. He'll ride out whatever initial jolt is delivered to his assumptions.

Harlesden's Victorian High Street was still elegant when you raised your eyes above the tired awnings and cluttered signage. Nina could picture him outside Mr Adonteng's minimart, beside plywood boxes of vegetables and fruit, his reflection another phantom in the dark window of the teeming shop. She saw him discussing coconut oil and turmeric at cash registers where twice a week she lined up with cat food and skimmed milk. Nina had always accepted the exotic abundance as a still life – shafts of light falling across a barrel of salt cod, the yams, sweet potatoes and green bananas – and its complicatedly spiced interiors as stage-managed atmosphere, no more a culinary matter than the swinging incense at a Roman Catholic Mass. Nina imagined Richard enjoying himself and coming out laden with aromatic carrier bags. She just hoped he wouldn't expect her kitchen to include an eye-level oven in a tower.

A taxi pulled up, its low-frequency vibrations throbbing uncomfortably through the flat. A metal door slammed. The gate clicked. The doorbell rang.

'Nina,' said Richard. 'How about we use this weekend to meet your mother?'

Having him here was dreamlike, literally: ungraspable. His face was becomingly flushed, and as they cuddled and murmured she encountered his skin scent, always elusive to her memory, soap and a spicy bedroom warmth. He glanced around him at her piano and the wall of books, their multi-coloured spines presenting an artwork of a thousand vertical brushstrokes. Outside he said, 'The famous garden,' examining its smudged stepping stones. One of her sweet-pea trellises leaned drunkenly where a tangoing guest had lost her balance.

'It will look better when it's grown back,' Nina told him, like someone speaking of a bad haircut. Over the wall, the recently hauled-away mattress had left its alter ego behind, an oblong of bleached grass – waxy and slimy like skin held too long underwater.

Nina's mother reacted predictably to the news that they were coming. 'Oh how lovely, dear! I'll put the kettle on.'

'Mum, rather than give you any trouble by staying the night, we'll book into a hotel.' Where we can sleep together, she mouthed at Richard who was stroking her hair.

'Extravagant, just like your father. Of course you will both stay here.'

Richard fell asleep in the car and Nina drove quietly, resenting every shudder that assailed his heartbreaking vulnerability. He woke as they neared the coast, and she was warmed by his eagerness to look, his fascination at the zigzagging pheasants, the distant trickling lines of houses marking ancient shorelines from before the land was reclaimed. And the winding lanes. 'But what are they winding to avoid?' he demanded, amused. 'There's nothing!'

Christine Hannay had brought out the bone china. 'How your father would have loved to be here,' she said.

Somehow, Richard's presence felt less outlandish in the setting of her mother's struggling gentility, her more accessible version of shabbiness.

'You're a doctor, Richard? So Nina's found her Dr Kildare. Did you know that your New England churches were based on our St Martin-in-the-Fields with the steeple over the portico?'

You owe me five farthings say the bells of St Martin's. Oranges and lemons say the bells of . . .

When Nina and her mother were making up the bed in the spare room, Christine said, 'There's something I need to ask you, dear. This place has *not* felt like home since Martin passed on.'

'I know, Mum.'

'Susan and André have been urging me to live with them on the Cape. I've always said no because it would mean leaving you. But perhaps, if you will be spending a lot of time in Boston . . . How do you feel about the idea?'

The starched pillowcase crackled in Nina's hand. I feel about the idea that Susan is a treacherous bitch whose blundering is about to splash our name across the world news – our name and Kaarlo Sippola's letter. With panic in her voice she said, 'Mum, Susan and André will scram at the first sight of a black president.'

'Now, Nina!'

'And what about poor Kruger? He couldn't re-enter this country without going into quarantine.'

Richard appeared in the doorway. Christine turned to him. 'Do you have brothers and sisters?'

'No, ma'am.'

She sighed with maternal bewilderment. 'I'm told siblings always scrap. Of course, it was difficult for Susan, coming along so very late and in Nina's wake. Their father loved them both to pieces, of course, but Susan could never see it. He was so devoted to music, you see. Nina was the same – she could play the violin and piano at the age of five but poor Susan had to inherit my tin ear. Nina even hears music in colour like he did. I've never come across anyone else with that gift, just Nina, Martin and Martin's Sibelius. No wonder Susan felt a failure. She always thought she had to achieve twice as much as her sister to get the same recognition. At Oxford the poor girl nearly worked herself into the ground. I would never say this to André, but part of his attraction was living six thousand miles away from the causes of Susan's inferiority complex. *So* silly, but we're all a little irrational in our heart of hearts, aren't we?'

Oh God, thought Nina. I get everything wrong. Everything's simpler than I think. And so bloody obvious that I miss it.

After lunch her mother was looking tired, so Nina took Richard and Kruger to the coast.

He said, 'Maybe it will ease your mind if your mother is settled, too. Darling, you know our future is together. By the way, why was she so interested in my Vietnam experience?'

The glorious import of his statement, said with the casual assurance of someone voicing the self-evident, was scuppered for Nina by one shadowy word that lay at its heart.

She said, 'Right now the future is something I'm scared to look in the face.' And she talked him through Mr Lowry's cheerful threats.

'Fuck,' said Richard.

'The latest from Usenet is mostly lofty terminology, but there's also news about Alejandro Santana: he was overheard behind yet another office door, this one the Dean's. He was being roasted.'

'Serves the bugger right,' said Richard.

But she didn't tell him about that dying soldier's letter. When Nina had heard herself say the words aloud on the phone to Helsinki they had soured the air in colours like a spreading bruise. She hadn't the courage to announce them to Richard and have them mingle with the mess of Usenet and plainclothes police. And watch him wrestle to arrange the pieces into one unified picture.

'Let's walk,' he suggested. 'This place is magnificent.'

They had arrived at the harbour. Kruger sniffed the wind, which was saline from the retreating tide. The three of them walked for hours. They walked until she no longer wanted to howl at her dead father.

Here on Nina's Finnish coastline it seemed an invidious injustice that the symphony couldn't just be set free, liberated into the arena of batons and interpretation, where its brothers in genius could sculpt the fine materials into subtly varying statuary, each sculptor bringing new meaning to the ambiguities, the half-smiles, the chiaroscuro of sunlight on marble. It was an affront to her soul that this couldn't be brought about without bemerding her father in the press and raining wretchedness upon her mother.

But perhaps here she could expiate one facet of her guilt. Nina considered returning to the coast with a Walkman and Greg, Greg who had been known to weep buckets over *Tapiola* yet had not given her symphony a single tear. Perhaps this coast would provide a respite, somewhere they wouldn't treat it as an intellectual puzzle or as the catalyst for ruin. Perhaps here they could cry.

Everywhere there were sailing boats. In the water, they bobbed or drifted. Others, beached, were being hauled along by men in soaking-wet lycra that would have had Tom of Finland reaching for his sketching pencil. There was an incessant frantic tinkling like wind chimes. Nina had never lived on this coast; its rhythms and routines were foreign to her. 'What's making that noise?'

Richard knew. 'It's the sound of halyards tapping on aluminum masts. The music of the harbour.'

Nina laughed. 'You can hear the next question coming, can't you?'

'A halyard is a rope,' he explained patiently. Then, 'What amazing vegetation.'

'That's called shrubby sea blite. And those birds will probably turn out to be twites and bearded tits. My poor father used to go into hysterics. It was probably some wildlife poster that triggered his heart attack.'

At Wells-next-the-Sea, Richard nearly had one of his own. The sight of the beach huts did it.

'It's a shanty town!'

'Oh, but a genteel one, please.' Nina was struggling to hold him up. A long wavy line snaked down the sands – two hundred sheds on high stilts, higgledy-piggledy. The best were perkily painted in blue, yellow or cherry red, Caribbean colours, like homes for cartoon characters singing 'Zippity Doo Dah'. Each had its flight of steps; many boasted twee, decorated verandas. There were jaunty names: Captain's Cabin, Sea Shanty, Dun Shrimpin.

'Do they get *postal deliveries*?' Richard stopped. 'Look at the name of that one!'

Sea View. They both lost it. They clutched each other, pointing and laughing at the gaudy madness of the huts.

'Had we better be going back?' suggested Richard eventually. Even the dog looked weary.

Her mother said gratefully, 'What a treat for Kruger. By the way, dear, before I move, would you help me clear out the loft? For a start there's a toy stethoscope and *Dr Kildare* telephone that should be in a jumble sale. I'm afraid that's another thing you inherited from your father. The tendency to store junk.'

59

Greg said, 'How does bar pianist in a top London hotel sound? Terrible hours, brilliant money. But you'd have to start tonight. They've been let down.'

Nina loved it. There were even tips ('You don't get that in the pharma industry,' she boasted to Duane). On the other hand the hours clashed with Boston's, so no phone calls. On the Friday after her Norfolk weekend she got a letter dated Tuesday.

My dearest Nina,
Today I have an eye patch. This piratical fashion accessory is part of the deal I made this morning with the surgeon – he agreed to laser my cataract if I agreed to the patch.

My sight has been deteriorating for months. They don't talk about double vision, the term is 'ghosts', so I was torn between handing myself over to a surgeon or an exorcist.

The procedure was successful but the run-up was not funny. Fear of blindness is a deep human terror, and I was almost as afeared of the surgery as I was of losing my sight. There's no let-up to that dread when you're seeing double all the time. Treble. Standing with you on the sands at Wells there was more than one line of beach huts. I asked myself: could this be my first *and last* sight of muzzy double British beach huts before darkness closes in?

The image of him frightened ravaged her. The desire to wrap Richard in her arms was stifling. Unable to do that, she phoned his office, which was quietly enjoying its night time, and left extravagant messages on his answer machine. Then she sank on to her sofa, sightless herself and trembling. She shook, and wept, and gulped for air like fish stranded on the sands of Holkham Bay.

Emerging an hour later she felt utterly dazed, wrung out. She wanted somebody to run her a hot bath, wrap her in fluffy towels, put her to bed with a milky drink and sing her to sleep. She was in danger of crying on and off all afternoon; she would turn up at the hotel bar with her face swollen like the loser of a fistfight. Only a comfort that reached to the bones could staunch this haemorrhage. Lu was at work. It would have to be music.

Not long ago at the dentist, paying for her long-term neglect with root-canal work, Nina had experienced a strange phenomenon. The radio was on, playing Beatles songs dating from the very worst days in Seaton Bois. Its calming effects reached across the years, bone deep. Yet this was counterintuitive: how can anything that's inseparable from the worst misery of your life bring such reassurance? Nevertheless it did. Now, she sat down at her piano.

The theme from *Dr Kildare* was for orchestra and bell, a grown-up Big Ben bell, tolling through the deep-blue music in shivering circles of gold. Nina hadn't heard it in a couple of decades. How did it open? With a clever descending figure. After four bars the strings swept in, subsuming the motif beneath the melody proper. Nina essayed some chords. She was off.

It felt good beneath her fingers, the luminous confidence

of its theme and leaping intervals, the abrupt splintering into figures that ran back and forth between her colluding hands.

That night Nina played it again, in a bar packed with American businessmen. Before its closing chords decayed, she had an audience round the Yamaha grand.

'You know any others? Did you people get *Perry Mason*?'

So Nina gave them a plashy rendition of *Perry Mason*, after which the crowd was four-deep and singing along to *The Flintstones*. By the time they concluded with a whooping, air-punching, head-'em-up, move-'em-out *Rawhide*, there were furious pyjama'd guests in the bar shouting and the duty manager was gesticulating like a one-man semaphore show. It didn't matter to Nina. She'd just made enough in tips to keep her for a month.

*

Lu nibbled her lip. 'Nina, I don't like the sound of that jealous tantrum after your party.'

They were in Nina's kitchen. It was Saturday morning. Lu had arrived at the door, taken one look at her friend, and wormed the story out of her. She had brought along a bag of *pains au chocolat*, which were now traduced to greasy crumbs and a smear across Lu's right palm. Nina's timid cat was curled in Lu's lap, purring like a lawn mower.

Nina said, 'Richard was so ashamed he caught the next plane to London. What more can a man do?'

'You left messages for five days. He wanted you to stew. He was punishing you, kiddo.'

'No. His house had burglars and—'

'You said it didn't. The burglars were scared off. Nina, I'm worried. You talk about living three thousand miles away from your friends in a town you don't know, and dependent on him. I've done it, kid, and it's no picnic even when the man's a sweetie. If there's even a *chance* he's an emotional manipulator, don't do it.'

'Richard is a sweetie at heart, Lu. Trust me.'

'All right then, what about this? You're walking along the beach at Wells in that special cosiness, deep in love, you think he's happy. Only actually he's seeing double and terrified about surgery and going blind.'

'Exactly,' said Nina. 'If only—'

'It strikes me there were two legitimate ways Richard could have dealt with it. He could have said, "Nina, I'm scared," and let you comfort him, which, incidentally, you would have loved to do. Or he could have chosen silence. After all, you'd got troubles of your own. He opted for another way. He waited till it was too late for you to do anything and wrote a letter carefully pointing out that while you were on the wings of love at Wells, he was scared shitless. Why bring the beach huts into it? If he'd been seeing double for weeks he could have cited anything. Why *Wells* – unless it was deliberate, to make you feel guilty somehow? I know you hate me for saying this, kid, but I still have to say it.'

'I don't hate you.' Nina produced the carcass of a smile. 'I might if you were right but you're wrong. When someone's scared, they don't think clearly.'

'He wasn't scared by the time he wrote you. The surgery was successful. That's my point. He's insecure, right? Is that because of his father?'

'I'm sure. Look, Lu, the unpalatable truth is I seem to fall for insecure men who need comforting. Nothing to be proud of but there you have it. Goes hand in hand with the Samaritans and—'

'And bandaging poor Tyger. I know, little Moomintroll, this is Lulu. But were you aware that Richard was insecure when you fell for him? I mean, did you see a guy crying out for TLC, and say, "That's the man for me!"?'

Nina didn't know how to answer.

'Let me tell you why I ask. In Toronto, I had a friend whose fiancé used to hit her. It wasn't her first taste of domestic violence: her father would come home drunk and beat up her mother. When at last she ditched the fiancé she had counselling and said she understood herself now, she was attracted to violent men because of her father. I knew it was bullshit. She *hated* being hit. She'd cower in corners, wetting herself. Don't tell me she was on the lookout for more. The thing is, the first time I met that guy I could *smell* that he was a bully. She was the one who couldn't. Signs that set off danger signals in me went unnoticed by her because she grew up with them as the wallpaper of her life.'

The cat stirred in Lu's lap. Lu kissed the top of its head and settled Fearless back on the floor. Nina thought distractedly, I have never managed that without having my thighs clawed like a knife attack.

Lu went on, 'I'm afraid there might be qualities in Richard that will near destroy you, and because of your history you won't pick up on them till it's too late.'

Nina, hot-faced, was biting back a reply. Lu tactfully turned away and caught sight of a sheaf of American quarto. '*Series 5*,' she read, '*William Shatner and Jack Nicholson.* Wow! Where'd you get this?'

60

Nina was in bed. She twisted under the duvet with a restlessness that felt willed from elsewhere, as though her worries were physical and weighty, roiling in her light frame, turning her over and over.

She had fits of exhausted mind-drifting. She believed she was practising *giros*. Her teacher in Buenos Aires never could pronounce the word 'axis'. 'Keep your ax straight as you turn!' she called out to Nina.

' "Careful With That Axe, Eugene," ' Nina replied.

'Yes, but the band couldn't follow up *Dark Side Of The Moon*, not in a virtual slump and a creative void. You can't write in a panic. The next album just wasn't up to snuff.'

Nina struggled free of the jangling dream. Believing she was awake, she heard Giancarlo say, 'Don't expect that symphony to heal anything. They were very troubled men, your father and Sibelius.'

Her mother was shouting about the loft. And suddenly, Nina knew why the footwork was so difficult to execute – Jussi's camera was blinding her. *Flash! Flash!* She could hardly make out the dance floor beyond the shining auras. *Flash! Flash! Flash!*

*

'It's Nina. I'm sorry to ask but could you think back to 1966? Not the best of times, I know. You cleared out the loft. Dad found out months later and went ballistic. You must remember.'

'I could hardly forget.'

'What did you chuck away?'

'Whatever you're looking for, my dear, it wasn't thrown out by me in Seaton Bois.'

'No, but can you—?'

'Just the things your poor father accumulated. Carrier bags weighing a ton, that he never touched and which I'd lugged all the way from Southend. You know I would never discard anything valuable. These were just photographs. I don't mean family portraits. Music. Full-plate photographs which the silly man must have carted all the way from Finland and never looked at again. Typical of your poor father. Just music.'

Beryl was out. Nina and Giancarlo walked in the garden, Gian dead-heading the roses.

Nina said, 'Not long after I found the symphony I was talking to Mum and I got to thinking about creativity and how you can't produce anything decent when you're agitated. Grief and misery are a boon, but no one can work in a sick panic. It was Dad I was thinking of, but I should have thought it through further. Because it has implications for Sibelius.'

Giancarlo looked up from his secateurs.

'You see, Gian, I didn't inherit all my father's talents. I'm no symphonist and I'm not even particularly discerning. Even less when I can bask in the beloved familiarity of the composer. When it failed to move anyone to tears I started by blaming the context and then I blamed the synthesizers. But I remember the first time you and I talked about the Eighth, and I referred to it as "this wonderful work of genius". You tried to put me off.' Gian was now completely still. 'I thought you were concerned I'd make myself unhappy stirring up old wounds. I was wrong, wasn't I? You didn't want me making too much of that symphony because you knew from Dad it wouldn't take the weight. That grown men would never weep over it. That it isn't up to snuff.'

Giancarlo slipped his fingers round an opening bud, carmine bleeding into a soapy cream. 'When you were little,' he said, 'somebody told you the legend of the rose breeder smuggling this out of occupied France, so you created an entire melodrama accompanied by violin. It was the night before Beryl and I flew to Melbourne. Lucia cried all night and we got about an hour's sleep between us.' He snapped the stem and handed it to Nina.

'At first,' he said, 'Martin tried to convince himself his instincts were wrong. It seemed impossible that such a composer could produce a second-rate symphony. What's the fashionable expression? Martin was in denial. Also, like you, he was infatuated with its familiarity. Eventually he had to accept the truth. Gusty was the word Martin used. Too many climaxes that just fell away and the music was going nowhere. The needlework was fine but the tapestry wasn't a picture. Your father put the failure down to illness or infirmity. Then in Seaton Bois he was in the midst of his own crisis and a hundred yards down the road was Giancarlo Clark in deadlock. Creative paralysis. For the first time, your father knew what had happened to Sibelius.' Giancarlo smiled. 'Of course I can't class myself with one of the century's best-known musical geniuses but I'm *nearly* that high-strung and difficult. Martin's insight was spot-on.'

'He told you it just didn't—?'

'Didn't hang together. I'm not a musician, Freddy, and anyway the discussion was really about me, but Martin explained that the clever stuff was embedded in far too much padding, and it just wasn't an entity. As mine was not. And the failure was made more apparent because the symphony purported to tell a story. To make that succeed you have to keep driving it forward. So, of course, your

346

father really could have been talking about my cabaret show.'

Nina fiddled with the rose. Its petals spilled from her fingers on to the irreproachably clipped lawn. She said, 'But the analogy doesn't . . . I mean, Sibelius did finish the Eighth whereas you—'

'Many times, I expect. Again and again. I would bet yours isn't the same symphony he burned, but merely one version out of several. If yours dates from the late 1930s, how long had Sibelius been working on it – more than a decade, you said? Well, by then it was full of reworked material but with fewer new ideas than in earlier drafts. I also expect his later ones got shorter as he despaired of entire sections and abandoned them. You told me he once gave a version to be copied by a professional. I'd say that was an attempt to put some distance between him and it. See the piece afresh.'

'Like filming it with a cine camera?' suggested Nina with a smile.

Gian smiled too. 'You remember that? Yes, it didn't work for me either.'

'I'll swear some of the passages are wonderful.'

'Oh, bound to be. Absolute gems. But getting fewer with every new draft as he lost the plot. As a creative unit it would never gel. Panic had set in.'

'A simple case of blue funk in the face of too many folk crying "What will the genius give us next?"'

'That's one way to put it. Sibelius must have realized he couldn't win. The project was so big, you see, and was always going to take too long. The longer he was silent . . . Well, he reached a point where it would make no difference what he produced, he knew what the critics would say.'

'But he was used to being trashed. Fear of bad reviews had never floored him before.'

'He'd never been trashed this way. He knew the very words they would use, and he would rather destroy the thing than hear them.'

'That he was in a virtual slump and a creative void?'

'No, sweetheart. You don't realize how trivial and vain the motivation can be that drives a catastrophe. They would have said about Sibelius what I so dreaded they would say about me when I hit fifty. "The old boy can't hack it any more, he's over the hill." That's what they would have said. "He's just too old." '

61

'Dr Hannay?'

'Yes?'

'I am Docent Kustaa Hahtela of Tampere University. I had a call from—'

'Yes!'

The voice was not young and sounded enough like her father to cause Nina pain.

'I believe I have your information, though it is not what you expect, I think.'

'I'm braced for that.'

'The book *Muistelmat* caused no scandal.' Then, 'Wait one moment, please.' There was a change in sound texture as he set down the receiver, then the noxious percussion as he picked it up again. 'A letter was written by one Kaarlo Sippola to a young lady named—'

'Elina,' broke in Nina. 'I know. The book generated a furore. The author was a significant local bigwig.'

'The Tampere newspapers made reference but very . . . cagey. And not the national papers. There was no *cause célèbre*.'

The words 'You must be wrong' swam into Nina's throat. She thought, I am about to contradict a specialist in post-war Finnish affairs about a post-war Finnish affair. Pains churned at her lower gut. Worry pains.

'Martti Hannikainen was my father,' she said. 'That's how I know he was driven out of Finland. I grew up with the iniquity.'

'I am sorry we are talking of your father but it was not from scandal. The allegation was serious and there was a full military inquiry. Rifleman Hannikainen was cleared without a stain on his character. Kaarlo Sippola was dead but the court determined he had been unreliable as a witness. His letter made it clear he *saw* nothing and was nearly mad with pain. His platoon sergeant described him as immature and emotional. Nurses from the field hospital testified that he had fever when he wrote the letter. Hannikainen himself gave a clear account, and there was no possible motive: the enemy was all around, Sippola was wounded, Veikko Virta was your father's only able-bodied compatriot. For a soldier in battle to kill his only fit companion would be inviting death.'

'So the investigation—?'

'Exonerated him.'

'Docent Hahtela, the story *did* cause uproar.'

'It did not. Dr Hannay, you must understand our situation in Finland. We were sick with war. The Soviets had broken our hearts. Even after defeat they managed to steal our land including most of Karelia, the heartland of our *Kalevala*. There was no appetite for pillorying a hero of Tolvajärvi. If there had been a case to answer, the law would have taken its course. There was none. Besides, we Finns do not turn upon our own people at a whim. We are slow to anger even against our enemies. We are not a nation given to hysteria and spite.'

It was as if Concorde had suddenly done another double thrust in mid-Atlantic and started flying backwards. Nothing made sense. People cover up scandals, but nobody has ever invented one, exiled himself needlessly from the homeland he loved, connived with his best friend for an unnecessary safe haven with strangers. Then Nina pictured her father throwing up in the garden as he waited for the police. He was so afraid, he never returned. Afraid of *what*?

Docent Hahtela said, 'If you give me your address I will post you a copy of the documents. Though of course they are in Finnish.'

The hall was packed. The woman taking money at the door didn't want to let Nina past.

'I'm a friend.'

'Then you should know better than to try and interrupt him.'

'I'm sorry, but I'm coming in.'

Jussi was going from couple to couple. 'I know I told you to eradicate that ballroom technique,' he was saying to a pair with indefatigable Blackpool smiles, 'but don't discard the neonate with the aqueous ablutionary fluid.' Then he caught sight of Nina steaming across the floor with her face set. 'Yeah?' His near-sighted eyes flicked around the room as if assessing the back-up available if she should spring.

'I'm not after you, love. I need Erik's phone number in Tampere.'

'He's here,' said Jussi.

Nina spun round.

'Not *here* here. My flat. Arrived back this morning.'

'Let me in, please.'

Nina slipped past into the big, airy, shabby flat. Erik looked tired. He was an old man. Nina didn't sit but crossed the room to the window, which meant that Erik, being of her father's generation, couldn't sit either. Suddenly she could see the men together in Essex, the huge, gentle bear and the short, slight man in the dog collar, like some Nordic take on Laurel and Hardy.

'I want you to tell me why my father left Finland in 1946. I've had Virta's book translated, and any day now I'll have the report of the military investigation that cleared Dad's name. What happened? Why did he leave his country to live with your relatives?'

Erik didn't look shocked. He said, 'I would like a drink, Nina. And you?'

'No.'

Jussi kept his bottles in the kitchen so Erik left her alone. There was a big bay window, its smeared glass mottled outside with the sooty tracks of dried rain. A choking rubber plant whose earth had shrunk away from the pot knocked at the glass whenever a lorry passed. The rest of the room showed a tidemark of unfinished tidying. Erik, no doubt. When he returned, pouring himself a stiff one, Nina regretted having been too proud to accept.

'You have to understand, there was no appetite for scandal.' Erik's cigarette crackled.

'That's what the historian said.'

'Frankly, Virta's book was in bad taste. A letter from a silly sick boy to his Girl Guide. But in print it could not be ignored. Wearily our military people did their duty. Martti gave a good account of himself, and there was the question – why should he turn his pistol on a fellow soldier, and in the height of battle with only Kaarlo there, who'd always been useless even when he hadn't just had his hand shot off? Martti left the court a free man. In Tampere there was much sympathy.'

'So why, Erik? If nobody believed it?'

'I did not say that. Somebody important believed it.'

'You mean . . . like the president? Or *Sibelius*? How would—?'

'No, Nina. It was worse. Martti's own parents believed it. Knew. They knew their only son was a cold-blooded murderer.'

Outside, laughter swelled above the plane trees. A crowd making for the Questors theatre, further down Mattock Lane.

'Not initially,' continued Erik. 'Not when first they heard the allegation. Outrageous. Scurrilous. Then they read Kaarlo's letter and they knew.'

And as Erik said it, so did Nina. The ring of truth. Not easy to define but unmistakable when you met it. She said, 'So Dad's parents, who knew him better than anyone, who had been living with him when he returned from that war, took one look at Kaarlo's letter and realized every word was true.'

'And were prepared to convince others. They were God-fearing people of the age that suffered under the last Tsar. Their generation won our independence. Murder was bad enough, but this was the slaughter of a fellow Finn while their beloved land, whose sovereignty they had so recently wrested from Russian oppression, was being raped. Martin told Christine his parents died soon afterwards of disgrace. This is not true. His father was very much alive until a year ago, past ninety but clear-witted.'

'My grandfather!' said Nina. 'I had a grandfather! Did I have a grandmother, too?'

'Until just a few years ago, my dear, yes.'

Nina sat down heavily, a brand-new grief building. She had had grandparents in Finland and now they too were dead. '*They* sent Dad away? Their only child?'

'Yes. But exile takes time to arrange. Uncle Timo agreed to give Martti sufficient money. That would be his punishment, to be banished. If Martti ever returned to the Finland he had betrayed, the family would go to Jorma Virta and let him publish their own condemnation.'

'Good God.'

'Still, Martti feared his parents might go to Virta anyway, so strong was their anger. Nina, try to understand, they probably felt the crime was somehow their fault. Parents do. And some try to push that guilt as far away from themselves as they can. Martti's pushed theirs to London.'

And when his parents didn't shop him, thought Nina, he became convinced the Almighty would provide the reckoning. Even becoming a clergyman could not atone.

'What about you, Erik? Did you believe it?'

'I didn't ask and didn't give a damn either way, Nina. Veikko Virta was a blot on the face of humanity. Whoever killed him, Soviet or Finn, deserved to be decorated. Afterwards, Martti gave the impression they had been friends. That, too, was untrue. For us both, Veikko was merely an alarming acquaintance.'

'My mother said he was into porn films. I presume they were imports and he knew crooks in the States.'

'Christine thought it was films? No. Photographs, and not imported. He needed no assistance; the pornography was his own. Filthy, degrading stuff. The girls weren't volunteers, they were conscripts. Veikko Virta was clever at coercion. He was a scoundrel.'

The dated expression, evoking another era's morality, was somehow fitting: a handsome war hero, brave as a lion, who was a scoundrel. Nina asked Erik for a cigarette.

Between her fingers it felt fatter than the cigarettes of her memory. The flame of Erik's lighter licked the end, and Nina drew in her first lungful of smoke for nearly a year. Her senses walked forward to meet the kick of the nicotine. They greeted it. They hurled themselves in its path as supplicants. White light slammed into Nina's head. Smoke trickled, carboniferous and aromatic, putting out spidery fingers like ink dropped into a pool. When the sensation subsided in a gradual dissolve, she was sorry to see it go. I'm a murderer's daughter. But Nina's mind-picture of the killing was still filmic. A chaos of dust hung in air artily softened by crepuscular light, and the sound-track was saxophone blue, achingly illustrating the soldier's loneliness. Had he shot Veikko through the heart, a ghastly parody of the description in his own letter to Jorma Virta? Or through the head, brain matter splattering the filthy air? But all of them had been steeped in gore and horror for weeks, so what was one more brain, one more heart, one more dead scoundrel? *But* he went on to construct a cover story, a survival strategy, an edifice of lies – and fed those lies to his family. It was this that stunned Nina: the painstaking manufacture of a transmissible disease that infected the wife and child he loved.

'Do you know why he killed Veikko?' she asked.

'I assumed I would never know, Nina. Then I came to Martti's funeral and you talked to me of a great symphony hidden in his desk. Of course I was suspicious. Martti had not written a symphony. When I saw the music, I knew it could only be the lost Eighth. And so much secrecy – this reeked of a racket of Veikko's. What would Martti keep secret even from me, but some hell-inspired collaboration with that creature? Taken together with Äglä järvi . . . I believe somewhere there is a motive to do with that symphony.' Erik's lenses wobbled over his drink. 'I must apologize. At first I could only see that this was the maestro's work and must be played to the world. I assumed the music itself would overshadow any interest in Martti and his past. That was stupid.'

'Photographs, you said. That means Veikko had the equipment and a darkroom. Erik, I now know Dad copied the music from photographs, a bag load. Full plate.'

'Yes? Then certainly the photographer was Veikko. Who else?'

'So somehow Veikko got his hands on the score, photographed it, and—'

'Intended selling it, no doubt. Veikko Virta would have sold his own grandmother for a box of cigars and a night with a tart. I beg your pardon, my dear.'

'I suppose he dragged Dad in as a copyist because a written transcript would be easier to sell than a bagful of photographs. The truth is, Erik, Veikko wouldn't have needed to resort to coercion there. Dad could never have resisted the chance to pore over the symphony.' Thinking this out, Nina went on, 'Of course, even if Dad had refused, he couldn't stop Veikko selling it anyway. Veikko had the negatives. He only had to run off another set of prints and find another accomplice.'

Erik recharged his whisky glass, and without asking poured one for Nina. 'Yes, Veikko would have sold the symphony,' he said. 'But then came war. And a farmhouse in Äglä järvi.'

'Dad hauled those photographs all the way to England and kept them until 1966, when Mum threw the whole lot out with the rubbish. Oh God. Presumably they showed either the original by the composer's hand or a professional copy which would have been annotated with Sibelius's corrections. What a treasure to have. Lugged off to the nearest landfill site. I wonder how long they took to putrefy.'

She saw a wife demented with worry, clearing out the

useless baggage of an over-encumbered life. Then Nina remembered her father smashing his record collection and howling.

'When Dad discovered the photographs had gone he couldn't tolerate any reference to Sibelius. He banned it from the house, destroyed his records, and put away his beloved violin. God, what a mess.' Then, 'How on earth did Veikko get hold of it in the first place?'

Erik shrugged. 'Maybe his father had acquaintances in that world. If so, the son would exploit them as he exploited everything he touched.'

'At least I can tell you why Dad killed him. Between the time he first saw the score and the battle of Äglajärvi, Dad was confronted with a reason to stop that symphony being made public.'

'I think I can guess. Since that night in Hampstead, I have wondered. Sibelius himself destroyed the work. Is it not of the best?'

'Exactly. According to an expert in these matters, its author kept reworking it until he did it to death.' Until he discarded the neonate with the aqueous ablutionary fluid, she thought bitterly.

Erik said, 'So, as Martti worked through the photographs he began to recognize this fact. And he would rather go against the first commandment than shame Sibelius. Martti himself expected to die, I am sure. By killing Veikko, he exposed himself to near-certain death. He foresaw self-sacrifice. Yet he survived.'

Nina remembered Giancarlo talking to her mother: when Martin reached his forties and had a healthy daughter, he decided his luck must be due to run out. From there it was a short hop, skip and a jump to the conclusion that it *had* run out. That he was dying of cancer. *We have done those things which we ought not to have done and there is no health in us.*

She ground the stub of her cigarette into Erik's ashtray. 'It just occurred to me. Those negatives would still have been in Tampere when Veikko died.'

'Along with many very disgusting pictures. Jorma Virta would not examine his son's photographs beyond that discovery, no father would. I imagine everything was burned. Later, to lessen his despair, he latched on to the story that his son was the victim of evil, rather than always its ringmaster. So he wrote his embarrassing book.'

'What happened to him?'

'His life rotted after Veikko's death. He went to his grave broken.'

'Dad knew that? Oh, Erik.' And his parents were lost to him. And to me. Then she remembered another childhood loss. 'Why did you stop coming to us when we left Seaton Bois?'

'Martti asked me to. It was the summer of 1967. Your sister was born and he wrote to me of starting a fresh life. This was wise. One time, my careless remarks nearly gave him away. I was talking of some poetry your father published. From what I said, anyone could have pinpointed the date to mid-1946, when he was supposed to be a pariah.'

Nina said, 'We might have asked ourselves why Uncle Timo, apparently so fond of his nephew, never wrote, never came to visit, never kept in touch.'

'Disgrace is an excellent alibi. Inventing a scandal in which you are innocent, to hide acquittal on a charge of which you are guilty. It is . . .' Erik searched for the expression. 'It is cast iron,' he said.

'But I still can't see how Veikko got that symphony out of Ainola. Nobody else had managed.'

Erik shrugged. He looked dog-tired, done in. 'We will never know. It is an unfortunate aspect of life, that some mysteries can never be solved.'

'What should I do with the score?'

'Sibelius is dead, Nina, and Martti is dead. Do what you must. And now I am very tired. I would like to be left alone for a while before my son returns with his relentless energy, and the sort of music to make Sibelius cringe.'

62

Dear Dr Hannay,
You wrote to Docent Kari Kilpeläinen with questions
about the 8th symphony of Sibelius. He asks me to
send the draft of his latest paper.

Followed by a signature from the University of Helsinki.
Nina had completely forgotten her correspondence with the
keeper of the Sibelius archives. He was kind enough to
remember me, she thought, and coloured. I have in my
possession the real thing – and it is second-rate. The
knowledge was hateful to her.

She skimmed the enclosed article. In the early 1930s,
Sibelius bought a mass of manuscript paper . . . Well yes, he
must have got through an entire Finnish forest for that
unhappy symphony. His family remembered taking com-
pleted sections to his copyist . . . There was an invoice dated
August 1938 . . . The conductor Nils-Eric Fougstedt
claimed to see the score on the shelves at . . .

Nina put the article aside and drove to Duane's.

He looked worse than she did. 'Jeremy and I had a row
last night,' he said. 'About whether he'll leave his wife.'

'You're asking him to?'

'What do you take me for? Jeremy says he's going to and I'm saying, "For God's sake, think of the children."'

They sat on his leather sofa with a drink and Nina told him what had happened.

'So *that* was what haunted your father all his life. Not ostracism and having his character assassinated in the press.'

'Which was all moonshine. I'm a murderer's daughter.' But even aloud it had a feel of penny-dreadful exaggeration like those imagined tabloid headlines of her mother's. It was a different four words that had the power to assault her soul. Jorma Virta's life rotted. That was the sin her father had lived with, the one that could never be expiated because the concept was meaningless: just two parallel miseries, Jorma Virta's, and her father's recognition of it as soon as he had a child of his own. Without Nina, maybe his life in the Church would have been enough to atone for his crime, but once she was born he began to understand what he'd done to another father, and it capsized him.

She said, 'At least I can stop driving myself crazy trying to figure it out.'

'I can't, though,' replied Duane dismally. 'All I ever wanted to know was how the fuck a porn merchant wormed his way into that house and snuck out again with a filched symphony.'

'Maybe Veikko coerced one of the servants. Apparently that's the sort of bastard he was.'

Duane said, 'Anyhow, here's the latest downloads. Just more speculation.'

```
. . . Sibelius was already moving away
from tonics and dominants. In his Fifth
the bulk of the exposition was written
in the tonic.
```

To which some wag had added:
```
Unlike his Sixth, which was written in
the gin.
```

It struck Nina that as they couldn't get hold of the real one they were all out there writing their own. 'Thanks,' she said, 'but you can stop now. I've got it quashed. The whole kerfuffle will die the death inside a week.'

'What?'

'It was simple, Duane. I invented conclusive proof that the symphony was Dad's after all, and then mailed it to MSM. Santana only has extracts, remember, and only photocopies, at that. Well, I doctored one of them, and sent it to him with a lot of other stuff.'

Simple in concept, maybe, but a pig of a job to execute. Forgery is a fiddly business. Nina had mocked up a page to make the whole thing look like the start of a student exercise – by her father at the Conservatoire.

It had taken two days to find paper that matched his, and then a week with Tippex and ink pen, trial and error, patience stretched to screaming point. But at the end of it she had something for Erik.

'Come on, Nina, it's your turn on the coffee shift,' he had said in her kitchen at two in the morning.

'Nah, I'll do it,' said Jussi. 'Only Finns know how to make coffee.'

Erik annotated Nina's new page with a critique in Finnish. By the end, the whole thing looked passable.

He assured her, 'Once Jussi puts it through another photocopier tomorrow, your Manhattan prof won't be able to see the joins. It *does* look convincing for 1939. I'd be fooled, and I was there.'

Nina now explained to Duane, 'When Santana translates Erik's notes, they will inform him that the work earned the student an A grade. Whereas Dad's violin sonata, which I've also included, and remember, it's in the self-same hand-writing, only merited a B minus. I'm sorry, Dad,' she said quietly, 'about the grade.'

'Santana will fall for that?'

'Why not? He must already be getting suspicious. He only has Susan's word that there ever existed an entire symphony and I bet by now he realizes (a) she's never set eyes on it, and (b) she knows sod all about music. It won't take much to convince Santana that Susan is just a stupid girl going off at half-cock. I think the violin sonata will swing it. That looks like Sibelius, too, though for different reasons. Poor Dad.' Nina waited for her voice. 'Anyway, to help things along I'm about to call Susan and put the fear of God into her. She'll be on the phone to MSM in a blind panic.'

'Nina, she can't get through. The switchboard's still jammed.'

'You don't know Susan. She'll get through.'

'What will you say?'

'Oh, tell her Mum misunderstood and those fourteen folders included every drib and drab Dad ever wrote. Even if she doesn't believe it, she'll realize she's done for and go into a tailspin. Actually, Duane, I run to a few words of Afrikaans, picked up from a pub in Earl's Court. My motto is, never miss an opportunity to learn "fuck off" in someone else's language. *Voetsak*, that's what I'm going to say. *Voetsak*.'

So it was all over. Summer, too, was closing down. Beyond the kitchen window her garden had an end-of-season look. Another month and the cosmea would be yellow and aetiolated, and Nina would have to dig it up. In Boston, autumn was beginning in scarlet and gold like the origami geisha Richard once sent her from Tokyo. He was driving her up to Vermont for the second week of October.

She tidied the kitchen. Slivers of Sellotape were stuck all over the table. As she passed the fridge, Nina dislodged the learned article so kindly sent her from Helsinki. It deserved a more dignified home than the fridge, anyway. She stooped to retrieve it.

And felt the ground fall away.

'*A bill dated August 1938, paid by Sibelius the following month, for . . .*'

Nina walked awkwardly to a chair and read.

In the archives was an invoice relating to a work entitled *Symphonic*. Seven volumes. The bill was from a Helsinki publisher, Weilin & Göös. But they weren't music publishers, the bill was for binding. In August 1938, the year before the Winter War, Sibelius's new symphony, just back from his copyist, was lying around in a Helsinki publishing house waiting to be bound into seven volumes.

Nina walked slowly to the phone. She would check with Erik but there was no rush, she knew what he would say: in the summer of 1938, when Uncle Timo found menial work for her father, it was at Weilin & Göös.

63

'So it was your *dad* who found it,' said Duane. 'Bloody hell. You've been on the wrong track from the start.'

'But you partly guessed. You always thought the story began and ended with Dad.'

There was a chill to the evening. In Greg's Adam fire-place, the quiet flames were pallid in the low-leaning light. Jussi had brought a bottle of burgundy. Greg accepted him now, a fellow sufferer, another reject of his irrational ex.

'Just imagine,' she told them. 'There's Dad, bored to sobs and wool-gathering – and one day among the stacks of paper: *Symphonic*, Jean Sibelius. The seven volumes mean individual parts as well.'

Nina remembered the binder who did her PhD thesis: five copies to be knocked together at prices that wouldn't provoke students into fainting away and cluttering up the premises in contravention of the fire regulations. She remembered the feel of the place with its tottering book stacks and smell of paper and leather and glue. She could picture her father among them.

'But what about Veikko?' asked the three men in unintended comic chorus.

'He was just the man with the camera. Like you said,

Duane, I made up scenarios that suited my prejudices. Dad must have realized instantly that the only way he could keep the manuscript long enough to study and wallow in it was by sneaking the papers out one stack at a time and getting the pages photographed. Of course, he couldn't do that himself, he didn't have the equipment, but back in Tampere was a fellow student with a professional camera, a darkroom and no scruples whatsoever. Dad didn't like him. Maybe he even loathed him. But it would only have taken one phone call.'

Greg said, 'But your father still knew Veikko was a crook and once he got him involved, Veikko would see dollar signs. Finnmarks.'

'Of course. Imagine the sheer time and cost of developing hundreds of full-plate photographs in 1938. Veikko would only have done it if he foresaw an enormous return on investment. As for Dad, the idea of publicizing the symphony probably wasn't anathema at first. Not until he realized the truth about the music. Too late by then, Veikko had the negatives. Then I suppose Dad played for time and convinced Veikko that a potential buyer couldn't perform from photographs, they'd have to pay to get the music transcribed, which would drive down the selling price. Better to provide a written transcript up front. It also explains why Dad copied out the entire mass. It never made sense before. It does if the exercise was designed to stonewall Veikko, who probably didn't understand about individual parts being supplementary. Most people wouldn't. Presumably Dad needed the whole lot photographed as back-up to help him whenever the pictures of the main score weren't clear. But he didn't have to transcribe it all. That was purely a stalling tactic.'

'And Sibelius knew the symphony wasn't good enough?'

'Oh yes. He had it professionally copied and bound to put some distance between himself and the music. He'd have known when he got it back from Weilin & Göös. And despaired. And rewrote it and despaired again. Until . . . *auto-da-fé*.'

Duane said, 'Obviously your father succeeded in stalling for twelve months, otherwise Veikko *would* have sold the photographs straight off.'

'I can't really believe Veikko was still hanging around waiting after a year, can you? I bet he'd given up on Dad and was already making plans to sell the photographs direct. Then . . . Well, then came the Battle of Äglä järvi.'

Greg put out his hand to her. 'Nina, I'm a musician myself. I can't blame your father.'

'I know. His judgement would have gone to pot by then. They'd been at the front for fifteen days, no let-up at all since Tolvajärvi. Even before that there were always skirmishes breaking out at night. Dad was a pathological insomniac, he wouldn't have been able to grab even the cat-naps that saved other soldiers from going round the bend. In that farmhouse he had no judgement left and no conscience.'

'But at least no more mystery,' said Greg. 'It's been driving you crazy.'

'And I've been driving you three crazy.'

'No,' said Duane and Greg.

'No,' said Jussi. 'Drink your wine.'

Erik had said, 'It is an unfortunate aspect of life that some mysteries can never be solved.' Had Nina solved hers? No, she realized. Fathers can't be solved. I've gone through all this to try to make sense of him, but even now I can only manage a sketch with some highlighting. I haven't explained the true chaotic configurations that made up the man. What I wanted was to analyse him, database him, and lock him up in a VAX-8600. Generally we take for granted that people are not explicable; it's only with fathers that we demand a denouement to every mystery. That's because what we are really trying to understand is ourselves.

She was visited by a dreadful wave of grief, not hot and passionate but cold and despairing and final. I shall never talk to him again. Gone. He is gone.

Greg was talking. 'He paid for it in misery, Nina.'

'So did his family,' she said, then added, 'and so did his dog.'

'Sorry?'

'When my mother threw out those priceless photographs, Dad was so harrowed he punished her by having our Labrador destroyed. Of course, Mum hadn't the remotest idea of what she'd done but he punished her anyway, never mind that he was as fond of the dog as she was, and never mind that the collateral damage included his ten-year-old daughter.' Nina stopped. Punishment. Lucia. *Pains au chocolat*. 'Oh, fuck,' she said quietly.

✳

'How many operatic sopranos does it take to screw in a light bulb?' laughed Richard at the other end of the phone. 'One. She just holds on and the world revolves around her. What's the difference between an operatic soprano and terrorists? You can negotiate with terrorists. What do you call an operatic—?'

'Richard.'

His happy babble stopped. Nina pictured his abrupt surprise.

'What is it?' he asked in a different voice.

'Darling, I need to talk to you.'

'You can have all the time you want.'

'It's about that day on the Norfolk coast. We were so close. It was one of the happiest of my life.'

'And mine.'

'Yes? When you wrote to tell me about your surgery, why did you make a point of explaining how you were terrified and seeing double at Wells? When you knew I'd thought we were blissful?'

Richard was silent. She had wondered how the question would sound to him. From the shape of Richard's silence she knew Lu had been right.

He said, 'Maybe I overplayed the sympathy angle.'

'I wouldn't mind that. You can have sympathy by the truckload. I think you wanted to ruin the day in my memory. That you were punishing me.'

'For what?'

'Perhaps for dancing the tango with a man at a party, perhaps for not being the sort of woman to impress your father. By the time you wrote that letter you even knew the man was gay, and of course you'd *always* known how your father would view me. So really, you were punishing me simply because you could.'

Richard said quietly, 'Look, maybe I milked the moment. I'm insecure, Nina.'

Insecure men. Images tumbled through her mind, of another man she had loved.

'You might like to know I'm having blackouts,' Greg was shouting at her. 'I didn't want to tell you in case you worried.'

'So you're telling me now. Now that we happen to be having a row about something else.'

And another day.

'So go ahead – walk out! You'll be responsible for what happens, you'll have to live with that for ever. If I top myself, how will you feel?'

Now, music started up from Sean and Victoria's flat. It was David Bowie, a track from his *Low* album. 'Always Crashing In The Same Car'.

Nina said into the phone, 'If I were someone else, perhaps I could cope with your insecurities as well as my own. But it's as if the things that happened to me when I was small cauterized a channel into my mind, and anything similar goes hurtling down that path like lightning finding the easiest route to earth. When you wrote your letter effectively telling me you had rejected my love and comfort that day at Wells, I was a little girl again, bandaging her pet dog because she was useless to help her daddy.'

'Nina, I love you!'

'I left urgent messages telling you something terrible had

happened and I needed you. You didn't phone back for five days. How is that loving me?'

Richard swore softly and at length. Then his hurt turned itself on her. 'Well, Nina, I can see how you might have a happier life on your own, in a flat worth half your mortgage in a location that's a slum.'

Down the phone line, Nina could hear the moneyed silence of Beacon Hill, its muffled seclusion. Behind her own flat, across the wasteland of back gardens came a random blast from a circling ice-cream van, 'Boys And Girls Come Out To Play'; its sagging amplified cacophony ding-donged like some electric bell-ringing display from Hades. Beacon Hill was what Richard had offered his wife, of course – and then he hated her for accepting it.

Yesterday evening at Greg's, Nina had thought of Richard's well-bred fireplace with its protective screen. No danger of falling into it, or its flames catching a passing hemline. If a symphonic score were burning in that grate, you wouldn't smell the scorch of the paper or the acrid sting of the smoke.

Greg's sitting room was Georgian like Richard's, but his fabrics were chosen for their unrestrained splashes of colour that changed with the light like the lagoons of Titchwell Marshes. In the watery green light from the dripping garden, the room had glowed with a colour so unearthly, Nina was reminded of reports of colour-blind people with synaesthesia, whose minds light up with colours they can't name because their retinas have never passed them on from the outside world. With no terrestrial counterparts for comparison, there is nothing to call them but 'Martian colours'. Nina had knelt at the fireplace, beside her the manu-script and tangle of tape wrenched from the cassette.

'*No.*' Greg was out of his chair.

Duane said, 'Nina, not now while you're so shocked. You can't make this kind of decision.'

'She can,' said Jussi.

The heaped papers, now humped and unstable from their

landslide in front of the hearth, were no longer the immaculate sheets she had stumbled upon nearly a year ago; by now they had the used look of a loved and reread book. Phrases and fragments looked up at her in her father's ink-work, asserting their disparate musical voices. The satisfying curls of the treble clefs, the backwards-looking ciphers of the bass, the flying wings of the phrase marks, and chords like tight-stacked little lozenges: these had been the language of her life, all her life, and had bound her to her father. So intimate, the sight of his meticulous script; so much of his personality slumped in front of the fire.

'Nina, I beg you,' said Greg.

They discussed it for an hour but she was both calm and decided.

Greg's colour had drained to a stippled anaemic grey. 'When Sibelius did this, his wife couldn't bear to watch, it nearly tore her heart out. Don't you owe anything to *her* memory?'

'Perhaps I should,' agreed Nina. 'But I can't take my lead from Aino Sibelius. I've never managed to understand her. But I have come to understand her husband a little.' She could hear his musical baritone, potent and apparently unruffled. And not without courage, given that every single listener to that interview knew he'd fizzled out years ago, defeated. 'Come on, let's set fire to it and break all the bylaws against burning smokeless fuel.'

But Greg couldn't. He stood by the grate in tears. 'Music is your heart and soul. How can you do this?'

Nina put an arm round him. 'Because it isn't a finished work of art. Just an offcut. If Dad had lived to old age he would have burned it himself rather than risk its public autopsy. And, sweetheart, you've heard it several times but this is the first time you've shed a tear.'

He turned away. 'Can we at least keep the ashes?' he said, and Nina agreed they could keep the ashes of Sibelius's eighth symphony.

Now, beyond her bay window in Harlesden, voices

shouted. Somebody called, 'Get me a strawberry ripple.' Ordinary people in an ordinary day. Nina remembered an autumnal Saturday all those years ago. Why is it that when you're suffering, other people's trivialities appear so excruciatingly out of kilter? *About suffering they were never wrong, The Old Masters.*

Nina said into the phone, 'On my own I'm going to be very unhappy for a while, Richard, but not as unhappy as trying to live with someone who punishes me whenever he's feeling insecure. I'm sorry I'm hurting you. I'll talk again tomorrow if you want, but right now I need some peace.'

After she hung up, Nina sat for a long time without moving. The ice-cream van trundled away, the voices subsided, mundane and happy and human. I was wrong to resent them for that, she realized. Auden's great poem doesn't apply. This is not suffering. This is suffering averted.

Lucia would be here later with her daughter, who had flown to London for some Canadian school trip. There was more comfort to come: next week, Nina was presenting her ideas about the skating system to the regulatory authority for ballroom dancing. Their preliminary opinion was that she'd got a solution. When autumn advanced she would collect Kruger. Her mother had finally acknowledged that Susan and André might indeed come scuttling over to England after majority rule, so instead of the Western Cape he had drawn Harlesden. And this coming Sunday night, the anniversary of her father's death, Nina was playing the organ in that beautiful church in the Saxonshore benefice, for a candlelit Evensong in memoriam. *The day thou gavest, Lord, is ended.* As Nina got up and walked to the kitchen, the hymn of peaceful acceptance took its place among the plangent colours and textures of her mind, like cleverly organized light in an oil painting.

PART IV

Oranges and Lemons

64

2002

Lucia said, 'Do you think your early Italian helped you learn Spanish?'

'Probably,' agreed Nina. 'Though at first I got very confused and couldn't always guarantee which would come out, a Spanish word or some long-lost Italian one. That was in the beginning. I don't do it now.' With which she turned to the waiter and ordered their drinks – in Italian. Lu shrieked.

They were in Confiteria Ideal. A few feet away danced the elderly couple Señor Ferrari had pointed out to Nina more than a decade ago, now perfectly at home among the trendy young, and the loud foreigners who flocked here for the tango revival. As Nina watched, the pair dropped their hold to dance forehead to forehead, arms at their sides, feet busy. An interesting variation on that *milonguero* triangle.

Señor Ferrari was also busy, organizing tonight's competitive events.

'When they filmed *Evita* here he taught Madonna to tango,' said Nina, forgetting for a moment who she was talking to.

'Gosh, *how* that would impress Mum and Dad!'

They both dissolved, just as the waiter returned. He set their glasses down and shuffled off, baffled.

They were in their middle forties; Lucia had unreasonably retained her air of naughtiness and sexiness, and Nina her elfin eccentricities. As for Beryl and Giancarlo (nearly seventy, nearly eighty-four!) they were out there in the October spring, last seen heading towards the violet blossom of Plaza de Mayo. They had heard crowds gathering for some demo, and toddled off to have a look. Whoever the demonstrators were, they would shortly have to give up their place to the Mothers of the Disappeared, who had it Thursday afternoons. The reign of the *junta* was long over. These days in Plaza de Mayo, you booked a slot.

Nina had been living here eight years. Back in London she had faced down the recession, surviving on music, but she knew her home was in clinical trials. It would never leave her, this need to be involved in drug research. Cancer. When the ice began to thaw, Nina saw a post advertised by a pharma company with an affiliate in Buenos Aires. She took an intensive language course, and after six months in the London office was borderline proficient, and she and Kruger flew south. To sell her Harlesden flat required every penny of her savings to pack the hole they called negative equity, but she did sell, and upped and left. 'I want to get away.' At last she knew where to.

Buenos Aires began to thrive. By the end of the nineties property prices were rocketing. Everyone implored Nina to stop throwing away money in rent, so she managed to secure a foreign loan and bought an apartment close to where she had once stayed with Jussi. Then the Argentinian government changed the banking laws overnight. Among its catastrophic effects was a spectacular crash of the property market, a collapse on a scale that shook the population into a daze, shell-shocked.

'I am *so* sorry!' Nina told her *porteño* friends. 'I do it everywhere. It's the Hannikainen money curse!'

She never would have any luck with money but Nina

never worried, something always came up. And despite the insane unpredictability of Buenos Aires, she adored it. From October to May she was inundated with guests from home, though Lucia was the only one who regularly hopped on a sixteen-hour flight for a long weekend.

Back in London, the revival predicted by Jussi had happened at last; when the show *Tango Argentino* finally arrived he was outside leafleting the after-theatre crowds ('Be there or be square'). It paid off doubly. Jussi was the best-known tango teacher in the country – and married one of the cast. Nina had not gone back to him after the split with Richard, despite the temptation, the comfortable nature of her love. There was a well-judged reason why it would never have been wise to marry him. But they met up every February, as Jussi still did his annual tango trips, nowadays with his wife and children.

The next wedding was Greg's, who married a singer in a girl-power band. 'She's far better at handling his insecurities than I ever was,' said Nina, delighted for him. Duane too was married, of a sort. His Jeremy did leave the wife. Or rather the wife left him.

'Duane, are you making this up? It's straight out of *The Code of Highwaymen*!'

'I assure you I can tell fact from fiction, Nina. Marigold fell in love with the au pair and they've moved to an all-female commune in Wales. Jeremy and I will have the children alternate weekends.'

'Well, I hope she didn't take his silk knickers with her,' responded Nina crisply.

Duane had also returned to oncology, though by now those VAX-8600s were obsolete. Technology had moved on. So had the communications industry. Like everyone else Nina knew, Duane couldn't leave home without his Nokia mobile. When the Finns' economy collapsed with the Soviet Union, they turned their hand to something appropriate. In fact, the economy was galloping along. Finland was indexed as the least corrupt country on earth and the most educated in Europe, but still nobody could get them to brag about it, and the world just assumed Nokia was Japanese.

Duane kept up his writing, though these days his output wasn't classed as gay porn. His latest novel concerned a young man phobic about sickbeds and helpless to stop his beloved leaving him for a better nurse when he tested HIV-positive. It wiped the board for literary prizes. Duane's acclaimed prose included a much-quoted scene in which two men dance a tango stripping naked as they do so – to the music of 'A La Gran Muñeca' by Carlos Di Sarli.

Nina was wrong about Susan and André: they did stay on after majority rule. Martina was now twelve and there was a Joshua. Even so, Nina didn't go to the Cape; she couldn't forgive Susan's treachery, and though Susan must surely have been ashamed of causing an international hullabaloo, she was never going to say so. Their mother came to Buenos Aires, though, flitting across the South Atlantic as many times a year as she and Nina could afford between them. The sight of her mother in Nina's apartment chatting to the Clarks and *laughing* was curative all by itself.

The only loss was Nonna, who had died shortly after her hundredth birthday. 'From that ocean of champagne at Mum's grandiloquent Roman party,' insisted Lu. 'It's a wonder we didn't lose you and Melanie!' This was a pointed allusion involving the Trevi fountain and a couple of epic hangovers.

And Richard? Nina had not heard of Richard in years. She knew he had started his own company in the biotech boom, and therefore she could find him by simply typing his name into Google, but the exercise would serve no purpose so she never did it.

Whatever, she had her Lu. 'Just think, Nina, a few years ago nobody outside Finland had heard of the Winter War, and now every bugger knows the battle of Ägläjärvi but thinks it was won by the Americans!'

There had been a Hollywood movie, massive budget,

depicting a kind of Wild West in the snow, in which the floundering Finns were rescued by the arrival of a troop of US volunteers. Decried in the European press, it was nevertheless the global smash hit of the year and won seven Oscars.

One of them was for original musical score. In his acceptance speech, Alejandro Santana laughingly recounted a story from 1990. He told the Academy how he was overheard on the phone talking about his musical tribute to Sibelius that would become the film score, and suddenly there were rumours that he possessed fragments of the eighth symphony! Nina couldn't avoid hearing Väinämöinen's storm. It was everywhere for months.

'Did it make you sorry?' asked Lu. 'For destroying the rest?'

'Never. And he always did inspire soundtracks: *The Jazz Singer*. *Psycho*. If only Dad had got his hands on an earlier version, like from when Sibelius was first promising it to Koussevitzky. I would love to know the colours.'

At least she now knew the colours of his landscape. She flew to Finland one summer to see Erik and Tampere – which now had a Moomintroll Museum. Then Helsinki. And Ainola.

On a windless day, Nina walked in Aino's flower gardens with their banks of rugosa roses, the sun soft as talcum, the air sweet as a light Chablis. She took with her a pretty stoppered bottle of ashes. Back in Hampstead it had sounded perfectly reasonable to promise Greg she would scatter the ashes across the garden, but Nina found she wasn't alone. It hummed. Besides which, the Finns are not the British: they are devoted to their environment. In Finland you don't stand in a public place in broad daylight tossing charred trash into the air. But that was just the first of many visits. The following summer she rented a summerhouse with Lucia.

They went to Saturday-night dances of tango finlandia in a community centre packed to the doors. It was always a bring-a-bottle party as Finnish alcohol laws banned the sale there of booze.

'Not entirely working, those laws,' pointed out Lu as a couple of young men collapsed in the car park.

Inside, women stood on one side, men on the other. Boyling point and girling point again. There was a kind of traffic-light system to let the women know when they could ask the men to dance. Otherwise, it was the men who swooped across to coax them into a gentle shuffle. Nina and Lu were astonished by their own alien conspicuousness. When they danced a flamboyant Argentinian tango together, Giancarlo's daughter leading, the rule-abiding Finns looked scandalized. But the second Saturday night brought the aurora borealis, the sky a bolt of fluttering green silk. Then everyone was outside and talking to everybody else.

Lu said of the landscape, 'It's beautiful but impersonal,' and Nina agreed. There was no welcoming invitation in this beauty. The granite underpinnings thrust out of the earth like the bones showing through, as if its life force were heaving. Here was the domain of gods who were beyond curiosity about the preoccupations of mankind. Nina could understand Soviet soldiers being rattled into despair.

On their next visit, at last they saw the country under snow. Nina and Lu walked out across the icescape of Helsinki Bay at sundown, a fizzing luminosity that turned the ice floor to purple for hours. The next day Nina returned to Ainola, alone. It wasn't open. She peered through the pines at the house in its red, white and green. And high across a hedge she threw the ashes of Sibelius's eighth symphony. They scattered, and blew, and then their speckled grey was just another shade of snow falling in a snowy world, across the graves of Aino and Jean Sibelius.

And in Brancaster, in a setting as English as Gray's *Elegy*, Nina set a bed of stones on her father's grave, glimmering rose-pink granite shaped by thirty degrees of frost, arranged round a bowl of peace roses.

*

'Will you really not marry Federico?' Beryl asked wistfully.

Lu said, 'Poor old Mum. She keeps buying wedding hats and they go out of fashion, unworn.' Lu was still with the handsome Tod but they hadn't married, either. 'No contracts, no fetters,' she said, to her parents' continuing disapproval.

'We only want to see you both happy!'

They were in Nina's apartment. Federico was a surgeon and had his own near the hospital. Tonight he was at a political protest meeting that was doubtless shaking the plaster off the ceiling. He would be enjoying himself. He was a man who did enjoy himself. It took me long enough, thought Nina, but I have learned what is and isn't nutritious. Still, she recognized that her present well-being was remission, not cure. As she wasn't in love with Federico, her passions would always be in danger of ambush, middle age notwithstanding; you can't constantly patrol the crannies and crawl spaces of your heart against the intrusion of some new man with ferocious intelligence and a wounded neediness. But she knew that when it happened, Federico would not force her hand as Jussi had done, he would hold on tight. That was the reason she had not dared to marry Jussi.

'*And* he's dazzlingly handsome.'

Lu said, 'Give the girl a break. Anyway, we've got work to do. Nina, can we move this *ryijy* rug? Will Kruger mind if I pull him along?'

Kruger was fourteen.

'I thought Irish wolfhounds lived to about eight!' Beryl had said, shocked.

'There are older ones on record,' explained Nina. 'But me, I think it's the redemptive powers of the southern sun.' The dog gave a small affirmative woof and thumped his tail on the wood-block floor. 'But why move the rug?'

'Because you're about to purfle on your seventeenth-century Jellicoed violin.'

Beryl cried out, 'You've taken it up again? Oh, lovey, we are *so*—'

'Yes, a couple of years ago.'

'And you two are going to waltz to it,' added Lu.

'Absolutely not,' said Gian and Beryl together.

'Don't even think of refusing. We've waited forty years.' Lu winked at Nina, who let out an ungainly hoot.

'What conspiracy is this?' demanded Gian.

Nina said, 'I think your daughter wants you to dance to the theme from *Dr Kildare.*'

Gian looked at Beryl. 'Are we going to be bullied into this?'

'No,' said his wife.

Outside, the mothy twilight was full of jacaranda and the warm street noise of a city just waking up for the night. Buses trundled late workers homebound and shift workers work-bound. A mess of music jangled from corner cafés, ghetto blasters, the radios of passing cars. Taxi drivers remembered past traffic jams and leaned on their horns. And in Nina's apartment, the world's most famous ballroom champions danced a perfect waltz on a postage stamp, the startling fact of their old age an accessory to their beauty, the man laughing, the woman tutting in poorly disguised amusement, the music rolling in inky waves. On they danced, impeccable floorcraft in a tiny space, hearing only Nina's competent bow-work and not the raucous competing soundscape from the sidewalk ten floors below.

But the violinist could hear the sidewalk, she could even discern one particular tune glittering across the square from an unguessable source. It was a London tune. '*Oranges and Lemons say the bells of St Clement's.*' And catching it, Nina was aware of no sinister resonance, just a nursery rhyme, a song for happy children, singing its benign trivialities to an evening rich with human noise and the scents of a summer just beginning.

ACKNOWLEDGEMENTS

Although this is a work of fiction, I tried not to play fast and loose with history – but I admit to poetic licence in citing the 'F major' stove as the location of the *auto-da-fé*.

For information on the eighth symphony, and for my shameless construction of it, I am indebted to the following: Erik Tawaststjerna, *Sibelius, Volume III: 1914–1957*, translated by Robert Layton (Faber and Faber, 1997); Erik Tawaststjerna, 'Sibelius's Eighth Symphony, an insoluble mystery', *Finnish Music Quarterly*, 1–2, 1985; Kari Kilpeläinen, 'Vielä hieman Sibeliuksen 8. sinfoniasta' *Synkooppi*, Op. 32 2/1989; Kari Kilpeläinen, 'Sibelius's Eighth – What happened to it?' *Finnish Music Quarterly*, 4, 1995. I am also grateful to the Sibelius Archives, University of Helsinki, for providing me with sketches associated with the Eighth.

For general information about the composer and his music I recommend: Erik Tawaststjerna, *Sibelius, Volume I: 1865–1905* and *Sibelius, Volume II: 1904–1914*, both translated by Robert Layton (Faber and Faber, 1976, 1991); Glenda Dawn Goss (ed.), *The Sibelius Companion* (Greenwood Press, 1996); Daniel M. Grimley (ed.), *The*

Cambridge Companion to Sibelius (Cambridge University Press, 2004); Robert Layton, *Sibelius* (Master Musicians series) 2nd edition (J. M. Dent and Sons, 1978); Santeri Levas, *Sibelius, A Personal Portrait*, translated by Percy M. Young (Lewisburg, Pa: Bucknell University Press, 1973); Harold E. Johnson, *Jean Sibelius* (Greenwood Press, 1959); Glenda Dawn Goss, *Jean Sibelius and Olin Downes* (Northeastern University Press, 1995); Timothy L. Jackson and Veijo Murtomäki (eds), *Sibelius Studies* (Cambridge University Press, 2001) and the website *Virtual Finland* (http://virtual.finland.fi). In addition, *Finnish Music Quarterly* was a mine of information, issue after issue, and its contact people were a joy to deal with.

I could not have written my storyline without William R. Trotter's authoritative work, *The Winter War: The Russo-Finnish War of 1939–40* (Aurum Press, 2002). I am also indebted to: Allen F. Chew, *The White Death, The epic of the Soviet–Finnish Winter War* (Michigan State University Press, 1971); Eloise Engle and Lauri Paananen, *The Winter War* (Stackpole Books, Michigan, 1972) and Pekka Parikka's award-winning film *Talvisota* (National Filmi Oy). I must also thank Pirjo at the Finnish Embassy for treating all my questions with such enthusiasm.

Anyone interested in the *Kalevala* in translation (John Martin Crawford, 1888) can find it at http://www. sacred-texts.com/neu/kveng/index.htm, where the ease of navigation is exemplary.

During the years in which Gian and Beryl reigned over the ballroom, the genuine champions were Bill and Bobbie Irvine, MBE. I was privileged to spend a day with them a few months before the lovely Mrs Irvine died; the charm, charisma and graciousness I gave the Clarks came directly from them. I also plundered the Irvines' autobiography for facts and figures (*The Dancing Years*, 1970). However, all other aspects of the Clarks' characters and career were purely my invention.

I must thank my long-suffering tango teachers, Paul

Lange in London and Lidia Ferrari in Buenos Aires. For technical information on dance I also recommend the following videos: Daniel Trenner, *Argentine Tango*, and Chris Morris, *Argentine Tango* (both from Dance Vision USA). The latter is from the series *Learn to Dance with the Champions*, which also provided me with numerous valuable videos on ballroom dancing. I also recommend the many videos with Marcus and Karen Hilton presented by Geoffrey Hearn for the Alex Moore Letter Service or for Hearn & Spencer Ltd, House of Dance; *Tango – Passion and Power* with William Pino and Alessandra Bucciarelli presented by Geoffrey Hearn for DSI Media, and videos of the Blackpool Dance Festival by Quasar Video.

In turning all this into a novel, I first ran the plot past my friends Peter Dunne and Martin Teale, whose advice was invaluable. Kirsty Fowkes provided a constructive review of an early draft, and Chloë Frayne did so for a later one. I am also grateful to Paul Abrahams, Hugh Trethowan, Michael Smith – and especially Emrah Tokalac who eradicated my Sibelian howlers. At Transworld I was blessed with three excellent editors: Diana Beaumont, Joanna Micklem and Sarah Turner. Thanks also to the unfailing eye of Deborah Adams. And my wonderful agent Véronique Baxter is, quite simply, one of the best things that ever happened to me.

Finally, the father's nervous breakdown. It was my own father's. I am therefore deeply grateful to my mother for her supportive attitude towards such a painful book. And although my father had died before I started it, there's no doubt he would have supported it, too.